For Rosalyn, Antonia and Francesca

First published in Great Britain in 1993 by The Bodley Head Children's Books
An imprint of Random House UK Ltd, 20 Vauxhall Bridge Road,
London, SW1V 2SA

Random House Australia (Pty) Limited
20 Alfred Street, Milsons Point, Sydney,
New South Wales 2061, Australia

Random House New Zealand Limited
18 Poland Road, Glenfield, Auckland 10,
New Zealand

Random House South Africa (Pty) Ltd
PO Box 337, Bergvlei 2012, South Africa

Typeset in Great Britain
Printed in Hong Kong

A catalogue record for this book is available from the British Library

ISBN 0 370 31759 9

Timid Tim
and the Cuggy Thief

John Prater

THE BODLEY HEAD
London

Tim was a shy little boy.

He wasn't very brave, and didn't like noisy, messy
fun or being splashed or rough and tumbles.

He didn't like big adventures.

He only wanted to be still and quiet,
with his special soft and sleepy blanket,
his cuggy. He took his cuggy
everywhere, and kept it close by
him always.

The other children would sometimes tease him by singing the CUGGY THIEF SONG!

Look out! Beware the cuggy thief
Who creeps around at night,
And steals away your favourite things
If you don't hug them tight!
They say he can be frightened off
If you put up a fight!
But none of us would ever dare
Face such an awful sight.

One dark and windy night Tim lay in bed, holding his cuggy tight.
But when he fell asleep, he tossed and turned – and let it go!

A chilling blast of air blew through the bedroom, and Tim awoke to find his cuggy gone.

He let out a little cry, which grew bigger, and bigger, and bigger…

until he yelled at the top of his voice,
"Come back you thief! You rascal!
Give me back my cuggy!"

Tim leapt out into the night to catch the thief.

The streets were dark and empty.

The wood was darker still.

The path was steep, the mud was
deep, and though his heart beat fast,
Tim never took his eyes off the
wicked rogue ahead.

The weather grew wild, and the waves crashed loud.

But Tim bravely kept going on. He knew that he was getting close to
the cuggy thief's dreadful lair.

He took a deep breath, then boldly entered the dim and rocky hole.
"Give me back my cuggy," he yelled.

Tim grabbed his cuggy.
"It's mine," he shouted.
    The startled cuggy thief
grew bigger, and bigger,
and bigger, let out a
horrid scream, and
turned to pounce . . .

But Tim did not run. He stood quite still, and faced that awful sight.

The horrid scream grew faint until it was no more than the distant whistling of the wind. His huge darkness grew pale and thin, until it was no more than the smoke curling from the fire.

"Phew!" said Tim. "Serves you right." He knew there was nothing left of that horrid villain. The cuggy thief was gone forever.

Tim gathered together all the cuggies, teddies and best-loved toys in the wicked robber's hoard.

The boat was full for the journey home.

Everyone cheered the hero Tim for being the bravest boy ever.

But even the bravest boy ever still cuddled cuggy for just a little longer.

YALE HISTORICAL PUBLICATIONS
Miscellany, 133

i

CHRISTIAN TRADE UNIONS
in the
WEIMAR REPUBLIC,
1918–1933
The Failure of "Corporate Pluralism"

William L. Patch, Jr.

YALE UNIVERSITY PRESS
New Haven and London

Designed by Margaret E.B. Joyner
and set in Caledonia type
by The Composing Room of Michigan.
Printed in the United States of America by
BookCrafters, Chelsea, Michigan.

Library of Congress Cataloging in Publication Data

Patch, William L., 1953–
    The Christian trade unions in the Weimar Republic,
1918–1933.

    (Yale historical publications. Miscellany ; 133)
    Revision of author's thesis (doctoral)—Yale
University, 1981.
    Bibliography: p.
    Includes index.
    1. Trade-unions. Catholic—Germany—History.
2. Germany—Politics and government—1918–1933.   I. Title.
II. Series.
HD6481.2.G3P38   1985   331.88′0943   84-27150
ISBN 0-300-03328-1 (alk. paper)

The paper in this book meets the guidelines for permanence
and durability of the Committee on Production Guidelines
for Book Longevity of the Council on Library Resources.

10 9 8 7 6 5 4 3 2 1

To My Parents
William and Barbara

Contents

Preface

This book is a substantially revised version of a Yale dissertation completed in 1981, based on archival research carried out in Germany in 1978–79. Thanks are due to the many German libraries and archives that provide remarkable freedom of access for foreign scholars, especially to the municipal library of Mönchen-Gladbach, the labor history library at the University of Bochum, and the library of today's German Labor Federation in Düsseldorf. Thanks also to Friedrich Freiherr Hiller von Gaertringen, who took time out from a very busy schedule to help me use the personal papers of his grandfather, Count Westarp. The German Academic Exchange Service and the Mrs. Giles Whiting Foundation provided generous financial support for the dissertation.

I wish to express my special gratitude to my dissertation adviser and friend, Henry Ashby Turner, and to Yale's other experts on modern German history, Hans Gatzke and Peter Gay. They are in large measure responsible for whatever insight into German society and culture I possess. I am also grateful to Tim Mason, who helped formulate the original topic, to Hans Mommsen for his unstinting advice and emotional support during my year of archival research, and to Gerald Feldman for his suggested improvements of the manuscript.

Introduction

A wide variety of friendly and hostile commentators in the 1920s agreed that the leaders of the relatively small blue-collar Christian trade unions enjoyed extraordinary political influence because they had established an extensive network of alliances with white-collar unions, religious organizations, and patriotic leagues. Yet these alliances struck many observers as unnatural, the unstable achievement of politically ambitious union functionaries who had forgotten the fundamental interests and values of their followers. Claims by Christian union leaders to have forged a "Christian-nationalist labor movement" uniting Catholic and Protestant, blue-collar and white-collar workers were received skeptically by contemporaries and strike most historians today as implausible. The Christian unionists' far more ambitious claim that their movement could forge a consensus in public opinion concerning the most divisive issues of the day seems utterly fantastic. They nevertheless came surprisingly close to achieving these goals.

The political strategy of the Christian unions rested on the fundamental premise that the intense class conflict of Wilhelmian Germany resulted from the temporary disorientation caused by Germany's intense urbanization during the late nineteenth century. Following the teaching of Catholic and Lutheran social theorists, Christian workers felt that rapid industrialization "uprooted" individuals and atomized society, and that this led directly to strife, riots, mass strikes, and lockouts. Social conflict could be expected to diminish in intensity as people gradually adjusted to the new urban industrial environment, rebuilding in new forms the associations for mutual aid common in the old society. The conflicts of interest between industrial employers and workers or between urban consumers and farmers were immediately apparent, but gradually they would learn of their shared interests as well, of the interdependencies linking the various sectors of a modern industrial economy.

Thus Christian workers subscribed to what Charles Tilly has termed the "breakdown" theory of the causes of social conflict. Tilly criticizes this view on the grounds that disoriented individuals are generally passive, that organization and solidarity, the essential prerequisites for becoming a contender in the political arena, have been the major sources of social conflict.[1] Tilly's arguments are persuasive within the time frame he chooses, ending in 1930, but a recent study of labor strife in Germany from 1864 to 1975 suggests that the expectations of Christian workers were not entirely unrealistic. In the period since 1949, when both employers and workers have been better organized than ever, the frequency and intensity of strikes and lockouts have declined dramatically. This state of affairs, predicted by Catholic social theorists ever since the 1880s, was slow to emerge, however. Indeed, the years from 1919 to 1923 witnessed the most intense strike activity in German history, while the following eight years were characterized by the most massive lockouts.[2] Christian trade unionists in the Weimar Republic therefore confronted a contradiction between their premise that social conflict would abate and the facts of strife around them. They concluded that politics and labor relations were rendered unnecessarily bitter by the survival of old habits of confrontation between "bourgeois" and "proletarian" camps that were no longer relevant to the vital issues of the day.

Efforts by the Christian unions to end the habits of confrontation took place on three levels. In the parliamentary arena, the old pattern of class polarization meant that every major issue pitting left against right tended to coincide with the fundamental antagonism between the Social Democratic Party (SPD) and the "bourgeois" parties. The determination of Germany's bourgeois liberals to combat the privileges of the aristocracy, clergy, and officer corps had ebbed away under the Empire. After 1880 the SPD remained the only consistent and aggressive critic of the established churches, discrimination against women, and excessive military expenditure.[3] Compulsory disarmament, suffrage for women,

1. Charles Tilly, Louise Tilly, and Richard Tilly, *The Rebellious Century 1830–1930* (Cambridge, Mass., 1975), pp. 4–6, 239–43. For the formulation of this theory that most influenced Christian workers in Germany, see Franz Hitze, *Kapital und Arbeit und die Reorganisation der Gesellschaft* (Paderborn, 1880).

2. Heinrich Volkmann, "Modernisierung des Arbeitskampfs? Zum Formwandel von Streik und Aussperrung in Deutschland 1864–1975," in Hartmut Kaelble et al., *Probleme der Modernisierung in Deutschland* (Opladen, 1978), pp. 123–27, 136–38.

3. See Friedrich Zunkel, *Der Rheinisch-Westfälische Unternehmer 1834–1879* (Cologne and Opladen, 1962); James Sheehan, "Conflict and Cohesion among German Elites in the Nineteenth Century," in James Sheehan (ed.), *Imperial Germany* (New York, 1976), pp. 62–92; and Richard J. Evans, *The Feminist Movement in Germany 1894–1933* (London, 1976), pp. 82–86, 167–90, 224–29.

and the disestablishment of the Evangelical Church in 1919 removed many of the grievances against which the Wilhelmian SPD had protested, but the impression lingered that the labor movement was the deadly enemy of Christian culture and national security. Many leading Social Democrats perceived that they should seek to dispel this impression in order to encourage acceptance of parliamentary democracy among the middle classes. Indeed, a faction within the SPD inspired by the writings of Eduard Bernstein had long been arguing that the party must abandon its Marxist rhetorical style and method of social analysis, which alienated small farmers, white-collar workers, clergymen, and idealistic patriots. This remained a minority view in the SPD of the Weimar Republic, however, although it eventually triumphed with the adoption of the Godesberg Program in 1959.[4] The danger of an anti-Marxist backlash among groups not directly involved in the conflicts of interest between management and labor was perceived more clearly by the Christian trade unionists.

On the level of economic interest groups, the old pattern of confrontation meant that all factions of businessmen and landowners joined ranks against the trade unions whenever important issues were debated. Thus, although the economic policies of the Wilhelmian government obviously discriminated in favor of heavy industry, the desire to preserve a united front of employers against the unions frustrated Gustav Stresemann's efforts after 1902 to organize an effective protest movement among manufacturers opposed to protective tariffs and monopoly prices.[5] Viable parliamentary democracy doubtless requires a more flexible attitude among the various factions of businessmen and landowners, a willingness to form ad hoc alliances that do not exclude trade unions as a matter of principle. In the 1920s the leaders of both the mammoth Free unions allied with the SPD and the Christian unions sought repeatedly, with some success, to reach agreement with the Reich Association of Industry on the broad outlines of national economic policy. Yet only the Christian unions undertook imaginative approaches to agrarian interests that created a highly fluid situation in the mid-1920s, when for a short time union representatives became full-fledged participants in the logrolling process whereby lobbyists for the various interest groups sought to muster parliamentary majorities.

The third level of class confrontation in imperial Germany, that of labor relations within the enterprise, generated the most difficult and enduring prob-

4. Hans Mommsen, "Die Sozialdemokratie in der Defensive. Der Immobilismus der SPD und der Aufstieg des Nationalsozialismus," in Hans Mommsen (ed.), *Sozialdemokratie zwischen Klassenbewegung und Volkspartei* (Frankfurt am Main, 1974), esp. pp. 119–21; Richard Hunt, *German Social Democracy 1918–1933* (New Haven, 1964), pp. 111–41; Harold Schellenger, Jr., *The SPD in the Bonn Republic* (The Hague, 1968).

5. Hans-Peter Ullmann, *Der Bund der Industriellen, 1895–1914* (Göttingen, 1976).

lems. No union could ignore its members' strong feelings about the basic issues of wages, hours, and authority over the work process, and the Christian unions generally cooperated closely with the Free unions at the collective bargaining table. The Christian unions made the first sustained effort within the German labor movement, however, to persuade workers to moderate their demands for higher wages and shorter hours so as to promote economic growth and prevent unemployment. Knut Borchardt has recently provoked lively controversy by reviving the argument that wage bills and welfare programs so expensive as to starve industry of investment funds were the major cause of the Great Depression in Germany.[6] Borchardt's argument is certainly one-sided, but the crucial fact underscored by him and stipulated by his critics, that real wages increased at a rate greater than national income from 1924 to 1929, remains noteworthy because it could not have occurred under the empire. Before World War I the Prussian monarchy banned all union activity among farmworkers and state employees. The army intervened massively in a few major strikes, and policemen and judges systematically harassed pickets. A favorable political climate enabled most of Germany's largest corporations to resist unionization drives, and no more than 15% of all industrial workers participated in collective bargaining. Even by exerting themselves to the utmost, the trade unions could barely if at all secure wage increases commensurate with the growth of corporate profits.[7] The situation was rather different in the 1920s, when the balance of social and political forces had changed to such an extent that, for the first time, trade unions had the power to ram through wage settlements that could contribute directly to inflation or unemployment. As the head of the Christian unions, Adam Stegerwald, warned his followers in 1924, they bore a far greater responsibility to exercise self-restraint now that they were powerful organizations in a very weak state.[8] The reaction to Stegerwald's plea was mixed even within the Christian unions, but Free union leaders displayed no comparable awareness of the damage that they could wreak.

In many ways the Christian trade unionists anticipated the analysis of Charles Maier, who has argued that the emergence of a new order of "corporate pluralism" in the 1920s rendered the traditional terms of debate between leftists and

6. Knut Borchardt, "Wirtschaftliche Ursachen des Scheiterns der Weimarer Republik," in *Wachstum, Krisen, Handlungsspielräume der Wirtschaftspolitik* (Göttingen, 1982), pp. 196–205. For a more detailed discussion, see below, pp. 157–59, 234.

7. See Klaus Saul, *Staat, Industrie, Arbeiterbewegung im Kaiserreich* (Düsseldorf, 1974); Klaus Schönhoven, *Expansion und Konzentration* (Stuttgart, 1980), pp. 80–141; Hartmut Kaelble and Heinrich Volkmann, "Konjunktur und Streik während des Übergangs zum Organisierten Kapitalismus in Deutschland," *Zeitschrift für Wirtschafts- und Sozialwissenschaften*, 92, no. 5 (1972), pp. 516–27, 536–41; and Volkmann, "Modernisierung?" pp. 131–52, 167–69.

8. See below, pp. 98f.

rightists throughout Western Europe obsolete. Maier holds that the leading representatives of big business, agriculture, and organized labor began in this decade to settle vital issues of economic and social policy among themselves. The crucial problems of the emerging order involved the danger of inflation, the relationship between parliamentary institutions and the economic "corporations," and the political powerlessness of groups that were weakly organized in the marketplace, not class conflict in the strict sense.[9]

Maier's conceptual model has been criticized for neglecting the important distinction between corporatism imposed by the state and that erected by voluntary associations. In Portugal, Austria, and some Latin American countries, dictators began during the 1930s to impose "state corporatism" in an authoritarian spirit that had nothing to do with "pluralism." Ulrich Nocken has suggested that we reserve the term "societal corporatism" for the development described by Maier, where a gradual increase in the power of voluntary lobbying associations shifted the locus of decision making, while recognizing that projects for "state corporatism" played a major role in the thinking of German conservatives and reactionaries.[10] The very ambiguity of Maier's original term seems indispensable for describing the outlook of Christian union leaders, however, which did not distinguish sharply between state and society. Christian labor leaders actively promoted state intervention in the economy, particularly in the field of labor arbitration, so as to compel employers to accept collective bargaining. They also urged parliament to delegate substantial regulatory powers to agencies created jointly by the lobbying associations of management and labor, thus encouraging the two to work together. Nevertheless, all their proposals for reform retained the principle of voluntary membership and self-government within the economic associations and insisted above all on the sovereignty of the democratically elected parliament.

This book will seek to show that the leaders of the Christian unions first perceived how a labor movement must behave if it rejects the project of social revolution in favor of parliamentary democracy and pluralism, that their policies were in some sense the "correct" policies for the Free unions as well. It must be noted at once, however, that this interpretation contradicts that of most existing accounts. East German historiography still upholds Lenin's dictum that the Christian unions were "organs of bourgeois reaction," the paid agents of employers and officials seeking to destroy the unity of the labor movement.[11]

9. Charles Maier, *Recasting Bourgeois Europe* (Princeton, 1975), esp. pp. 510–15, 579–93.
10. Ulrich Nocken, "Corporatism and Pluralism in Modern German History," in Dirk Stegman et al. (eds.), *Industrielle Gesellschaft und politisches System. Festschrift für Fritz Fisher* (Bonn, 1978), pp. 37–56.
11. Herbert Gottwald, "Gesamtverband der christlichen Gewerkschaften Deutschlands

Western historians who identify themselves more or less closely with the SPD have recently offered more plausible reasons to consider the Christian unions unrealistic or misguided. Günter Plum has advanced a sociological critique in his study of the Catholic population in Aachen and its environs. He argues that the Christian unions derived their support primarily from workers who had no experience of the social problems resulting from large-scale industry and massive urbanization, that is, rural and small-town workers.[12] Michael Schneider, who recently published the first comprehensive history of the Christian unions, has compiled a great deal of material from their resolutions and manifestoes in an effort to demonstrate that they failed to develop a coherent political or economic program. He strongly emphasizes the confusion of socially progressive with nationalistic, monarchist, patriarchal, and nostalgic ideas in the movement,[13] but confines his attention almost exclusively to the sources generated by the unions themselves, neglecting to study in depth the activities of Christian trade unionists as members of political parties, church organizations, and patriotic leagues. This book seeks to make sense of the debates and tactical maneuvers that Schneider interprets merely as signs of confusion. Finally, some Catholic historians have concluded from the eagerness of the Christian union leaders to involve industrialists and agrarians in government coalitions that they were fundamentally antidemocratic, that they stood on the right wing of the Center Party against such "enthusiastic republicans" as Matthias Erzberger and Joseph Wirth.[14]

We shall return to the issue of realism at the conclusion of this book, to the question of whether the Free or Christian unions more accurately assessed the trends of the times. We should not exaggerate the importance of "realism," however, in our desire to understand the emergence of the world in which we live. Schneider correctly emphasizes that certain policies can be both an anticipation of later developments and a terribly misguided approach under the conditions of the 1920s. Indeed, even if veterans of the Christian labor movement could prove that they were objectively correct in all their prognostications, we might still find that their program was sterile, that it lacked any power to moti-

---

1901–1933," in Dieter Fricke (ed.), *Die bürgerlichen Parteien in Deutschland* (Leipzig, 1968), esp. p. 113, and Dieter Fricke, "Zur Förderung der christlichen Gewerkschaften durch die nichtmonopolistische Bourgeoisie," *Zeitschrift für Geschichtswissenschaft*, 29 (1981), pp. 814–19.

12. Günter Plum, *Gesellschaftsstruktur und politisches Bewußtsein in einer katholischen Region 1928–1933* (Stuttgart, 1972), esp. pp. 18–34, 67–70.

13. Michael Schneider, *Die Christlichen Gewerkschaften 1894–1933* (Bonn, 1982), pp. 388–408, 497–506, 684–87, 707–19.

14. Ellen Evans, "Adam Stegerwald and the Role of the Christian Trade Unions in the Weimar Republic," *Catholic Historical Review*, 54 (1974), pp. 602–26.

vate the masses or alter the course of events. The conciliatory ideals of the Christian-nationalist labor movement never attracted the allegiance of more than one-sixth of Germany's unionized workers. Crisis situations repeatedly jeopardized the cohesiveness of the Christian unions themselves. From 1918 to 1924 Catholic and Protestant members responded with very different emotions to military defeat, revolution, Communist uprisings, hyperinflation, and the French occupation of the Ruhr. In the even more desperate situation after 1930, nobody resolved to risk life and limb in the struggle against Hitler from the conviction that German workers could someday move to the suburbs and watch color television. "Corporate pluralism" in the Weimar Republic existed as a pious wish in the minds of Christians and, in somewhat different form, as a goal for hardheaded lobbyists who felt that it should be possible to establish rational mechanisms for resolving conflicts of interest with a minimum of damage to the economy. It had a real foundation in the facts of industrial concentration and social organization that enabled a few dozen men to speak on behalf of big business, agriculture, and labor. It was not, however, an inspiring cause, and people in those troubled times sorely needed inspiration.

ACRONYMS

ADGB	Allgemeiner deutscher Gewerkschaftsbund (General Association of German Unions, umbrella organization for the blue-collar Free unions from 1919 to 1933)
AfA	Allgemeiner freier Angestelltenbund (General Association of Free Employees, umbrella organization for Free white-collar unions from 1921 to 1933)
BVP	Bayerische Volkspartei (Bavarian People's Party)
CSVD	Christlich-sozialer Volksdienst (Christian Social People's Service)
DAF	Deutsche Arbeitsfront (German Labor Front, 1933–45)
DDP	Deutsche Demokratische Partei (German Democratic Party)
DGB	Deutscher Gewerkschaftsbund (German Labor Federation, umbrella organization for both blue- and white-collar Christian-nationalist unions from 1919 to 1933)
DHV	Deutschnationaler Handlungsgehilfen-Verband (German Nationalist Union of Commercial Employees)
DNAB	Deutschnationaler Arbeiterbund (German Nationalist Workers' League)
DNVP	Deutschnationale Volkspartei (German Nationalist People's Party)
DVP	Deutsche Volkspartei (German People's Party)
GcG	Gesamtverband der christlichen Gewerkschaften Deutschlands (League of Christian Unions)
GDA	Gewerkschaftsbund der Angestellten (League of Employees' Unions, liberal white-collar ally of the Hirsch–Duncker unions)
KPD	Kommunistische Partei Deutschlands (German Communist Party)
KVP	Konservative Volkspartei (Conservative People's Party)
NSBO	Nationalsozialistische Betriebszellen-Organisation (National Socialist Factory Cells Organization)
NSDAP	Nationalsozialistische Deutsche Arbeiterpartei (National Socialist German Workers' Party)
RLB	Reichslandbund (Reich Agrarian League)
SA	Sturmabteilung (Storm Section, Nazi paramilitary league)
SPD	Sozialdemokratische Partei Deutschlands (German Social Democratic Party)
WAZ	Westdeutsche Arbeiter-Zeitung (West German Workers' Gazette)
ZAG	Zentralarbeitsgemeinschaft der gewerblichen Arbeitgeber und Arbeitnehmer Deutschlands (Central Association of Industrial Employers and Employees)

1

The Origins of Christian Trade Unions
in Imperial Germany

The Christian trade unions had no chance whatsoever of putting their ideas into practice during the first two decades of their existence. Indeed, in Wilhelmian Germany the prospect that organized labor would ever be accepted by the lobbying associations of industry and agriculture as an equal partner in setting the guidelines for public policy in social and economic affairs was so remote as to appear utopian. We must therefore digress a bit to discuss the special circumstances attending the birth of the Christian unions before resuming the discussion of "corporate pluralism," which suddenly came very close to reality at the end of World War I.

The first explanation given by Social Democratic commentators for the emergence of separate "Christian" trade unions in Germany during the 1890s was that the Roman Catholic clergy had organized them in order to retain its hold on the Catholic masses. In this view, the spread of the Social Democratic Party into the predominantly Catholic regions of Germany had caused priests and bourgeois Catholic politicians to imitate the outward forms of trade unionism in paternalistic organizations dedicated to preventing the emergence of authentic class consciousness among Catholic workers.[1] Gradually, however, a consensus has emerged that this explanation is inaccurate. Clergymen and bourgeois politicians did play an important role in founding the Christian unions, to be sure, and antisocialism figured prominently in the complicated mixture of their motives. The Christian unions soon attracted thousands of energetic working-class activists, however, which distinguished them from the dozens of other organizations

---

1. See August Erdmann, *Die christlichen Gewerkschaften* (Stuttgart, 1914).

1

founded to wean German workers from Marxism. By 1900 the Christian unions were firmly controlled by the blue-collar members and sought primarily to serve their economic interests. This development occurred because the spread of a militantly anticlerical ideology in the socialist Free unions aroused genuine indignation among the churchgoing minority of workers.

THE RISE OF SOCIALIST ANTICLERICALISM

The attitudes of German workers in the late nineteenth century toward Christianity remain enigmatic. Most apparently had ambivalent feelings about their religious heritage. Young, unmarried industrial workers seem to have been the most aggressively blasphemous and irreverent element of the population, but later in life many of these same workers accepted church weddings and permitted their children to be baptized and receive some religious instruction. Probably no more than 10% of the urban population attended church with any regularity, yet the vast majority remained nominal members of the established churches. Despite the opportunity to avoid paying church taxes by declaring oneself "confessionless," 62% of the entire German population was Evangelical and 36% Catholic at the turn of the century.[2]

The policies of the established Evangelical Churches (Landeskirchen), which were usually set by conservative royal officials, undoubtedly tended to estrange workers from Christianity in predominantly Protestant regions. The patriarchal attitude common among the clergy aggravated strains between workers and institutional Christianity. Because the local priest or pastor was usually the only person with a university education who dealt with workers on a personal level, it was often an unpleasant encounter with him that opened their eyes to the pervasiveness of class prejudice in German society. By 1870 most workers in Berlin, Hamburg, and other major cities imitated the skeptical elements of the educated middle classes who turned their backs on church life and ridiculed the clergy.[3] Bourgeois Protestants, moreover, were reared with concepts of order that produced an extremely hostile reaction to the first initiatives of the socialist

2. See Annemarie Burger, *Religionszugehörigkeit und soziales Verhalten* (Göttingen, 1964), pp. 212f., 356–59; Heiner Grote, *Sozialdemokratie und Religion* (Tübingen, 1968), pp. 110–18, 146–49; and Antje Kraus, "Gemeindeleben und Industrialisierung. Das Beispiel des evangelischen Kirchenkreises Bochum," in Jürgen Reulecke and Wolfhard Weber (eds.), *Fabrik, Familie, Feierabend* (Wuppertal, 1978), pp. 274–80.
3. William O. Shanahan, *German Protestants Face the Social Question* (Notre Dame, 1954); Herwart Vorländer, *Evangelische Kirche und soziale Frage in der werdenden Industriegroßstadt Elberfeld* (Düsseldorf, 1963), pp. 26–33; Klaus Pollmann, *Landesherrliches Kirchenregiment und soziale Frage* (Berlin and New York, 1973), pp. 104–06; Wolfgang Köllmann, "Aus dem Alltag der Unterschichten in der Vor- und Frühindustrialisierungsphase," in Reulecke and Weber (eds.), *Fabrik, Familie, Feierabend*, pp. 33–36.

labor movement. The *Reformed Weekly* of Elberfeld, for example, described industrial strikes in 1873 as "exercises on the parade ground in preparation for civil war."[4] Lutheran pastors in Saxony and Brunswick exploited their control of cemeteries for heavy-handed reprisals against the early supporters of the Social Democratic Workers' Party, founded in Eisenach in 1869. Some pastors refused to bury party activists or their children, and all prohibited graveside speeches by comrades. In response the Social Democrats began to transform funeral processions into party rallies that attracted thousands of workers and sought to demonstrate unconcern for the threat of fire and brimstone.[5] Such purely negative responses to the rise of socialism could only spread the impression that the clergy regarded itself as part of the ruling class and would lash out at any effort to undermine traditional patterns of deference.

The early leaders of the Social Democratic movement displayed a hostility toward Christian doctrine that surpassed the anticlericalism common among workers, however. August Bebel, Wilhelm Liebknecht, and many of their colleagues began their political careers in the educational workers' clubs founded by liberal notables in the 1860s, where they read a wide range of anti-Christian tracts in the spirit of the Enlightenment. When the majority of German liberals decided in 1866 to support Bismarck and the Hohenzollern dynasty, these activists felt that the ideals of the Enlightenment had been betrayed by a bourgeoisie that sought to prop up the reactionary aristocracy and clergy in order to prevent progress toward democracy.[6] At the first party congress of the Social Democratic Workers' Party in 1869 and the Gotha unification congress of 1875, where it merged with the Lasallean faction to form the SPD, militant atheists demanded that all party members be required to renounce church membership. Bebel and Liebknecht sympathized with the demand but decided that such a rule would hamper recruitment. The Gotha Program adopted instead a relatively restrained article declaring that "religion is a private matter" and calling for complete separation of church and state. But even this secularist platform, retained in subsequent party programs until 1925, proved highly offensive to Catholics and orthodox Protestants. Furthermore, the SPD leadership granted militant anti-Christian propagandists access to the party press and publishing houses.[7]

August Bebel denounced Christianity in increasingly strident terms during

4. Vorländer, pp. 82f.
5. Grote, pp. 131–34.
6. See Vernon L. Lidtke, "August Bebel and German Social Democracy's Relation to the Christian Churches," *Journal of the History of Ideas*, 27 (1966), pp. 246–51, and Richard Reichard, *Crippled from Birth: German Social Democracy, 1844–1870* (Ames, Iowa, 1969), pp. 222–35.
7. Grote, pp. 101–22, and Herbert Christ, "Der politische Protestantismus in der Weimarer Republik," Ph.D. diss. (Bonn, 1967), pp. 285–91.

the 1870s as the *Kulturkampf*, the campaign by Bismarck to subject the Catholic Church to state control, aroused passionate controversy. While condemning Bismarck's repressive methods, Bebel was also anxious to prevent his followers from sympathizing with the victims of Bismarck's persecution. When a conciliatory Catholic priest wrote in 1873 that the clergy worked to abolish the same abuses and achieve the same goals as the SPD, Bebel replied with an impassioned denunciation of religion in root and branch, which would become one of the SPD's most widely disseminated pamphlets. Bebel wrote that Christianity "has diverted humanity from its purpose of perfecting itself in every way, . . . has held mankind in bondage and oppression. It has been used and has willingly served as the foremost tool of political and social exploitation up until the present day."[8] The German churches may have deserved harsh criticism of their political attitudes, but Bebel advanced a more dubious second line of argument. The bulk of his pamphlet offered a facile survey of recent discoveries in anthropology, geology, biology, and Bible criticism in order to show that "the irrefutable facts established by the natural sciences . . . destroy the foundation on which Christianity stands and bring it down."[9] Bebel's reading of Auguste Comte and the philosophes had convinced him that science must supplant religion. Unable to conceive of organized religion as an enduring force that should be conciliated if it became more sympathetic to organized labor, he concluded with the famous declaration that "Christianity and socialism confront each other like fire and water."[10] These words later figured prominently in the propaganda of the Christian unions.

During its period of illegality (1878–90), banned by Bismarck's Socialist Law, the SPD toned down its attacks on religion in order to distance itself from anarchism. The influence of Marxism on the party leadership increased dramatically during these years, and Friedrich Engels warned his German supporters against preoccupation with anti-Christian polemics on the grounds that only the abolition of capitalism would cause the religious impulse to wither.[11] But the spread of Marxism in the SPD did not facilitate cooperation with progressive Christians. The party's dominant theoretician, Karl Kautsky, had undergone a conversion to Darwinism prior to and in some ways more fundamental than his conversion to Marxism. Kautsky rejoiced to find in the writings of Darwin and his

8. August Bebel, "Christentum und Sozialismus" (Berlin, 1901, first published in 1873), p. 13. See also Klaus Kreppel, *Entscheidung für den Sozialismus* (Bonn-Bad Godesberg, 1974), pp. 40–46.
9. Bebel, p. 7.
10. Ibid., p. 16. Kreppel, p. 45, claims that Bebel confined his attacks to institutional Christianity, but contrast Lidtke, pp. 253–55, and Grote, pp. 62f.
11. Lidtke, pp. 252–58.

more daring, aggressively materialistic commentators like Ernst Haeckel the proof that man's moral impulses derived from the social instincts observable in the animal kingdom. Kautsky considered this insight essential to "scientific" socialism because it demonstrated that all forces in human history were governed by immutable laws. He schooled party functionaries in a deterministic and materialist world-view profoundly hostile to Christianity.[12]

A few Lutheran pastors joined the SPD between 1890 and 1914, seeking to promote détente between it and the Evangelical Church, but they encountered fear and hostility in both camps. In 1893 a young seminarian in Stuttgart urged all true Christians to support the SPD, issuing an indictment of throne-and-altar Christianity. In response the editor of the Cologne organ of the SPD, August Erdmann, denied that a genuine Christian could be a genuine Social Democrat. Erdmann reasoned that the proletariat could be sustained in its class struggle only by a belief in economic determinism that was utterly incompatible with faith in God. "Only one thing can support me, can give me motivation and dedication: the insight into the natural necessity of social development, into the inevitability of the goal we strive for, and finally the certainty that power and victory must sooner or later lie on the side of natural necessity."[13] In 1905 Friedrich Stampfer then published the most detailed explanation of the SPD's attitude toward religion. He acknowledged the presence of some idealistic Christians in the party but associated himself with "the majority of modern socialists," who believed that "their world-view is incompatible with Christian dogma."[14] Although more diplomatic in tone, Stampfer's pamphlet reiterated much of the substance of Bebel's broadside against Christianity thirty years earlier. Indeed, during the first two decades of the twentieth century formal organizations of "proletarian freethinkers" seeking to draw workers out of the established churches proliferated and increased their influence within the socialist labor movement. The incorporation of the Gotha Program's religious article into the SPD's revised Görlitz Program of 1921 underscored the continuity in the philosophical views of the SPD leadership. An anticlerical and rationalist outlook was essential for promotion within the party hierarchy.[15]

12. Hans-Josef Steinberg, *Sozialismus und deutsche Sozialdemokratie* (Hannover, 1967), pp. 45–75.

13. August Erdmann, "Ein Wort der Entgegnung auf Th. v. Wächter's 'Stellung der Sozialdemokratie zur Religion'" (Elberfeld, 1894), pp. 16f. See also Richard Sorg, *Marxismus und Protestantismus in Deutschland* (Cologne, 1974), pp. 89–99, and Manfred Schick, *Kulturprotestantismus und soziale Frage 1890–1914* (Tübingen, 1970), pp. 130–35.

14. Friedrich Stampfer, "Religion ist Privatsache. Erläuterungen zu Punkt 6 des Erfurter Programms," 2d ed. (Berlin, 1919), pp. 5f.

15. H. Christ, pp. 246–96, and Hartmann Wunderer, "Freidenkertum und Arbeiterbewegung. Ein Überblick," *Internationale wissenschaftliche Korrespondenz zur Geschichte der Arbeiterbewegung*, 16 (March 1980), pp. 1–6.

Social Democratic anticlericalism did not create a serious dilemma for the churchgoing minority of workers, however, until the Free unions forged a close alliance with the SPD and spread rapidly into all regions of Germany after 1890. The pioneers of unionization in Germany between 1862 and 1878 had displayed little interest in political programs. The most effective socialist union organizers maintained their distance from both the Lassallean and Marxist parties, and the moderate unions founded by the liberal politicians Max Hirsch and Franz Duncker flourished. In the 1880s, however, after the police invoked the Socialist Law against most existing unions as well as the SPD, militant young socialists reorganized the Free unions in the large cities of central and northern Germany, while thousands of hitherto apolitical workers concluded that they could secure no improvement of their economic condition without a fundamental transformation of the state. Their union statutes continued to proclaim political neutrality, but after 1890 the overwhelming majority of Free union officials belonged to the SPD and regarded it as the sole political representative of the working class. The Hirsch–Duncker unions were relegated to the role of a small sect on the fringes of the labor movement. This new cooperation between SPD and union officials achieved spectacular successes, as the party electorate grew from 1.5 million voters in 1890 to 4 million in 1912, while Free union membership surged from 200,000 to 2.5 million.[16] This rapid growth after 1890 brought many churchgoing workers into contact with the socialist labor movement for the first time.

There were, to be sure, significant debates over tactics between the SPD leadership and the General Commission of the Free Unions, organized by Carl Legien in 1890. Many party intellectuals believed that strikes could never improve the material condition of the working class but should be employed for political purposes. Legien and his colleagues sharply opposed political strikes and believed that the SPD did too little to advocate legislation for the immediate amelioration of the worst abuses of capitalism.[17] Although often described as indifferent to socialist theory, however, these trade unionists obviously perceived some positive value in the orthodox Marxism of Kautsky. The unions cooperated enthusiastically with the SPD in educational projects designed to wean workers from religion and spread a scientific world-view. Legien and most of his colleagues came from the most irreligious cities in Germany and shared the

---

16. See Ulrich Engelhardt, *"Nur vereinigt sind wir stark"* (Stuttgart, 1977), and Gerhard A. Ritter and Klaus Tenfelde, "Der Durchbruch der Freien Gewerkschaften Deutschlands zur Massenbewegung im letzten Viertel des 19. Jahrhunderts," in Gerhard A. Ritter, *Arbeiterbewegung, Parteien und Parlamentarismus* (Göttingen, 1976).

17. John A. Moses, *Trade Unionism in Germany from Bismarck to Hitler, 1869–1933* (Totowa, N.J., 1982), vol. 1, pp. 113–33, and Heinz Josef Varain, *Freie Gewerkschaften, Sozialdemokratie und Staat* (Düsseldorf, 1956), pp. 14–34.

SPD leadership's distaste for Christianity. They also seem to have shared August Erdmann's view that only a materialist creed could inspire workers to make sacrifices for the movement.[18] Reformist union organizers nevertheless remained somewhat more willing than party intellectuals to reconsider their views on Christianity should the churches offer meaningful support for welfare legislation in the future.

Kautsky's deterministic doctrine may have been inspirational, but its dissemination by the SPD apparently had unintended consequences. A vague faith in scientific progress and hostility toward religion were often the only elements of socialist ideology that could capture the imagination of members in the rank and file. Such intellectual influences often prompted abusive treatment of churchgoing workers on the job. When asked late in life why they had joined Christian trade unions, many veteran activists responded that insults, practical jokes, and occasional blows from "enlightened" colleagues had made their lives miserable until they banded together with other Christian workers. Frequent admonitions by leading Social Democrats against crude anticlerical insults confirm these charges.[19] Thus the Christian unions arose in large part as a defensive reaction against currents in Social Democracy that demanded conformity from all workers in philosophical matters not directly related to the SPD's party platform.

PARTNERS OR PATRONS? CLERICAL ORGANIZATIONS FOR WORKERS

The Social Policy Association (Verein für Sozialpolitik), founded in 1872, helped to create a climate of public opinion favorable to the emergence of Christian trade unions. The small but illustrious group of professors and civil servants in this association sought to improve the living standard of workers so that they would have no reason to support the radical socialist labor movement. A few of its members, most notably the liberal economist Lujo Brentano and the conservative Lutheran economist Adolf Wagner, argued eloquently that the state should encourage moderate trade unionism in order to save Germany from

18. See Gerhard A. Ritter, *Die Arbeiterbewegung im Wilhelminischen Reich* (Berlin, 1959), pp. 218–27, and Steinberg, pp. 129–42.

19. See the autobiographical articles by Adam Stegerwald, Carl Schirmer, and Franz Behrens in Gesamtverband der christlichen Gewerkschaften Deutschlands (Hg.) (hereafter abbreviated GcG), *25 Jahre christlicher Gewerkschaftsbewegung* (Cologne, 1924), and by Jakob Minter in *Der Deutsche Metallarbeiter*, 1 January 1927, p. 5. See also August Erdmann, "Ein Wort der Entgegnung," pp. 22f.; Stampfer, pp. 37–44; and Schneider, *Die Christlichen Gewerkschaften 1894–1933*, pp. 214–20.

destruction through class warfare. Brentano's writings in praise of the English trade unions and the English Christian Social movement became a major influence on Christian labor leaders and progressive civil servants. Most members of the Social Policy Association sought to avoid political controversy, however, when prominent businessmen denounced the views of Brentano and Wagner. The association could not adopt a unified stance regarding trade unionism or political reform, confining its activities by and large to the study of urban conditions and the formulation of specific legislative proposals to improve housing and job safety. It made no effort to mobilize a popular constituency for social reform.[20]

The Catholic clergy contributed more directly to the birth of the Christian trade unions by preserving a large reservoir of practicing Christians in the industrial labor force. For a variety of reasons, Catholic priests displayed more sympathy for the problems of working-class parishioners than did Lutheran pastors. Most of Germany's Catholic population lived in economically depressed regions and played little role in the early development of industry. Romantic anticapitalism and nostalgia for medieval society prompted Catholic thinkers early in the nineteenth century, most notably Adam Müller and Franz Baader, to demand a "corporatist" reform of society, a *ständische Ordnung*. All such corporatist theories involved efforts to protect artisans and small farmers from the ravages of free competition, but they varied greatly in thrust, ranging from Müller's frankly reactionary plea to revive the influence of the clergy and nobility to Baader's forward-looking program for state action to strengthen the position of wage earners on the labor market.[21] In 1849 a former cobbler turned priest, Adolf Kolping, set a precedent for practical efforts to protect Catholic workers from economic dislocation by founding clubs for journeymen artisans, whose recreational activities and vocational training were praised even by August Bebel. Sixty thousand artisans belonged to these clubs by the time of Kolping's death in 1865.[22] In the 1860s Wilhelm Ketteler, bishop of Mainz, infused Catholic anticapitalism with a new vigor by studying socialist literature and seeking dialogue with industrial workers in his diocese. Influenced by Lassalle, he developed a program for social reform through universal suffrage and producers'

20. See Karl Erich Born, *Staat und Sozialpolitik seit Bismarcks Sturz 1890–1914* (Wiesbaden, 1957), pp. 33–47, and Schick, pp. 49–63.

21. Ralph Bowen, *German Theories of the Corporative State* (New York and London, 1947), pp. 33–38, 46–53; Emil Ritter, *Die katholisch-soziale Bewegung Deutschlands im neunzehnten Jahrhundert und der Volksverein* (Cologne, 1954), pp. 30–53; Franz Focke, *Sozialismus aus christlicher Verantwortung* (Wuppertal, 1978), pp. 29–34.

22. Emil Ritter, pp. 88–91; Eric Dorn Brose, "Christian Labor and the Politics of Frustration in Imperial Germany," Ph.D. diss. (Ohio State University, 1978), pp. 12–17; August Bebel, *Aus meinem Leben*, 5th ed. (Berlin, 1978), pp. 35f.

cooperatives. When Catholics formed the Center Party in 1870 to defend themselves against the Protestant majority in a newly unified Germany, Ketteler joined its first Reichstag delegation. Isolated among Catholic leaders because of his democratic tendencies, Ketteler nevertheless inspired a host of younger priests. [23]

Ketteler was the first German bishop to recognize the vital importance of a ministry to industrial workers for the future of Catholicism. By the 1870s massive industrial growth in the predominantly Protestant cities of Rhineland-Westphalia, Baden, Württemberg, and Hesse was attracting large numbers of Catholic workers from surrounding rural areas. Their migration significantly altered the ratio between Catholics and Protestants in many industrializing cities. As a result the urban Catholic population was composed mostly of blue-collar workers by the end of the century, and the clergy was compelled to retain their confidence if it did not want to lose all foothold in the cities. [24] Moreover, the family origin of parish priests was generally humbler than that of Evangelical pastors, they enjoyed somewhat more independence from wealthy parishioners, and priests did not have to worry about saving money for children or launching them in good careers. Finally and most important, the Catholic Church in Prussia was far more independent from and critical of the Hohenzollern monarchy than was its Protestant counterpart. All these factors tended to counteract the conservative instincts of the higher Catholic clergy, who were usually from the aristocracy or upper middle class.

Rhineland-Westphalia proved exceptionally fruitful ground for Ketteler's ideas because of the coincidence there between intense industrialization and the *Kulturkampf*. For most priests in the rural areas surrounding the Ruhr basin, modern industry appeared in the 1870s as a hostile force that disrupted families in the parish and threatened the faith of youths who migrated to the mushrooming cities. Such concerns impelled gifted young priests like Franz Hitze, Wilhelm Hohoff, and the younger August Pieper to study socialist literature seriously. [25] At the same time, the Catholic Church was locked in combat with Bismarck and his National Liberal allies, who included most industrialists in the region. All Catholic spokesmen responded by denouncing "liberalism," and some included under this heading the expropriation by capitalists of the petite

---

23. Emil Ritter, pp. 95–107, and Brose, pp. 19–44.

24. The national census of 1907 showed that the proportion of Catholics who were blue-collar industrial workers nearly equaled that of Protestants (34.4% vs. 35.5%) despite the fact that far fewer Catholics lived in urban areas (40.6% vs. 49.4% in Prussia in 1910, for example). Thus there were relatively few bourgeois Catholics: see Kreppel, pp. 12f., and Burger, pp. 321, 340. See also Hans Graf, *Die Entwicklung der Wahlen und politischen Parteien in Groß-Dortmund* (Hannover and Frankfurt am Main, 1958), pp. 16–19, and Kraus, pp. 281–84.

25. See Kreppel, pp. 30–34.

bourgeoisie, the determination of wage levels according to supply and demand rather than the needs of the workers, and all forms of unearned income condemned by Thomas Aquinas. The Catholic Church enjoyed a surge of popular sympathy when the Prussian police began in 1873 to exile or imprison recalcitrant clergymen, and the Center Party scored massive electoral gains at the expense of both the SPD and National Liberals, consolidating an electoral base among industrial workers along the Rhine and Ruhr that it never lost.[26]

Class tensions flared up within the Center Party, however, when Christian workers sought to establish independent organizations. Radical young curates inspired by Ketteler began in 1869 to help workers form Christian Social clubs, which attracted 3,000 members each in Aachen and Essen and smaller followings in a dozen other cities. These clubs admitted Protestant as well as Catholic workers, and their leaders boldly demanded the abolition of all legal restrictions on trade unions, a voice for workers in regulating factory conditions, and legal restriction of the working day to ten hours. In the Reichstag election of 1877, the Christian Socials of Essen scored an unprecedented victory by defeating the official nominee of the Center Party and electing a metalworker, Gerhard Stötzel. The Center Party then accepted Stötzel into its Reichstag delegation, where he served with one interruption until his death in 1905. The first Christian Social movement collapsed at the end of the 1870s, however. In 1878 the Aachen club went bankrupt, while the Essen club erupted into controversy over efforts by Christian miners to form an ideologically neutral trade union with Social Democrats. The police harassed the Christian Social clubs severely after the passage of the Socialist Law, and the episcopate sternly discouraged radical attacks on the existing social order as the *Kulturkampf* began to wind down.[27]

The decline of the radical Christian Social movement persuaded the priest and sociologist Franz Hitze to formulate, in cooperation with progressive Catholic industrialists, a moderate doctrine of "Christian socialism" compatible with technological progress and entrepreneurial initiative. Hitze sought to persuade the Catholic populace to support the development of modern industry while reviving the spirit of association and mutual aid that industrialization threatened to destroy. He joined the Center Reichstag delegation in 1884 and became its leading spokesman on social policy. Hitze's youthful writings were ambiguous because they described his goal sometimes in terms of "state socialism" and

26. J. D. Hunley, "The Working Classes, Religion and Social Democracy in the Düsseldorf Area, 1867–78," *Societas—A Review of Social History*, 4 (Spring 1974), pp. 131–49; Erich Schmidt-Volkmar, *Der Kulturkampf in Deutschland 1871–1890* (Göttingen, 1962), pp. 135–87; Kreppel, pp. 17–21, 50–64.

27. Focke, pp. 35–43; Klaus Tenfelde, *Sozialgeschichte der Bergarbeiterschaft an der Ruhr im 19. Jahrhundert* (Bonn/Bad Godesberg, 1977), pp. 514–22; Emil Ritter, pp. 68–76; Brose, pp. 45–65.

sometimes as a revival of the medieval guilds. But he consistently argued that the Catholic understanding of natural law required all Christians to oppose the anarchy of contemporary capitalism, to encourage associations of workers and artisans that could counterbalance the overwhelming power of industrial capital, and to endorse state intervention against the exploitation of workers.[28] In 1891 Pope Leo XIII endorsed these views in his famous encyclical on social questions, *Rerum novarum*, which greatly enhanced Hitze's prestige. However, the pope described the Catholic "mixed unions" of France, which included employers and renounced strikes, as the ideal form of organization for workers.[29]

Hitze was more inclined to endorse English trade unionism as a model for German workers, but he felt that they could not yet manage their own affairs responsibly. In 1884 he began to coordinate efforts by Catholic bishops to establish church-affiliated workers' clubs in each parish, dedicated to education, recreation, and devotional life. These clubs satisfied a hunger among workers for self-improvement, and the clergy's enthusiastic efforts organized 80,000 Catholic workers by 1895, mostly in Rhineland-Westphalia, and 430,000 by 1912, all over Germany. As the clubs grew they offered some leadership role to elected representatives of the members and hired a few full-time functionaries of working-class background, but the clergy continued to dominate them.[30] In 1890 Hitze and other Center Party leaders founded the Volksverein für das katholische Deutschland (Popular League for Catholic Germany), headquartered in Mönchen-Gladbach, an organization devoted to social reform and anti-Marxist apologetics that embraced 800,000 members by 1913. Formally independent of the Church, the Volksverein nevertheless depended on the willingness of bishops to allow socially engaged priests to devote their time to it. The Volksverein differed from the Social Policy Association in that it attracted a mass membership and lobbied for some controversial reforms. Nevertheless, its leadership remained firmly in the hands of clergymen and bourgeois politicians, and when the Catholic workers' clubs of Munich proposed in 1891 that Christian workers should establish their own trade unions, the Volksverein successfully opposed the idea. Hitze was willing at this time to accept only "trade groups" of workers under clerical supervision within each workers' club, a form of organization that made meaningful union actvity impossible.[31]

The Lutheran pastor Adolf Stoecker, the son of a sergeant who rose to

28. See Emil Ritter, pp. 58–61, 120–26, and Bowen, pp. 90–116.
29. Brose, pp. 83f.
30. Emil Ritter, pp. 281–85; Hans Dieter Denk, *Die christliche Arbeiterbewegung in Bayern bis zum Ersten Weltkrieg* (Mainz, 1980), pp. 47–62; Kreppel, pp. 22–27; Dieter Fricke (ed.), *Die bürgerlichen Parteien in Deutschland. Handbuch* (Berlin, 1970), vol. 2, pp. 255ff.
31. See Horstwalter Heitzer, *Der Volksverein für das katholische Deutschland im Kaiserreich 1890–1918* (Mainz, 1979); Denk, pp. 55–58; and Brose, pp. 78–82.

become a preacher at the imperial court, encountered fierce resistance among German Protestants when he sought to emulate Hitze. In January 1878 Stoecker staged a rally in Berlin to proclaim the formation of a Christian Social Workers' Party. His party program avoided any call for democratic political reforms but raised sweeping social demands similar to those of Hitze. It favored mandatory insurance for widows, orphans, invalids, and the aged, progressive income and inheritance taxes, a ban on Sunday labor and regulation of work hours during the rest of the week, and the formation of workers' associations in each trade guaranteed the right of collective bargaining.[32] Stoecker's campaign had little impact on the mostly unchurched workers of Berlin, however, and Bismarck sharply opposed his program as too radical. Embittered by reactionary currents at the imperial court, which he refused to blame on true aristocrats, Stoecker began to attack the baneful influence of "modern Jewry" in the cosmopolitan press and high finance. Such speeches proved popular in many cities, less among workers than the lower middle class, and attracted the sympathy of the Conservative Party, which helped Stoecker win the Reichstag seat for the Siegerland in 1881. Stoecker's constituency in this traditional center of metallurgy and Pietism was composed largely of workers who owned their own homes or a small farm and played an active role in congregational life.[33]

During the 1880s the development of Protestant workers' clubs expanded the base for the sort of workers' party originally envisioned by Stoecker. In 1882 Protestant miners in Gelsenkirchen formed the first such club because they resented Catholic domination of the local Christian Social club. These workers found a vigorous ally and skillful organizer in Ludwig Weber, pastor of Mönchen-Gladbach and a friend of Stoecker. In 1890 the Evangelical Church leadership urged pastors all over Germany to imitate Weber after the young Kaiser Wilhelm II discharged Bismarck and announced a new policy of reconciling workers to the state. The Protestant workers' clubs grew from 50,000 members in 1890 to 140,000 in 1914, more than one-third of them in Rhineland-Westphalia.[34] The heterogeneous nature of the clubs prevented them from developing a coherent social program, however. In central and eastern Germany they were often

32. Karl Kupisch, *Adolf Stoecker* (Berlin, 1970), pp. 28–36. The best account of Stoecker's world-view remains that of Walter Frank, *Hofprediger Adolf Stoecker und die christlichsoziale Bewegung*, 2d ed. (Hamburg, 1935), pp. 13–35.

33. Kupisch, pp. 39–46; Richard S. Levy, *The Downfall of the Anti-Semitic Political Parties in Imperial Germany* (New Haven and London, 1975), pp. 17–23; Gottfried Mehnert, *Evangelische Kirche und Politik 1917–1919* (Düsseldorf, 1959), pp. 20f.

34. Ernst Faber, "Die evangelischen Arbeitervereine und ihre Stellungnahme zu sozialpolitischen Problemen," Ph.D. diss. (Würzburg, 1927), pp. 69f. See also Gert Lewek, *Kirche und soziale Frage um die Jahrhundertwende. Dargestellt am Wirken Ludwig Webers (1846–1922)* (Neukirchen, 1963), and Pollmann, pp. 93–100.

founded at the behest of employers or government officials who desired to inoculate workers against trade unionism. Most clubs admitted members of the *Mittelstand* as well as blue-collar workers, and some included factory owners too. Workers seeking to forge an effective instrument for representing their interests apparently predominated in the clubs of western and southwestern Germany.[35]

Taking advantage of an enthusiastic public response to the kaiser's call for social reform, Stoecker and Ludwig Weber secured the participation of a broad spectrum of the Protestant intelligentsia in the Evangelical Social Congress, founded in May 1890. Its declared purpose was "to investigate social conditions in our nation, to measure them against the ethical and religious demands of the Gospel, and to make those demands more fruitful and effective in today's economic life,"[36] but even many participants in the congress doubted that this was possible. Most Lutheran theologians agreed with Adolf von Harnack that Protestants "must adhere to the rule of Luther that the spiritual and the worldly are not to be mixed, and therefore that an economic program may not be proposed in the name of religion."[37] Opposition from conservative industrialists and agrarians also weakened the Evangelical Social Congress and prevented it from becoming the Protestant counterpart to the Volksverein, as Stoecker had hoped. Radical pronouncements by young pastors from southern Germany, led by Friedrich Naumann, elicited a torrent of complaints to the kaiser about "socialist" currents in the clergy. Disappointed that workers did not forsake the SPD as soon as he offered them his protection, Wilhelm renounced his policy of conciliation in 1895. In December of that year the leadership of the Prussian Evangelical Church followed suit by condemning "efforts to improve the world" by pastors and ordering them to preach "that welfare and contentment rest on pious acceptance of the worldly order and government ordained by God . . . , that, on the other hand, envy and lust after the goods of one's neighbor violate God's command."[38] In 1896 the most influential advocate of social reform, the Prussian minister of commerce Hans von Berlepsch, was pressured out of office. The

---

35. Eberhard Wächtler, *Zur Geschichte des Kampfes des Bergarbeiterverbandes in Sachsen* (Berlin, 1959); Denk, pp. 23–46; Eckehart Lorenz, "Reaktionen der evangelischen Kirche auf die Entwicklung der sozialistischen Arbeiterbewegung. Mannheim 1890–1933," D.D. diss. (Heidelberg, 1976), pp. 1–100. See also the complaints against the influence of bourgeois elements in the Protestant workers' clubs by Emil Hartwig in *21. Kirchlich-sozialer Kongreß (April 1918)* (Leipzig, 1918), pp. 82f., and Franz Behrens in "Strömungen in den evangelischen Arbeitervereinen und ihre gewerkschaftliche Wertung," a memorandum for Catholic union colleagues written about 1909 and found in the Volksverein Bibliothek.

36. Schick, pp. 76–80.

37. Ibid., pp. 27f., and Pollmann, pp. 111–16.

38. The circular from the Evangelische Oberkirchenrat to all pastors in December 1895 is reprinted in Günter Brakelmann (ed.), *Kirche, soziale Frage und Sozialismus. Band I: 1871–1914* (Gütersloh, 1977), p. 192. See also Pollmann, pp. 120–209, and Born, *Sozialpolitik*, pp. 90–118.

Christian Socials were compelled to leave both the Conservative Party and the Evangelical Social Congress, and Stoecker found his dreams of reconciling the aristocracy with the urban proletariat shattered.[39]

Although Stoecker's fortunes sank in Berlin, a new initiative by coal miners on the Ruhr provided an excellent opportunity for practical cooperation between Catholic and Protestant social reformers. Miners had long been active in religious clubs and were reputedly the most pious group of workers because they faced mortal danger on a daily basis. Churchgoing miners played a major role in the great Ruhr strike of 1889 and the subsequent efforts to organize a unified trade union for all miners.[40] They found, however, that militant Social Democrats eliminated them from all powerful positions in the new union. In 1894 the Ruhr miners' union sent delegates to an international miners' congress in Berlin organized by the SPD. One of its founding members, the Catholic August Brust, responded by proclaiming the formation of a new Union of Christian Miners at a rally of the Catholic and Protestant workers' clubs of the Ruhr.[41] Brust realized that his initiative required the goodwill of the churches to succeed but feared, as he confided to a friend, that the clergymen active in the church-affiliated workers' clubs hoped to use him "as a battering ram against Social Democracy" but would "hold themselves back when it comes time to advance the interests of miners."[42]

Brust initially adopted union statutes that were poorly suited for militant action in order to win toleration from church and state authorities. Dues were set at one-half the level of the socialist miners' union, now known as the Old Union, in order to show that Christian miners were not building a war chest for a major strike, and Brust created an advisory council for clergymen and other bourgeois notables. Although the National Liberal press persuaded many Protestant workers' clubs in the Ruhr to oppose the new union, Brust secured the energetic support of Ludwig Weber by guaranteeing Protestants half the seats on the executive committee.[43] However, the blue-collar union leaders soon achieved successes that forced their clerical patrons to adjust their thinking. In 1897 Brust began to threaten strike action, and he organized a successful strike in Osnabrück in April 1898. Brust's militant new course angered Hitze and Ludwig Weber,

    39. Kupisch, pp. 78–80.
    40. Tenfelde, *Sozialgeschichte,* pp. 345–96, 573–97, and Albin Gladen, "Die Streiks der Bergarbeiter im Ruhrgebiet in den Jahren 1889, 1905 und 1912," in Jürgen Reulecke (ed.), *Arbeiterbewegung an Rhein und Ruhr* (Wuppertal, 1974), pp. 112–31.
    41. Max Jürgen Koch, *Die Bergarbeiterbewegung im Ruhrgebiet zur Zeit Wilhelms II.* (Düsseldorf, 1954), pp. 33–60, and Brose, pp. 99–113.
    42. August Brust to Hermann Köster, 8 April 1894, reprinted in GcG, *25 Jahre,* pp. 124f.
    43. Koch, pp. 60–64; Brose, pp. 109–22; Schneider, *Die christlichen Gewerkschaften,* pp. 58–63.

who resigned from the advisory council, but union membership surged to 21,000, compared with 18,000 for the Old Union. Brust found champions within the Catholic clergy in Heinrich Brauns, a gifted young priest in Essen who understood the rationale for strikes, and August Pieper, executive secretary of the Volksverein. Moreover, Adolf Stoecker lent his considerable talents as a public speaker to the union, and in 1898 he retained his Siegerland Reichstag seat despite Conservative opposition largely because of support from Christian workers.[44] A new era of partnership between the German clergy and Christian workers was dawning.

THE CHRISTIAN UNIONS' STRUGGLE FOR AUTONOMY

Various groups of Christian workers in Rhineland-Westphalia and Bavaria soon imitated Brust's initiative without any central direction. Catholic textile workers along the lower Rhine formed a union in 1898. Heinrich Brauns, himself the son of a master tailor who suffered from the competition of ready-made clothes, advised the founders of this union and later wrote a doctoral dissertation on the mechanization of the Rhenish textile industry. The union organized more than twenty strikes by 1901 and succeeded in compelling many Catholic textile industrialists to abandon their patriarchal standpoint and participate in collective bargaining. It admitted Protestant workers after 1900 and included 37,000 members by 1906, outnumbering its socialist rival in the Rhineland while offering strong competition in Baden and Alsace as well.[45]

In 1899 the Catholic steelworker Franz Wieber founded what was to become the largest Christian union in the early 1920s among his colleagues in Duisburg. Wieber embodied a mixture of militant activism and pious Catholicism distinctive to the Christian labor movement. Born in 1858 the son of a poor Hessian peasant, he entered the Ruhr steel industry as a teenager and rose to become a skilled molder (*Former*). Wieber joined a Kolping Club for artisans but found it powerless to improve the material condition of the labor force. Sacked in 1889 for attempting to form a Christian trade union, Wieber joined the Free metalworkers' union from 1890 to 1895. He later wrote that "in economic matters I

---

44. Brose, pp. 130–39; Hubert Mockenhaupt, *Weg und Wirken des geistlichen Sozialpolitikers Heinrich Brauns* (Munich, 1978), pp. 32–35; Frank, p. 290f.; Irmgard Steinisch, "Der Gewerkverein christlicher Bergarbeiter," in Hans Mommsen and Ulrich Borsdorf (eds.), *Glück auf, Kameraden!* (Cologne, 1979), pp. 274f.

45. Schneider, *Die christlichen Gewerkschaften*, pp. 75–85. See also the highly sympathetic account by Otto Müller, *Die christliche Gewerkschaftsbewegung Deutschlands* (Karlsruhe, 1905), pp. 51–82, 157–78, and Mockenhaupt, pp. 15f., 47f.

could agree with a great deal of what the Social Democrats said" but that their attacks on the Church disgusted him.

> I regarded Christianity not merely as a means for salvation in the afterlife, but rather as the foundation on which the true interests of workers could be advanced and preserved. Our old teacher [in the village school] had showed us how Christianity had abolished slavery and recognized the equal rights of workers. Thus it could not be true that Christianity was the enemy of workers.[46]

Wieber's view of church history, which contrasted so sharply with that of Bebel, may not have been strictly accurate, but he obviously encountered a concern for social problems in the clergy that made it plausible.

Bavaria was a second cradle of the Christian unions, but its importance to the movement soon declined. Here the formation of Christian unions was coordinated by a political club for the Catholic workers of Munich, founded in 1896 by the locksmith Carl Schirmer in order to protest against their neglect by the Bavarian Center Party. Schirmer organized a Bavarian Christian textile workers' union in 1897 and later assisted in the formation of unions for woodworkers, tailors, leatherworkers, and potters. He eventually won a Reichstag seat for the Bavarian Center in 1907, but in 1912 his Christian unions still had only one-tenth the membership of the Bavarian Free unions, and most of their followers lived in small towns and villages. This failure resulted largely from the hostility of the local clergy. The predominantly Catholic employers of Bavaria usually opposed all trade unions, and the clerical supervisors of the Catholic workers' clubs proved extremely reluctant to endorse strike tactics when industrialists as well as workers belonged to the parish. In 1902 the founder of the Christian woodworkers' union, Adam Stegerwald, responded to clerical indifference by moving his headquarters from Munich to Cologne, an action soon imitated by the other Christian unions founded in Bavaria.[47]

Stegerwald's arrival in Cologne accelerated a process of centralization in the Christian unions that began in 1897 at an international congress on social reform in Zürich. Among the German delegates were representatives of both the SPD and Center Party, including a Catholic machinist from Cologne named Johannes Giesberts, Brust, Schirmer, and Matthias Erzberger, a gifted young journalist and head of the Catholic workers' clubs of Württemberg. The Catholic workers

---

46. Wieber's reminiscences in GcG, *25 Jahre*, esp. p. 173, and Schneider, *Die christlichen Gewerkschaften*, pp. 88ff., 168f.

47. Denk, pp. 250–93; GcG, *25 Jahre*, p. 8; Heitzer, pp. 50–55.

played a largely passive role, however, and felt ashamed that their colleagues, unlike Social Democratic workers, still required clergymen and bourgeois politicians to serve as their spokesmen. They returned home determined to establish a nationwide network of independent unions.[48] In 1899 the four allies from Zürich organized the first national congress of Christian unions in Mainz, which adopted guidelines that repudiated calls by a few delegates for explicit commitment to the Center Party or Catholic doctrine.

> The trade unions shall stand on the foundation of Christianity but will be interconfessional, i.e., embrace members of both Christian confessions. The trade unions shall also be nonpartisan, i.e., affiliated with no particular political party. The discussion of partisan political issues is to be avoided, but the implementation of legal reforms on the basis of the existing social order shall be discussed.

These Mainz Guidelines expressed a desire for amicable accord with employers but endorsed the use of strikes "as a last resort and if success seems probable." The congress also established a League of Christian Unions (Gesamtverband der christlichen Gewerkschaften Deutschlands, or GcG) to lobby for social reform and coordinate organizing drives.[49]

At the second congress of the Christian unions, which met in Frankfurt in 1900, Brust and Giesberts declared that ideologically neutral trade unions for all workers were their ideal, that merger between the Christian and Free unions could occur if the latter would "renounce Marxism" and sever their ties with the SPD. Brust even declared, in a statement highly offensive to the Catholic clergy, that "we can calmly strike the word 'Christian' from the trade union movement" because "neither the Christian nor the socialist Weltanschauung belongs in the union."[50] Giesberts and Brust dared take such a stand because of the ferment within the socialist labor movement. Eduard Bernstein had published his famous "revisionist" attack on the economic determinism of Marx and Kautsky in 1899. Arguing that socialism should be considered an ethical imperative rather than a logical deduction from facts, Bernstein urged closer cooperation between the SPD and idealistic social reformers in the liberal parties and clergy. At the same time, the emergence of Christian unions had prompted extensive self-criticism among Free union leaders, many of whom deplored anticlerical propaganda and

---

48. See the accounts by Stegerwald in GcG, *25 Jahre*, p. 9, and Giesberts in GcG, *12. Kongreß der christlichen Gewerkschaften* (Berlin, 1929), p. 87. See also Klaus Epstein, *Matthias Erzberger und das Dilemma der deutschen Demokratie*, rev. German ed. 1962 (Ullstein Verlag, 1976), pp. 26–29.
49. Schneider, *Die christlichen Gewerkschaften*, pp. 123f., 134–37.
50. Brose, pp. 180–83.

demanded more scrupulous adherence to the political neutrality clauses in union statutes.[51] These developments also encouraged bourgeois social reformers such as Friedrich Naumann, Hans von Berlepsch, and Lujo Brentano to anticipate the fission of the SPD into a small band of dogmatic social revolutionaries and a large, moderate labor party allied with the unions. In 1899 Hans von Berlepsch and the Catholic Volksverein founded a new Society for Social Reform uniting progressive bureaucrats, academics, and bourgeois politicians with Christian and Hirsch–Duncker trade unionists. Although the Free unions refused to join, Bernstein approved of the new society. Berlepsch hoped someday to win the support of all moderate trade unionists, and the Frankfurt speech by Giesberts, who sat on the society's executive committee, reflected this strategy.[52]

Thus the charges in the SPD press after the Frankfurt Congress that Brust and Giesberts did not mean what they said about neutral unions, that they merely sought to conceal the clerical domination of the Christian unions, were unfair. This propaganda proved highly effective, however. Bernstein's remained an isolated voice in the SPD. Trade union delegates at party congresses consistently joined with the executive to condemn Revisionist doctrinal heresies in exchange for enhanced autonomy in tactical decisions. The inner cohesion of the socialist labor movement, the refusal by moderate socialists to provoke a schism when it seemed highly unlikely that the empire's ruling elite would ever accept substantial reforms, confounded the ambitious plans of Berlepsch and his confederates. The GcG was compelled to carry on with the difficult task of competing against a much larger and wealthier socialist rival for the allegiance of workers, and neutral unions did not arise in Germany until after World War II.

The GcG found an energetic leader for this difficult task when Adam Stegerwald became its general secretary in 1903. Born in 1874 near Würzburg, like Wieber the son of a poor peasant, Stegerwald was a skilled cabinetmaker who found in a Kolping Club the first satisfaction of his hunger for learning and self-improvement. In Munich he attended Brentano's economics lectures from 1900 to 1902, and he combined a knowledge of history and economics most unusual for a self-educated worker with a gift for expressing himself in direct language and earthy imagery. He proved an able administrator and persuaded the GcG's member unions that they must surrender a good deal of autonomy in order to marshal their resources efficiently. Under his leadership the GcG grew steadily

51. Steinberg, pp. 87–106; Moses, vol. 1, pp. 135–38; Schneider, *Die christlichen Gewerkschaften*, pp. 214–20.
52. Brose, pp. 158–75, and Rüdiger vom Bruch, "Bürgerliche Sozialreform und Gewerkschaften im späten deutschen Kaiserreich. Die Gesellschaft für soziale Reform 1901–1914," *Internationale wissenschaftliche Korrespondenz*, 15 (December 1979), pp. 582–608.

from 108,000 members in 1904 to 343,000 in 1913, far outstripping the Hirsch–Duncker unions.[53]

The member unions of the GcG also learned after 1900 that they must imitate the militant strike tactics of the Free unions in order to survive. Christian hopes for the peaceful arbitration of labor disputes were consistently disappointed, most notably by the leaders of heavy industry, who refused to engage in collective bargaining with any unions. Blacklists, the wholesale arrest of picketers, and the importation of strikebreakers remained common.[54] When August Brust resigned as chairman of the Christian miner's union in 1904 in order to enter the Prussian parliament for the Center Party, militant young activists abolished the advisory council of bourgeois notables and raised dues to the same level as the Old Union's in order to build up a strike chest. The Christian miners cooperated closely with the Old Union in the Ruhr miners' strike of 1905. The Christian union's stance stimulated a groundswell of sympathy for the strikers in the bureaucracy, the lower middle class in Ruhr cities, and the Protestant and Catholic clergy that deeply alarmed the mine operators, and its ties with the Center Party were instrumental in securing legislation on hours and working conditions that satisfied many of the strikers' demands. The membership of the Christian miners' union had stagnated after 1897, but this reorganization enabled it to keep pace with Old Union gains thereafter.[55] The most effective spokesman for the new leadership of the Christian miners' union was Heinrich Imbusch, editor of its journal and later union chairman from 1919 to 1933. Born in Oberhausen in 1878, Imbusch was one of the few second-generation industrial workers among the Christian union leaders and displayed unusual sensitivity to any sign of discrimination against workers. Imbusch felt disgusted by the condescending treatment accorded Gerhard Stötzel as the token worker in the Center Party leadership and prodded the GcG to demand a quota of labor representatives in all Center Party organs. Imbusch considered the Center Party's grant of three Reichstag seats to Christian unionists in 1907 and five in 1912 inadequate.[56]

53. Josef Deutz, *Adam Stegerwald* (Cologne, 1952), pp. 20–26; "Adam Stegerwald," in GcG, *25 Jahre;* Helmut Schorr, *Adam Stegerwald* (Recklinghausen, 1966), pp. 30–33.
54. See Müller, pp. 83–86; Saul; and Hans Mommsen, "Soziale Kämpfe im Ruhrbergbau nach der Jahrhundertwende," in Mommsen and Borsdorf (eds.), *Glück auf!*.
55. Koch, pp. 96–110; Gladen, pp. 134–40; Born, *Sozialpolitik*, pp. 184–91; Günter Brakelmann, "Evangelische Pfarrer im Konfliktfeld des Ruhrbergarbeiterstreiks von 1905," in Reulecke and Weber (eds.), *Fabrik*, pp. 302–14; Steinisch, p. 274f.
56. See Imbusch's reminiscences in GcG, *25 Jahre*, pp. 195–99, and Ludwig Frey, *Die Stellung der christlichen Gewerkschaften Deutschlands zu den politischen Parteien* (Berlin, 1931), pp. 72–88.

Not all the clergymen who had supported church-affiliated organizations for workers would cooperate with militant and independent Christian trade unions. The Volksverein did. Franz Hitze accepted the Christian unions after they became an established fact, and August Pieper helped Johannes Giesberts establish a mass circulation weekly for Catholic workers in 1898, the *Westdeutsche Arbeiter-Zeitung*, disseminated the writings of Brentano and other pro-union economists, and inaugurated annual summer seminars for Christian labor leaders. Led by Heinrich Brauns after 1904, these two-month seminars involved the study of economics, labor law, and the history of the labor movement. The alumni included most of the leading Catholic trade unionists of the Weimar Republic and a few of their Protestant colleagues.[57] Any cooperation between the Christian and Free unions in strike action outraged many senior clergymen, however, especially in Silesia and the Saar, where powerful Catholic industrialists and magnates played a major role in Church life. In 1902 the conservative prince-bishop of Breslau, Cardinal Kopp, and Bishop Korum of Trier decided to combat the spread of the Christian unions. They maintained that the pronouncements of the Church hierarchy should guide Catholic workers in all their economic and political activities, a position that came to be known as "integralist." Kopp and Korum preached that participation in strikes tempted workers to rely on material force instead of faith, and that cooperation with Protestants, who, one of their spokesman explained, had "no authority or firm principles in these important questions but are governed by their passions," would corrupt the morals of Catholic workers even more.[58] Kopp and Korum encouraged the Catholic workers' clubs of their dioceses to forbid membership in the Christian unions and to revive Franz Hitze's old idea for purely Catholic "trade groups" under clerical supervision. The integralist Berlin Wing of the Catholic workers' clubs attracted 130,000 members by 1913, although its Trade Groups remained much smaller. The archbishop of Cologne stoutly defended the Christian unions, but the integralists enjoyed the sympathy of the antimodernist Pope Pius X and hoped that their opponents would be branded as heretics.[59]

Integralist attacks severely damaged the credibility of the Christian unions by confirming the worst fears among Protestants concerning ultramontanism and among Catholic workers concerning capitalist influence in the Church. They

57. Heitzer pp. 42–66, 239–41; Mockenhaupt, pp. 46–53; Oswald Wachtling, *Joseph Joos* (Mainz, 1974), pp. 5–27.

58. See Rudolf Brack, *Deutscher Episkopat und Gewerkschaftsstreit 1900–1914* (Cologne and Vienna, 1976), pp. 57–68 (quotation on p. 66), and Ronald Ross, *Beleaguered Tower* (Notre Dame, 1976), pp. 68–75.

59. Brack, pp. 75–82, and Emil Ritter, pp. 314–25.

especially complicated Adolf Stoecker's efforts to rally Protestant support for the GcG. In 1897 Stoecker began to rebuild an independent Christian Social Party and a Free Clerical Social Conference, a small but well-organized pressure group of orthodox Protestants and social activists that imitated the activities of the Volksverein on a small scale. In the conference Stoecker found colleagues who could articulate a theological rationale for social activism that overcame some of the inhibitions among Lutheran pastors, such as the professor of church history at the University of Berlin, Reinhold Seeberg, and Stoecker's son-in-law, Reinhard Mumm. The Clerical Social Conference sought in particular to encourage the emergence of Protestant labor leaders, and in 1898 it raised money to hire Franz Behrens, a gardener in Mecklenburg and executive secretary of a small gardeners' union who was involved in a dispute over affiliation with the Free unions, as a full-time organizer for the Protestant workers' clubs.[60] But the integralist controversy encouraged attacks on Stoecker by progressive and reactionary Protestants alike. Friedrich Naumann polemicized against the idea that a trade union could be "Christian" and established close ties with the Hirsch–Duncker unions and the Protestant workers' clubs of Baden-Württemberg.[61] Leaders of heavy industry organized a more dangerous threat to the Christian unions in the form of "Yellow" company unions, which spread rapidly within heavy industry between 1905 and 1914. Some Protestant workers' clubs and local branches of the National Liberal Party conducted vigorous propaganda on behalf of these company unions, denouncing the GcG as ultramontane. By 1914 their membership far exceeded that of the Hirsch–Duncker unions and began to rival that of the GcG.[62]

Convinced that integralism prevented their unions from growing, Stegerwald and other GcG leaders responded in angry speeches, offensive even to their sympathizers in the episcopate, that bishops must not presume to make judgments in economic matters. But Stegerwald also proved a skillful tactician in forging alliances designed to isolate the integralists and to demonstrate that the GcG could promote social reform in cooperation with bourgeois moderates. In

60. Schick, pp. 37–44, 91–94; Pollmann, pp. 284f.; Reinhard Mumm, *Der christlich-soziale Gedanke* (Berlin, 1933), pp. 21–60; "Franz Behrens," in GcG, *25 Jahre*, pp. 153–60.

61. Dieter Düding, *Der Nationalsoziale Verein 1896–1903* (Munich and Vienna, 1972), pp. 104–31; Pollmann, pp. 209–13; Born, *Sozialpolitik*, pp. 62–75; Rennie Brantz, "Anton Erkelenz, the Hirsch-Duncker Trade Unions, and the German Democratic Party," Ph.D. diss. (Ohio State University, 1973), pp. 13–33.

62. See Klaus Mattheier, *Die Gelben* (Düsseldorf, 1973), esp. pp. 220–34. The Christian unions enjoyed the sympathy of the National Liberal Party chairman Ernst Bassermann and his lieutenant Gustav Stresemann, however, who helped arrange an alliance with the Bochum Center Party in 1912 to replace the socialist Otto Hue with a Protestant member of the Christian miners' union: Brose, pp. 314–17.

1903 Stegerwald and Behrens secured the participation of a broad front of non-socialist organizations in a German Labor Congress, including the Catholic and Protestant workers' clubs and the white-collar union that became the GcG's most important ally in the Weimar Republic, the Nationalist Union of Commercial Employees (Deutschnationaler Handlungsgehilfen-Verband) or DHV. The founders of the DHV in 1893 had been deeply involved in the anti-Semitic German Social Party and the chauvinist Pan-German League, but now a pragmatic faction in the leadership led by Hans Bechly, the union's chairman from 1909 to 1933, sought to disengage it from such causes and to concentrate instead on the material interests of white-collar workers.[63] Although the Hirsch–Duncker unions refused to participate, the congress received enthusiastic attention in the bourgeois press, established a standing committee under Franz Behrens, and persuaded Reich Chancellor Bülow to receive its leaders and promise sympathetic attention to their demands for the abolition of legal restrictions on union activity.[64] In order to document its commitment to interconfessionality, the Christian miners' union hired Behrens as its general secretary in 1905. In 1906 he became vice-chairman of the GcG, and he won a Reichstag seat from Wetzlar in 1907 for the Christian Social Party. Although Protestants comprised only 15–30% of GcG members before World War I, Behrens secured a somewhat larger quota of leadership positions for them.[65] Stegerwald also won energetic support against the integralists from the leadership of the Center Party, which desired to underscore its independence from the Church in order to facilitate parliamentary alliances and the appointment of Catholic civil servants by the Crown.[66]

However, the GcG, Volksverein, and Society for Social Reform failed to win the meaningful progress in social legislation that alone could create a real impression on the working class. In 1907 the last powerful advocate of legislation that would encourage trade unionism, Reich Interior Minister Posadowsky-Wehner, was forced out of office, and in 1909 the Center Party formed a Reichstag coalition with the Conservatives that embarrassed the GcG by blocking proposals for Prussian suffrage reform and increasing the burden of indirect taxation on the poor.[67] Stymied in their pursuit of legislative reform, the Christian unions hoped

63. See Iris Hamel, *Völkischer Verband und nationale Gewerkschaft* (Frankfurt am Main, 1967), pp. 110–22.

64. Schneider, *Die christlichen Gewerkschaften*, pp. 236–44, and Brose, pp. 221–32. See also the documentation by Dieter Fricke, "Bürgerliche Sozialreformer und die Zersplitterung der antisozialistischen Arbeiterorganisationen vor 1914," *Zeitschrift für Geschichtswissenschaft*, 23 (1975), pp. 1177–98.

65. Brose, pp. 241–47. Brose estimates that in 1906, 75,000 of 245,000 members were Protestant, but the Prussian police and the Volksverein leadership both believed the proportion to be lower than 20%: Ross, p. 83.

66. Brack, pp. 116–24; Ross, pp. 33–42, 125–27; Schorr, pp. 40–45.

67. Brose, pp. 282–87, and Heitzer, pp. 127–31. See also Reinhard Patemann, *Der Kampf um die preußische Wahlreform im Ersten Weltkrieg* (Düsseldorf, 1964), pp. 15f.

at least to weaken the position of radical socialists by winning acceptance for collective bargaining in heavy industry.[68] In March 1912 the Christian miners' union went to the greatest lengths to demonstrate its goodwill by actively opposing a strike in the Ruhr, launched by the Old Union against its advice. The Christian union acted in part from a realistic assessment of the prospects for a strike but raised the issue to the ideological plane by denouncing the Old Union's claim that German miners should take advantage of strikes by their English colleagues in order to force German industrialists to their knees. Franz Behrens declared on the floor of the Reichstag that Christian workers valued the health of the national economy above the utopian ideal of international proletarian solidarity. Christian miners willing to work appealed for protection against striking colleagues, thus encouraging the government to crush the strike with a massive show of force.[69] Instead of promoting acceptance of collective bargaining, the Christian miners' stance merely encouraged conservative politicians and reactionary industrialists like Alfred Hugenberg, chairman of the board of directors of the Krupp combine, to hope for a merger between the Christian and Yellow unions. In July 1913 the heavy industrialists who categorically rejected collective bargaining joined with leading agrarians to organize a Cartel of Productive Estates, which agitated for stringent new legislation against picketing. Curiously, they invited the Christian unions to enroll as charter members.[70]

Renewed attacks on trade unionism within the Catholic Church coincided with this intensification of labor strife. Panic gripped the Christian unions and their allies when Pope Pius X publicly lauded the principles of integralism in May 1912. Persuaded that roughly 800,000 Catholic workers had already joined the Free unions, mostly in regions where there were no Christian unions to offer a meaningful alternative, the archbishops of Cologne and Munich mobilized the vast majority of German bishops to petition the Vatican on behalf of the GcG. Reich Chancellor Bethmann Hollweg, responding to an appeal by Behrens, and Center Party leaders also intervened. They persuaded the pope to include in the encyclical *Singulari quadam* of September 1912 a grudging declaration that individual bishops might "tolerate" interconfessional Christian unions if extraordinary local conditions prevailed, which effectively ended the controversy.[71]

Alarmed by the polarization of German society, the leaders of the Christian unions rediscovered the important interests they shared with the SPD and Free

68. See Elaine Glovka Spencer, "Employer Response to Unionism: Ruhr Coal Industrialists before 1914," *Journal of Modern History*, 48 (September 1976), pp. 403–07, and Brose, pp. 307f.

69. Koch, pp. 121–32; Gladen, pp. 143ff.; Saul, pp. 271ff.

70. Mattheier, pp. 248–69; Brose, pp. 321–25, 374–83; Saul, pp. 370–94; Dirk Stegmann, "Hugenberg contra Stresemann," *Vierteljahrshefte für Zeitgeschichte*, 24 (October 1976), pp. 346–64.

71. Brack, pp. 257–337; Denk, pp. 305–24; Ross, pp. 112–16.

unions. They felt disillusioned when the Center Party press and even Matthias Erzberger commented favorably on the Cartel of Productive Estates. Far from joining it, the GcG dropped all attacks on Social Democrats in the summer of 1913 and devoted the Third German Workers' Congress in December to criticism of the cartel. In May 1914 the Free, Christian, and Hirsch–Duncker unions participated in a mass rally against proposed antiunion laws, organized by the Society for Social Reform, the first such act of public cooperation among the feuding unions.[72] Perhaps for the first time, anger with government policies, with the labor relations practices of heavy industry, and with reactionary currents in the churches clearly outweighed the desire to weaken Social Democracy in the minds of Christian labor leaders.

THE TRADE UNIONS AND THE WAR EFFORT

Most nonsocialist labor leaders and bourgeois social reformers adopted an emphatically nationalistic stance during the increasingly grave diplomatic crises of the decade before the war. They felt that workers had to demonstrate a fervent patriotism before they could win true civic equality, and their efforts to persuade workers that prosperity and social progress depended in large measure on Germany's attaining the status of a true "world power" apparently enjoyed considerable success.[73] The stance of the Christian unions in particular doubtless strengthened the belief of Carl Legien and other skeptical Free union leaders that the ideals of the Second International found little echo in the German working class. Far from preparing a general strike, on August 2, 1914, the General Commission resolved to oppose all strikes for the duration of the war. Thus it anticipated and in a sense determined the SPD's decision to approve war credits in the Reichstag and to accept the German government's claim that Russia was the aggressor.[74] The kaiser then declared that he no longer recognized distinctions of party or class, and all factions agreed to a domestic political truce, a *Bürgfrieden*.

The historic decision by the socialist labor movement to support the war effort greatly facilitated cooperation between the Free and Christian unions. By enhancing the legitimacy of organized labor in the eyes of both the authorities and middle-class public opinion, it also brought Germany much closer to the system of corporate pluralism described by Charles Maier. The war created new

72. Bruch, pp. 603–08; Brose, pp. 379–95; Schneider, *Die christlichen Gewerkschaften*, pp. 226–30, 251ff.
73. See Schneider, *Die christlichen Gewerkschaften*, p. 254; Düding, pp. 68–78, 112–13; and Heitzer, pp. 212–19.
74. Moses, vol. 1, pp. 163–89; Susanne Miller, *Burgfrieden und Klassenkampf* (Düsseldorf, 1974), pp. 48–51; Varain, pp. 71–78.

opportunities for practical cooperation between socialists and nonsocialists in efforts to alleviate the material distress of the civilian population. In January 1915 every major trade union participated in the formation of a new War Committee for Consumers' Interests, which lobbied to hold down food prices. Stegerwald proved willing to provoke sharp clashes with agrarian interests in the Center Party over this issue, both in public and in private. He also entered the governing board of the War Food Office, created in May 1916 to monitor the food supply and to control prices, where he collaborated with the Social Democrat August Müller.[75] In the spring of 1915 the General Commission adopted a portentous new strategy when it opened a campaign to implement a new system of labor exchanges controlled jointly by management and labor. For the first time, the Free unions formulated their legislative proposal in consultation with the Christian and Hirsch–Duncker unions, made significant concessions to their views, and thereby won support from a Reichstag majority composed of the SPD, Center Party, and left liberals. Thereafter it became standard practice for the three trade union associations to submit joint petitions to the government on a variety of issues.[76]

The most successful collaboration between the Free and Christian unions occurred late in 1916 during the parliamentary debate over the Patriotic Auxiliary Service Law, a measure designed to mobilize the labor force more efficiently. A large Reichstag majority sympathetic to the trade unions amended the government's bill in order to create workers' committees in each large factory that met with management in order to regulate working conditions and the allocation of labor. General Wilhelm Groener of the War Office for the economy instructed his subordinates to encourage the election of union representatives to the workers' committees and to exclude the Yellow unions and integralist Catholic Trade Groups. Thus the government compelled heavy industrialists, for the first time, to recognize union officials as the representatives of their workers. This policy contributed to a dramatic increase in the prestige, influence, and membership of the unions in war-related industries.[77]

The collaboration between the Free and Christian unions after 1914 took place in the midst of intensifying class conflict, aggravated by serious food shortages, and an increasingly savage public debate over war aims. This polarization of

75. Hans-Joachim Bieber, *Gewerkschaften im Krieg und Revolution* (Hamburg, 1981), vol. 1, pp. 194ff.; and Gerald Feldman, *Army, Industry, and Labor in Germany 1914–1918* (Princeton, 1966), pp. 109–15. For Stegerwald's firm line against agrarians in the Center Party, see Carl Bachem's notes on a conference of Rhenish Center leaders on 7 January 1916, NL Bachem/854, and Stegerwald to Giesberts, 22 September 1916, NL Otte/6/183–87.

76. Bieber, vol. 1, pp. 150–53.

77. Feldman, *Army*, pp. 204–325; Varain, pp. 89–97; Mattheier, pp. 188–212.

society was reflected in the schism of the SPD during 1916 between the prowar majority and the pacifist Independent Social Democrats, and caused serious disputes in the Center Party as well. Many agrarian and bourgeois Catholics supported the annexationist propaganda financed by the economic interest groups in the Cartel of Productive Estates. Catholic labor leaders believed that such propaganda merely prolonged the war, however, and desired to leave the door open for a negotiated compromise peace. In September 1915 Stegerwald arranged the first of many private conferences with the leaders of the Rhenish Center in order to protest against annexationist resolutions by local party meetings. He expressed astonishment that the Christian peasants' clubs had signed petitions to the government demanding the annexation of territory on the western front containing 17 million inhabitants without giving them any voice in Reich affairs: "Such a policy might be possible with African Hottentots, but not with the Belgian and French populations, which look back on a tradition of political liberty lasting more than a century."[78] Despite this protest, the agitation for annexations and unrestricted submarine warfare intensified in the Center press, led by Carl Bachem's *Kölnische Volkszeitung*. In another Rhineland conference in April 1916, Stegerwald led a blistering attack on Bachem's editorial policies that was supported by Giesberts, Heinrich Brauns, and other labor representatives. Although Bachem had supported the Christian unions during their prewar confrontation with the Vatican, their leaders interpreted his annexationism as evidence of an "anti-worker outlook," and Bachem's account of the episode to his agent in Berlin reveals that he did indeed hope to prevent democratic reform by achieving total victory. However, the unexpected force of this attack persuaded him to moderate his public criticism of the government.[79]

The same war weariness among workers that impelled union leaders to demand a prompt, compromise peace also impelled them to demand democratization of the constitution. Ever since the fall of 1914, Chancellor Bethmann Hollweg had promised to reward the patriotism of workers with a "new orientation" of domestic policy after the war. The SPD publicly demanded the immediate implementation of equal suffrage in Prussia when the fighting entered its second year. In December 1915 the Volksverein leadership responded by submitting a confidential memorandum, probably written by Stegerwald, to the national committee of the Center Party. This document described in detail the intensification of class conflict in Germany on the eve of the war and warned that

---

78. Stegerwald to Carl Trimborn, 11 September 1915, NL Marx/222/24–27. Stegerwald referred to the memorandum of May 1915 by the "Six Trade Associations" discussed by Fritz Fischer, *Germany's Aims in the First World War* (New York, 1967), pp. 165–73.

79. Carl Bachem to Hans Eisele, 27 April 1916, NL Bachem/854.

the Center Party could be torn to pieces by this trend. "For the great mass of the population, social progress and the representation of economic interests depend so strongly on a liberal reform [freiheitliche Gestaltung] of the Prussian suffrage law . . . that this issue has become the cardinal point for our political development." The author warned that the Center might cease to be a "people's party" if it failed to seize the initiative on this issue. [80]

The Center Party took no initiative, however, and Stegerwald encouraged the organ of the Christian miners' union to criticize its stance publicly in the summer of 1916. The Christian unions' senior parliamentarian, Johannes Giesberts, who had inherited Stötzel's Reichstag seat for Essen in 1905 and also sat in the Prussian parliament, expressed concern that this tactic would jeopardize party unity, but Stegerwald replied that the GcG must adopt a policy of "confrontation and public spectacle [Krach und Theater]" in order to compel the Center to recognize that the time had come to grant workers equal rights. [81] Stegerwald rejoiced when Chancellor Bethmann Hollweg persuaded the kaiser to call for abolition of Prussia's three-class suffrage in his Easter Address of 1917, but Giesberts and the leaders of the Center delegation to the Prussian parliament sought to minimize the impact of this initiative by drafting a compromise bill with the Conservative Party that gave extra votes to property owners and heads of families. Stegerwald nevertheless mobilized all other Catholic labor leaders to agitate for equal suffrage, a principle endorsed by the chancellor in July 1917. The Catholic workers' clubs of western Germany cooperated closely with the GcG in organizing a network of Political Committees for workers in the Center Party and staging mass rallies for equal suffrage. [82]

At this juncture the political scene was thrown into confusion when Matthias Erzberger, a former annexationist, decided to reveal the desperate nature of Germany's military situation to the public in order to secure passage by the Reichstag of an antiannexationist Peace Resolution. This initiative diverted public attention to international relations and led directly to the fall of Bethmann Hollweg, whose incompetent successor Michaelis blocked any reform initiative

80. Teilnachlaß Pieper 15/1/4, pp. 973ff. See also Emil Ritter, p. 366, and Patemann, *Kampf,* pp. 20–37.

81. [Stegerwald] to Giesberts (unsigned carbon copy), 22 September 1916, NL Otte/6/186f. See also Carl Bachem's praise for Giesberts' willingness to subordinate suffrage reform to Church interests and party unity in notes of November 10, 1916, on a conference of Rhenish party leaders, NL Bachem/851.

82. Patemann, *Kampf,* pp. 71–74; Heitzer, pp. 133–36; *Zentralblatt,* 21 May 1917, p. 83; [Theodor Brauer] to Giesberts, 13 March 1917, NL Otte/6/179; Cologne Archdiocese, "Arbeitervereine"/V, "Protokoll der Sitzung des Diözesankomittees," May 22, 1917. Michael Schneider, *Die christlichen Gewerkschaften,* pp. 392–94, grossly underestimates the strength of agitation for suffrage reform by the Christian unions and Catholic workers' clubs.

during three critical months. Historians have never been able to explain fully why Erzberger, supposedly the head of the left wing of the Center Party, cooperated with General Ludendorff in order to topple Bethmann just when the latter had resolved to press energetically for democratic reforms.[83] Stegerwald's suspicion that Erzberger sought to support the effort by his friend Giesberts to delay any consideration of suffrage reform in the interest of Catholic unity may provide the explanation. At any rate, Stegerwald deeply regretted the departure of Bethmann Hollweg, whom he considered the only leader capable of implementing significant reforms, and feared that the Peace Resolution would merely undermine morale further without accomplishing anything positive. These policy differences of July 1917 later ripened into an intense personal antagonism between Erzberger and Stegerwald.[84]

Erzberger's Peace Resolution also embarrassed the interconfessional Christian unions by encouraging a public debate over war aims that divided Catholic and Protestant workers. In September 1917 annexationists responded to the Peace Resolution by founding the Fatherland Party, a mass movement appealing for the suspension of all domestic debates for the sake of total victory. While acquiring financial control of many newspapers, Hugenberg and other right-wing industrialists secretly organized and funded the new party, whose patriotic rhetoric masked plans for reversing the trend toward democratization in Germany.[85] In October Stegerwald rallied a united front of Christian union leaders, including Protestants, to oppose the policies of the Fatherland Party at the Fourth German Labor Congress, held in Berlin. The congress demanded equal suffrage in Prussia and collective bargaining throughout the Reich, while condemning both annexationist propaganda and the pacifism of the Independent Socialists.[86] In December the GcG went further by joining with the Society for Social Reform and the Free and Hirsch–Duncker unions to form the antiannexationist People's League for Freedom and the Fatherland, in which Gustav Bauer of the General Commission served as first vice-chairman and Stegerwald as second. The GcG organ explained the need for active opposition to the Fa-

83. The best attempts are by Epstein, pp. 206–29, and Rudolf Morsey, *Die Deutsche Zentrumspartei 1917–1923* (Düsseldorf, 1966), pp. 61–72.

84. See *Zentralblatt*, 30 July 1917, pp. 121–23, and 3 June 1918, p. 94. Even before 1914 the priorities of reformers in the Volksverein, who wanted to increase popular participation in state and local government without necessarily impinging on the constitutional prerogative of the kaiser, had differed significantly from those of south German democrats like Erzberger, who desired above all to parliamentarize the government of the Reich.

85. Dirk Stegmann, "Zwischen Repression und Manipulation. Konservative Machteliten und Arbeiter- und Angestelltenbewegung 1910–1918," *Archiv für Sozialgeschichte* 12 (1972), pp. 376–89.

86. *Bericht über die Verhandlungen des 4. Deutschen Arbeiter-Kongresses, 28.–30. Oktober 1917* (Cologne, 1918), esp. pp. 11–34, 69.

therland Party by linking annexationism with patriarchal approaches to labor relations. "In heavy industry the employer wants to dictate unilaterally while the worker is supposed to obey blindly. We oppose this spirit in labor relations, we struggle against this spirit in our political life, and we also condemn this spirit in our foreign policy."[87] This analysis suggests a convergence of outlook between the core membership of the Christian unions and Social Democratic workers. The Protestant clergy counted among the most enthusiastic supporters of the Fatherland Party, however, including the Christian Socials Weber, Seeberg, and Mumm, and their views enjoyed much influence within the Protestant workers' clubs. In principle the Christian Socials supported suffrage reform and trade unionism, but they accepted uncritically the Fatherland Party's claim that all squabbling over reforms represented a breach of patriotic duty in time of war.[88] Moreover, the Nationalist Union of Commercial Employees (the DHV) was so angered by the participation of the GcG in the People's League that it considered resigning from the German Labor Congress. The DHV decided to content itself with a press release to the effect that the white-collar unions in the congress were in no way bound by the GcG's action, but this dispute highlighted important differences in outlook that were later intensified by defeat and revolution.[89]

The People's League failed to influence German foreign policy because Russia's military collapse at the end of 1917 revived hopes for total victory. Hunger riots and wildcat strikes during 1917 and the frightening example of the Russian Revolution nevertheless persuaded government leaders and a substantial Reichstag majority that they must support organized labor's demand for suffrage reform. The Hertling cabinet formed in November promptly presented a bill for equal suffrage to the Prussian parliament. Moreover, Stegerwald was appointed to the Prussian House of Peers, the first and last worker to sit in that body. The agrarian wing of the Center's Prussian parliamentary delegation, encouraged by Cardinal Felix Hartmann of Cologne, continued to support the conservative opposition to the government, however. In the decisive vote of June 11, 1918, 33 of 93 Center delegates present joined the majority in favor of the Conservative Party's rival bill for plural suffrage. The Political Committees for workers in the Center Party responded with mass rallies in western Germany, where labor leaders pledged to prevent the reelection of all foes of equal suffrage in the

87. *Zentralblatt*, 14 January 1918, p. 12. See also Varain, pp. 98–102, and Bieber, vol. 2, pp. 533–39.
88. See Mumm, *Der christlich-soziale Gedanke*, pp. 72–87, and Mehnert, pp. 43–74.
89. "DHV Verwaltung: Auszüge" (DHV Archiv, Hamburg), pp. 64f. Two recent accounts exaggerate the strength of annexationist currents in the Christian unions by generalizing the attitude of DHV activists and Christian Social pastors: see Schneider, *Die christlichen Gewerkschaften*, pp. 388–91, and Bieber, vol. 1, pp. 249–53.

party.[90] Once again the vacillating conduct of Giesberts, who pledged support of equal suffrage in April 1918 but then endorsed plural suffrage in June, outraged his colleagues. Intimidated by opposition to equal suffrage in the episcopate and Supreme Army Command, fearful that the militant tactics of the GcG would merely reinforce radical currents in the working class, Giesberts quietly resigned from its executive committee.[91]

The dispute over suffrage reform generated the most intense conflict in the Archdiocese of Cologne. Cardinal Hartmann believed that equal suffrage would enable an anticlerical majority of liberals and socialists in the Prussian parliament to cripple the Church. By the end of 1917 most of Hartmann's colleagues in the episcopate felt that continued opposition to suffrage reform was futile, but he carried on the fight with private letters to Center Party leaders and public praise for the Catholic nobility.[92] He also selected several conservative priests as chairmen of workers' clubs, who promptly began fueding with their membership. However, Monsignor Otto Müller, the popular leader of the workers' clubs in the archdiocese, strongly supported Stegerwald's political line. In May 1918 he persuaded a national congress of club chairmen to endorse equal suffrage, and he then urged Hartmann to dismiss any chairman who opposed it. Müller's enemies responded by telling Hartmann that Müller and Stegerwald were plotting to end clerical supervision of the Catholic workers' clubs.[93] A secret memorandum of August 13, 1918, apparently drafted by Hartmann for distribution to the other Prussian bishops, endorsed this charge. It stated that the bishops had accepted interconfessional unions only on the condition that the Catholic workers' clubs would check radical currents in them, but that the clubs had proved too weak for this task. Catholic members of the Christian unions had taken on a "radical materialist tinge" in their struggle for higher wages. "Now a second movement of the materialist kind is to be introduced among Catholic workers," the movement led by the Political Committees that sought to transfer political power to the working class.[94]

90. Patemann, *Kampf*, pp. 189–96; Schorr, p. 53; "Bericht über die erste Tagung der Arbeiter-Zentrumswähler Westdeutschlands in Bochum am 23. Juni 1918," Volksverein Bibliothek.

91. See Brauer to Giesberts, 4 July 1918, Giesberts' reply of July 11, and the rough draft for Brauer's response in NL Otte/6/156–62. Giesberts apparently rejoined the committee in the fall of 1918.

92. Reinhard Patemann, "Der deutsche Episkopat und das preußische Wahlrechtsproblem 1917/18," *Vierteljahrshefte für Zeitgeschichte*, 13 (October 1965), pp. 346–66.

93. "Erster allgemeiner Präsidestag des Kartellverbandes katholischer Arbeitervereine West-, Süd- und Ost-Deutschlands, 22.–23. Mai 1918," Volksverein Bibliothek; Otto Müller to Cardinal Hartmann, 25 March 1918, KAB Archiv; Cologne Archdiocese, "Arbeitervereine"/vol. V, Müller to Hartmann, 11 June 1918, Houben to Hartmann, June 18, and von Weschpfennig to Hartmann, June 20 and August 10, 1918.

94. Cologne Archdiocese, "Arbeitervereine"/vol. V, anonymous memorandum of August 13, 1918, marked "Geheim" and printed in the same format as circulars to the Fulda Bishops' Conference, which Hartmann headed.

After a stormy interview on August 24, 1918, Cardinal Hartmann dismissed Müller as the chairman of the workers' clubs of the Archdiocese of Cologne on the grounds that Müller had politicized what should be purely religious associations. This action provoked a storm of indignation in the Catholic press, and Müller won support from some moderate bishops, Center Party leaders, and a united front of Catholic labor leaders, including Giesberts. In a gesture of defiance, the interdiocesanal association of the Catholic workers' clubs of western Germany elected Müller as its chairman to replace August Pieper.[95] In September 1918 Müller and Carl Walterbach of Munich drafted a new democratic program for a national association of Catholic workers' clubs. The Fulda Bishops' Conference refused to ratify it, however, and the war's end found the clubs in total disarray with morale very low. Not until September 1919 did they complete a reorganization with a program that supported parliamentary democracy and granted more power to elected representatives of the membership.[96]

Catholic workers were bitterly disappointed by the strength of patriarchal currents in the Center Party. When Franz Hitze refused to permit the trade unionist Carl Schirmer to represent the Center Reichstag delegation in negotiations for a bill to establish chambers of labor in September 1918, Stegerwald advised him to give Hitze the following lecture:

> You don't seem to have realized that the workers' maturity and determination to emancipate themselves have leapt ahead by two generations during the war. At the present time a much greater transformation is taking place within the labor movement than that represented by the emancipation of the serfs during the Wars of Liberation 100 years ago. But you believe that the labor movement can still be treated as you would treat a child.[97]

The consistent fulfillment of Stegerwald's predictions that resistance to reform and radical annexationism would ruin morale on the home front greatly enhanced his reputation among moderate leaders of the Center Party, but it required the collapse of the German war effort before Stegerwald and his associates could become a major force shaping party policy.

The stance of Cardinal Hartmann naturally intensified the frustration felt by

95. See Focke, pp. 61–63, and KAB Archiv, "Aussprache des Diözesanpräses mit Sr. Eminenz, Herrn Kardinal v. Hartmann, am 24. August 1918," and "Vorgänge die sich nach der Amtsenthebung des Herrn Dr. Müller ereigneten."

96. See Hartmann's circular to the Fulda Bishops' Conference, 27 September 1918, and the replies in Cologne Archdiocese, "Arbeitervereine"/vol. V, and the *Bericht des 12. Verbandstages der kath. Arbeiter- und Knappenvereine Westdeutschlands, 14.–15. September 1919* (Mönchen-Gladbach, 1919), pp. 46–61.

97. [Stegerwald] to Schirmer, September 13, 1918, NL Otte/6/244.

Christian workers. The burning question in their minds was whether Hartmann represented the last of a vanishing breed in the episcopate or merely gave the most open expression of views shared by more tactful colleagues. The rising lights in the Prussian hierarchy, the younger bishops Bertram and Schulte, had consistently opposed the most reactionary positions of Kopp and Hartmann, but there remained some grounds for suspicion that they were merely intelligent elitists with a fine sense for when to bow to the inevitable.[98] August Pieper, for one, decided that Hartmann expressed a widespread hostility in the clergy toward the emancipatory aspirations of Catholic workers. In December 1918 he resigned as director of the Volksverein because he felt that the clergy was no longer willing to support clubs, devotional exercises, or publications geared specifically to the mentality of workers, techniques essential to the Volksverein's strategy for integrating the working class into civil society.[99]

A heightened sense of solidarity with socialist workers naturally resulted from the feeling among Christian workers that their allies in the clergy and bourgeois parties had proved unreliable during the war. The leaders of the Hirsch–Duncker unions, who feared that their organization was doomed to extinction, repeatedly proposed a permanent association of all three union leagues in the years 1915–17. Although the GcG rejected this suggestion, it also declared that relations with the Free unions were now based on the principle of "healthy competition" in which each side sought not to weaken the other but to strengthen the labor movement as a whole.[100] The joint petitions submitted to the government by the three union leagues in 1917–18 went beyond the issues of the day to propose detailed plans for social insurance and government regulation of the economy after the war, plans implying sustained political cooperation among the rival unions.[101] GcG leaders remained fearful, however, that the moderate leadership of the Free unions would be forced to make major concessions to the growing leftist opposition in its ranks, and they denounced the Free unions during the great Berlin metalworkers' strike of January 1918 for failing to prevent the disruption of the munitions industry.[102]

Despite their many failures, the Christian trade unionists could also pride

---

98. Karl Schulte of Paderborn (archbishop of Cologne after 1919) wrote Hartmann to oppose the democratic tendency of Müller's new program for the Catholic workers' clubs on September 30, 1918, as did Bertram of Breslau on October 2 (Cologne Archdiocese, "Arbeitervereine"/vol. V). See also Emil Ritter, pp. 369f.

99. Teilnachlaß Pieper 15/1/4, pp. 979f., and 15/1/5, pp. 1012–15.

100. *Zentralblatt*, 23 April 1917, pp. 66f., and 18 June 1917, pp. 99f. See also Bieber, vol. 1, pp. 254–59.

101. Friedrich Zunkel, *Industrie und Staatssozialismus* (Düsseldorf, 1974), pp. 117–24, and Varain, pp. 109f.

102. *Zentralblatt*, 11 February 1918, p. 29. For background see Bieber, vol. 1, pp. 441–86.

themselves on some achievements suggesting that they made a unique contribution to social progress. Whereas many clergymen had denounced all strikes in the 1880s, by March 1918 even Cardinal Hartmann was persuaded that strikes had come to be considered "normal" and that he should not oppose union efforts to abolish restrictions on picketing and the right to unionize. The old argument by employers that the law must protect the strikebreaker's "right to work" had obviously lost much of its moral authority.[103] The Christian unions and their allies in the Volksverein, Society for Social Reform, and Christian Social Party were the most successful popularizers of the ideas of progressive economists like Lujo Brentano. They persuaded large segments of a hostile bourgeois audience, inculcated with individualistic and voluntarist ideals, that welfare legislation and collective action by trade unions were ethically justified. In 1917 the General Commission of the Free unions recognized the importance of such influence by joining the Society for Social Reform, and GcG leaders interpreted this act of imitation as proof that they represented the most forward-looking faction of the labor movement.[104] Indeed, if the goals of labor were to be achieved through the politics of compromise rather than social revolution, the experience and temperament of the Christian trade unionists made them ideal labor spokesmen. As the war drew to a close, Stegerwald and his colleagues felt uniquely qualified to promote the peaceful integration of the working class into German society, and this sense of mission inspired them with a political ambition out of all proportion to the size of their movement.

103. The integralist Catholic workers' clubs of Berlin petitioned Cardinal Hartmann on March 7, 1918, to oppose the trade unions' agitation for repeal of Article 153 of the Commercial Code, which prohibited "compulsion" to join unions and had been used to jail picketers. Hartmann issued a negative reply after receiving a memorandum from his staff on March 18 that portrayed a long-term increase in the incidence of strikes as inevitable (Cologne Archdiocese, "Arbeitervereine"/vol. V). The Reichstag repealed the article in April 1918: see Ludwig Preller, *Sozialpolitik in der Weimarer Republik* (Düsseldorf, 1978, first published 1949), pp. 49f.

104. *Zentralblatt*, 29 January 1917, pp. 17–19, and Varain, p. 91.

2

The Founding of the Weimar Republic

Christian workers applauded the formation of a parliamentary monarchy in October 1918 under the chancellorship of Prince Max of Baden. This government appeared to correspond exactly to the ideal of the "social monarchy" long propagated by the Christian unions, the Volksverein, and the Society for Social Reform. The General Commission of the Free unions agreed to accept governmental responsibility by dispatching its vice-chairman, Gustav Bauer, into the cabinet as secretary of labor, with Johannes Giesberts as his undersecretary. Both the Free and Christian unions then exhorted the populace to carry on the war effort for weeks after General Ludendorff had abandoned all hope. Moderate trade unionists therefore reacted with shock and indignation to the series of mutinies that led to Wilhelm's abdication on November 9. In later years many leaders of the Christian unions openly declared the view that figures on the right wing of the socialist labor movement privately expressed: that the German Revolution had been "completely unnecessary."[1]

The anxiety with which Christian workers witnessed the departure of the kaiser soon found a definite focus when many of the new revolutionary workers' and soldiers' councils, which for the moment constituted the only armed power in the land, exhorted all workers to unite in the socialist trade unions. Meeting in Berlin on November 13, the national committee of the GcG adjusted to the new situation by calling for prompt elections to a constitutional convention and urging followers to seek influence within the workers' and soldiers' councils. Many activists in the Christian unions heeded this call, but their efforts to infiltrate the

---

1. See Varain, pp. 112–19; GcG, *10. Kongreß 1920*, pp. 65f.; and Gewerkverein christlicher Bergarbeiter, *15. Generalversammlung 1919*, pp. 67f.

councils, which often limited membership to socialists or communists, enjoyed only limited success. The GcG soon concluded that the councils were fundamentally undemocratic.[2]

The regime of workers' and soldiers' councils tempted some functionaries of the Free unions to employ coercion against Christian workers, occasionally in the form of strikes to compel employers to discharge them. The senior leadership of the Free unions sternly discouraged such initiatives, however. Far from seeking to suppress the Christian unions, Carl Legien and the General Commission were determined to cooperate with them in efforts to deny the workers' councils any role in collective bargaining and to prevent spontaneous factory occupations.[3] The leaders of both the Free and Christian unions hoped above all to achieve a new, cooperative relationship with employers. The SPD's decision to insist on prompt elections to a constitutional convention against the opposition of the Independent Socialists also created an environment highly favorable to the growth and influence of the Christian unions.

NEW CHANNELS OF INFLUENCE FOR THE CHRISTIAN UNIONS

The Stinnes–Legien Agreement of November 15, 1918, launched the most remarkable social experiment of the Weimar Republic. Even before Germany's military collapse, a few captains of industry such as Hugo Stinnes, Albert Vögler, and Walther Rathenau advocated recognizing the trade unions as collective bargaining agents in heavy industry if they would support efforts to dismantle the government's system of wartime economic controls. But important differences between management and labor remained. Employers were particularly reluctant to grant demands by both the Free and Christian unions for the suppression of the Yellow company unions. On November 5 Carl Legien and Adam Stegerwald nevertheless agreed in principle with business leaders in Berlin to form the Central Association of Employers and Employees (the Zentralarbeitsgemeinschaft or ZAG), which would take over responsibility for supervising demobilization from the unpopular Economic Office of the old War Ministry. Legien ended the dispute over the Yellow unions by insisting that they be excluded from the Central Association while offering to renegotiate the matter if they survived for

2. *Zentralblatt*, 18 November 1918, pp. 193–95, and 2 December 1918, pp. 206f. See also Varain, p. 128, and Eberhard Kolb, *Die Arbeiterräte in der deutschen Innenpolitik 1918–1919*, 2d ed. (Frankfurt am Main, 1978), pp. 83–98.
3. Heinrich Potthoff, *Gewerkschaften und Politik zwischen Revolution und Inflation* (Düsseldorf, 1979), pp. 33–40, and Moses, vol. 1, pp. 230–39. In a detailed report on "red terror" against its members, the Christian metalworkers' union could find only six cases where such strike threats were actually carried out, and in three of them Social Democratic government officials or union leaders promptly intervened. Many of the cases involved actions by "Spartacist" workers against the secretaries of the Free and Christian unions alike: Christlicher Metallarbeiterverband, *Bericht des Verbands-Vorstandes, 1918–1919*, esp. pp. 50–59, 282f., 416–20.

six months without any support from employers.[4] The abdication of the kaiser on November 9 persuaded even Alfred Hugenberg and the coal mine operators to make major concessions. The final agreement of November 15 announced the implementation of the eight-hour day in all branches of industry, and employers pledged that they would "not support the company unions either directly or indirectly." Legien assured the industrialists who signed the declaration that the unions would oppose factory occupations by radical workers. This agreement gained the force of law when the provisional government led by Friedrich Ebert reissued it in the form of a decree.[5]

Although Carl Legien was the primary architect among labor leaders of the ZAG, the response to it was much more enthusiastic among Christian workers than socialists. The Stinnes–Legien Agreement secured important gains for organized labor but also obliged the unions to defend employers against the radical left and to accept responsibility for the welfare of the economy as a whole. Nothing in the prewar traditions of the Free unions prepared their members for such a role. Legien sought to portray the ZAG as a giant step forward on the path to socialism, but the growing Independent Socialist faction within the Free unions denounced it as a continuation of the General Commission's wartime policy of naive self-abnegation.[6] Their case was strengthened when many leading businessmen soon began to speak of the Central Association as a temporary expedient, which could be discarded as soon as the danger of revolutionary upheaval had passed. Moreover, many industrialists never had any intention of disowning their company unions and accepted the ZAG only because the leaders of their business associations assured them misleadingly that Carl Legien had promised to admit Yellow unions after six months. The survival of company unions in major steel plants outraged union members and helped Independent Socialists to gain control of the mammoth socialist metalworkers' union in October 1919. Their first act was to resign from the Branch Association for the metal industry, a step soon imitated by the socialist construction workers and five smaller craft unions.[7]

The leaders of the Christian unions, on the other hand, could rely on their

4. Gerald Feldman, "German Business Between War and Revolution: The Origins of the Stinnes–Legien Agreement," in Gerhard A. Ritter (ed.), *Entstehung und Wandel der modernen Gesellschaft* (Berlin, 1970), pp. 312–41, and Zunkel, *Industrie und Staatssozialismus*, pp. 177–88.

5. Gerhard A. Ritter and Susanne Miller (eds.), *Die deutsche Revolution 1918–1919. Dokumente*, 2d ed. (Hamburg, 1975), pp. 237–41, and Zunkel, *Industrie*, pp. 189–92.

6. See Potthoff, pp. 66–85.

7. Mattheier, *Die Gelben*, pp. 294–99; Zunkel, *Industrie*, pp. 193f.; Potthoff, pp. 180–83. See also the indictment of the company unions at the Krupp Works of Essen and the Bochumer Verein in Christlicher Metallarbeiterverband, *Bericht des Verbands-Vorstandes 1918–1919*, pp. 222f., 239.

members to accept the ZAG as a natural step in the course of social evolution long predicted by Christian theorists. Carl Legien complained bitterly to his colleagues that none of them displayed the energy and dedication with which the leaders of the Christian unions hurled themselves into the task of administering the Central Association and organizing new Branch Associations.[8] The contrast in attitudes emerged most strikingly in the Christian metalworkers' union, which proudly accepted the role of primary representative of labor in its Branch Association after the departure of the socialists. Despite his anger over the survival of Yellow unions, Franz Wieber consistently sought to generate enthusiasm among workers for their new "partnership" with employers. At the first postwar congress of Christian metalworkers, held in Essen, he recounted the rags-to-riches story of Alfred Krupp, emphasizing that his achievements had created thousands of jobs, and concluded that the one great failing of the pioneers of the steel industry, their lack of "genuine contact with their workers," had been corrected by the formation of the Central Association.[9] This attitude apparently caused no debate within Wieber's union. Thus the Christian unions were temperamentally prepared to exploit whatever opportunity for exerting new influence that active participation in the ZAG offered.

The talks leading to the Stinnes–Legien Agreement also fostered contacts among Germany's various nonsocialist unions, which were drawn together by the fear of red terror. The leader of the Hirsch–Duncker unions, Gustav Hartmann, and Adam Stegerwald organized a mass rally in Berlin on November 20, 1918, to proclaim the formation of a new German Democratic Labor Federation, which included almost every nonsocialist union for blue- and white-collar workers in Germany. The federation's succinct program sought to forge a consensus with the right wing of the SPD by demanding parliamentary democracy based on proportional representation, the subdivision of large agricultural estates, the nationalization of mineral wealth, and state control of syndicates. The new federation was loosely knit, however. Its founders admitted frankly that they were less interested in forging a new organization than in making declarations on behalf of an imposing number of workers, a combined total of 1.5 million members. Only such a demonstration, they felt, could inspire liberal and Christian democrats with the courage to return to political activity. Stegerwald sought to galvanize his followers to political action with enthusiastic praise for the historic "world revolution" that had "brought democracy to power all the way from Belgium to Siberia" and created unprecedented opportunities for the laboring masses to abolish the "abuses of capitalism."[10]

8. Potthoff, p. 180.
9. Christlicher Metallarbeiterverband, *9. Generalversammlung, August 1920*, p. 21.

The primary purpose of the new federation of nonsocialist unions was to promote democratic reform of the nonsocialist political parties. As Christian labor leaders sensed, there could be no genuine partnership between management and labor unless the leaders of Germany's "bourgeois" parties agreed to display new regard for their working-class constituents and to actively discourage industrialists and agrarians from adopting confrontation tactics. Stegerwald fervently hoped that the ZAG and the German Democratic Labor Federation could serve as the foundation for a broad new political party that would unite progressive Catholics, liberals, and Christian Social Protestants. He hoped that such a party would help consolidate parliamentary government, but he also thought in more selfish terms that it would facilitate efforts to organize the millions of farmworkers, white-collar workers, and state employees who had been prevented from joining unions under the monarchy. The greatest handicap to organizing drives among such workers, who were most often Protestant, was the widespread identification of the Christian unions as agents of the Catholic Center Party. Thus it was natural that Stegerwald's closest allies in the effort to form a new, interconfessional political party were leading Protestants in the old German Labor Congress: Hans Bechly, chairman of the Nationalist Union of Commercial Employees, Friedrich Baltrusch, the GcG's spokesman for economic affairs, and Wilhelm Gutsche, chairman of the union for railroad workers affiliated with the GcG.[11]

Stegerwald's political ambitions, although not publicly discussed, were an open secret among politicians in Berlin, and he conferred frequently with Friedrich Naumann, Gustav Stresemann, Walther Rathenau, and others at the time of the kaiser's abdication. In the third week of November 1918, Stegerwald, Gutsche, and Behrens sought to pave the way for a new party by helping Rathenau form a Democratic People's League with a small group of intellectuals and industrialists who actively supported the principles of the ZAG. The wartime writings of Rathenau in favor of a "communal economy" (*Gemeinwirtschaft*) with new forms of economic planning impressed Stegerwald deeply. Stegerwald sought like this "conservative socialist" to find some blueprint for the economy that would restrain competition, improve the status and morale of workers, and at the same time preserve high levels of productivity by retaining the services of Germany's experienced entrepreneurs. The difficulty of this task immediately became apparent, however, when Hugo Stinnes and most other industrialists in the league flatly refused to endorse any sort of "socialization" of the economy.

    10. *Zentralblatt*, 2 December 1918, pp. 203–05. See also 6 January 1919, pp. 3f., and Verband der deutschen Gewerkvereine (Hirsch–Duncker), *20. Verbandstag, Juni 1919*, pp. 75–80.
    11. For the rest of this section, compare Larry Eugene Jones, "Adam Stegerwald und die Krise des deutschen Parteiensystems," *Vierteljahrshefte für Zeitgeschichte*, 27 (January 1979), pp. 1–29.

This rebuff prompted the sensitive Rathenau to dissolve his league in late November.[12] Stegerwald was then compelled to postpone any effort to found a new party because simultaneous initiatives by Catholic, left liberal, and conservative politicians each attracted the allegiance of a significant portion of the workers in the German Democratic Labor Federation.

The most important obstacle to Stegerwald's plan was the continued loyalty of many Catholic workers to the Center Party. Heinrich Brauns supported Stegerwald on November 13 by writing the leaders of the Rhenish Center on behalf of the Volksverein to demand that the party drop its old name, deny any role to those who had opposed suffrage reform in Prussia during the war, and adopt a revised program to attract Protestants. But Johannes Giesberts and Matthias Erzberger publicly urged voters to hurl themselves into the task of strengthening the good old Center Party.[13] After a conference in Cologne on November 18 between bourgeois and working-class leaders of the Rhenish Center, the Reichstag delegate Johannes Becker-Arnsberg of the Christian construction workers' union telegraphed an appeal not to participate in the formation of any new party to his friend Stegerwald in Berlin. Becker explained that all party leaders in the west were willing to accept the essential programmatic demands of Brauns, but that the old party name must be retained in order to prevent Integralists from misusing it. Becker invited Stegerwald to recruit Protestant trade unionists and socially progressive conservatives for the task of drafting a new party program.[14] In such a matter names were highly important because any German Protestant who joined the party forged in the *Kulturkampf* would expose himself to strident attacks, but Stegerwald acquiesced.

Stegerwald found the Center Party an eager suitor under the revolutionary circumstances and must have been gratified by the results of his decision to reenter the fold. He and Brauns enjoyed tremendous influence over nominations for the election to the National Assembly in January 1919. They succeeded in persuading the judges and lawyers who led the party, men like Carl Trimborn and Peter Spahn, that "everything that leaned toward the right in the past must go!"[15] Whereas the Christian unions sent only five spokesmen into the Center's 91-member Reichstag delegation of 1912, the 90 delegates of 1919 included 24

---

12. Lothar Albertin, *Liberalismus und Demokratie am Anfang der Weimarer Republik* (Düsseldorf, 1972), pp. 29–31, and reminiscences by Stegerwald in *25 Jahre Christlicher Gewerkschaftsbewegung*, pp. 38f. See also Heinrich Brüning, *Memoiren 1918–1934* (Stuttgart, 1970), pp. 49f., and Klemens von Klemperer, *Germany's New Conservatism*, 2d ed. (Princeton, 1968), pp. 59–66, 83–88, 107–11.

13. Heinrich Brauns to Wilhelm Marx, 13 November 1918, NL Marx/222/72f., and Rudolf Morsey, *Die Deutsche Zentrumspartei 1917–1923* (Düsseldorf, 1966), pp. 79–98.

14. Becker-Arnsberg to Stegerwald, 19 November 1918, NL Marx/222/78–83, and Morsey, *Zentrumspartei 1917–1923*, pp. 99–104.

15. NL Bachem/854, "Provinzialausschuß der rheinischen Zentrumspartei," 8 January 1919.

Christian trade unionists, 18 of them active union functionaries, in addition to the clerical patrons of the movement, Hitze and Brauns. Among the parliamentary newcomers who were to become fixtures of the republican Reichstag were Stegerwald, Wieber, Imbusch, and Joseph Joos, editor of the *Westdeutsche Arbeiter-Zeitung*. No members of the landed nobility entered the Center delegation of 1919, and Catholic farmers and the *Mittelstand* found their representation sharply reduced.[16] When the Center Party entered a coalition govenment led by the SPD soon after this election, Johannes Giesberts entered the cabinet as Reich postal minister, where he remained until 1922. Stegerwald became the first Prussian welfare minister in a similar coalition government on the state level.

Despite this dramatic new political recognition of the Christian unions, the Center Party proved highly resistant to change on the local level. The Rhineland was the province with the greatest concentration of blue-collar Catholic workers, who provided 30–40% of the party vote, but workers received only 9 of 98 seats on the provincial committee when local party organs were reconstituted in April 1919. Civil servants, priests, and small businessmen continued to set the tone, and no laborite was elected chairman of a county committee. Even when party locals acknowledged the need to increase the workers' share of leadership positions, they often ignored trade union secretaries, the most vigorous labor representatives, in favor of "simple workers" or relatively inexperienced employees of the Catholic workers' clubs.[17] The *Westdeutsche Arbeiter-Zeitung* complained bitterly of the lingering "caste mentality" in Center Party locals.[18] Thus the Christian unions found it difficult to consolidate their political influence even where the internal structure of the Center Party was most democratic. In Southern Germany the Center never became a genuine mass membership party and continued to rely heavily on the support of the clergy and the Christian peasants' leagues. Here the workers' difficulties multiplied. Indeed, the peasants' resentment against the increasing political influence of the trade unions constituted the primary cause of the secession by the Bavarian People's Party from the Center in January 1920, which left Catholic workers in that state politically isolated.[19]

16. Frey, pp. 88, 108, and Morsey, *Zentrumspartei 1917–1923*, pp. 154–56. For the role of Christian workers in reviving the Center Party, see Herbert Kühr, *Parteien und Wahlen im Stadt- und Landkreis Essen in der Zeit der Weimarer Republik* (Düsseldorf, 1973), pp. 57–61, and Wolfgang Stump, *Geschichte und Organisation der Zentrumspartei in Düsseldorf 1917–1933* (Düsseldorf, 1971), pp. 26–33.

17. NL Bachem/850: "Provinzialausschuß der rheinischen Zentrumspartei," 24 April 1919, and "Kommunalpolitische Vereinigung der Rheinischen Zentrumspartei," 27 August 1920. The Rhenish Center compiled figures in August 1920 showing that a respectable 15 of 88 nominees with good prospects in the upcoming municipal elections were workers, but a detailed breakdown revealed that only 3 of them were trade unionists.

18. *WAZ*, 6 February 1919, p. 9, and 6 March 1919, pp. 27f.

19. Klaus Schönhoven, *Die Bayerische Volkspartei 1924–1932* (Düsseldorf, 1972), pp. 25–27,

The senior Protestant in the leadership of the Christian unions, Franz Behrens, had an independent political base in the small but dedicated band of Christian Social activists. Behrens and his closest associates, such as Emil Hartwig and the pastor Reinhard Mumm, admired Stegerwald's idea for an interconfessional party but doubted the willingness of Catholic workers to participate. In 1916 a young Christian Social fighting on the front, Wilhelm Lindner, had written Behrens and Hartwig to propose the merger of all "parties of the right" into a strong new nationalist front, suggesting as a name the German Nationalist People's Party (Deutschnationale Volkspartei, DNVP). Behrens encountered enthusiasm for the idea on November 13, 1918, when he met a group of conservative politicans by chance at the funeral of a parliamentary colleague. Merger talks among the Conservative, Free Conservative, Christian Social, and German Social (anti-Semitic) parties began in earnest on November 19, immediately after Johannes Becker's discouraging telegram to Stegerwald. The reconstitution of the Center Party left Behrens free to pursue an old Christian Social dream: to convince the Conservative Party that it had been foolish to expel Adolf Stoecker in 1896 and turn its back on Protestant workers.[20]

The Conservative leader, Count Kuno von Westarp, deeply resented Behrens' claim during the merger talks to predominant influence over the program and propaganda of the new party, observing that the Christian Socials represented a mere 200,000 voters as opposed to the Conservative Party's 1.2 million.[21] Most Conservative back-benchers realized, however, that their party had been thoroughly discredited by Germany's defeat and that they had no hope for influence in the future if they continued to rely on their old electoral base in Prussia's rural eastern provinces. The chairman of the new DNVP, the conciliatory Prussian bureaucrat Oskar Hergt, felt that the Christian Socials possessed unrivaled experience in agitating among the urban wage- and salary-earners who must be attracted if the party was to grow, and he permitted Behrens to draft most of the electoral platform published on November 24, 1918. This document endorsed private enterprise while urging the socialization of suitable (unspecified) branches of industry, and demanded land for peasant homesteads, "the expansion of our social programs," freedom of coalition for all workers, and the

---

66–76. See also the bitter debate between agrarians and trade unionists in Deutsche Zentrumspartei, *1. Reichsparteitag 1920*, pp. 19, 36f., 69, 89.

20. Amrei Stupperich, *Volksgemeinschaft oder Arbeitersolidarität* (Göttingen, 1982), pp. 17f.; Lewis Hertzman, *DNVP: Right-Wing Opposition in the Weimar Republic 1918–1924* (Lincoln, Nebraska, 1963), pp. 24–35; Deutschnationaler Arbeiter-Bund (DNAB), *Die deutschnationale Arbeiter-Bewegung, ihr Werden und Wachsen* (Berlin, ca. 1926), p. 10.

21. Kuno von Westarp, "Konservative Politik in der Republik," unpublished MS in NL Westarp, pp. 6–10.

encouragement of social mobility through scholarships for higher education. The Christian Socials were disappointed by their failure to secure a plank in the party platform explicitly endorsing trade unions as opposed to company unions, but they included such a statement in the Westphalian party program and played a dominant role in the organization of party locals in western Germany. The party's 44 delegates to the National Assembly included 5 Christian trade unionists and several more middle-class Christian Socials, a dramatic increase in political representation for Protestant workers.[22]

Franz Behrens sought to clarify the DNVP's attitude toward trade unionism with a spirited defense of the principles of the Stinnes–Legien Agreement at the first national party congress in July 1919. He assured his listeners that both the Free and the Christian unions would oppose plans for centralized economic planning but insisted that the principle of "self-help" gaining ever more acceptance among both employers and employees could not be reconciled with Yellow unions: "Whoever believes in free enterprise must also believe in trade unions for workers and must also recognize the right to unionize and the right to strike." Behrens also defended the principle that the government should delegate regulatory powers to the voluntary associations of management and labor against both the adherents of councils democracy and the reactionary advocates of "state corporatism": "In general I am not a supporter of Darwinism, but I must say that here the principle of natural selection is proper. In national and economic life, natural selection occurs when those people genuinely interested in their trade and the economy demonstrate that interest by banding together with their fellows to secure representation."[23] This position was supported by moderate DNVP politicians from the Free Conservative Party and by industrialists who favored the ZAG, such as J. W. Reichert, Paul Lejeune-Jung, and Walter Rademacher, but the Pan-German League mounted a sustained press campaign against all trade unions, blaming them for Germany's defeat. Moreover, the resentment against trade unions already noted in the Center Party was much stronger in the DNVP, where most party locals were dominated by small property owners who displayed a pathological fear of social change and the trade union secretaries who symbolized it most vividly. Behrens encountered a bitter disappointment when the party congress insisted on including two Yellow labor leaders in the new six-member Workers' Committee of the DNVP. When the com-

22. Werner Liebe, *Die Deutschnationale Volkspartei, 1918–1924* (Düsseldorf, 1956), p. 18; Ritter and Miller (eds.), *Dokumente*, pp. 296–98; Emil Hartwig, "Die Deutschnationale Volkspartei und die Arbeiterschaft," DNVP pamphlet no. 156 (1924), pp. 9f.; Gisbert Gemein, "Die DNVP in Düsseldorf, 1918–1933," Ph.D. diss. (Cologne, 1969), pp. 1–9.
23. Franz Behrens, "Arbeiterschaft und Deutschnationale Volkspartei," DNVP pamphlet no. 23 (1919), pp. 5–8.

mittee staged its first rally in November 1919 in Berlin, the proceedings soon degenerated into a shouting match between Yellow unionists and the supporters of Behrens.[24]

It is not clear whether the Hirsch–Duncker unions' agreement to enter the German Democratic Labor Federation involved any sort of commitment to support Stegerwald's plan for a new political party. Apparently not, since Gustav Hartmann was a founding member of the German Democratic Party (Deutsche Demokratische Partei, DDP), whose left liberal organizers excluded groups that Stegerwald hoped to include by condemning all former annexationists, including Stinnes and Gustav Stresemann, while demanding complete separation of church and state. Four Hirsch–Duncker leaders joined the 75-member DDP parliamentary delegation in January 1919 along with 4 representatives of liberal white-collar unions. Anton Erkelenz, the most talented journalist and public speaker among the liberal trade unionists, devoted himself full-time to the task of building up the party organization.[25] Friedrich Naumann and other prominent leaders of the DDP spoke frequently of the need for "building bridges" between bourgeois and proletarian Germany, advocating a new system of "industrial parliamentarianism" within the economy. The DDP relied heavily on the financial contributions of big business, however, and many veterans of the old liberal parties in its ranks believed that it should frankly espouse the economic interests of the middle classes against the SPD. The Hirsch–Duncker unions never succeeded in mobilizing significant numbers of activists to participate in party work, and many observers concluded that they lacked esprit de corps as well as numerical strength.[26] Workers enjoyed much less influence in the DDP than in either the Center Party or the DNVP.

The consolidation of the DNVP and DDP left the most enthusiastic supporters of Stegerwald's plan, Baltrusch, Bechly, and Gutsche, in some confusion. They sympathized with Gustav Stresemann's efforts to transform the National Liberal rump into a new German People's Party (Deutsch Volkspartei, DVP), however, because of his outspoken criticism before 1914 of the autocratic labor relations policies of heavy industry and his wartime efforts to promote suffrage reform in Prussia. On December 12, 1918, Baltrusch offered Stresemann the

24. Stupperich, *Volksgemeinschaft*, pp. 21f., 55–67, and Stegmann, "Zwischen Repression und Manipulation," pp. 392–410.

25. Albertin, *Liberalismus und Demokratie*, pp. 55–69, and Brantz, pp. 60–80.

26. Albertin, pp. 181–90; Ernst Lemmer, *Manches war doch anders* (Frankfurt am Main, 1968), pp. 86–89; Heinz Landmann, "Die Entwicklung der Hirsch–Dunckerschen Gewerkvereine nach dem Kriege," Ph.D. diss. (Freiburg, 1924), pp. 39–54. Only a dozen of the 800 delegates to the first party congress of the DDP were workers or union functionaries: see the list of delegates and their occupations in DDP, *Bericht über die Verhandlungen des 1. Parteitages* (Berlin, no date).

support of all "nonconservative" Protestant trade unionists. Stresemann warned Baltrusch in reply that he had already conferred with the head of the Krupp company union, Fritz Hess, an old party colleague. Stresemann declared that he would not actively support the Yellows but could not afford to reject any group of workers willing to support him.[27] Wilhelm Gutsche sought to persuade Stresemann that the Yellow unions would soon die out as a result of the Stinnes–Legien Agreement, warning that trade unionists could not remain in the DVP if it granted parliamentary seats to Yellow labor leaders because "we would lose all credibility in the labor movement." Despite failure to resolve this issue, the Christian union leaders decided to support Stresemann because he published a campaign platform on December 15 that resembled their program much more closely than did that of the DDP.[28]

However, Stresemann proved unable to secure significant parliamentary representation for trade unionists. Only one laborite entered the DVP delegation to the National Assembly, a humble Christian miner named August Winnefeld, nominated at the initiative of his party local rather than the Christian unions because of his record of loyalty to the National Liberal Party.[29] Stresemann promised to redress this imbalance in the next election and urged the central committee of the DVP in April 1919 to add Gutsche, Otto Thiel of the DHV, and several other representatives of white-collar unions to its ranks. But this suggestion produced a stormy debate and demands for equal treatment of the Yellow unions. Hess and Fritz Geisler, the most prominent prewar Yellow leader, were then added to the central committee alongside Stresemann's nominees. This debate casts a revealing light on the apparently harmonious proceedings of the DVP's first party congress, which began the next day, where several speakers proclaimed grandiloquently that the Stinnes–Legien Agreement had paved the way for genuine reconciliation between the classes.[30]

Any sign of DVP sympathy for the Yellows weakened the influence of the Christian unions still further by discouraging their members from becoming active in party locals. In August 1919 Winnefeld came under fire at a convention

27. Baltrusch to Stresemann, 12 December 1918, and reply of 13 December in NL Stresemann (microfilm) 3068/6892/134018–21. See also Henry A. Turner, *Stresemann and the Politics of the Weimar Republic* (Princeton, 1963), pp. 15–26.
28. Gutsche to Stresemann, 14 December 1918, NL Stresemann 3068/6892/134089–91; Jones, "Adam Stegerwald," pp. 10f.; Ritter and Miller (eds.), *Dokumente*, pp. 316–19.
29. Albertin, *Liberalismus und Demokratie*, pp. 73f., 110–12, and DVP Geschäftsführender Ausschuß, 29 January 1919, BAK R45II/50/1–5.
30. DVP Zentralvorstand, 12 April 1919, BAK R45II/34/33–51, and DVP, *1. Parteitag, April 1919*, pp. 78f., 87–94. Geisler had reconstituted a formally autonomous Deutscher Arbeiterbund at the end of 1918, issuing unreliable membership claims of 57,000 in 1921 and 79,000 in 1923: see Mattheier, *Die Gelben*, pp. 297–99.

of Christian miners for having addressed a rally of Yellow workers who supported the DVP, and many of his union colleagues declared themselves unwilling to have any dealings with the party.[31] At the second party congress of the DVP in October, only 10 of 460 delegates represented labor, including several Yellow unionists, and Fritz Hess persuaded the delegates to condemn "terrorism" against "nationalist workers" in blanket terms that could be applied to the Christian unions as well as the Free.[32] Blue-collar trade unionists had little chance of establishing a power base in either of the liberal parties.

BROADENING THE BOUNDARIES OF TRADE UNIONISM

While the Christian unions encountered frustrations within the bourgeois parties during the twelve months after the revolution, the membership of the Free unions surged from 4 to 8 million. These developments convinced Stegerwald and his associates that they must have a more centralized union federation in order to coordinate organizing drives among previously nonunionized workers and to consolidate their political influence. The programmatic differences between the liberal and Christian unions concerning the role of religion in society apparently reflected considerable tension between their members, which made cooperation difficult. In March 1919 Christian trade unionists insisted that the word "Democratic" be dropped from the title of their umbrella organization in order to avoid identification with the DDP.[33] A schism became inevitable during the summer, when merger talks between the DHV and the liberal white-collar unions collapsed because of the DHV's insistence on separate organizations for men and women, and for technical and commercial employees. The liberal white-collar unions then merged to form the League of Employees' Unions (Gewerkschaftsbund der Angestellten, GDA), which admitted all types of employees, and the DHV resolved to seek closer ties with the League of Christian Unions, its old associate in the prewar German Labor Congress.[34] In November 1919 the German Labor Federation (Deutscher Gewerkschaftsbund, DGB) was reconstituted with the blue-collar League of Christian Unions, which had grown to embrace a million members, a white-collar federation with 450,000 members

31. *Gewerkverein christlicher Bergarbeiter, 15. Generalversammlung 1919*, pp. 56–61, 127, 209f.

32. See *DVP, 2. Parteitag, Oktober 1919*, list of delegates and pp. 87–96, 155–57, and the protests by Otto Thiel in DVP Geschäftsführender Ausschuß, 16 October 1919 and 28 January 1920, BAK R45II/50/345–47, and 51/165–67. Lothar Döhn has compiled data on 3,298 DVP activists in the 1920s, finding that only 1.5% were blue-collar workers and 1.5% white-collar: *Politik und Interesse* (Meisenheim am Glan, 1970), p. 79.

33. Michael Schneider, *Die Christlichen Gewerkschaften*, p. 488.

34. Hamel, pp. 172f., and "DHV Verwaltung: Auszüge" (DHV Archiv) 24 July 1919, p. 80.

led by the DHV, and a new federation for employees of the public sector under Wilhelm Gutsche, which grew out of the unions for postal and railroad workers founded by the Christian unions and claimed 350,000 members. In the following year the liberal unions followed suit by forming the Trade Union Ring, in which white-collar unions predominated, while the Free unions formed two federations, the General Association of German Labor (Allgemeiner Deutscher Gewerkschaftsbund, ADGB) for blue-collar unions and the League of Free Employees (Allgemeiner freier Angestelltenbund, AfA) for white-collar.[35]

Stegerwald, Bechly, and Gutsche proudly declared that the DGB represented no mere reaction against the threat of "red terror" like its predecessor, but rather a unified movement based on commitment to shared "Christian-nationalist" values. They hired Stegerwald's assistant at the Prussian welfare ministry, the trained economist Heinrich Brüning, to coordinate their lobbying activities as the DGB's executive secretary. The offspring of a conservative bourgeois Catholic family in Münster who served as a company commander during the war, Brüning had no trade union background. But he had conceived a great admiration for unions as bastions of order during the revolution and found Stegerwald's plans for an interconfessional political party exciting. He confided to a friend that, although Stegerwald operated from different premises as a "Bavarian and a democrat," they could reach agreement on most issues.[36] Despite the rhetoric of its founders, however, the alliance between the Christian unions and the DHV rested more on shared interests than a community of ideas. Most DHV members did not take Christian social theory seriously. As Max Habermann observed, for many of them the "völkische Weltanschauung" had become "a complete substitute for religion."[37] But Hans Bechly and his aides supported the DGB enthusiastically because they needed a network of firm political alliances in order to implement their demands for special treatment of white-collar workers in social legislation. During the war the DHV played a leading role in the turn toward collective bargaining and strike action by white-collar workers, but its pragmatic chairman encountered a backlash among old-fashioned members who still considered commercial employees nascent entrepreneurs. Bechly found that his followers would accept trade unionism only if he secured self-administration for white-collar workers in the social insurance system and separate seats on the various public bodies that represented orga-

35. Wilhelm Wiedfeld, *Der Deutsche Gewerkschaftsbund* (Leipzig, 1933), pp. 25–28; Landmann, pp. 147–53; Potthoff, pp. 59f.

36. Brüning quoted in Gottfried von Treviranus, *Das Ende von Weimar* (Düsseldorf and Vienna, 1968), p. 40. See also *Zentralblatt*, 8 December 1919, p. 202, and Brüning, pp. 40f., 56–61.

37. Max Habermann, "Der Deutschnationale Handlungsgehilfen-Verband im Kampf um das Reich," unpublished MS (1934), DHV Archiv, p. 5.

nized labor. Adam Stegerwald's willingness to support such demands earned Bechly's gratitude.[38]

Leaders of the Christian unions found in turn that affiliation with the predominantly Protestant DHV protected them against the charge of ultramontanism and encouraged Protestant workers to join. Whereas only about one-sixth of the Christian union membership was Protestant in 1912, by the mid-1920s 300 of 700 union functionaries and nearly one-third of the membership belonged to that confession.[39] The DHV had strong locals in Berlin, Hamburg, and other large cities in central and northern Germany where the Christian unions had never taken root, and the DHV maintained joint DGB offices for legal aid and political lobbying in cities where the Christian unions were weak. Whereas more than 60% of all Christian union members lived in Rhineland-Westphalia in 1919, only 43% did so in 1929, with 24% in southern and southwestern Germany, 17% in central and northern Germany, and 15% east of the Elbe. Thus the DHV helped the Christian unions to become more a national rather than a merely regional movement.[40]

At the time of the formation of the German Labor Federation, the leaders of the Christian unions and DHV had high hopes of challenging the Free unions for primacy within the labor movement. Hundreds of thousands of previously unorganized and apolitical white-collar workers, farmworkers, and public sector employees turned toward trade unionism between 1917 and 1919. These groups

38. Habermann MS, pp. 6–19, and Hamel, pp. 167–92.

39. The GcG kept the exact proportion of Protestants among its members a secret, but Jakob Kaiser declared in January 1921 that 800,000 of the 2 million members of the DGB as a whole belonged to that confession: *Kölnische Volkszeitung*, 11 January 1921, no. 26. See also Theodor Cassau, *Die Gewerkschaftsbewegung* (Halberstadt, 1925), pp. 32–35, and the report by General Secretary Grunz of the Evangelical workers' clubs in *Die Verhandlungen des 37. Evangelisch-Sozialen Kongresses, Juni 1930* (Göttingen, 1930), pp. 149f.

40. GcG, *Jahrbuch der christlichen Gewerkschaften 1930* (Berlin, 1930), p. 132. The following figures on membership in selected cities, taken from pp. 173–79 and from DHV, *Der DHV in Jahre 1929* (Hamburg, 1930), p. 303, illustrate the importance of the DHV for filling regional gaps in the organization of the Christian unions:

	ADGB	GcG	DHV
Aachen	13,050	16,596	1,128
Cologne	62,421	24,618	4,510
Dortmund	26,201	15,307	2,386
Düsseldorf	31,772	10,469	3,124
Essen	31,502	28,775	3,045
Munich	81,201	13,187	6,729
Berlin	393,564	7,858	27,340
Hamburg	213,385	1,998	15,183
Leipzig	118,756	3,179	8,585.

stood outside the distinctive subculture of the socialist labor movement, and the DGB anticipated great success among them by combining effective trade union- ism with the defense of dominant cultural values. The DGB's ideological opposi- tion to socialism did prove an asset among white-collar workers. Egalitarian pronouncements and attacks in the socialist press against the real or imagined privileges of white-collar workers represented a chronic source of embarrass- ment for the AfA-Bund of white-collar unions.[41] Stegerwald and other DGB leaders persuaded the blue-collar Christian unions, on the other hand, to pro- vide financial and logistical support for organizing drives among white-collar workers by stressing the influence of technical and supervisory personnel on workers in the factory, arguing that the spread of socialist unions among white- collar workers would jeopardize the position of the blue-collar Christian unions. The publications and rallies of the Christian unions consistently sought to reduce tensions between blue- and white-collar workers by explaining the economic importance of administrative functions and defending the right of better edu- cated employees to somewhat higher pay.[42]

Although the AfA-Bund initially provided stiff competition, the DGB soon emerged as by far the most popular union federation for white-collar workers in the Weimar Republic. The DHV embraced a large majority of all unionized male commercial employees, although technical personnel preferred the AfA- Bund:[43]

	DGB			AfA			GDA
				ZdA *(commercial)*			
		VwA *(female)*					
	DHV		Technicians	Male	Female	Technicians	*(mixed)*
1920	250,469	122,673	4,500	196,302	167,219	93,552	300,357
1922	285,879	102,626	9,750	148,363	148,028	76,500	302,254
1924	253,032	67,547	6,046	92,831	82,578	57,801	260,796
1926	291,486	66,332	9,500	79,982	69,277	53,720	275,352
1928	346,703	77,431	9,921	92,368	83,844	59,139	301,967
1930	404,009	92,390	14,258	105,010	105,370	63,115	327,742

The DGB's good showing among female office personnel is surprising because the DHV was militantly sexist. Here the principle of separate organization

41. Hans Speier, *Die Angestellten vor dem Nationalsozialismus* (Göttingen, 1977), pp. 66–71.
42. See Gewerkverein christlicher Bergarbeiter, "Protokollbuch" (IGBE-Bibliothek, Bochum), Vorstandssitzung, 7 February 1920; GcG, *10. Kongreß 1920*, pp. 157–59, 326–28; *Zentralblatt*, Beilage "Betrieb und Wirtschaft," September 1920, p. 14; DGB, "Aus der Arbeit des D.G.B." (Berlin, 1925), p. 22.
43. *Statistische Jahrbücher des Deutschen Reichs*, 1921–32.

appears to have given women a somewhat larger leadership role in the DGB than they enjoyed in the Free unions, where male chauvinism remained the rule in practice if not in theory. Habermann complained bitterly of their independent attitude.[44] The DGB also sponsored a secession from the German Foremen's Union when it decided at the end of 1918 to affiliate with the Free unions. The Christian-nationalist foremen's union attracted only 15,000 members, but its larger rival was sufficiently concerned by the competition to lobby militantly within the Free union camp against any identification with the SPD. The Free foremen blamed the steady decline of the AfA-Bund after 1920 on the Marxist politics of its chairman, Siegfried Aufhäuser. White-collar workers who wanted to retain their jobs could not afford association with such a radical.[45]

Organizing efforts by the DGB among state employees also showed great promise after the revolution struck down legal barriers to trade unionism in the public sector. Lower level civil servants had suffered great deprivation during the war and were eager to imitate the forms of organization that had apparently made blue-collar workers the dominant power in the new republic.[46] The Christian railroad workers' union under Wilhelm Gutsche pioneered in efforts to unite civil servants and state-employed wage earners in the same union, arguing that railroad workers must not permit themselves to be divided by the administration's practice of granting civil service status to strategic categories of skilled workers. By 1920 it attained a membership of 230,000, roughly 20% of all railroad workers.[47]

Controversy over public sector strikes soon divided the DGB, however. Government spokesmen, higher ranking civil servants, and all the bourgeois parties insisted in the years 1919–22 that strikes by civil servants remained illegal and pernicious despite the new constitutional guarantee of freedom of association.[48] Highly publicized shutdowns of utilities and public transport during wildcat strikes embarrassed the Free and Christian unions alike and prompted the government to create an Emergency Technical Service in September 1919 to maintain vital services. The ADGB opposed this new agency after some hesitation, but the Christian unions felt compelled to endorse it.[49] When so-

---

44. Habermann MS (DHV Archiv), p. 82, and Brian Peterson, "The Politics of Working-Class Women in the Weimar Republic," *Central European History*, 10 (1977), pp. 87–111.

45. See Johannes Breddemann, "Der Deutsche Werkmeister-Verband. Vom wirtschaftsfriedlichen Unterstützungsverein zur sozialistischen Klassenkampfgewerkschaft" (Essen, 1924), and Mommsen, "Die Sozialdemokratie in der Defensive," pp. 119f.

46. See Jürgen Kocka, *Klassengesellschaft im Krieg* (Göttingen, 1973), pp. 66–74.

47. See *Die deutsche Gewerkschaft*, 11 January 1919, p. 2, and *Statistisches Jahrbuch des Deutschen Reichs*, 1921.

48. See Deutsche Zentrumspartei, *1. Reichsparteitag 1920*, p. 13; DVP, *1. Parteitag 1919*, pp. 82f.; and *Akten der Reichskanzlei. Das Kabinett Fehrenbach* (Boppard am Rhein, 1972), pp. 417–20.

49. Potthoff, pp. 159–70, and *Zentralblatt*, 21 July 1919, pp. 115f., and 24 November 1919, pp. 193–95.

cialist railroad workers unleashed a major strike on January 31, 1922, the government promptly responded with a presidential proclamation declaring all strikes by civil servants illegal. The Free and Hirsch–Duncker unions sought to persuade the railroad workers to abandon their strike, and the GcG went further by demanding strict legislation based on the principle that "civil service and the right to strike are two irreconcilable concepts." The government insisted on prosecuting numerous "ringleaders" after the strike collapsed. The Christian railroad workers' union repudiated this strike but rejected the government's case with equal heat.[50] Gutsche and his lieutenants felt that their blue-collar comrades had betrayed the cause of trade unionism for state employees, but Stegerwald considered the preservation of state authority and a good public image for the older unions more important than the unity of the DGB.

Relations between the civil servants and the other two groups in the DGB deteriorated steadily after 1922. The GcG and DHV often sought to promote consensus with business and agrarian representatives by attacking the swollen bureaucracy and demanding money-saving administrative reform. Friction with them strengthened the arguments of higher ranking civil servants that identification with the working class was a dangerous fallacy for public officials. In November 1926, reluctantly responding to pressure from discontented members, Gutsche led 200,000 civil servants out of the DGB into the politically neutral League of Civil Servants, while the 120,000 wage earners he had led affiliated directly with the GcG.[51]

Germany's 3 million landless farm laborers composed the third major group new to the ranks of organized labor in the Weimar Republic. Strict laws had prevented union activity among them in the Kingdom of Prussia, despite considerable discontent among the 1.2 million farmworkers on large East Elbian estates.[52] The Christian unions began in the summer of 1918 to subsidize a major organizing drive by Franz Behrens among them because, as the *Westdeutsche Arbeiter-Zeitung* explained, "Here is the chance to alter the balance of power between the two trade union currents in favor of the Christian labor movement."[53] DGB leaders assumed that socialist ideology and ignorance of rural

50. *Zentralblatt*, 20 February 1922, pp. 45f., 49f.; Potthoff, pp. 304f.; *Akten der Reichskanzlei. Die Kabinette Wirth* (Boppard am Rhein, 1973), pp. 534–59, 587–89, 699f.; *Akten der Reichskanzlei. Das Kabinett Cuno* (Boppard am Rhein, 1968), pp. 192f., 280f., 299f.

51. Wiedfeld, pp. 48–50, and *Zentralblatt*, 29 November 1926, p. 344. See also the antiunion arguments in the DNVP's Reichsausschuß der deutschnationalen Beamtenschaft, circular of 31 May 1926, StA Osnabrück/C1/87/25f.

52. See Johann Beßler, "Die Streikbewegung in der deutschen Landwirtschaft, unter besonderer Berücksichtigung Ostelbiens und Mitteldeutschlands," Ph.D. diss. (Erlangen, 1927), pp. 26–29, and Hagen Schulze, *Otto Braun oder Preußens demokratische Sendung* (Frankfurt am Main, 1977), pp. 96–99.

53. WAZ, 8 November 1919, p. 166, and Zentralverband der Landarbeiter, *1. Verbandstag, 1920*, p. 33.

conditions would handicap the Free unions in the countryside. The Christian farmworkers' union attained 90,000 members in 1920 and 104,000 by the end of 1921. Meanwhile, the socialist farmworkers' union mushroomed to more than 600,000 members, but the rapid decline of this union confirmed the prediction that the Free unions would find it difficult to take root among farmworkers. After the economic crisis and labor strife of 1923, the Christian farmworkers' union retained 77,000 members while its socialist competitor shrank to 102,000.[54]

Franz Behrens hoped that his position as cofounder of the DNVP would facilitate the acceptance of collective bargaining among estate owners. He diplomatically instructed his agents to request permission from an employer before approaching his workers, and he braved the wrath of urban Christian workers by advocating the decontrol of food prices.[55] Many landowners nevertheless refused to believe that they must choose between cooperating with Behrens or watching their "servants" become revolutionary socialists. The reactionary agrarians in the Pomeranian Landbund (Agrarian League) launched a frontal assault against agricultural trade unionism in the spring of 1919. They sought to induce farmworkers to join a Yellow union by offering payment in kind, which was advantageous to laborers in times of inflation but encouraged them to identify with the interests of their employers by making them small marketers of produce. Paramilitary bands recruited by the landowners from the Free Corps supplied even more powerful arguments against trade unionism by beating labor organizers and wrecking their offices. By the end of 1920 the Workers' Group of the Pomeranian Landbund had attained 55,000 members, as many as the socialist farmworkers' union in the province, and Pomeranian landowners recognized it as the sole collective bargaining agent for their workers. Yellow farmworkers' unions then spread to Brandenburg, Mecklenburg, Saxony, and Silesia, merging with the Pomeranian organization at the end of 1920 to form the Reich Farmworkers' League with 100,000 members.[56]

The rise of the Farmworkers' League threatened the Christian unions more than the Free. Its leader, Johannes Wolf, had been an official of the Christian factory workers' union until he was discharged under a cloud in 1910. The propaganda of this alumnus of the Volksverein training program discredited the Christian unions by twisting their religious and patriotic ideals into an apology

54. Wilhelm Vogler, "Probleme des Klassenkampfes zwischen den Landarbeitern und Gutsbesitzern im Regierungsbezirk Merseburg (1918–1923)," Ph.D. diss. (Halle, 1973), p. 334.

55. Zentralverband der Landarbeiter, *1. Verbandstag 1920*, pp. 49–61.

56. Jens Flemming, "Grossagrarische Interessen und Landarbeiterbewegung," in Mommsen, Petzina, and Weisbrod (eds.), *Industrielles System*, pp. 751–58; Horst Hildebrandt, "Die Rolle der sogenannten 'wirtschaftsfriedlichen' Landarbeiterbewegung in Ostelbien während der Weimarer Republik," Ph.D. diss. (Rostock, 1969), pp. 45f., 82–87; Eberhard Voß, "Revolutionäre Ereignisse und Probleme des Klassenkampfes zwischen Landarbeitern und Gutsbesitzern in den Jahren 1921 bis 1923 in Deutschland," Ph.D. diss. (Rostock, 1964), pp. 49–59.

for hierarchical labor relations.[57] Although socialist unions might survive or even benefit from polarization in the countryside, the Christian farmworkers' union won almost no followers in the strife-torn province of Pomerania. The DGB leadership concluded that it must persuade landowners to abandon Yellow experiments by convincing them that Christian workers understood and would promote their legitimate economic interests. The DGB climaxed its anti-Yellow lobbying effort in December 1921 by bringing 200 landowners to Berlin, where Stegerwald told them that they needed a strong trade union movement among farmworkers as a bridge between city and country that would promote future acceptance of agricultural tariffs by urban workers.[58] This plea had no immediate result, but the alliance urged by Stegerwald would become a potent force in German politics in 1925–27.

The leading agrarians of Silesia and Saxony scoffed at the notion that they required the services of mere trade unionists to help them arrive at a consensus with industrialists regarding tariff policy, but they concluded realistically that they had no chance to eliminate trade unionism in their provinces and should seek instead to drive a wedge between the Christian and socialist unions. Late in 1921 they signed a "Village Community" (Dorfgemeinschaft) agreement with Behrens that established joint welfare projects to aid the rural poor, while compelling their small Yellow unions to merge with his organization. However, these landowners embraced the Christian farmworkers' union only in the hope of isolating and weakening it. The new National Agrarian League (Reichslandbund) offered Behrens an agricultural version of the ZAG only if he would sever all links with urban unions.[59] Patriotic fervor in the isolated province of East Prussia helped the Christian unions to win more sincere support from landowners there. Provincial administrators and DNVP functionaries warmly praised Behrens' patriotism, even though they expected his union to behave like its socialist rival in collective bargaining, and most landowners rejected the Reich Farmworkers' League. The province soon became the bastion of the Christian farmworkers' union, providing nearly one-third of its total membership in the mid-1920s.[60]

57. See Johannes Wolf, "Kampforganisation oder Wirtschaftsbund," (Berlin, no date, ca. 1921), and Stupperich, *Volksgemeinschaft*, p. 266.

58. Zentralverband der Landarbeiter, "Die christlich-nationale Landarbeiterbewegung und die Hebung der landwirtschaftlichen Produktion als Voraussetzung des deutschen Wiederaufstiegs" (Berlin, 1922), pp. 16f.

59. ZStA/RLB/55a/29–31, 228–37: conference of 15 December 1921, memorandum of 12 December ("Wege zur Stärkung der nationalen Landarbeiterbewegung"), and social program of 12 April 1922. See also Flemming, "Grossagrarische Interessen," pp. 759f.

60. DNVP Landesverband Ostpreußen, circular of 23 January 1919, Forschungsstelle zur Geschichte des Nationalsozialismus (Hamburg), DNVP/7533; Freiherr von Gayl to Stegerwald, 10 August 1920, NL Stegerwald/001/Bd. 1919–20/no. 82; Hildebrandt, pp. 72f.; Beßler, pp. 43f.

Christian labor leaders were ultimately disappointed in their hopes that farmworkers would greatly strengthen their movement, however. Behrens' efforts to conciliate landowners exposed him to sharp attacks in the socialist press, which accused him of adopting Yellow practices as a result of his Village Community agreement. Meetings of Christian workers in western Germany also criticized Behrens, disclaiming any sympathy for the political views of East Elbian landowners.[61] Moreover, after 1923 neither the Christian nor the socialist farmworkers' union could generate enough revenue to sustain its thinly spread organization, and some leaders in the GcG grumbled when called upon to cover Behrens' annual deficit of RM 50,000–60,000.[62] Thus the Christian farmworkers' union represented a somewhat dubious asset, although Behrens' contacts with Nationalist landowners proved extremely valuable to the DGB during the parliamentary debates over social legislation in the mid-1920s.

Whereas antisocialist ideology helped the DGB grow among white-collar workers at the expense of the Free unions, it conferred no benefit among industrial workers. The membership ratio between the blue-collar Christian and Free unions remained more or less constant at 1:6 throughout the Weimar period. All blue-collar unions grew in times of full employment and suffered losses during recessions, although membership fluctuation was somewhat milder in the GcG.[63] The ideal of a unified trade union movement exercised a perennial fascination among younger Christian industrial workers, and their leaders therefore sought to demonstrate solicitude for the strength and cohesion of the labor movement as a whole by cooperating closely with the Free unions at the collective bargaining table and in the great majority of strikes.[64] Radical currents among Ruhr workers compelled the two major miners' unions in particular to cooperate closely. By the end of 1919 the syndicalist Free Union of Workers attracted the allegiance of tens of thousands of Ruhr miners, and its agitation for the six-hour shift and factory occupations jeopardized both established unions. In response Imbusch and the leaders of the Old Union agreed to avoid all forms of competition that might discredit trade unionism and to establish uniform

61. See *Zentralblatt*, 16 October 1922, pp. 277–79, and *WAZ*, 26 January 1924, p. 16. Hildebrandt, pp. 26f., reprints a letter of March 1919 in which a functionary of the Christian farmworkers' union solicits contributions from landowners, but this appears to have been an extraordinary instance. Behrens responded to such charges in Zentralverband der Landarbeiter, *3. Verbandstag 1926*, pp. 39–47.

62. NL Otte/7/260, GcG Vorstand, 11 October 1926, and Reichsverband ländlicher Arbeitnehmer (formerly Zentralverband der Landarbeiter), *Geschäftsbericht zum 4. Verbandstag 1929*, pp. 11f.

63. Michael Schneider, *Die Christlichen Gewerkschaften*, pp. 140f., 448f.

64. See Gewerkverein christlicher Bergarbeiter, *15. Generalversammlung 1919*, pp. 127, 189f.; Christlicher Metallarbeiterverband, *Geschäftsbericht 1918–19*, pp. 92–94, 312f.; and Schneider, *Die Christlichen Gewerkschaften*, pp. 532–38, 620f.

levels of dues and support payments. In at least one instance, Imbusch discharged a union functionary for attacking the Old Union.[65] The larger member unions of the GcG could not afford to permit their movement's leaders in Berlin to go too far in emphasizing ideological differences with the socialist labor movement.

EFFORTS TO RENOVATE THE SOCIAL ORDER

The Christian unions took great pride in the presence of 30 of their representatives in the National Assembly, who held the numerical balance between the socialist and nonsocialist parties. Stegerwald received a unique opportunity to put his ideals into practice when he was appointed in March 1919 as the only trade unionist on the 28-member committee of the National Assembly that drafted the Weimar Constitution, where he cochaired the subcommittee on socialization.[66] The demand for socialization had involved 300,000 Ruhr coal miners in a wildcat strike in February, and the movement later spread to Berlin and central Germany. In order to appease the strikers, Social Democratic government leaders had reduced the miners' shift from eight to seven hours, created a National Coal Board to give labor and consumers a role in setting prices, and pledged to establish a definite economic role for "workers' councils" in the constitution. Carl Legien furiously denounced the last concession, claiming that it would cripple trade unionism, but Stegerwald, Giesberts, and both miners' unions agreed with the SPD leadership that a new name and somewhat expanded powers for the workers' committees made mandatory in all large factories during the war would appease radical workers by protecting them against authoritarian employers without harming the economy or undermining collective bargaining.[67]

The socialization articles drafted by Stegerwald and Franz Hitze were adopted with little change by the constitutional convention. They rejected a Social Democratic suggestion that the constitution mandate public ownership of all mineral wealth but permitted the Reichstag to expropriate property with or

---

65. Gewerkverein christlicher Bergarbeiter, "Protokollbuch," Hauptvorstand, 28 August 1919, and *Außerordentliche Generalversammlung 1920*, pp. 37–39. For background see Klaus Tenfelde, "Linksradikale Strömungen in der Ruhrbergarbeiterschaft, 1905 bis 1919," and Steinisch, in Mommsen and Borsdorf (eds.), pp. 218–23, 282–88.

66. See the committee assignments in the meeting of March 5, 1919, in the transcripts of the proceedings of the constitutional committee: Hajo Holborn Papers, box 18, folder 158.

67. Potthoff, pp. 123–34, and Peter von Oertzen, *Betriebsräte in der Novemberrevolution* (Düsseldorf, 1963), pp. 99–150.

without compensation, to provide land for peasant homesteads, and to nationalize businesses or compel them to band together in self-administering syndicates, all through a simple majority vote (Articles 153, 155, and 156).[68] This extraordinary emphasis on the economic powers of parliament derived logically from the ideals of Christian workers, who had no settled views concerning the advisability of public ownership of the means of production, but who felt strongly that the principles of free enterprise must be modified or suspended whenever they undermined human dignity. In the words of Friedrich Baltrusch, Christian workers rejected "the capitalist view of the state," according to which it existed "primarily to protect private property," believing instead that "the economy is the object of politics, not its subject." Baltrusch explained further that it was the state's duty to promote social equality by creating economic "strongholds for those without property, . . . thus creating given facts, to which the economy must adjust, just as it must adjust to the facts of nature or existing state borders."[69] These strongholds were discussed in Article 165 of the constitution, which promised that subsequent legislation would establish economic powers for factory councils, regional workers' councils, and a National Economic Council.

When the Weimar Constitution was ratified in August 1919, the cabinet ministers of the SPD, DDP, and Center Party had already agreed on a factory councils bill that would require employers to consult their councils before making any decision that affected workers, and that guaranteed the councils access to the confidential corporate balance sheet and the right to name two members of the board of directors. Stegerwald urged support for the bill with the following warning to bourgeois politicians: "Many people imagine that the revolution is over. That is a fallacy. The political revolution has more or less reached a conclusion, but the social and economic revolution is just beginning."[70] Opposition to the bill from the business community resulted in the first major test of the relative influence of industrialists and organized labor in the bourgeois parties. In the Center Party the Christian unions clearly held the upper hand. Rudolf ten Hompel, the owner of a large cement plant in Münster, led an uncompromising campaign against the bill by the Center's Committee for Commerce and Industry, but found to his chagrin that party leaders always capitulated on crucial issues when Stegerwald reminded them that 60–70% of their voters were blue-

68. See the transcript of the crucial debate of May 30, 1919, in Holborn Papers, box 18, folder 159, and Hermann Mosler (ed.), *Die Verfassung des Deutshen Reichs vom. 11. 8. 1919* (Stuttgart, 1968), pp. 49–51.
69. Friedrich Baltrusch, "Unsere Wirtschaftsauffassung," in GcG, *25 Jahre*, p. 107.
70. *Kölnische Volkszeitung*, 3 November 1919, no. 861, and *Akten der Reichskanzlei. Das Kabinett Bauer* (Boppard am Rhein, 1980), pp. 156–58.

or white-collar workers.[71] Indeed, many Catholic industrialists disapproved of ten Hompel's intransigence because they relied on the Volksverein and its allies in the Christian unions to combat the antimodernist sentiments, the hostility toward all technological innovation and large-scale industry, simmering within the Catholic *Mittelstand* and clergy. Far from denouncing the Factory Councils Law, Florian Klöckner, brother of one of the leading steel magnates of the Ruhr, eagerly sought the support of the Christian metalworkers' union for the upcoming Reichstag elections. He apparently pledged to support cooperative agencies like the ZAG and factory councils if the Christian metalworkers would oppose any plan to socialize the steel industry.[72]

On the other hand, in October 1919 business lobbyists succeeded in persuading the DDP to demand that factory councils be denied access to the corporate balance sheet or the right to appoint members of the board of directors. In this matter the DDP's parliamentary leaders pursued a confrontational course even though they realized that it might force liberal trade unionists out of the party. Similarly, the handful of Christian trade unionists in the DVP had no hope of winning that party's support for the bill after the leaders of heavy industry condemned it.[73] More surprising perhaps was the reaction of the DNVP, in which even relatively moderate party spokesmen such as Martin Schiele denounced the bill as an effort to impose "Bolshevism in pure form." The bill finally passed on January 18, 1920, after the SPD and Center secured the support of the DDP leadership by restricting the councils' access to confidential information. The Christian Social delegates absented themselves from the vote because they could not support the DNVP's negative stance.[74]

In its final form the Factory Councils Law outraged the radical left even more than the business community. The Christian unions may have been the only group that truly believed the idealistic principles enunciated in the law, according to which the factory councils would protect workers' rights while giving them new insight into economic problems so that they would be more willing to

71. Deutsche Zentrumspartei, *1. Reichsparteitag 1920*, pp. 52–59, 65, 86f., and NL ten Hompel/1: "Errinerungen," chap. 4, p. 4.

72. See the remarks by Klöckner and Franz Wieber in *Kölnische Volkszeitung*, 11 January 1921, no. 28. See also Teilnachlaß Pieper/5/1036f., speech by Heinrich Brauns to Volksverein Vorstand, 19 February 1920, and Emil van den Boom, "Industrie und Zentrum," (Volksverein-Verlag, Mönchen-Gladbach, 1925), pp. 9–12.

73. Albertin, *Liberalismus und Demokratie*, pp. 181–85; *Das Kabinett Bauer*, pp. 276–78, 422f.; DVP, *2. Parteitag, Oktober 1919*, pp. 89f., 108–17.

74. Amrei Stupperich, "Volksgemeinschaft oder Arbeitersolidarität. Studien zur Stellung von Arbeitern und Angestellten in der Deutschnationalen Volkspartei (1918–1933)," Ph.D. diss. (Göttingen, 1978), pp. 97–102. This episode is one of the many details omitted from the published version.

"support the employer in fulfilling the factory's purposes." The Free unions decided that they could live with the law, however, and both factions of organized labor devoted considerable energy to electing union nominees to the councils and then training them in the principles of accounting and labor law.[75] The task of collectivist economic reform continued with the creation of two new bodies in the spring of 1920, the National Economic Council promised in the constitution and an Iron Trades Federation. The former was created to advise the government on social and economic legislation. It included equal numbers of representatives of management and labor, appointed by the ZAG, and a smaller group of consumer advocates and economists. Thirty-seven of the 320 members belonged to the DGB, and they banded together in a quasi-parliamentary caucus led by Friedrich Baltrusch. The Iron Trades Federation was created to regulate prices and included three groups of equal size representing the producers of raw iron and steel, organized labor, and the merchants and manufacturers who purchased those products.[76] Taken together, these reforms encouraged Christian trade unionists to believe that the Weimar Republic was achieving a historic compromise between capitalism and socialism, a *Gemeinwirtschaft* (communal economy) in which Christian ideals of solidarity would triumph over selfishness.

The enthusiasm of Christian workers for these reforms encouraged them to believe that all the economic problems of the young republic could be solved in a spirit of cooperation, even if this required persuading workers to surrender some of the gains made during the revolution. In December 1919 Johannes Giesberts confidentially explained the crippling effects of Germany's coal shortage to the GcG's chief theoretician, Theodor Brauer, and suggested that the GcG press should exhort the miners to work overtime, beginning in the following spring "when our domestic situation will bear such a debate."[77] The thinking of the Christian union leadership was expressed more openly by its ablest spokesman in the DVP, Georg Streiter, who promised industrialists that, if they carried out the provisions of the Factory Councils Law in good faith, this would help the "reasonable workers in the major trade unions to expel the radical elements" and commence the crucial tasks of restoring piece-rate wages and permitting exceptions to the eight-hour day.[78] However, early in 1920 the Social Democratic government leaders Bauer, Schlicke, and Carl Severing decided that they could

75. *Zentralblatt*, 15 March 1920, pp. 42–45, and 21 June 1920, p. 122, and Potthoff, pp. 156–58. The best account of the councils' workings is still Nathan Reich, *The Organization of Industrial Relations in the Weimar Republic* (New York, 1938), pp. 156–237.

76. *Zentralblatt*, 19 July 1920, pp. 141–43; Preller, p. 251f.; Gerald Feldman, *Iron and Steel in the German Inflation 1916–1923* (Princeton, 1977), pp. 140–59.

77. Giesberts to Brauer, 20 December 1919, NL Otte/6/150f.

78. DVP, *2. Parteitag, Oktober 1919*, pp. 153f.

wait no longer for the mood of workers to improve. Instead they employed threats of massive military intervention in order to pressure the miners' unions into accepting an overtime agreement that retained the principle of the seven-hour shift but obliged all miners to work two extra half-shifts per week. Heinrich Imbusch charged that the "socialist representatives of the new democracy have succumbed to the allures of the old authoritarian government."[79] There was an element of posturing in this charge, but it does appear that the leaders of the Christian unions retained more faith in the character of the average worker than did the leaders of the SPD and Free unions, exasperated by their fratricidal struggle against the radical left.

In an atmosphere made tense by the imposition of overtime in the mines, a band of rightist freebooters returning from the wars in the Baltic republics chased the elected government out of Berlin on March 13, 1920, and proclaimed an East Prussian official prominent in the wartime Fatherland Party, Wolfgang Kapp, as Germany's new chancellor. The participation of a few army units in the affair and their colleagues' decision to observe a stance of "neutrality" proved a terrible blow to the prestige of the founders of the Weimar Republic. The leaders of the SPD and Free unions soon regained the initiative, however, by proclaiming a general strike that resulted in the most impressive display of the power of organized labor in German history and forced Kapp to abandon his adventure within five days. The Hirsch–Duncker unions endorsed the general strike appeal, but the DGB would only authorize regional strikes where they would hamper the rebels most while doing the least damage to the economy. Most Christian workers supported the strike, and Gutsche's railroad workers' union played a major role in shutting down rail traffic in central and eastern Germany on March 15.[80]

The Christian and Hirsch–Duncker unions promptly called for a resumption of work when the Kapp Putsch collapsed on March 18, but Carl Legien announced that the Free unions could not persuade indignant workers to end the general strike unless the government granted "decisive influence" for the unions over the composition of the cabinet, a purge of all reactionary elements in the bureaucracy, socialization of the coal mines, and the suppression of all "counterrevolutionary military formations." These demands outraged the representatives of the DDP, Center Party, and even many Social Democrats, but they felt

79. See Gewerkverein christlicher Bergarbeiter, *Außerordentliche Generalversammlung, Februar 1920*, p. 64, and Gerald Feldman, "Arbeitskonflikte im Ruhrbergbau 1919–1922. Zur Politik von Zechenverband und Gewerkschaften in der Überschichtenfrage," *Vierteljahrshefte für Zeitgeschichte*, 28 (April 1980), pp. 171–83.

80. Potthoff, pp. 262–64; Varain, p. 173; *Zentralblatt*, 29 March 1920, pp. 53f., 59; GcG, *10. Kongreß 1920*, pp. 161–63; Brüning, pp. 62–66.

compelled to endorse Legien's program in slightly modified form on March 20, when Chancellor Bauer and Defense Minister Gustav Noske were pressured out of office in deference to his wishes. Legien's tactics bore fruit to the extent that this agreement mollified the workers of Berlin and enabled the ADGB to terminate the general strike in most regions.[81] Radical workers assumed leadership of the strike movement in the Ruhr, however, organizing a "red army" to suppress all "counter-revolutionary forces." The Reichswehr (regular army) bloodily suppressed this revolt in early April. The Kapp Putsch and outbreak of civil war in the Ruhr thwarted Giesberts' hopes for an amicable agreement between management and labor concerning revision of the eight-hour day, and gravely deepened the divisions within the working class. Moderate members of both the Free and Christian unions in the Ruhr greeted the Reichswehr troops as liberators and complained bitterly that the government had delayed too long in ending the regime of the "terrorist minority," the "dictatorship of the rabble."[82] To hundreds of thousands of workers disillusioned with trade unionism, however, it seemed that the government employed antirepublican troops to mow down workers who had idealistically responded to its appeal to defend the republic.

Heinrich Imbusch and Friedrich Baltrusch accepted a measure of direct responsibility for pacifying the workers of the Ruhr when they entered the new Socialization Commission created at the end of March in order to fulfill the government's pledges to the Free unions. The Christian miners' union had endorsed public ownership of the mines ever since March 1919, while expressing concern that levels of productivity not be reduced. In the commission's first round of talks, Imbusch eloquently sought to persuade Hugo Stinnes and Albert Vögler to renounce private ownership, to accept the inevitability of socialization and dedicate themselves to the service of the new economic order "like our old professional officers, who remained in the harness even after the revolution in order to save Germany from greater disaster."[83] Imbusch's faith in the altruism of the mineowners and the inevitability of socialization was misguided, however.

The Reichstag election of June 1920 gravely weakened the campaign for socialization. The DVP and DNVP doubled their strength, from 16 to 32% of the vote, while the SPD lost nearly half its voters, mostly to the Independent Socialists. Although the parties of the Weimar Coalition retained a small majority, the stunned leaders of the SPD promptly renounced governmental responsi-

81. *Das Kabinett Bauer*, pp. 710–25, and Potthoff, pp. 270–84.
82. See the reception for representatives of the Ruhr populace on April 8, 1920, *Akten der Reichskanzlei. Das Kabinett Müller I* (Boppard am Rhein, 1971), pp. 49–55.
83. Transcript of the proceedings of the commission on 22–24 April 1920, NL Imbusch/3, p. 49. See also *WAZ*, 28 March 1919, p. 37, and Gewerkverein christlicher Bergarbeiter, *15. Generalversammlung 1919*, pp. 170–72.

bility in order to nurse their wounds. The Center Party's Konstantin Fehrenbach formed a weak minority cabinet with the support of the DDP and DVP.[84] Fearful of labor unrest under the first "bourgeois government" of the Weimar Republic, Fehrenbach sought to strengthen the advocates of socialization in his cabinet by appointing Heinrich Brauns as labor minister, a highly influential post that Brauns retained until 1928. However, the economics, justice, defense, and interior ministries passed into the hands of liberal politicians firmly opposed to socialization. They blocked any legislative initiative for socialization despite popular agitation for it by the SPD, pending the outcome of a complicated round of negotiations in the Socialization Commission and the National Economic Council. These talks merely demonstrated the inability of management and labor to reach agreement on truly controversial issues in the absence of a major external threat.[85]

By November 1920 the Socialization Commission had published three conflicting proposals: a straightforward plan for nationalizing the mines drafted by the Social Democrats; a plan by Rathenau for gradual transfer to public ownership over a period of thirty years; and the Stinnes–Silverberg plan, which most observers agreed would merely place the government's seal of approval on the process of vertical concentration already occurring in heavy industry, although it also offered workers profit sharing. In this confused situation Imbusch and Baltrusch sought to forge a compromise by endorsing the Stinnes–Silverberg plan with the crucial proviso that ownership of mineral wealth be transferred to the national government while the current owners continued to operate as leaseholders. With this proposal Imbusch revived a suggestion he had made in July 1919 to adopt the Royal Prussian Mining Ordinance of 1794 as a model for socialization. Although the Free unions charged that this would merely alter the method by which taxes were collected, Imbusch believed that governmental authority to revoke the leases of delinquent operators would enable miners to secure adequate safety precautions, the removal of unfair overseers, and improved vacation time. Equally important in his view, it would raise productivity by convincing miners that they served "not the pursuit of individual profit, but rather the good of the whole."[86]

84. Maier, pp. 171–73.

85. *Das Kabinett Fehrenbach*, pp. 27f.; Mockenhaupt, pp. 161–65; Peter Wulf, "Die Auseinandersetzungen um die Sozialisierung der Kohle in Deutschland 1920–21," *Vierteljahrshefte für Zeitgeschichte*, 25 (January 1977), pp. 53–89.

86. Heinrich Imbusch, "Die Sozialisierung des Kohlenbergbaus," *Deutsche Arbeit*, 4, no. 7 (1919), pp. 304f. See also *Germania*, 27 October 1920, no. 473, and 13 November 1920, no. 500, and the pamphlet published in 1921 by the socialist miners' union, "Giesberts und Imbusch für Sozialisierung!" (IGBE Bibliothek), pp. 9–11.

Imbusch sought to marshal broad public support for his plan at a DGB rally held in Duisburg on January 9, 1921. It adopted a resolution, however, whose convoluted language suggested inner doubts, demanding "the implementation of a collective organization of our economy (socialization)," on the condition that "state domination and bureaucratization must be avoided, as well as the suppression of free initiative."[87] Despite valiant efforts to maintain a united front in public, the socialization issue caused considerable controversy within the DGB and Center Party. Heinrich Brüning and the DHV leadership apparently opposed any form of socialization, and the Berlin organ of the Center Party suggested delicately that Imbusch should pay more attention to the need for increasing productivity.[88] The provincial party congress of the Rhenish Center convened on January 10, 1921, and there Florian Klöckner attacked state ownership of the coal mines in any form. Franz Wieber explained somewhat apologetically that the Christian unions had been forced to support Imbusch's program because of the danger that the "500,000 Social Democratic workers who oppose the 100,000 Christian workers" in the Ruhr "would proclaim the general strike and civil war." Such halfhearted support reflected the fact that workers in many other trades resented the miners' high wages and seven-hour shifts, feeling that miners collaborated with employers on the National Coal Board in order to push up wages and prices regardless of the damage to the economy as a whole.[89]

Strangely enough, the controversy over socialization died down almost overnight after a government panel of legal experts reported in February 1921 that a transfer of the mines to public ownership would expose them to confiscation by the Western powers in lieu of reparations under the terms of the Treaty of Versailles. Imbusch formally endorsed this argument at a congress of Christian miners in July 1921, after the French and British governments had sobered all the German factions by insisting on a total reparations bill of 132 billion gold marks at the London Conference.[90] The momentum behind economic reform had been checked. Many Christian workers began to question the value of the existing organs of "communal economy," of the National Economic Council, where management and labor seemed to wrangle endlessly, of the regulatory

87. *Kölnische Volkszeitung*, 10 January 1921, no. 23.
88. Heinrich Brüning had criticized the enthusiasm of Labor Minister Brauns for socialization in a letter to Stegerwald on July 30, 1920, NL Stegerwald/001/Bd. 1919–20/no. 78. See also NL Diller/6, "Richtlinien deutschnationaler Sozialpolitik," 15 October 1920, and *Germania*, 10 January 1921, no. 14, and 13 January, no. 19.
89. *Kölnische Volkszeitung*, 11 January 1921, no. 28. See also Feldman, "Arbeitskonflikte im Ruhrbergbau," pp. 171–74, 222f., and the attacks on the miners in Zentralverband christlicher Bauarbeiter, *11. Generalversammlung 1920*, p. 26.
90. Wulf, "Sozialisierung," pp. 92–98; Gewerkverein christlicher Bergarbeiter, *16. Generalversammlung 1921*, pp. 236–44; Maier, pp. 237–43.

boards for the coal and iron industries, whose powers were undermined by private understandings between producers and consumers, and of factory councils. By the end of 1920, some had begun to doubt the power of Christian ideals to transform the economy.[91] Their dreams of forging a new social order were supplanted by nagging worries about how to control inflation and balance the budget while financing welfare programs and reparations. In this atmosphere the tough-minded nationalism of Heinrich Brüning and the leaders of the DHV gained influence. In August 1921 Brüning wrote to Stegerwald in the following terms of his hopes for the DGB:

> If our trade unions would resolve to base their agitation on a strongly patriotic platform, rejecting bourgeois-pacifist ideas, it would undoubtedly be possible to tear large chunks out of the edifice of the Social Democratic trade unions. . . . At heart, 70% of the German workers care nothing for Marxism or anti-Marxism, socialization or free enterprise any more. They are overwhelmed with such slogans and perceive today that the programs of all parties and trade unions contain the same kernel, while an ever stronger pressure from abroad weighs upon the German people, meaning that none of the lovely promises can be fulfilled.[92]

The growing pessimism in the Christian unions matched the mood of the inner circle of government leaders, including President Ebert and Prussian premier Otto Braun of the SPD. The confidential program of the Wirth cabinet, constituted on the basis of the Weimar Coalition in May 1921, was to prevent economic disaster by persuading workers to surrender the eight-hour day in exchange for acceptance by property owners of effective direct taxation. Postal Minister Giesberts had long been preaching the need for longer hours directly to workers' rallies, and now Labor Minister Heinrich Brauns drafted a law authorizing state labor arbitrators to grant exemptions from the eight-hour day, which failed to win support from either the Free unions or industrialists.[93] The issue caused open conflict between the Free and Christian unions in the spring of 1922, when the socialist metalworkers' union launched a major strike in southern Germany to resist the prolongation of the work week from 46 hours to the 48 hours normal in the rest of the country. Sensitive to the growing sympathy for

91. See the sharp exchange between the pessimistic Hüskes and Friedrich Baltrusch in GcG, *10. Kongreß 1920*, pp. 303f., 318f.

92. Brüning to Stegerwald, 4 August 1921, NL Stegerwald/018 (unordered).

93. *Die Kabinette Wirth*, pp. 406f., cabinet meeting of 15 November 1921, and Preller, pp. 272–74. See also Giesberts' speeches in Gewerkverein christlicher Bergarbeiter, *Außerordentliche Generalversammlung 1920*, pp. 12–15, and WAZ, 30 July 1920.

employers in the government and public opinion, the Christian metalworkers' union opposed the strike but could not prevent its socialist competitor from winning majorities of 90% in two successive strike ballots. The result was a costly defeat for the unions, but the bitter determination of the strikers, who held out for up to twelve weeks, highlighted the emotional importance of the shortened work week as the most tangible gain for workers from a revolution that had disappointed so many of their hopes.[94] This thorny issue would strain the capacity of the Weimar system for promoting compromise beyond its limits.

THE DGB'S CAMPAIGN FOR PARTY REFORM

The deteriorating relations between management and labor made the task of strengthening the influence of Christian workers in the political parties more urgent than ever. Adam Stegerwald undertook a major new initiative to this end in November 1920, at the Essen Congress of the Christian unions, by publicly calling for the formation of a new political party to unite Protestants and Catholics. The idea first received public expression in April 1920 when an admirer of Stegerwald in the Munich office of the DGB, Lorenz Sedlmayr, wrote that the DGB should bring together the appropriate politicians to form a "Christian Nationalist People's Party" that would unite Protestant and Catholic workers with the progressive elements of the peasantry and *Mittelstand*.[95]

Stegerwald obviously feared that his followers were encountering such frustration in the bourgeois parties that they might lose faith in the conciliatory ideals of the Christian unions. The nominations process for the Reichstag election of June 1920 heightened this frustration. The DVP elected only two Christian unionists, Winnefeld and Georg Streiter, alongside two Yellow leaders, Fritz Geisler and Otto Adams. The DGB considered this sort of parity humiliating.[96] Only the successful Reichstag candidacy by Otto Thiel of the DHV gave the DGB a certain edge over the Yellow unions in Stresemann's party. Alarmed by its lack of direct influence on social legislation in the National Assembly, the DHV exhorted its members in the spring of 1920 to choose one of the two "national" parties (DVP or DNVP) and enter its cadre. A remarkable percentage of DHV members discovered a taste for political activism, and Thiel was soon

94. Christlicher Metallarbeiterverband, *11. General-Versammlung 1925*, pp. 52, 77f., and Gerald Feldman and Irmgard Steinisch, "Die Weimarer Republik zwischen Sozial- und Wirtschaftsstaat. Die Entscheidung gegen den Achtstundentag," *Archiv für Sozialgeschichte*, 18 (1978), pp. 364–79.

95. "Her mit der christlich-nationalen Volkspartei!" *Deutsche Arbeit* (GcG monthly devoted to social theory), 5, no. 4 (1920), pp. 137–42.

96. Franz Behrens to Gustav Stresemann, 4 May 1920, NL Stresemann 3089/6927/238639f.

able to defend joint trade union interests with the support of DVP employees' committees all over Germany.[97]

More serious strains emerged within the DNVP in the aftermath of the Kapp Putsch. Count Westarp and other prominent Conservatives supported the rebels. After the revolt collapsed, outraged trade unionists threatened to leave the DNVP unless it purged such reactionaries and repudiated the Yellow farmworkers' unions, but the party's central committee flatly rejected these demands on April 9. Franz Behrens could secure only a subtle concession, persuading party chairman Hergt to insist that the East Prussian provincial association of the DNVP accept him as its Reichstag delegate rather than an uncompromising landowner sponsored by Count Westarp.[98] This decision helped Behrens to make East Prussia the bastion of his farmworkers' union, but rumors continued to circulate that he would lead a Christian Social secession from the DNVP.

The elections of 1920 even produced an alarming threat to the Christian unions in their political stronghold, the Center Party. In April conservative Catholics formed a new Christian People's Party in the Rhineland, which outraged class-conscious Catholic workers with its combination of Integralist rhetoric and reactionary social views. The party had no future, but the threat seemed serious when the Bavarian People's Party formed an electoral alliance with it.[99] At the end of May the DGB responded with the following declaration in a confidential circular for its officials:

> Economic and political conditions have not stabilized sufficiently in the year-and-a-half since the end of the war to clear the path for a progressive and comprehensive development of the German nation in the spirit of the ethical, patriotic, economic and social goals of the DGB. The reform of the existing party system in this spirit is our most pressing task. We can recognize the existing party system, inherited from a completely different age, as nothing more than a transitional state.[100]

This grandiloquent manifesto ended on a cautious note by urging its readers to continue to seek influence in the existing parties for the time being.

Powerful opposition to Stegerwald's plan emerged within the church-affili-

---

97. NL Diller/6: DHV Verbandstag resolution of 16 May 1920 and circular by Lambach and Thiel of 5 May; Döhn, pp. 132–38.

98. Hertzman, pp. 100–05; Westarp MS, "Konservative Politik," pp. 52–58; and Westarp to Heydebrand, 20 October 1919 and 25 March 1920, in NL Westarp.

99. See Sedlmayr to Jakob Kaiser, 31 May 1920, NL Kaiser/250, and Morsey, *Zentrumspartei 1917–1923*, pp. 315f.

100. NL Diller/6: "Richtlinien des D.G.B. für die Reichstagswahlen," in DHV circular of 19 May 1920.

ated Catholic and Protestant workers' clubs, however. The leaders of the Catholic clubs of western and southwestern Germany resented what they saw as efforts by the Christian unions to usurp their traditional role as the political representatives of Catholic workers. At a club rally in September 1919, Joseph Joos chided the Christian unions for trying to cooperate with monarchists in the DNVP who were incapable of accepting modern political realities. While agreeing that the Center Party required further democratization, Joos declared that, if the Christian unions wanted to unite their members in a single party, that party must be the Center.[101] Like the Swabian populists Erzberger and Joseph Wirth, these club leaders supported the Weimar Coalition enthusiastically. Although this fact has prompted many commentators to consider them the only good democrats in the Center Party, it must be understood that the Erzberger faction supported the Weimar Coalition largely as a means to the end of preserving Catholic unity, threatened by massive working-class defections to the SPD. They felt that the Church could retain the loyalty of workers only by avoiding conflict with the Social Democrats, while Stegerwald and Heinrich Brauns believed that public controversy with the SPD was sometimes necessary to underscore the distinctive identity of the Christian labor movement. Joos and Msgr. Otto Müller restored close ties with the episcopate after the death of Cardinal Hartmann late in 1919. The new archbishop of Cologne, Carl Joseph Schulte, was a friend of theirs but distrusted the ecumenicists in the Volksverein and Christian unions.[102] The leaders of this "left wing" of the Center Party sometimes went to absurd lengths in efforts to preserve Catholic unity, as when Giesberts blamed the high price of potatoes in Cologne during the war on the Junkers rather than the nearby Catholic peasantry, and when Joos later blamed the secession of the Bavarian People's Party from the Center on "East Elbian intriguers."[103] On the deepest level the Erzberger faction adhered to the very old view that the primary mission of the Center Party was to plug leaks from the Catholic reservoir. In this respect the ecumenicists Stegerwald and Brauns displayed a better grasp of long-term historical trends.[104]

Joos and Müller nevertheless succeeded in persuading some Christian union

---

101. Verband der katholischen Arbeitervereine Westdeutschlands, *12. Verbandstag 1919*, pp. 32–38, and Wachtling, pp. 57–65.

102. See Teilnachlaß Pieper, vol. 5, pp. 989, 1022–24, 1062, 1192, and Ernst Deuerlein, "Heinrich Brauns, Schattenriß eines Sozialpolitikers," in Ferdinand Hermens and Theodor Schieder (eds.), *Staat, Wirtschaft und Politik in der Weimarer Republik* (Berlin, 1967), p. 55.

103. See [Stegerwald] to Giesberts, 22 September 1916, NL Otte/6/186f., and *WAZ*, 1 October 1921, p. 154.

104. Compare Thomas Knapp, "Joseph Wirth and the Democratic Left in the German Center Party 1918–1928," Ph.D. diss. (Catholic University of America, 1967), pp. 245–56, and see below, pp. 135–41, 154f.

leaders that party reform would only encourage dangerous social radicalism. They portrayed the advocates of a Christian Nationalist People's Party as mostly young hotheads who desired a new labor party devoted to proletarian class struggle, a splinter party that would inevitably drift into the Marxist orbit.[105] Stegerwald and his spokesmen denied any thought of founding a class-based party and urged consolidation instead of secession, but some excited DGB activists did speak of a new "workers' party," either misunderstanding or misrepresenting Stegerwald's intentions. At the congress of the Christian metalworkers' union in August 1920, Franz Wieber denounced an unauthorized circular from the Hanover office of the DGB in which junior officials threatened to appeal to the membership over the heads of union leaders if they hesitated to form a new party. This showed, in Wieber's view, that Sedlmayr's magazine article had been "a provocation to the masses that has had a very dangerous impact." The congress resolved to condemn any DGB initiative to form a new party despite a spirited defense of Sedlmayr by Stegerwald's spokesmen Brauer and Kaiser.[106]

Stegerwald realized that the divided loyalties of Catholic workers made it impossible to found a new party without the cooperation of the Center leadership. A confidential memorandum by him for DGB leaders, written in September 1920, emphasized that Christian workers enjoyed a far better position in the Center than in any other party. The Center should be the "starting point" for the Christian Nationalist People's Party because "a large popular bloc is already united in it that represents an appropriate mixture and is of good will."[107] This modest plan for changing the Center Party's name in order to attract disgruntled Protestant workers could be supported by all Catholic labor leaders, but their united front promptly disintegrated at a meeting of the Center Reichstag delegation on October 19, when Rudolf ten Hompel demanded that Matthias Erzberger not be reelected to its executive committee. Erzberger had failed to clear his name of corruption charges in a notorious libel suit against Karl Helfferich of the DNVP and was the target of vicious attacks in the nationalist press. The Catholic workers' clubs had won much popular sympathy for Erzberger by portraying him as the victim of capitalists angry over progressive taxation and Protestant bigots who considered all Catholics potential traitors.[108] Now Stegerwald supported ten Hompel by arguing before the delegation that Erzberger

---

105. *WAZ*, 22 May 1920, p. 82, and 28 August 1920, p. 138, and Cologne Archdiocese, *Mitteilungen an die Präsides der katholischen Arbeitervereine*, October 1920, pp. 85, 93f.

106. Christlicher Metallarbeiterverband, *9. Generalversammlung 1920*, pp. 76f., 137–49.

107. "Arbeiterbewegung und Politik," September, 1920, NL Stegerwald/001/vol. 1919–20, and Jones, "Adam Stegerwald," pp. 12f.

108. Epstein, pp. 392–413, and *WAZ*, 7 February 1920, pp. 21f.

should retire from politics for a while in order to promote the formation of a "new party of reconstruction," but Giesberts retorted that "the Catholic workers would not sacrifice Erzberger for the sake of the grand political goals discussed by Stegerwald."[109]

The debate over Erzberger resumed in the broader forum of the Center's national committee on October 31 and November 1, 1920. Here Stegerwald sought to promote consensus by portraying the formation of a new party as a substitute for socialization.

A socialization plan that brings a decline in production is utterly unacceptable. On the other hand, we must reckon with 80% of the whole population as wage- and salary-earners. The socialization question is therefore essentially a psychological question. . . . The German people must go through a vale of suffering in the next ten years such as few can imagine today. In this situation something extraordinary must happen, and this I can see only in *party reform*.[110]

Erzberger's strongest supporter, Finance Minister Wirth, retorted that "the chasm between the confessions is still unbridgeable" because reactionary elements dominated the Protestant camp. Party chairman Carl Trimborn, on the other hand, readily agreed to prepare a definitive new party program and to encourage Protestants to participate. As in November 1918, however, he insisted that the old party name be retained. His skillful tactics, conciliatory tone, and underlying firmness of purpose probably doomed Stegerwald's initiative even before it was publicly announced.[111]

The tenth congress of the Christian unions, which convened in Essen on November 20, nevertheless improved the morale of Christian trade unionists considerably. Stegerwald's keynote address, written largely by Brüning, sought to make the turbulent events of the last two years understandable in terms of traditional Christian teaching. Stegerwald lumped liberal employers and proletarian socialists, Lenin and Poincaré together as "materialists," advocates of class struggle, cold-blooded rationalists obsessed with power and domination.[112] He painted a harsh but realistic picture of Germany's economic distress and argued that the task of reconstruction required the formation of a broad new

109. Morsey, *Zentrumsprotokolle 1920–25*, pp. 54–58.
110. NL ten Hompel/16/101f.
111. NL ten Hompel/16/114–16. See also Hermann Cardauns, *Karl Trimborn. Nach seinen Briefen und Tagebüchern* (Mönchen-Gladbach, 1922), esp. pp. 184–88.
112. Adam Stegerwald, "Deutsche Lebensfragen," in GcG, *10. Kongreß 1920*, pp. 186–88, and Morsey, *Zentrumspartei 1917–23*, pp. 368–70.

party of the middle to ensure continuity and realism in government policies. The new party should be "German," meaning that it would urge revision of the Treaty of Versailles, "Christian," meaning that it opposed "the materialist and mechanistic theory of history," "democratic," meaning that it favored increased popular participation in government, and "social," meaning that it advocated the "recognition of the worker as a subject and equal partner in production."[113] Several union leaders seconded Stegerwald's appeal with concrete suggestions for how to promote reconstruction and social partnership in collective bargaining and factory councils. The congress concluded with a theoretical address by Theodor Brauer on the contradictions between Christianity and socialism, a speech that effectively ended the widespread flirtation with the slogan of "Christian socialism" after the revolution.[114]

Stegerwald's speech electrified contemporaries of many different political persuasions. The liberal press responded enthusiastically, and Anton Erkelenz championed the "Essen Program" as a means to save the DDP from plutocracy. Moreover, many idealistic nationalists such as Artur Mahraun of the Young German Order began to look to Stegerwald as a man who could correct the abuses of party politics.[115] The Essen Congress also announced several concrete measures to increase the political leverage of the Christian unions. It established a newspaper, *Der Deutsche*, the only trade union daily in Germany, a German People's Bank to collect workers' savings and invest them in progressive enterprises such as producers' cooperatives, and a new political committee to coordinate the activities of the various parliamentary representatives of the DGB.[116] In December 1920 Stegerwald exhorted the Center to dissolve itself in order to clear the path for party reform, and the Christian union press reported that DGB members could not be restrained from organizing independent Christian labor tickets in communal elections as long as "conditions in the political parties are unsatisfactory."[117]

Some confusion remained, however, concerning just what had been decided in Essen. Johannes Giesberts sought to avoid controversy by describing the essence of Stegerwald's program as "No new party, but rather a permeation of politics with the ideals of the Christian-nationalist labor movement," appealing

113. GcG, *10. Kongreß 1920*, p. 231.
114. Theodor Brauer, "Christentum und Sozialismus," in GcG, *10. Kongreß 1920*, pp. 406–32, and Focke, pp. 69–77, 91–110.
115. *Frankfurter Zeitung*, 23 November 1920; Anton Erkelenz, "Wie Schafft man eine Erfüllungsmehrheit?," *Die Hilfe*, 5 July 1921, pp. 291f.; Klaus Hornung, *Der Jungdeutsche Orden* (Düsseldorf, 1958), pp. 25–33; Brüning, pp. 71–73.
116. Morsey, *Zentrumspartei 1917–23*, p. 372, and Treviranus, pp. 52–54.
117. *Zentralblatt*, 20 December 1920, pp. 301–03, and 14 February 1921, p. 52.

for closer cooperation between the Center and the DVP and DDP. Trimborn also portrayed himself as an enthusiastic admirer of Stegerwald who sought to implement the Essen Program through closer cooperation with the liberal parties in the Reichstag.[118] Stegerwald heightened the confusion at the end of 1920 by signing an electoral appeal to support the Center Party in the upcoming Prussian provincial elections. In February 1921 the Center's vote held firm in the working-class districts of Rhineland-Westphalia, and a relieved Trimborn concluded after the elections that Stegerwald's initiative had fizzled.[119]

Stegerwald also encountered unexpected difficulty in securing the cooperation of Christian Socials in the DNVP. Many activists from the Protestant workers' clubs and the DHV in that party distrusted Catholic workers for their "pacifism" and willingness to cooperate with Social Democrats. Since the end of 1919, Count Westarp had become skillful at promoting the integration of such workers into the DNVP by arguing that "the fight against the Versailles Treaty is the class war of an entire nation reduced to proletarian status against its exploiters."[120] Westarp's rhetoric was imitated after June 1920 by the DHV's new representative in the DNVP Reichstag delegation, Walther Lambach, and the Christian Social leader Paul Rüffer, one of the few working-class Christian Socials who had never held union office. In October 1920 they transformed the second party congress of the DNVP into an impressive demonstration of class harmony by denouncing the Treaty of Versailles while securing the party's approval for a bill to impose profit sharing on industry as a corollary to the need for national unity. Stegerwald's closest ally in the DNVP, Franz Behrens, displayed a curious reticence in the months before and after the Essen Congress. He was absorbed in the delicate negotiations that led to the signing of the Village Community agreement with the Reichslandbund (Reich Agrarian League) and apparently refused to undertake any initiative that might strain relations with his agrarian party colleagues.[121]

Lambach and Rüffer, while emphasizing their loyalty to the DNVP, also sought to exploit concern over Stegerwald's initiative at Essen in order to pres-

118. *Germania*, 27 November 1920, no. 523, and *Kölnische Volkszeitung*, 11 January 1921, nos. 26, 27.

119. *WAZ*, 8 January 1921, p. 6, and 22 January, pp. 14f.; *Der Deutsche*, 28 September 1921; Trimborn to ten Hompel, 5 April 1921, NL ten Hompel/17.

120. Hertzman, pp. 205f.

121. Walther Lambach, "Unser Weg zur deutschen Volksgemeinschaft," DNVP pamphlet no. 79 (1920), esp. pp. 3–5, and Paul Rüffer, "Deutschnationale Arbeitertagung in Hannover am 26. Oktober 1920," DNVP pamphlet no. 88. Brüning, who strongly desired to engineer a schism of the DNVP in order to implement the Essen Program, wrote Stegerwald on 4 August 1921 that "from this standpoint I have the strongest possible reservations concerning the Behrens policy toward the *Landbund*" (NL Stegerwald/018).

sure the Yellow unionists out of their party. In this campaign they apparently advertised Stegerwald to the leaders of the DNVP as the one man who could lead the Christian unions and Center Party into a united rightist bloc, dedicated to combating the SPD, thus misunderstanding or misrepresenting him.[122] At the end of 1920 the DNVP founded a new biweekly for workers to be edited by Rüffer. The first issue praised Stegerwald's program but claimed that the DNVP corresponded most closely to his ideal. Rüffer appropriated three of Stegerwald's slogans, German, Christian, and social, but replaced "democratic" with "nationalist." He also predicted the imminent outbreak of "the decisive struggle between the Social Democratic and Christian-nationalist labor movements."[123]

In the spring of 1921 Stegerwald decided realistically that his call for party reform had been premature and devoted himself to the more modest goal of promoting a Grand Coalition from the SPD to the DVP. He believed that a coalition between the leaders of management and labor would represent "the greatest success for both foreign and domestic affairs since the Revolution" and prove "that the German Republic is no mere episode." It would also serve the aims of the Essen Program by renewing the willingness of industrialists to cooperate with trade unions and by weakening the political cross currents that threatened to disrupt the DGB.[124] To this end Stegerwald accepted the office of Prussian prime minister in April, after the Center's Prussian parliamentary delegation decided that the Weimar Coalition must be broadened rightward to reflect the changing mood of voters, despite fears by his advisers that the Center merely sought to deflect him from the pursuit of party reform. Stegerwald quickly reached agreement with Otto Braun of the Prussian SPD on the composition of a Grand Coalition cabinet, but Otto Wels and Hermann Müller vetoed this solution because most Social Democrats were not yet ready for the idea of cooperation with Stresemann's party. On April 21 Stegerwald therefore presented a Center-DDP minority cabinet to the Prussian parliament and offered to resign. In an unexpected development, after intense lobbying by the Christian Socials within their party, Stegerwald was reelected prime minister with the support of the DNVP against the votes of the SPD.[125] His minority cabinet

122. See the cryptic description of internal party conferences in NL Diller/6: "Mitteilung des Reichs-Angestellten-Ausschusses der DNVP," December 1920, and circular of 14 January 1921 for the "Staatspolitische Arbeitsgemeinschaft" of the DNVP.

123. *Deutsche Arbeiterstimme*, January 1921, pp. 1–4, 14f.

124. See Stegerwald to Francisco Mühlenkamp (a financial backer of *Der Deutsche* who lived in South America), 8 October 1921, NL Stegerwald/018.

125. Helga Grebing, "Zentrum und katholische Arbeiterschaft 1918–1933," Ph.D. diss. (Berlin, 1953), pp. 94–100; Schulze, pp. 325–37; Morsey, *Zentrumspartei 1917–23*, pp. 356–58. Brüning anticipates later developments in his *Memoiren*, p. 75, when he claims that Stegerwald pursued a coalition with the DNVP at this juncture.

remained in office for six turbulent months, trying to achieve a Grand Coalition while the new Reich chancellor, Joseph Wirth, pursued the same goal on the national level. Only such a coalition could create the political foundation necessary for stabilizing the economy through some prolongation of work hours combined with effective tax reform.

Stegerwald's unusual fund of goodwill on both the left and the right was soon exhausted. The Social Democratic press attacked him as a reactionary for accepting the support of the DNVP, and a bitter Stegerwald concluded that "in all decisive moments the 'statecraft' of the SPD and its ministers consists of adjusting their policy to that of the tumultuous streets."[126] The worst blow for Stegerwald was the assassination of Erzberger by radical nationalists on August 26, 1921. Joint rallies of the Christian unions and Catholic workers' clubs in western and southwestern Germany hailed Erzberger as a martyr and portrayed the DNVP as a den of assassins. This in turn provoked angry Christian Social workers to charge that the Christian unions had abandoned confessional neutrality. Wilhelm Lindner observed that Protestant workers were willing to honor distinguished Catholic social reformers like Hitze and Brauns but considered Erzberger "the most harmful man in our nation." In private correspondence he contemplated founding independent Protestant trade unions if Stegerwald pressed forward with his efforts to disrupt the DNVP.[127] Stegerwald's credibility within his own party suffered further when his monarchist friend, the Catholic corporatist intellectual Martin Spahn, defected from it to the DNVP and publicly urged Stegerwald to follow him. Joseph Joos then launched an unprecedented public attack on the leader of the Christian labor movement, accusing him of ignoring antidemocratic currents in the rightist parties. Joos claimed that Stegerwald had lost the confidence of Catholic workers in western Germany by neglecting union affairs in his efforts to play the statesman.[128]

Stegerwald considered these charges unjustified, but the DGB undoubtedly experienced an organizational crisis in the summer of 1921. Stegerwald had secured the approval of Christian union leaders for his political adventure by transferring control of the daily operations of the League of Christian Unions to a new general secretary, the Catholic chairman of the Christian textile workers' union, Bernhard Otte.[129] Friction soon developed between the offices of Otte and Heinrich Brüning, both of whom claimed primary responsibility for coordi-

126. GcG, *25 Jahre*, pp. 145–47, and Schulze, p. 338.
127. *Deutsche Arbeiterstimme*, October 1921, pp. 155–57, and Lindner to DNVP Ortsgruppe Eberswald, 19 April 1922, ZStA/DNVP/170/52–57.
128. *Germania*, 23 September 1921, no. 587.
129. *Zentralblatt*, 25 April 1921, pp. 120f.

nating the lobbying activities of the individual Christian unions. Some blue-collar Christian unions also refused to fulfill their pledges of financial support for *Der Deutsche*, feeling that neoconservative intellectuals patronized by Brüning and the DHV enjoyed too much influence over its editorial content. A discouraged Hans Bechly wrote Stegerwald that the blue-collar Christian unions were crippling the DGB with their campaign of "passive resistance" and predicted that the federation would soon disintegrate unless Stegerwald resigned from political office and actively wooed the blue-collar unions. Brüning also complained that the DGB had developed no inner cohesion and submitted his resignation in November 1921, although he returned to his post after a long vacation.[130]

Although Stegerwald remained convinced that he could strengthen the DGB by holding high political office, the DDP doubtless did him a favor by toppling his Prussian cabinet in November 1921. The DGB leadership was forced to acknowledge the limitations of its authority, to recognize that it could not simply issue orders that would change the political marching route of the hundreds of thousands of Catholic workers in the Center or Protestant workers in the DNVP. Instead it supported efforts during 1922 to consolidate the position of workers in both parties. The Christian unions reached a new modus vivendi with the Catholic workers' clubs in the Center Party, organizing a network of workers' committees on a parity basis that enabled the unions and clubs to speak with a single voice in political debates.[131] In a more dramatic development, the third party congress of the DNVP in September 1921 authorized Emil Hartwig, Lindner, and Rüffer to establish the German Nationalist Workers' League (Deutschnationale Arbeiter-Bund, DNAB) with the authority to organize its own local branches independent of the party cadre, levy its own dues, schedule separate rallies for workers, and distribute its own electoral propaganda. This arrangement, unique among German parties, made the DNAB the only political mass organization specifically for workers in the Weimar Republic.[132]

Fritz Geisler and other Yellow union leaders succeeded in alarming members of the DNVP by charging that the Christian unions planned to gain control of the workers' and employees' committees of the DVP and DNVP so that they could split those parties when the command came down to form the "Stegerwald

130. Bechly to Stegerwald, 28 September, and Brüning to Stegerwald, 24 September 1921, NL Stegerwald/014/Nachtrag nos. 4 and 6; Brüning to Stegerwald, 23 November 1921, NL Stegerwald/018; GcG circular of 9 May 1922, NL Otte/1.
131. *WAZ*, 4 March 1922, pp. 34f., 18 March, p. 41, 16 September, p. 128, and 18 November 1922, p. 157.
132. See the DNAB statutes in "Aufbau und Tätigkeit des Deutschnationalen Arbeiterbundes," DNVP pamphlet no. 213 (1925).

Party." Such charges compelled Walther Lambach to take a sharp stand against Stegerwald in public, repudiating the political middle of the Essen Program in favor of a strong right,[133] while compelling DNAB leaders to maintain the appearance of neutrality in all quarrels between the Christian and Yellow unions. Even Franz Behrens extended an olive branch to the Yellow unions by writing for the DNVP press that all "occupational associations" deserved the party's support "insofar as they clearly and unambiguously commit themselves to Christianity, to German values, and to the *Volksgemeinschaft.*"[134] Supporters of the Christian unions nevertheless secured eight of ten seats on the DNAB's executive committee, and its secretary Wilhelm Lindner quietly sought to persuade local leaders of the DNVP to recruit Christian trade unionists as organizers of new DNAB branches, arguing that they were intellectually and morally superior to Yellow workers. Growth was slow at first, limited to cities that already had a strong party organization such as Breslau, Bremen, Hamburg, Danzig, Dortmund, and Stettin. At the end of 1922 the DNAB claimed a modest 45,000 dues-paying members, but the French invasion of the Ruhr in 1923 provided it with the impetus for growth to more than 300,000.[135]

The reaction by bourgeois politicians to the assassination of Foreign Minister Rathenau in June 1922 revealed that the Essen Program still enjoyed influence. His brutal murder by a group of ex-officers sparked imposing mass demonstrations and protest strikes in which, for the first time, the Communist Party cooperated with the SPD and Free unions. Alarm in the bourgeois parties over this "proletarian unity front" caused a revival of interest in the Essen Program. On July 23 the new chairman of the Center Party, Wilhelm Marx, published a proclamation written by Heinrich Brauns that announced the formation of an Association of the Constitutionalist Middle with the DVP and DDP, in which the three parties promised to enter and leave government coalitions as a unit. Marx also pledged that the Center would promote the "simplification and consolidation of the German party system."[136] The new association demonstrated the growing influence of Brauns and Stegerwald over the shape of parliamentary coalitions, following the strategy they had advocated since 1920 of forging a large centrist bloc able to form ad hoc alliances with either the left or right.

133. See Nationalverband deutscher Berufsverbände, *2. Reichstagung 1921*, pp. 25f.; NL Diller/6: "Mitteilung des Reichs-Angestellten-Ausschusses der DNVP," 1 November 1921, and circular from Georg Brost, "Der Wiesenbund," 10 November 1921.

134. *Deutsche Arbeiterstimme*, September 1921, p. 130.

135. Stupperich, *Volksgemeinschaft*, pp. 74–78; *Deutsche Arbeiterstimme*, November 1922, pp. 3f.; DNAB, *Werden und Wachsen*, pp. 24–26. See also the correspondence between Lindner and party locals in ZStA/DNVP/167/192f., 199/70, 210/138, and 210/195.

136. Potthoff, pp. 307–11; *Kölnische Volkszeitung*, 23 July 1922, no. 565; NL Marx/230/6, Brauns to Marx, 19 August 1922.

Stegerwald's campaign to involve the DVP in government strengthened the position of DGB representatives in the People's Party dramatically. Although Wilhelm Gutsche resigned from the DVP on the eve of the Essen Congress, Otto Thiel reaffirmed his loyalty to the party leadership, blandly asserting that Stegerwald merely wanted to improve parliamentary cooperation between it and the Center, on the condition that it repudiate the Yellow unions.[137] Fritz Geisler's supporters still included some of the most powerful industrialists in the party, however, and the Christian unions remained so weak on the grassroots level that they could not even muster a majority on the DVP workers' committee.[138] The atmosphere in the DVP changed abruptly after the formation of the Association of the Constitutionalist Middle. In order to explain the significance of the new association, Stresemann opened the columns of his own journal to Thiel, who wrote that the Center, DDP, and DVP had agreed on a long-range government program and that the DGB would provide redoubled support for all three parties. "Of course the parties belonging to the new association must realize that there is no room for Yellow unions of workers next to the Christian-nationalist trade union movement, nor for those extremist elements in the business community that can imagine cooperation only with a Yellow clique, not with self-confident workers. Their place would be in an opposition party on the extreme right wing."[139]

Geisler and his lieutenants counterattacked by calling for a "national front" of the DVP and DNVP, but moderates in the DVP won the upper hand in the autumn of 1922, when the Center loyally insisted on the DVP's inclusion in the national government even at the expense of toppling its own Chancellor Wirth.[140] Thereafter the Center and DVP cooperated in every coalition government of the Weimar Republic. The mounting tension between Stresemann and the advocates of a "national front" erupted into open conflict after he decided to form a cabinet of the Grand Coalition in August 1923. Geisler and the pro-Yellow syndic of the Essen chamber of commerce, Reinhold Quaatz, were expelled from the DVP for disloyal opposition to its leader's policies. Several other Yellow leaders followed Geisler out of the DVP and sought asylum in the

137. BAK R45II/54/405–09, DVP Geschäftsführender Ausschuß, 1 December 1920.

138. The committee elected Professor Paul Moldenhauer as chairman to break the deadlock between Winnefeld and Geisler: BAK R45II/56/39–45, DVP Reichs-Arbeiter-Ausschuß, 3 December 1921.

139. *Deutsche Stimmen*, 6 August 1922, pp. 502f. For Stresemann's growing interest in the Grand Coalition, see Turner, *Stresemann*, pp. 81–111.

140. Erich Schmidt, "Klassenkampf oder Volksgemeinschaft! Der Weg zur vaterländischen Befreiung der Arbeitnehmerschaft" (Hannover and Leipzig, 1922), pp. 20f., 33–37; Morsey, *Zentrumspartei 1917–1923*, pp. 484–90.

DNVP, where fanatical opposition to Social Democrats was no vice.[141] The handful of DGB activists in the party were the official labor representatives thereafter. Thus Stegerwald's prediction that the Grand Coalition would help spread acceptance for trade unionism found striking confirmation.

The DNVP would never consider cooperation with the SPD, but the desire of many leading Nationalists to participate in a right-of-center parliamentary coalition provided the Christian Socials with a lever similar to that used so effectively by Otto Thiel. The nationalist press treated Stegerwald with kid gloves as a possible bridge toward such a coalition.[142] After the Rathenau assassination party chairman Hergt and Karl Helfferich agreed with the Christian Socials that they must expel the three most radical anti-Semites from the DNVP Reichstag delegation in order to cultivate respectability. The trio enjoyed much sympathy from party locals, but industrial and agrarian lobbyists eager to influence legislation also opposed them. The Christian Socials rejoiced when the party congress of October 1922 expelled all three, who then led several hundred activists out of the DNVP into a new "Racial Freedom Party."[143]

However, any pressure to transform the DNVP so as to make it more acceptable to coalition partners provoked angry reactions from a large corps of fanatical party activists, a phenomenon not encountered in the DVP. Coalition considerations often enabled the Christian Socials to arrive at a consensus with representatives of the Reichslandbund and Reich Association of Industry, but their maneuvers provoked outrage among the rank and file over "materialism" in the party, that is, the sacrifice of sacred nationalist principles to economic or political expediency. Moreover, the Christian unions' role as the symbol of alarming social change always made them the special target of this resentment. Even when urging the same policies as other interest groups, the trade unionists somehow seemed more materialistic. In towns where numerous meetings and social events organized by the local DNVP sought to create a soothing atmosphere of a *Volksgemeinschaft* (national community) totally free from social conflict, only deferential workers could win acceptance.[144] This widespread abhorrence of any dealings with laborites constituted one of the most important obstacles to the achievement of "corporate pluralism" in Germany.

141. Döhn, p. 242, and *Zentralblatt*, 18 June 1923, pp. 95f.
142. Hertzman, pp. 166–74, and DNVP, *Korrespondenz*, 19 July 1922, p. 164.
143. Hertzman, pp. 141–55, and Liebe, pp. 66–70.
144. See the reaction to the party crisis in Gottfried Traub to Westarp, 24 July 1922, NL Westarp, and Reinhard Behrens, "Die Deutschnationalen in Hamburg: 1918–1933," Ph.D. diss. (Hamburg, 1973), pp. 93–97.

3

The Stabilization Crisis of 1923–1924

The French occupation of the Ruhr in January 1923 precipitated a year-long economic and political crisis in Germany, the most serious of the Weimar Republic before its fall. The Christian unions hoped at first that this international crisis would revive the wartime spirit of national unity and facilitate the quest for economic reform, for the *Gemeinwirtschaft*. Instead, economic distress and the kindling of nationalistic passions benefited the extremists of left and right. The DGB leadership reacted to this polarization by making substantial concessions to employers in order to preserve the organs of conciliation between management and labor that it had worked so hard to forge. For a time the Christian unions diverged significantly from the policies of the Free unions in pursuit of the vanishing mirage of national unity. However, this course soon provoked a reaction in favor of renewed cooperation with the Free unions among blue-collar Christian workers.

THE EROSION OF THE SPIRIT OF SOCIAL PARTNERSHIP

Demands by employers for abolition of the eight-hour day had already paralyzed the ZAG when the French occupied the Ruhr. In 1921–22 both the employers' associations and the Free unions rejected compromise proposals by the Labor Ministry for a law to grant limited exemptions from the rigid eight-hour limit imposed by the demobilization decrees of November 1918. As inflation reached alarming proportions in the autumn of 1922, the industrialists Hugo Stinnes and August Thyssen insisted publicly that only a ten-hour day could stabilize the economy.[1] At a meeting of the ZAG executive committee on November 10, management spokesmen explicitly repudiated the politics of consensus with organized labor for the first time. Hermann Bücher opened the meeting by declaring that "we have not developed a positive economic policy because we wanted to do justice to everyone's opinion, therefore we have no leadership." Fritz Tänzler added that only the restoration of prewar work hours and cuts in real wages below prewar levels could save the German economy.[2] Friedrich Baltrusch of the Christian unions expressed willingness to relax the eight-hour day on the terms proposed by the Labor Ministry but demanded in exchange increased influence for labor and consumer representatives on the pricing policies of cartels and syndicates as well as labor representation in the chambers of commerce. Baltrusch argued forcefully that only greater labor participation in management decisions could promote voluntary acceptance of longer work hours, and this approach enjoyed some support from moderate industrial spokesmen such as Hans von Raumer. But Peter Graßmann of the ADGB rebuked Baltrusch for abandoning the eight-hour day. He blamed inflation entirely on Germany's cartels and the failure by industrialists to promote technological innovation. Graßmann also warned that the widespread belief among Free union members that heavy industry profited from inflation and contributed vast sums to the Nazi Party and Yellow unions made it extremely difficult for union leaders to continue participation in the ZAG.[3] The arguments of the ADGB leaders were dominated by fear of radicalism among the rank and file rather than consideration of Germany's economic problems.

In December 1922 industrialists on the National Economic Council abandoned efforts to reach agreement with the trade unions, relying instead on support from academics and consumer advocates to push through a report on the government's work hours bill that urged total deregulation. Otto Thiel of the DHV warned industrialists that such reliance on "accidental majorities" would simply destroy the influence of the Economic Council. He and Baltrusch appealed to their fellow ZAG leaders to make one last effort to reach a genuine compromise, predicting correctly that the Reichstag parties would not be able to agree on a work hours law while the differences between management and labor remained unbridged. The Free unions agreed to such talks, but employers

---

1. See Feldman and Steinisch, "Die Weimarer Republik zwischen Sozial- und Wirtschaftsstaat," esp. pp. 381–84.
2. ZStA/ZAG/31/71f., 83–86.
3. ZStA/ZAG/31/77–90. See also Feldman, *Iron and Steel*, p. 394, and the published version of Baltrusch's plan in *Zentralblatt*, 17 September 1923, pp. 129f.

insisted that the majority report of the Economic Council stand unchanged.[4] Thus the DGB found itself unable to revive the sentiment that had been the motive force behind the formation of the Central Association: that management and labor must cooperate in order to keep major economic policy decisions out of the inexpert hands of the politicians and bureaucrats.

At the end of 1922 the debate over work hours was overshadowed by Germany's diplomatic confrontation with France over reparations. The two issues were not unrelated, because some leaders of big business opposed measures to resolve the international crisis in the hope that it would facilitate their campaign for the abolition of the eight-hour day. In November 1922 Reich Chancellor Wirth admitted that he could accomplish nothing because of the uncooperative attitude of the business community and French intransigence, and the non-socialist parties of the Reichstag created a conservative "cabinet of experts" under the leadership of Wilhelm Cuno, managing director of the Hamburg-America Line, in a bid for business support. Baltrusch sought to mediate between the ADGB leadership and Cuno by persuading the former to soften a list of demands to the government on financial policy while reminding the latter that he required active trade union support if he hoped to present a united front to the foreign enemy.[5]

When French troops entered the Ruhr on January 11, 1923, in order to compel Germany to step up its reparations payments, the Christian and Hirsch–Duncker unions persuaded the ADGB to publish a joint declaration with them urging nonviolent resistance to the foreigner. Patriotic Free union leaders resolved to organize anti-French strikes in occupied territory despite widespread sympathy among socialist workers for the call by the German Communist Party (Kommunistische Partei Deutschlands, KPD) to "fight reaction on the Ruhr and on the Spree!" that is, to oppose both the French and German governments as equally blameworthy in the affair.[6] The willingness of Ruhr industrialists to make sacrifices for the national cause and the firm example set by the Christian unions, which embraced about one-fourth of the organized workers of the Ruhr, then served to win over wavering hearts. As the Christian miners' and railroad workers' unions led in organizing strikes to shut down the coal pits and work-to-rule actions to disrupt public transport, all three union leagues and all political parties

---

4. ZStA/ZAG/47/38, Thiel to ZAG Zentralvorstand, 19 December 1922, and replies in 47/25–39.
   5. See Maier, pp. 244–66, 285–300, and *Akten der Reichskanzlei. Das Kabinett Cuno* (Boppard am Rhein, 1968), pp. 95–99, for reception for union leaders on 28 December 1922.
   6. See the ADGB's account in Lothar Erdmann, *Die Gewerkschaften im Ruhrkampf* (Berlin, 1924), pp. 84f.; *Das Kabinett Cuno*, pp. 186–88; and Freya Eisner, *Das Verhältnis der KPD zu den Gewerkschaften in der Weimarer Republik* (Cologne and Frankfurt am Main, 1977), p. 15.

from the SPD to the DNVP joined ranks to explain to German workers that the future of the eight-hour day and their prosperity in general depended on the struggle against French militarism and Entente capital in the Ruhr.[7]

For Labor Minister Brauns and many DGB leaders, the Ruhr conflict represented an opportunity to save cooperative social institutions from paralysis through a revival of the wartime spirit of national unity. In late January they joined management spokesmen to persuade Theodor Leipart, chairman of the ADGB since Legien's death in 1920, to authorize the proclamation of a joint Ruhr Aid fund-raising drive by the Central Association on behalf of the unemployed. In February and March Brauns persuaded the cabinet to entrust direction of the economic struggle on the Ruhr to the voluntary cooperation of management and labor, and the Labor and Economics ministries then established parity boards in occupied territory that decided which factories should close and administered welfare payments to idle workers. The government also agreed to compensate union secretaries who were banished or imprisoned by the French as if they were civil servants.[8] The Ruhr Aid collection failed miserably, however, because of rumors that workers' donations were being diverted to support the Yellow unions and other reactionary organizations sponsored by employers. The Free unions of Berlin and the entire socialist metalworkers' union decided to boycott any fund-raising drive administered jointly by management and labor, and this dampened the generosity of employers. In April the ZAG abandoned its collection after raising only one-fifth the sum anticipated. This failure revealed a startling deterioration in the authority of the ADGB leadership and demonstrated that the struggle on the Ruhr could not create an atmosphere of mutual trust between management and labor in central and eastern Germany.[9] Thereafter the government relied solely on the printing press to finance welfare payments in the Ruhr, adding fuel to inflation.

The economic distress caused by inflation soon destroyed the trade unions' enthusiasm for passive resistance. Already on February 7, 1923, the Christian unions jolted the Cuno cabinet with a harshly worded warning that the government must tax property owners more effectively and curb the liberal credit policies that encouraged inflation profiteering: "The belief that government and high finance have worked hand in glove in the last years is spreading rapidly in

7. See Feldman, *Iron and Steel*, pp. 351ff.; *Das Kabinett Cuno*, pp. 236f.; and WAZ, 10 February 1923, pp. 19f.
8. Uwe Oltmann, "Reichsarbeitsminister Henrich Brauns in der Staats- und Währungskrise 1923–24," Ph.D. diss. (Kiel, 1968), pp. 50–52, 79–81, 114–21; ZStA/ZAG/31/34–43, meetings of 23–24 January 1923; Potthoff, pp. 324–30.
9. See the protest letters from Free union locals to ADGB headquarters in BAK NS 26/933, and Lothar Erdmann, pp. 112–17.

the populace, endangers the will to resist, and is suited to bring about chaotic economic and social conditions."[10] In mid-April Leipart and the socialist miners' union pressured Cuno to make France a serious reparations offer, warning that the sufferings of Ruhr workers might cause the collapse of passive resistance within a week. Stegerwald and Otte barely succeeded in dissuading the ADGB from making such demands in public.[11]

Cooperation between management and labor disintegrated completely in the summer of 1923, as inflation ran out of control. The Cuno cabinet sought the assistance of the business community in raising a foreign loan to stabilize the mark, but on May 25 the Reich Association of Industry announced a highly partisan set of conditions for such aid, including the total deregulation of work hours and the return of Germany's railroads to private ownership. The Free and Hirsch–Duncker unions denounced the industrialists for disrupting national unity, and even the Christian unions concluded that most industrialists had abandoned any commitment to the ideals of the ZAG.[12] By July at least one-third of the industrial workers in the Free unions supported the Communist opposition to their union leaders.[13] Discipline was much better in the Christian unions, but echoes of KPD attacks on the union bosses could sometimes be heard in their meetings as well. Reports of Communist gains induced the cabinet to instruct state labor arbitrators to push up wages as quickly as possible in their race with consumer prices, but this measure could only postpone briefly the abandonment of passive resistance, which imposed incomparably more privation on the German populace than on the French. By midsummer serious arguments broke out within the GcG leadership concerning the feasibility of continued resistance. The militant patriot Jakob Kaiser, Stegerwald's representative in the GcG regional office for Rhineland-Westphalia, reported indignantly to his friend Sedlmayr that Giesberts and others had "fallen completely into the mentality of November 1918: surrender at any price."[14] Christian Socials and DHV activists were even more critical of "defeatist" currents among Catholic workers.

In late July and August a wave of Communist-inspired strikes and demonstra-

10. *Das Kabinett Cuno*, pp. 228–30. State Secretary Eduard Hamm forwarded the petition to the Finance, Economics, and Agriculture ministries, noting that it was of "very serious political significance."

11. *Das Kabinett Cuno*, pp. 376f., 417–19.

12. Ibid., pp. 512f., 537–40; Maier, pp. 369–71; Lothar Erdmann, *Die Gewerkschaften im Ruhrkampf*, pp. 148f.; *Zentralblatt*, 18 June 1923, pp. 81–87.

13. Eisner, pp. 144–60, and Martin Martiny, "Arbeiterbewegung an Rhein und Rubr (1920–1930)," in Jürgen Reulecke (ed.), *Arbeiterbewegung an Rhein und Ruhr*, pp. 255–58.

14. NL Kaiser/250, Kaiser to Sedlmayr, 22 February 1924. See also the undated report by Wilhelm Elfes from the spring of 1923 on morale in the Ruhr, KAB Archiv; *Zentralblatt*, 18 June 1923, pp. 93–95, 109; and *Das Kabinett Cuno*, pp. 455–57, 597, 612–28.

tions contributed to the fall of the Cuno government. The government and the trade unions sought desperately to reinforce each other's authority during this crisis.[15] In mid-August Gustav Stresemann facilitated government-union cooperation by forming a Grand Coalition cabinet dedicated to the termination of passive resistance and restoration of economic normalcy. The new cabinet relied on the trade unions to explain its policies to workers in occupied territory, but inflation now reached such grotesque proportions that union treasuries melted away and revenues dwindled to a trickle. As Ernst Lemmer wrote in a petition to the government from the Hirsch–Duncker unions, "If the trade unions are to help preserve law and order, their organizational apparatus must be protected from disruption." The government secretly granted the three union leagues hundreds of thousands of gold marks in "loans" repayable in depreciated paper money from August through October.[16] For the ADGB this close cooperation with the government represented an embarrassing departure from tradition, justified only by the extraordinary crisis. For many officials of the Christian unions, however, such ties reinforced feelings of personal loyalty to Labor Minister Brauns, fostering a tendency to view themselves as public servants rather than interest group representatives. This self-image hindered them from responding effectively to the grave social conflicts of the autumn and winter.

THE CRISIS OF PARLIAMENTARY GOVERNMENT

While the Stresemann cabinet deliberated measures for stabilizing the economy, the militant right wing of the Christian-nationalist labor movement, which opposed any cooperation with the SPD, strove to modify the policies of the DGB. Workers in the DNVP shared the tendency of radical nationalists to entertain unrealistic hopes regarding Germany's ability to resist France and to blame the alleged weakness or treachery of socialist workers when those hopes were disappointed. In February 1923 the chairman of the DNAB, Emil Hartwig, urged all DNVP members to boycott the Ruhr Aid collection by the Central Association. Charging that the ZAG discriminated in favor of socialist workers, Hartwig launched his own fund-raising drive to finance acts of sabotage and to

15. *Das Kabinett Cuno*, pp. 692f., and *Zentralblatt*, 20 August 1923, pp. 123f. Labor Minister Brauns instructed all government officials, for example, to refuse to receive deputations of unemployed workers without the mediation of union officials.

16. Wilhelm Ersil, "Über die finanzielle Unterstützung der rechtssozialistischen und bürgerlichen Gewerkschaftsführer durch die Reichsregierung im Jahre 1923," *Zeitschrift für Geschichtswissenschaft*, 6 (1958), pp. 1228–45, quotation from a petition of 10 September 1923 on pp. 1238f. See also the revealing exchange of reproaches between Franz Behrens and the head of the socialist farmworkers' union in the Reichstag debate of 26 March 1926, *Verhandlungen des Reichstags*, vol. 390, pp. 6730–36.

support unemployed party comrades.[17] The Christian unions officially opposed acts of violence that might lead to French reprisals, but Heinrich Brüning and Wilhelm Gutsche initially sought, like Hartwig, to support "active" as well as "passive" resistance. They cooperated with army officers to provide DGB intelligence reports and at least one demolitions expert to aid the volunteers undertaking nocturnal raids against French army transport.[18] The Reich government displayed an ambiguous attitude toward these efforts, but in the spring of 1923 Prussian Interior Minister Carl Severing, a Social Democrat, ended the campaign of sabotage by outlawing the Racial Freedom Party and paramilitary organizations active in the Ruhr. Radical nationalists and even some Christian union members considered this action treasonable, but Wilhelm Gronowski, provincial prefect of Westphalia and a former leader of the Catholic workers' clubs, loyally executed the orders of his Prussian superiors. Wilhelm Lindner demanded thereafter that the Catholic workers of the west choose once and for all between cooperation with the "nationalist" and the "internationalist" factions in German politics.[19]

In 1923 the most serious strike movement ever in East Elbian agriculture generated serious tensions between the Free and Christian unions and encouraged the self-assertive spirit on the right wing of the DGB. In mid-May a threat of food shortages emerged when numerous locals of the socialist farmworkers' union in Silesia rejected a provincial labor contract negotiated by union leaders and launched a strike that spread to about 50% of all Silesian estates. The socialist farmworkers' union disclaimed responsibility for the strike, which involved breach of contract, but declared its solidarity with the strikers. Franz Behrens denounced the strike as illegal and unpatriotic, and the Christian farmworkers' union strove with substantial success to keep Christian and unorganized farmworkers on the job. The strike movement spread to East Prussia and Pomerania in June, generating intense public concern over interruption of harvests. The DNVP helped organize armed protection for estates and recommended the two "nationalist farmworkers' organizations," that is, Behrens' Christian union and Johannes Wolf's Yellow farmworkers' league, to landowners all over Germany as antistrike allies.[20] Most of the strikes collapsed in July after the government's Emergency Technical Service intervened on behalf of landowners. Smaller strikes flared up again in the winter, however, prompting martial law comman-

17. DNAB circulars of 3 February and 21 April 1923 in StA Osnabrück C1/84/4f.
18. Treviranus, pp. 57f.
19. See *Das Kabinett Cuno*, p. 339; DVP Zentralvorstand, 7–8 June 1923, BAK R45II/38/17–33; and Lindner in *Kirchlich-soziale Blätter*, July 1923, p. 3.
20. Beßler, pp. 34–47; Voß, pp. 148–56; DNVP circular of 27 July 1923, StA Osnabrück C1/17:I/45; *Zentralblatt*, 20 August 1923, p. 125.

ders in East Elbia to threaten draconian penalties for strikers and to urge Labor Minister Brauns, unsuccessfully, to grant government recognition to the Yellow farmworkers' league.[21] As a result of the strike wave the Christian farmworkers' union renounced cooperation with the socialist union in Silesia and East Prussia, forming instead voluntary arbitration boards with employers. This stance encouraged landowners to refuse recognition to the socialist union, and the SPD press attacked the Christian farmworkers' union for marching into the Yellow camp.[22]

The political and economic crisis attending the termination of passive resistance in September 1923 encouraged Behrens to campaign against continued participation by the SPD in government. The DNVP, paramilitary leagues, and some extremists in the DVP considered Stresemann a traitor for urging "surrender." On September 23 Hergt and Westarp of the DNVP urged the Reichswehr commander, General Hans von Seeckt, to establish a military dictatorship, hoping that he would renounce the Treaty of Versailles and arm the paramilitary leagues in order to escalate the struggle against France. Behrens and Gutsche visited Seeckt the next day, apparently to second this appeal on behalf of nationalist workers. The substance of their talk is not known, but they obviously persuaded Seeckt that he should seek DGB support if he assumed the chancellorship. Stegerwald's name appeared on a list of cabinet ministers drafted by Seeckt, but the general's aides eventually persuaded him to renounce political ambitions.[23]

The DNVP's program for a military dictatorship linked with a suicidal foreign policy had no chance of winning acceptance from moderate DGB leaders, but economic concerns made them uncomfortable with the Grand Coalition. Labor Minister Brauns and most economists agreed with businessmen that some prolongation of work hours was essential to revive industrial production, but the SPD seemed unwilling to permit any exceptions to the eight-hour day. Moreover, the widespread belief in agrarian circles that socialist influence on the government fostered disorder and that the eight-hour day for urban workers was ruining the economy fueled Bavarian separatism and discouraged East Elbian landowners from making food deliveries to the cities.[24] In this tense situation the national committee of the DGB convened in Berlin on September 25. The

21. General Seeckt to Heinrich Brauns, 7 January 1924, reply of 6 February, and related documents in ZStA/RAM/6509/68–80.

22. *Vorwärts*, 16 June 1923, no. 277, 17 June, no. 279, and 13 May 1924, no. 222.

23. Günter Arns, "Die Krise des Weimarer Parlamentarismus in Frühherbst 1923," *Der Staat*, 8 (1969), pp. 182f., 203–06; Hans Meier-Welcker, *Seeckt* (Frankfurt am Main, 1967), pp. 374f.; *Akten der Reichskanzlei. Die Kabinette Stresemann* (Boppard am Rhein, 1978), pp. 1176–79.

24. See *Die Kabinette Stresemann*, pp. 93–98, 1177.

Center Party's *Germania* reported indignantly that Behrens and other committee members belonging to the DNVP exploited the absence of many union leaders from western Germany (i.e., Catholic members of the Center Party) in order to ram through a resolution opposing the Grand Coalition. The Christian union press denied that any political resolutions had been adopted, but Stegerwald's arguments in the Center Reichstag delegation meetings of the following days doubtless reflected an agreement reached by the majority of DGB leaders at that meeting. Stegerwald and Brauns told their party colleagues that the government must win the active cooperation of industrialists and agrarians in order to stabilize the currency and revive production, that prolongation of work hours and the appointment of an agriculture minister who enjoyed the confidence of the Reichslandbund were the minimum conditions for such cooperation, and that the moderate parties should form a "bourgeois" government if the SPD continued to oppose these measures.[25]

On October 1, 1923, Heinrich Brauns proposed to the cabinet a plan for the regulation of work hours. He advocated the extension of the coal miners' shift underground from seven to eight hours, retention of the eight-hour day for "heavy and unhealthy work," in particular for blast furnace and coking plant workers, and virtual deregulation of work hours elsewhere. Brauns and Stegerwald believed that quick agreement on this formula represented the only chance of protecting workers against still greater losses.[26] The Social Democratic cabinet ministers were receptive to the plan, but Brauns saw his worst fears confirmed the next morning when Hermann Müller announced that the SPD Reichstag delegation wanted to postpone any discussion of the issue. Ernst Scholz of the DVP promptly escalated the conflict by demanding extension of the Grand Coalition to include the DNVP. He apparently sought to drive the SPD out of the cabinet without even attempting to formulate a work hours plan, contrary to the wishes of his party chairman and Reich Chancellor Stresemann. Scholz's position appeared very strong because the DDP supported his demands, and Brauns and Stegerwald sought to persuade the Center Reichstag delegation to endorse a coalition of the bourgeois parties. The Grand Coalition cabinet resigned on October 3.[27]

Stegerwald and Brauns remained isolated within the Center Party, however. Wilhelm Marx, Joseph Wirth, and Joseph Joos sympathized strongly with Stresemann and the SPD, as did most Catholic workers, and other party leaders feared the diplomatic repercussions of a coalition with the DNVP. The Center

25. *Germania*, 2 October 1923, no. 273; *Zentralblatt*, 22 October 1923, p. 143; *Zentrums-protokolle 1920–25*, pp. 482–85.
26. *Die Kabinette Stresemann*, pp. 428–31, and Oltmann, pp. 198–200.
27. *Die Kabinette Stresemann*, pp. 436–62, and Arns, pp. 193–200.

Reichstag delegation quickly reached agreement with Hermann Müller that a bill should combine the substance of the Labor Ministry's proposal with a preamble affirming the principle of the eight-hour day. Negotiations faltered when the SPD demanded the right to propose amendments to the bill on the floor of the Reichstag and then abstain on the final vote, since this would give the Free unions a propaganda advantage over the Christian unions. But a chastened Hermann Müller accepted the bill on October 5, after SPD leaders realized that industrialists planned to fight for more sweeping concessions. This decision permitted Stresemann to reassemble a Grand Coalition cabinet that same day.[28]

Nonetheless, a clumsy effort by Ruhr industrialists to reimpose prewar work hours unilaterally prevented implementation of the government's compromise program. On September 30 the Ruhr mine operators resolved to defy German law and violate their collective labor contract by imposing an eight-and-a-half-hour shift for miners underground and a ten-hour day in surface installations, beginning October 8. The operators expected the Grand Coalition to be replaced by a more conservative government that would ratify their action. Placards appeared at the pitheads on October 6 to inform workers of this decision, but employers found themselves isolated in the face of unexpectedly strong popular resentment. The French army refused to support their action, and the revived Stresemann cabinet and much of the German press condemned it vigorously.[29] Heinrich Imbusch of the Christian miners' union had warned his DGB colleagues ever since the beginning of passive resistance that the Ruhr industrialists might exploit the crisis to impose such measures, and he now saw his worst suspicions concerning their autocratic tendencies confirmed.[30] Labor Minister Brauns responded by summoning representatives of management and labor to Berlin. The delegates of both the Christian and Free miners' unions declared on October 10 that, although they had been prepared to accept one hour of overtime, the operators' arbitrary action made it impossible to urge any revision of work hours on union members.[31] On October 11 Brauns persuaded the mine operators to rescind their work hours decree and await legislative action. Their attempted coup had so poisoned the atmosphere, however, that even the Christian miners' union decided to oppose the government's work hours bill, and the Grand Coalition fell apart before the Reichstag could consider it.[32]

Concern over the rightward drift of many industrialists strengthened Steger-

28. *Die Kabinette Stresemann*, pp. 484f.; *Zentrumsprotokolle 1920–25*, pp. 488–92; NL Marx/55/66f., autobiographical MS.

29. Feldman, *Iron and Steel*, pp. 408–16, and *Die Kabinette Stresemann*, pp. 474–76, 513–18.

30. Brüning, pp. 88f.

31. ZStA/RAM/290/28f.

32. NL Imbusch/2: Gewerkverein Hauptvorstand, 4 November 1923, and Feldman, *Iron and Steel*, pp. 427–30.

wald's desire to involve the DNVP in parliamentary government. On October 5 the SPD's *Vorwärts* accused him of turning against the Grand Coalition because he hoped to join a dictatorial cabinet being assembled by Hugo Stinnes, the DNVP, and the army. The charge was plausible because Stegerwald's closest associates, Brüning, Kaiser, Brauns, and Theodor Brauer, all expressed extreme pessimism concerning the viability of parliamentary institutions during this crisis.[33] It was unfair, however, because Stegerwald consistently advocated a rightward extension of the cabinet coalition precisely in order to preserve parliamentary rule at a time when powerful forces were agitating for dictatorship. He received a chance to implement his plan after the SPD withdrew from government early in November 1923. With the support of Catholic agrarians and industrialists, Stegerwald then succeeded, much to the surprise of party chairman Marx, in persuading a solid majority of the Center Reichstag delegation to endorse a coalition with the DNVP. After three weeks of indecision President Ebert requested Stegerwald on November 27 to form a coalition government of the bourgeois parties. The DNVP made significant concessions, agreeing to swear loyalty to the Weimar Constitution and to accept Stresemann as foreign minister, but it also insisted on admission to the Prussian government as the price for supporting Stegerwald's Reich cabinet. On November 28–29 the Prussian parliamentary delegations of the DDP and Center Party refused to withdraw support from the cabinet headed by the Social Democrat Otto Braun, and Stegerwald resigned his commission.[34]

Count Westarp's personal notes show that DNVP chairman Hergt attempted to salvage a rightist coalition in a private conversation with Stegerwald on the evening of November 29, after the official failure of his candidacy. Hergt suggested that Stegerwald persuade Seeckt and Ebert to threaten to install a Reich commissar in the provincial government of Prussia as they had in Saxony and Thuringia, in order to pressure the Prussian Center and DDP into toppling Otto Braun. It seems highly improbable that Ebert would have cooperated, although he was furious with the SPD leadership for toppling the Stresemann cabinet. At any rate, Stegerwald refused to consider the plan, declaring that he would be condemned as a militarist by his working-class followers were he to associate himself so closely with the army. Stegerwald predicted that the middle-of-the-road minority government being formed by Marx would not survive long, how-

33. See *Vorwärts*, 5 October 1923, no. 466; WAZ, 27 October 1923, pp. 141–43; *Der Deutsche*, 25 October 1923; Brüning, pp. 86–92; and Kaiser to Sedlmayr, 15 October 1923, NL Kaiser/250.

34. Morsey, *Die Zentrumspartei 1917–1923*, pp. 551–54; NL Marx/55/36, memoirs, and 58/4f., notes of 29 November 1923 on a conference with Prussian Center leaders.

ever, and both men expressed the hope that a coalition between the Center and the DNVP could be achieved in the future.[35]

A report of a second confidential conference held during Stegerwald's candidacy for the chancellorship further documents his resistance to antiparliamentary schemes. Clemens Lammers, the liaison between the Center Party and the Reich Association of Industry, shared the Ruhr mine operators' belief in the need for restoration of prewar work hours. He brought Friedrich Minoux, a former executive in the Stinnes combine, to explain to Stegerwald his program for economic stabilization under a "directorium." The Minoux plan for currency reform, total deregulation of the economy, and the appointment of an "economic dictator" to head the Labor, Economics, and Agriculture ministries had already fascinated General Seeckt. Stegerwald's only response, however, was to ask ironically whether Minoux would be willing to follow him to GcG headquarters and repeat his remarks before an audience of trade unionists. Lammers later fumed among fellow businessmen: "In this, Germany's most fateful hour, this man in whom all of Germany had placed its hopes could not rise above the niveau of a trade union secretary!"[36] The neoconservative intellectuals befriended by Stegerwald and Brüning during and after the war, such as the Catholic corporatists Eduard Stadtler and Martin Spahn, also expected Stegerwald to endorse the Minoux plan or rival schemes to transfer sovereignty from the Reichstag to a committee of leading industrialists, agrarians, and trade unionists, but they also found themselves bitterly disappointed.[37]

The paralysis of the German government left most workers without any legal safeguards regarding work hours when the demobilization decrees lapsed on November 17, 1923, and the restoration of prewar work hours in strategic branches of industry counted among the conditions for support of Marx's minority government by the DVP.[38] Determined to increase coal production, Brauns summoned delegates of the Ruhr mine operators and miners' unions to another conference in Berlin on November 29. The trade unionists soon accepted eight hours "voluntarily" when Brauns hinted that the government might impose an $8\frac{1}{2}$-hour shift if they remained obstinate. When some locals of the Old Union

35. The Westarp Papers contain two sets of handwritten notes on the talks of 27–29 November 1923, with one version for the press and the other confidential.

36. NL Dessauer/1, Adolf Hermkes to Friedrich Dessauer, 10 November 1924, reporting statements by Lammers to the Center Committee for Commerce and Industry. See also Meier-Welcker, pp. 390–93.

37. See Eduard Stadtler, "Werksgemeinschaft als soziologisches Problem" (Berlin, 1926), pp. 3–21.

38. See NL Marx/58, handwritten notes on talks with Scholz and Petersen, undated (30 October–1 November 1923), and ZStA/RAM/290/38, conference on 23 November 1923 between representatives of the Labor and Economics ministries.

rejected the agreement, Brauns secured compliance by threatening to terminate all welfare payments to the Ruhr.[39] Brauns also went beyond his self-proclaimed role as honest broker in a meeting of December 13, when he delivered a lengthy speech to the assembled representatives of management and labor from the Ruhr iron and steel industry that portrayed substantial increases in work hours as an economic necessity. After difficult negotiations in which the unions could win concessions only on wages, management and labor agreed on a 58- or 60-hour week for most categories of workers, not including rest periods. This enabled employers to reimpose the two-shift system prevalent before the war in their continuously operating plants, forcing workers to accept six 12-hour shifts a week. This settlement was rejected by an overwhelming majority of the members of the socialist metalworkers' union, but a lockout in the Ruhr soon compelled them to submit.[40] In 1920 the Christian unions had chastised a Social Democratic labor minister for imposing overtime on Ruhr miners, but they found that this economic crisis elicited an even harsher response from their mentor.

Heinrich Brauns intended the two collective labor contracts for Ruhr heavy industry to set precedents for voluntary agreements throughout Germany, but their terms naturally proved extremely unpopular with union locals. Hoping to reassure workers that the new settlements represented temporary emergency measures, Brauns persuaded the cabinet to issue a Work Hours Decree on December 21, 1923. It described the 8-hour day as the norm and empowered the labor minister to define at some future date those unhealthy or strenuous occupations for which it should be mandatory, but it also gave state labor arbitrators virtually unlimited power to grant exemptions. This provision was vitally important because an emergency decree of October 30, 1923, had greatly strengthened and centralized the state labor arbitration system, creating a nationwide network of arbitrators appointed by the labor minister, whose settlements he could declare legally binding. The Labor Ministry privately encouraged the arbitrators to act decisively.[41] In December and January a series of harsh arbitration decrees for heavy industry throughout Germany established wage rates roughly 20% below prewar levels and restored the two-shift system, even in some places where it had been abandoned before the war. The Free unions usually rejected the decrees, forcing the labor minister to assume direct respon-

39. ZStA/RAM/290/44–48, and *Akten der Reichskanzlei. Die Kabinette Marx I und II* (Boppard am Rhein, 1973), pp. 21–23. See also Feldman and Steinisch, "Die Entscheidung gegen den Achtstundentag," pp. 405–08.
40. ZStA/RAM/290/130–33, and Feldman, *Iron and Steel*, pp. 433–39.
41. Oltmann, pp. 327–29, and Preller, pp. 274–76.

sibility for declaring them binding. State arbitrators and lockouts by employers also implemented a 54- or 56-hour week in most branches of manufacturing, although the unions remained strong enough in a few trades to defend the 8-hour day. Thus Germany was transformed within a few months from the most advanced to one of the most backward industrial nations with regard to the length of the working day. These and other government austerity measures succeeded in stabilizing the currency, but at great cost to German workers, whose extraordinary losses in 1923–24 must be born in mind when discussing subsequent wage increases.[42]

All trade unions agreed in denouncing the autocratic Ruhr industrialists, but the Christian unions isolated themselves within the labor movement by defending the labor minister. In January 1924 the Free and Hirsch–Duncker unions launched polemics against Brauns for siding with industrialists and violating the spirit if not the letter of his own Work Hours Decree. The press of the Christian unions, on the other hand, defended the prolongation of work hours as a temporary emergency measure and urged workers not to rely on state protection but to rebuild their trade unions.[43] Local leaders of the Christian unions even collaborated with the authorities against the Free unions. In bargaining sessions for the iron and steel industry outside the Ruhr, the Christian metalworkers' union consistently supported the proposals of the state labor arbitrator against fierce opposition from its socialist rival. The Christian union's attitude encouraged state arbitrators to predict that the metalworkers' resistance would crumble if the Labor Ministry issued binding decrees.[44] In at least two cases, involving arbitration decrees that imposed twelve-hour shifts for the lignite strip mines of Cologne and Hesse, the Labor Ministry actually refused to declare the decree binding because the tough stance of the Old Union made it fear that miners would defy a government order. Only when the local leaders of the Christian miners' union privately assured the authorities that miners were incapable of further resistance did the Labor Ministry proceed.[45] Although the Christian unions had occasionally opposed strike actions by the Free unions in the past, these efforts to snatch defeat from the jaws of victory reflected a new sense of panic over the collapse of state authority.

The stabilization crisis of 1923–24 weakened Germany's unions so drastically

42. Documentation in ZStA/RAM/290; Bernd Weisbrod, *Schwerindustrie in der Weimarer Republik* (Wuppertal, 1978), pp. 301–09; Oltmann, pp. 338–43; Maier, pp. 361–64, 380f.
43. *Zentralblatt*, 21 January 1924, pp. 1–4, and 18 February 1924, pp. 10f.
44. See the reports on bargaining sessions for the Klöckner steel mills of Osnabrück and northern Westphalia in ZStA/RAM/291/143–56.
45. ZStA/RAM/291/168f., State Arbitrator Schneider (Cologne) to Labor Ministry, 21 January 1924, and memoranda of 2 February and 28 February in RAM/291/179 and 292/74–76.

as to produce a long-term shift in the balance of power between management and labor. The unions' financial impoverishment and inability to protect workers stimulated mass defections after the summer of 1923. The membership of the ADGB peaked at 8 million in 1920. In June 1923 it retained 91% of that figure, but by the end of the year it retained only 72%, 60% in March 1924, and 50% at the end of 1924. The decline began somewhat later in the Christian unions, but by the end of 1923 they too retained only 73% of their maximum membership of 1.1 million, dropping to 55% at the end of 1924.[46] Conscious of increased strength, the business community insisted that the new regulation of work hours represented the essential foundation for Germany's prosperity throughout the foreseeable future. The Christian metalworkers' union, which was suffering especially heavy membership losses, petitioned Brauns respectfully in the spring of 1924 to make use of his power to restore the eight-hour day for coking plant and blast furnace workers. Such strong resistance emerged from industrialists, the DVP and DDP, the Economics Ministry, and the Prussian Ministry of Commerce, however, that Brauns decided to await the outcome of international negotiations before undertaking any amendment of the Work Hours Decree.[47] The realization spread in the Christian unions that a long hard fight would be necessary to win back the ground lost so suddenly during the winter.

THE REVIVAL OF CLASS CONSCIOUSNESS IN THE CHRISTIAN UNIONS

After weeks of mounting pressure from his member unions, Theodor Leipart announced to the executive committee of the ZAG on November 27, 1923, that the ADGB would withdraw from that body to protest the work hours policy of heavy industry. The chairman of the Reich Association of Industry, Kurt Sorge, responded by expressing the hope that the ZAG could "hibernate" and be revived when social tensions diminished. Bernhard Otte agreed with Sorge that the ADGB bore much of the responsibility for the rupture because it had obstructed a reasonable compromise, and Sorge's attitude encouraged Otte and Stegerwald to suggest that employers continue their association with the DGB even if the other unions withdrew.[48] However, the drift rightward among indus-

46. GcG, *Jahrbuch 1925*, p. 21, and *Statistische Jahrbücher des Deutschen Reichs*. See also Brian Peterson, "The Social Bases of Working-Class Politics in the Weimar Republic: The Reichstag Election of December 1924," Ph.D. diss. (University of Wisconsin—Madison, 1976), p. 104.

47. See the documentation in ZStA/RAM/292/284–321, and Weisbrod, pp. 309–13. The membership of the Christian metalworkers' union declined from 200,000 to 77,000 between 1923 and 1925.

48. ZStA/ZAG/31:1/65–78. This suggestion was first raised in an unsigned article doubtless written by Stegerwald in *Der Arbeitgeber*, 15 October 1923, pp. 305–07.

trialists and Protestant workers in 1924 increased the influence of hard-line nationalists over the fate of the ZAG, and they preferred forms of association that would prevent Social Democrats from ever joining it again. Stegerwald's efforts to appease them provoked growing resentment among his followers.

Even before World War I, Count Westarp and other prominent conservatives had hoped to promote a merger of the Christian and Yellow unions in a united front of patriotic workers. Early in 1922 Wilhelm Schmidt, an official of the Stoeckerite Evangelical Social School in Spandau, persuaded Westarp and other DNVP leaders that the Protestant wing of the DGB leadership should be strengthened in order to facilitate such a fusion.[49] This goal became more realistic in 1923 as the objective differences between the Christian farmworkers' union and the Yellow farmworkers' league diminished. In October 1923, while they were promoting a Stegerwald chancellorship within the DNVP, Behrens, Lambach, and Baltrusch also sought to muster support for a "National Association" of industry, agriculture, and the DGB to replace the dissolving Central Association. As a corollary to this proposal, the DHV leadership instructed Lambach to explore the possibility of a rapproachement between the Christian and Yellow unions.[50] This idea naturally encountered resistance among Catholic unionists. The GcG denounced Wilhelm Schmidt in mid-November when he called publicly for a merger between the Christian and Yellow unions, but Otte apparently sought to prepare his followers for a surprising change of course a few weeks later by writing that an influx of sound trade unionist elements had altered the Yellow unions and made them potentially valuable allies.[51] At the year's end, Otte, Behrens, and Baltrusch began to negotiate with Fritz Geisler and other Yellow leaders, apparently indicating willingness to renounce strikes in agriculture but rejecting Geisler's demand that they terminate cooperation with the Free unions in industrial labor disputes.[52]

However, opposition from Pan-German elements in the DNVP prevented the Protestant DGB leaders from implementing their plan for a "National Association." Success seemed near at the ZAG executive committee meeting of February 15, 1924, called to arrange the dissolution of that body. When the ADGB proposed that the three union leagues form their own association to assume labor's share of the nominating powers for the National Economic Council formerly enjoyed by the ZAG, Friedrich Baltrusch declared in ringing terms that the DGB would never join any association organized on class lines. The

49. NL Westarp, Wilhelm Schmidt to Westarp, 28 March 1922, and Westarp to von Wrisberg, 3 April 1922.
50. "DHV Verwaltung: Auszüge," meetings of 19 October and 1 November 1923, pp. 119f.
51. *Zentralblatt*, 19 November 1923, pp. 151f., and 17 December 1923, pp. 153f.
52. See the contradictory accounts in *Zentralblatt*, 14 April 1924, p. 45, and Wilhelm Schmidt's *Deutsche Werksgemeinschaft*, 16 March 1924, pp. 3–6.

hard-line nationalist Ernst von Borsig, the chairman of the League of Employers' Associations, then indicated that employers would negotiate with the DGB concerning the status of the Central Association after the Free unions left.[53] But on March 4 the Pan-German *Deutsche Zeitung* effectively sabotaged these efforts by announcing that Wilhelm Schmidt had led a momentous exodus of all "rightist elements" of the Christian unions into Geisler's National Association of German Unions. Schmidt did not in fact lead anyone except for a few union functionaries laid off because of budget cuts, but he became Geisler's chief aide and founded his own magazine with financial support from right-wing businessmen, the *Deutsche Werksgemeinschaft*. Its enthusiastic reporting on tough speeches by leading industrialists suggests that Geisler and Schmidt had lost all interest in a merger with the DGB because they expected big business to reject collective bargaining in general and return to prewar methods for dealing with organized labor.[54] The Christian unions denounced the Yellows for abandoning any semblance of trade unionism, and a DGB-Yellow accord became impossible.

Otte probably felt compelled to participate in these talks because of the growing popularity of radical nationalism, which became manifest in the Reichstag election of May 1924, when the DNVP rose from 14.9 to 19.5% of the vote, while the National Socialist and allied Racial Freedom parties polled 6.5%. The SPD failed to attract any of the large Independent Socialist vote of 1920, declining from 21.6 to 20.5%, despite the affiliation with the SPD of the majority of Independent Socialist leaders in 1922. The Communist Party won about one-half the Independent Socialist vote, growing from 2.1 to 12.6% of the electorate, but roughly 2 million votes seem to have flowed directly from the radical left to the radical right.[55] All indications are that the DNVP's gains were spread broadly among all classes, with blue-collar workers contributing a large share. The membership claims of the Nationalist Workers' League soared from 45,000 in 1922 to 300,000 in 1924, and DNAB leaders won widespread acceptance for their claims that 1.5 to 2 million blue-collar workers and their dependents voted for the DNVP in 1924. The DNAB leaders also believed that they were attracting so many disillusioned adherents of the Marxist parties that the SPD and KPD might well sink into political impotence.[56] The new Reichstag delegation of the DNVP contained 11 DGB members, compared to 17 for the Center Party, 3 for the Bavarian People's Party, 2 for the DVP, and 2 DHV members in the National

53. ZStA/ZAG/31:1/28–32.
54. *Deutsche Werksgemeinschaft*, 16 March 1924, p. 1, and 20 April 1924, pp. 2f.; *Der Deutsche*, 14 March and 30 June 1924.
55. Maier, pp. 450–55.
56. Stupperich, *Volksgemeinschaft*, p. 95, and Emil Hartwig, "Die Deutschantionale Volkspartei und die Arbeiterschaft," DNVP pamphlet no. 156 (1924).

Socialist delegation.[57] Thus, for the first time, the DGB had almost as many Protestant as Catholic representatives.

Many different types of workers were streaming into the DNVP. Farmworkers constituted the largest component. The failure of the strike movement of 1923 discredited the SPD among farmworkers in East Elbia, and in 1924 the socialist farmworkers' union lost a greater proportion of its membership than any other union, 80%.[58] Farmworkers could not account for more than about 50% of the party's blue-collar vote, however. The DNAB was an organization of urban workers. Its social composition cannot be determined, but membership lists from two DNAB locals indicate a diverse mixture of unskilled casual laborers, skilled workers, and artisans or plant foremen. The proportion of unskilled workers seems to have been higher than that for the cadres of either the SPD or KPD.[59] Richard Comfort has argued persuasively that the Free unions, after greatly broadening their base of support in 1919–20, contracted to their original clientele of skilled workers in 1923–24. This development occurred in part because activists in the rank and file who merely advocated reducing the wage differential between skilled and unskilled workers were expelled as the Free union leadership adopted strict disciplinary action against "Communist agitators" during the stabilization crisis. Disillusioned with trade unionism, millions of unskilled and semiskilled workers adopted a stance of sullen hostility to all the institutions of the Weimar Republic. The obvious beneficiary of this process was the KPD, which received massive electoral support from such workers without really organizing them effectively.[60] The DNVP also appears to have benefited from this process to a much greater extent than is generally recognized.

Indifferent to the growth of the DNVP and hostile to the conciliatory policies of the DGB leadership, the Christian miners' union courted confrontation with employers and the Labor Ministry in the spring of 1924. Imbusch and his colleagues had prepared for the onset of hyperinflation ever since November 1919 and displayed remarkable business acumen in 1923, seeking in their own small

---

57. *Zentralblatt*, 19 May 1924, pp. 60f.
58. See Peterson, pp. 285–88, 385f.
59. In 1925, 33 of 46 members of the Osnabrück local of the DNAB were unskilled workers who merely listed "Arbeiter" as their trade (StA Osnabrück C1/84/15). In 1924 subscription lists for the *Deutsche Arbeiterstimme* in the county of Mansfeld, Saxony, recorded 65 skilled workers or artisans (*Schlosser, Dreher,* and so forth), 72 unskilled or semiskilled workers, 34 miners (who should also be considered semiskilled), 27 foremen or overseers, and 15 nonworkers: ZStA/DNVP/170/119–25. For the social composition of the socialist and communist membership, see Hunt, pp. 99–107, and Hermann Weber, *Kommunismus in Deutschland 1918–1945* (Darmstadt, 1983), pp. 67–70.
60. Richard Comfort, *Revolutionary Hamburg* (Stanford, 1966), pp. 109–66. See also Eisner, pp. 166–209, and Peterson, pp. 87–100.

way to imitate the dynamic investment policies of Hugo Stinnes. When the currency was stabilized, the Christian miners' union preserved a significantly greater share of its assets than did any other major union, Christian or Free.[61] Moreover, Imbusch felt personally betrayed by Heinrich Brauns, who had assured him in 1922 that the government would not seek prolongation of the miners' shift beyond seven hours. The stabilization crisis made the Christian miners intensely suspicious of the ideal of social partnership and convinced Imbusch that he could never trust a friend or associate who went away to work in the corrupting "Berlin atmosphere."[62]

A labor dispute in the Siegerland iron ore mines caused a public breach between the Christian miners' union and the Labor Ministry. Local mine operators employed a lockout to impose an eight-and-a-half-hour shift, which they refused to abandon even after Labor Minister Brauns declared an arbitrator's decree in favor of eight hours binding. Brauns assured the Christian miners' union that the owners acted illegally and promised to seek to provide unemployment benefits for the idled miners. But legal experts in the Reich and Prussian governments concurred that the government could not give financial support to one of the parties in a labor dispute, regardless of the merits of the case. As the resistance of Siegerland miners crumbled in early March, the Christian miners' union launched unprecedented public attacks on Brauns.[63]

In May 1924 the Christian and socialist miners' unions undertook a major trial of strength with employers in the Ruhr. After weeks of futile negotiations over work hours, the unions instructed their members to leave the pits at the end of the seventh hour of work when their collective labor contract expired at the end of April. Employers responded with a lockout affecting 93% of the Ruhr miners. The cabinet and much of the press, assuming that trade unions sought above all to preserve order, believed that Communist agitation had caused the strike. Even the DGB's *Deutsche* exhorted the miners' unions to explain the necessity for longer hours to their members.[64] Much to the public's surprise, the miners' unions accepted full responsibility for the struggle and succeeded in maintaining

61. At the end of 1924 the Christian miners' union retained assets of RM 25.07 per member, compared with 1.99 for the Christian metalworkers' union and 7.13 for the textile workers. The Old Union succeeded best among the Free unions with RM 18.63; calculations based on *Statistisches Jahrbuch des Deutschen Reichs, 1926*, pp. 466f. See also Gewerkverein christlicher Bergarbeiter, "Protokollbuch," 22 November 1919, and *17. Generalversammlung 1924*, pp. 108–17.

62. NL Imbusch/2, Gewerkverein Hauptvorstand, 22 December 1923; Gewerkverein christlicher Bergarbeiter, *17. Generalversammlung 1924*, pp. 38–44; *Die Kabinette Marx*, pp. 631f.

63. *Der Deutsche*, 6 March 1924; Oltmann, pp. 330–45; documentation in ZStA/RAM/290/182–217, and 292/120–27, 140–52.

64. See the remarks by Brauns and Jarres in the cabinet meeting of 8 May 1924, *Die Kabinette Marx*, pp. 627f., and *Der Deutsche*, 10 May 1924.

strike support payments for four weeks. Coal shortages idled 250,000 metal-workers by the end of May, prompting the government to intervene. The arbitration decree of May 27 defined the eighth hour of the shift as overtime subject to frequent review. Although employers were not required to pay a bonus for this first hour of overtime, miners received a 20% wage hike across the board, a major increase in the postinflation era. Under the circumstances Imbusch had a right to hail the result as a victory that would help end the trade unions' decline in membership and morale. [65]

In June 1924 Ernst von Borsig issued a sort of ultimatum to the trade unions on behalf of the League of Employers' Associations, predicting that employers would refuse to participate in collective bargaining unless the unions dropped their doctrinaire demand for the eight-hour day and acknowledged the economic necessities imposed by reparations and the task of national reconstruction. [66] This threat of intensified social conflict induced Adam Stegerwald to make one last effort to revive the Central Association in a public exchange with Borsig. Stegerwald insisted that employers distinguish between the reasonable, patriotic DGB and the sometimes doctrinaire Free unions and promised to do justice to all the legitimate economic concerns voiced by Borsig in the context of a revived ZAG. In reply Borsig publicly demanded a merger between the Christian and Yellow unions, observing that the Christian unions had in the past been every bit as militant as the Free in their competition for the workers' allegiance. This hostile response brought the public exchange to an abrupt end. [67] In September Stegerwald arranged a private conference in Essen between Christian unionists and prominent (but unnamed) industrialists to seek agreement on basic principles of economic policy as a foundation for reviving the ZAG. Heinrich Imbusch considered this action a "betrayal of the other unions" that had belonged to the ZAG, however, and the Christian miners' union boycotted the meeting. Refusal by the strongest and most militant Christian union to participate in the talks made employers lose all interest in an agreement. [68] This development compelled Stegerwald to acknowledge the demise of the ZAG.

For the Catholic leaders of the Christian unions in western and southern Germany such as Imbusch, the leftward radicalization of many industrial workers represented the most significant result of the stabilization crisis. Although the Christian unions did not suffer directly from the Communist Party's largely

65. *Gewerkverein christlicher Bergarbeiter, 17. Generalversammlung 1924*, pp. 34f., and Feldman and Steinisch, "Die Entscheidung gegen den Achtstundentag," pp. 412–30.
66. *Der Arbeitgeber*, 15 June 1924, pp. 221–23.
67. *Der Deutsche*, 29 June 1924, no. 151; *Der Arbeitgeber*, 15 July 1924, pp. 316–19; *Zentralblatt*, 7 July 1924, pp. 97f., and 4 August, pp. 137f.
68. NL Imbusch/2, Gewerkverein Hauptvorstand, 4 October 1924.

successful propaganda against the Free union bureaucracy, a similar disciplinary problem emerged for them with the appearance of a radical party of Catholic populists, the Christian Social Commonwealth (Christlich-soziale Volksgemeinschaft). This party was founded in the summer of 1922, when Catholic workers in several Westphalian towns found that Center Party leaders refused to nominate workers in communal elections. Although it nominated candidates in only a few electoral districts, it won 124,000 votes in May 1924, gaining over 10% of the vote in some working-class neighborhoods of the Ruhr.[69] The new party called for a united front of all "productive elements" in the populace against the capitalists and feudal aristocracy. It proclaimed adherence to Adam Stegerwald's Essen Program of 1920 but argued that the losses suffered by workers during the stabilization crisis proved the bankruptcy of Stegerwald's strategy of cooperation with the bourgeois parties: "Is it not a fact that the labor representatives in the old parties, in the Center, the People's Party, the Democratic and Nationalist Parties, are every bit as compromised in the eyes of workers today as the representatives of other social groups?"[70] The rise of the new party alarmed the leaders of the Christian unions and Catholic workers' clubs alike. The WAZ denounced it for fostering a "class conflict mentality," and Heinrich Brauns implored Cardinal Schulte to muzzle radical priests in the Ruhr who encouraged Catholic workers to blame their sufferings on the "mammonist spirit" of employers rather than on the material consequences of the war.[71] The Christian Social Commonwealth's vote declined sharply in December 1924, when economic revival weakened all the radical parties, but its appearance demonstrated that many Catholic workers felt estranged from the DGB leadership.

The leaders of the Christian miners' union opened an offensive to regain the confidence of the rank and file at the Christian miners' congress of August 1924. Imbusch and his lieutenants publicly aired their grievances against the editorial policies of *Der Deutsche* and against the willingness of Stegerwald and Brauns to make concessions to employers. They further declared that the Christian unions of western Germany would never change their principles to suit labor organizers in central and eastern Germany, where unusually harsh class conflict had fomented antisocialist hysteria. To underscore this message, the Christian miners' union suspended payment of dues to the League of Christian Unions, boycotted the meetings of its central committee, and dispatched emissaries to persuade the congresses of other Christian unions to adopt more militant policies.[72]

69. Focke, pp. 115–20, and Kühr, pp. 223–25.

70. *Die Volksgemeinschaft*, 5 April 1924 (NL Stegerwald 002/Bd. 1922–23/no. 264).

71. WAZ, 5 January 1924, p. 2, and Heinrich Brauns to Archbishop Schulte, 15 August 1924, Cologne Archdiocese, "Arbeitervereine"/6.

72. Gewerkverein christlicher Bergarbeiter, *17. Generalversammlung 1924*, pp. 41–45, 102f.,

Although the miners' offensive increased the danger of confrontation between the wings of the DGB, severe conflicts within the DNVP were teaching
Protestant workers not to underestimate the danger that their nationalistic ideals
could be manipulated by social reactionaries. After the DNAB refused to support
a Reichstag candidacy by the Yellow leader Wilhelm Schmidt, forcing him to
accept a seat in the Prussian parliament instead, Schmidt and his patrons blocked
a Reichstag nomination for Friedrich Baltrusch on the grounds that he had
permitted his daughter to marry a Jew.[73] The Pan-German *Deutsche Zeitung*
warned all DNVP locals against the DNAB as a dangerous "state within the
state" that abused its organizational autonomy to permit recruitment of Nationalist workers by the Christian unions. Local party chiefs who sympathized
with the Yellow unions flatly refused to have any dealings with the DNAB,
preventing its spread to Pomerania, Brandenburg, and other areas.[74]

In the summer of 1924 the controversy over the Dawes Plan for financing
reparations caused major conflicts of conscience within the Nationalist Workers'
League. The Christian union leadership publicly urged the DNVP to demon-
state its moderation by accepting the Dawes Plan and thus earn entry into the
right-of-center parliamentary coalition propagated by Stegerwald. However, the
DNVP launched a strident propaganda campaign against the plan as the "second
Versailles," and trade unionists within the party came under massive pressure to
demonstrate their independence from union colleagues on such a matter of
nationalist principle. Some Protestant trade unionists therefore boycotted the
joint strategy sessions arranged by Stegerwald for DGB parliamentarians, and
rumors circulated that Franz Behrens would lead a secession of Protestants from
the League of Christian Unions.[75] The DNVP delegation split down the middle
on the Dawes issue, and most of the DGB members in it eventually decided to
join their union colleagues in other parties to approve the amendment. Pan-
Germans and other extremists responded with a campaign to purge the DNVP of
the "yea-sayers" who had supported the government, and they directed their
heaviest fire against the trade unionists among them. As during the controversy
of 1922 over the expulsion of the radical anti-Semites from the DNVP, the trade

---

126–28, and NL Imbusch/2, Gewerkverein Hauptvorstand, 2 March, 14 May, and 19 July 1924. See
also the debate between Bernhard Otte and the miners' emissary, Franz Rotthäuser, in Zentralverband christlicher Bauarbeiter, *13. Generalversammlung 1925*, pp. 180–91.

73. Stupperich, *Volksgemeinschaft*, pp. 91–94.

74. See the hostile letters to the DNAB from local DNVP leaders in ZStA/DNVP/167/76
(Kreis Belgard-Pommern), 210/168f. (Niederlausitz-Brandenburg), and 176/55 (Kolberg-Körlin).

75. *Der Deutsche*, 21 May 1924; *Deutsche Arbeiterstimme*, June 1924, p. 6, and August 1924,
p. 6; *Zentralblatt*, 4 August 1924, p. 141, 18 August, p. 145, and 27 October, p. 242.

unionists had adopted the same policy as the leading spokesmen of industry and agriculture but became the special target of resentment against "materialism" among the party faithful.[76] DNAB leaders found themselves involved in ever sharpening polemics with the right wing of their own party and came to agree with party chairman Hergt that the divisions in the DNVP could be healed only by sharing government power in a coalition with the Center Party. The DNAB and Walther Lambach therefore undertook a campaign to convince all party locals that support for the progressive social legislation sponsored by the Christian unions would complete the process of discrediting the Marxist parties in the eyes of workers and would induce the Center to adhere permanently to a rightist bloc.[77] By the end of 1924 the Christian Socials again sought to cooperate closely with their Catholic colleagues, although their intentions remained rather different.

In October 1924 Adam Stegerwald responded to the secessionist tendencies displayed by both the Christian miners' union and Protestant workers by transforming a celebration of the twenty-fifth anniversary of the founding of the League of Christian Unions into a summit conference on the future of the movement. Here Stegerwald sought to persuade Catholic workers that they had more in common with the Protestant workers, peasants, and pastors in the DNVP than with the "uprooted" intellectuals who molded the policies of the SPD and DDP. While those intellectuals propagated an "abstract" concept of democracy based on the omnicompetent parliament, which merely opened the way for the capitalists to manipulate public opinion through the mass media at election time, orthodox Protestants and Catholics could cooperate to implement "the democracy of self-administration in the commune, in the province, in the economy," based on Baron Karl vom Stein's ideal of citizen participation. "We want the National Economic Council, the district economic councils, equal representation for workers in the chambers of commerce and agriculture. We want the transfer of governmental regulatory functions to an association of employers and employees. We want to see the idea implicit in the factory councils law . . . more fully developed." Thus Stegerwald anticipated the ADGB's adoption of a program for "economic democracy" in 1927–28.[78]

Stegerwald also struck a note alien to the deliberations of the Free unions, however, by admonishing his followers that every increase of influence for work-

76. Hertzman, pp. 213–23, and Stupperich, *Volksgemeinschaft*, pp. 95f. In December 1924 Wilhelm Lindner was demoted from the Reichstag to the Prussian parliament.

77. Walther Lambach, "Fragen zur Werksgemeinschaft," 5 July 1924, and circular of 3 September, NL Diller/8; DNAB circulars of 3 November 1924 and 25 February 1925, StA Osnabrück C1/84/27f., 34–39.

78. *Zentralblatt*, 27 October 1924, pp. 232f. Regarding "economic democracy", see below, pp. 124–26.

ers entailed increased responsibility. Under the empire, when trade unions confronted extremely hostile leaders of big business collaborating closely with the strongest army and police force in the world, it was entirely appropriate for the labor movement to exert its strength to the utmost.

> Before we had a strong state, now a weak one, before a strong economy, now a weak one. . . . In a weak state, strong organizations are a terrible danger for the community if they do not exercise discipline and display a sense of responsibility for the public welfare. We must all understand that trade union work is, in the long term, a labor of Sisyphus without a stable state and a secure economy.[79]

Thus Stegerwald focused attention on the crucial fact that Germany's trade unions now, for the first time in their history, enjoyed enough power to impose wage settlements that might contribute directly to unemployment or inflation. But he addressed an audience made skeptical by the traumatic experiences of the previous year. Heinrich Imbusch replied stoutly that the Christian unions should concern themselves exclusively with the material interests of their members, adding that discussion of the shape of parliamentary coalitions was inappropriate at a union rally. He pointed out that Stegerwald's friends in agrarian and industrial circles did not mean the same thing as he by the slogan of the *Volksgemeinschaft*, and that no other interest group displayed the tender concern for the public welfare that Stegerwald preached. Giesberts, Joos, and Heinrich Fahrenbrach, chairman of the textile workers' union, supported the position of Imbusch, while Bernhard Otte, Behrens, and Franz Wieber proclaimed their loyalty to Stegerwald. The most knowledgeable observer present, Ludwig Heyde, reported that the sympathies of the delegates. were evenly divided.[80]

Neither Stegerwald nor Imbusch could "win" this debate because the movement could prosper only if their strategies and talents complemented one another. Realizing this, Stegerwald made significant concessions in order to placate his left-wing critics. In November he fired Brüning's friend Hermann Ullmann as editor of *Der Deutsche* and brought Imbusch onto a reorganized board of directors. DNVP spokesmen attacked Stegerwald for weakly permitting the Christian unions to return to the quasi-socialist policies they had pursued during the revolution,[81] but he realized that he must become more militant on bread-and-butter issues in order to retain the credibility needed to promote his plan for

79. Ibid., pp. 236f.
80. Ibid., pp. 243–46, and *Soziale Praxis*, 30 October 1924, columns 915–18.
81. NL Imbusch/2, Gewerkverein Hauptvorstand, 10 November 1924; Treviranus, p. 54; *Deutsche Tageszeitung*, 4 and 12 November 1924.

integrating the DNVP into the parliamentary system. Stegerwald dedicated himself to winning support from Catholic workers for a right-of-center coalition by guaranteeing that it would promote the reduction of work hours and strengthen Germany's system of social insurance. Most importantly, he persuaded Labor Minister Brauns to join him in publicly pledging to eradicate the two-shift system in heavy industry.[82]

As Gerald Feldman has observed, participation by the ADGB in the Central Association represented the first stage in a long-term "learning process" whereby the Free unions came to combine self-restraint in demands on wages and hours with a comprehensive critique of the cartel and investment policies of big business, a strategy designed to demonstrate that the unions understood the interests of the economy as a whole better than did the selfish entrepreneurs. Germany's unions eventually won great influence over managerial decisions and government economic policy after World War II by demonstrating a willingness to defend unpopular measures needed to promote economic growth.[83] Nevertheless, Feldman tends to exaggerate the extent to which ADGB leaders were guided by such dispassionate calculations in 1922–23. The Christian unions had advanced much further on this scale of modernity. Baltrusch's plan to link concessions on the eight-hour day with increased labor participation in management decisions probably represented the only chance for a genuine compromise between management and labor during the stabilization crisis, but ADGB leaders vetoed any concessions on the grounds that they would be too unpopular. This stance exasperated Stegerwald, Behrens, Brauns, Baltrusch, Thiel, and Otte, who concluded that the ADGB neither understood nor cared about the concrete economic problems facing Germany. In 1924 they therefore felt justified in seeking to cultivate a special relationship with employers, and relations between the Free and Christian unions reached their nadir.[84]

These DGB leaders themselves had much to learn about the psychological foundations of the labor movement, however. In 1924 only "archaic" union leaders like Imbusch, who took a clear stand against the bosses and refused to worry too much about economic recovery, could succeed in reviving morale among the rank and file. At the congress of the Christian construction workers' union in 1925, for example, Chairman Wiedeberg made a tough speech in the

82. See *Zentralblatt*, 27 October 1924, pp. 244f., and Adam Stegerwald, "Christliche Gewerkschaften und Politik," *Deutsche Arbeit*, December 1924, pp. 397–404.
83. Gerald Feldman, "Die freien Gewerkschaften und die Zentralarbeitsgemeinschaft, 1918–24," in Heinz Oskar Vetter (ed.), *Vom Sozialistengesetz zur Mitbestimmung* (Cologne, 1975), pp. 243–51.
84. See the bitter attacks on Stegerwald in the ADGB's *Gewerkschafts-Zeitung*, 8 November 1924, p. 445.

spirit of Imbusch. One delegate then responded warmly that now each member could say to himself: "There stands the old *Prolet*, who not only founded our movement but whose whole heart is still with us. Then confidence in the movement grows again."[85] Most blue-collar labor organizers in the field sensed that their unions' vitality required clear-cut battle lines between workers and employers. Even within the Christian farmworkers' union, district leaders angered by the intransigence of employers returned to cooperation with their socialist colleagues at the collective bargaining table during 1924.[86] Theodor Brauer articulated the insights of such labor organizers when he argued that all trade unions had overextended themselves since 1918 through political action and by seeking to organize white-collar workers and civil servants. To be successful, he reasoned, unions must be animated by a passion for social reform that was alien to commercial employees and postal inspectors. They must return to their original base among blue-collar workers and their original goals of emancipating this downtrodden class, securing equal access to education, and transforming the wage relationship so as to protect them from the vicissitudes of the capitalist labor market.[87]

85. Zentralverband christlicher Bauarbeiter, *13. Generalversammlung 1925*, pp. 182–85, 201. This congress is remarkable for the frequent use of class terminology instead of the alternate corporatist vocabulary of Catholic social theory (*Klasse* instead of *Stand*).

86. See Gustav Hülser's lively account of a bargaining session in Silesia in December 1924, when his socialist colleagues finally appealed to him to preach a little "advent sermon" in order to move the stony-hearted employers: "Memoiren: Tarifverhandlung Advent 1924 in Breslau," handwritten MS, Splitternachlaß Hülser, DGB-Bibliothek, Düsseldorf.

87. Theodor Brauer, *Krisis der Gewerkschaften*, 2d ed. (Jena, 1924), esp. pp. 3–8, 14–20. A dramatic decline in strike participation by white-collar workers and farmworkers after 1923 confirmed Brauer's analysis: see Volkmann, pp. 128f.

4

Welfare Legislation under the Bürgerblock

The DGB played a pivotal role in the right-of-center government coalitions of the mid-1920s. Leaders of the Center and Nationalist parties needed vigorous support from the Christian unions in order to counter the explosive charge that their coalition represented a *Bürgerblock* (bourgeois bloc) dedicated to "class warfare from above." The DGB leadership exploited this situation skillfully to win acceptance as an almost equal partner with the Reich Association of Industry and the Reichslandbund in negotiations that produced several pieces of constructive reform legislation, recently cited by historians as evidence for the stabilization of the Weimar Republic.[1] The frustrations encountered by the Christian unions in 1927 strongly suggest, however, that even at the time of its greatest prosperity, the Weimar Republic was returning to the condition of extreme polarization along class lines that had so often paralyzed the political system of imperial Germany.

THE CHRISTIAN UNIONS AND THE FORMATION OF THE LUTHER CABINET

By the end of 1924, most agrarians and industrialists in the DNVP demanded a share of government power because Germany had passed through the period of mandatory free trade imposed by the Treaty of Versailles and would soon regain the freedom to legislate protective tariffs. Party chairman Hergt considered participation in the government the only way to restore party unity, disrupted by

---

1. Michael Stürmer, *Koalition und Opposition in der Weimarer Republik, 1924–1928* (Düsseldorf, 1967), pp. 32f., 278–83, and Maier, pp. 579–94.

the controversy over the Dawes Plan in the summer of 1924, and the DVP supported the idea in the hope of bringing the Nationalist Party to accept the basic principles of Gustav Stresemann's foreign policy.[2] In October 1924 Stegerwald and Heinrich Brauns joined DVP leaders in advocating a center-right coalition, but Joseph Wirth and the Catholic workers' clubs of western and southwestern Germany sharply opposed any coalition with the DNVP. The Reichstag election of December 1924 failed to break the parliamentary deadlock because the DNVP emerged unweakened. Stegerwald and Brauns then risked conflict with the "enthusiastic republicans" on the left wing of the Center Party by helping Hans Luther to end the government crisis in January 1925 with a "cabinet of experts" that included four representatives of the DNVP and Brauns as labor minister. Imbusch and Wirth voted against the Luther cabinet when it took office, and many Center leaders viewed it skeptically.[3]

The formation of the Luther cabinet generated intense pressure on industrial spokesmen in the Center Party and DNVP to prove that they had a social conscience. In its first official act the new government sought to overcome suspicions that it pursued reactionary policies by restoring the eight-hour day for workers in blast furnaces and coking plants. Brauns had long sought to issue such a decree but had not prevailed against the objections of Ruhr industrialists. Now the new economics minister, Karl Neuhaus of the DNVP, broke with the policy of his predecessor from the DDP by acknowledging that political considerations made issuance of the decree imperative.[4] Moreover, Brauns received confidential data from his party comrades, the Klöckner brothers, to refute the claims by other Ruhr industrialists that the decree would cause a disastrous increase in production costs. Clemens Lammers of the Center Party then warned the League of Employers' Associations that it must accept the decree in order to preserve the Christian unions as a voice of moderation in the labor camp, while J. W. Reichert of the DNVP warned steel industrialists that it represented the minimum price for survival of the rightist parliamentary coalition. Although the three-shift decree affected only a small minority of workers in heavy industry, it lent some credibility to Stegerwald's claim that the social composition of the DNVP made it far more attentive to labor interests than either of the two liberal parties.[5]

2. Hertzman, pp. 213–29, and Stürmer, p. 287.
3. *Germania*, 1 October 1924, no. 422, 16 January 1925, no. 25, and 17 January, no. 27; and NL Marx/60/78 and 66/34, 66–68, memoirs.
4. *Die Kabinette Marx I und II*, pp. 1185–88, 1244, and *Akten der Reichskanzlei. Die Kabinette Luther* (Boppard am Rhein, 1977), pp. 2–6.
5. Weisbrod, pp. 314–18; NL Dessauer/1, circular from Lammers to Center Party industrialists, 7 November 1924; NL Dessauer/2, Theodor Drösser to Dessauer, 17 January 1925; *Zentralblatt*, 2 February 1925, pp. 38f.

The Christian unions were soon compelled to pay their own price for political alliances when the Luther cabinet took up the issue of agricultural tariffs. Most urban workers sharply opposed any tariff on food and still felt bitter resentment against farmers because of alleged hoarding and profiteering during the war. Nevertheless, DGB leaders realized that the Luther cabinet would never survive to consider the legislation on work hours and unemployment insurance they desired unless the DGB exposed itself to attacks from the Free and Hirsch–Duncker unions by supporting a tariff compromise. Stegerwald maneuvered skillfully on this issue by combining stiff opposition to agrarian demands in private talks with a press compaign to prepare Christian workers for agricultural protectionism by depicting the sufferings of farmers and stressing the interdependence of the various sectors of the economy.[6] Thus his conduct contrasted with the often clumsy tactics of socialist labor leaders, whose verbal radicalism merely earned them bitter reproaches from the membership when they were compelled to compromise. Agrarians representing the Nationalist Reichstag delegation conferred repeatedly with labor leaders from the Center in the spring and summer of 1925, deciding at length to exempt frozen meat imports from the stiff new tariffs, to reduce the sales tax from 1.5 to 1% in order to limit the rise in grocery prices, and to devote tariff revenue to the state health insurance system. The Christian union leaders loyally defended the resulting government bill against attacks from the left, although they privately considered its rates excessive.[7] Whereas many industrial lobbyists had shown themselves capable ever since 1918 of allying either with agrarians or with organized labor, this was the first sign of a similar flexibility among union leaders.

However good the rationale for cooperation with the Reichlandbund might have been, it certainly did violence to the feelings of Catholic workers. The political dangers of the tariff issue for the Christian unions increased dramatically when Joseph Wirth resigned from the Center Reichstag delegation in August 1925. Since January he had quarreled repeatedly with rightist party colleagues as he sought to defend the Center's alliance with the SPD in the Prussian parliament and in the second round of the presidential elections, in which the SPD supported the Catholic Wilhelm Marx against Field Marshal von Hindenburg. Wirth considered the government legislation of August 1925, which in addition to setting protective tariffs also shifted some of the tax burden from direct to indirect taxes, confirmation of his worst fears concerning the *Bürgerblock*. Writ-

6. *Die Kabinette Luther*, pp. 101f.; Stürmer, pp. 99–102; *Zentralblatt*, 1 September 1924, p. 165, and 19 January 1925, p. 25; and WAZ, 3 January 1925, p. 5.
7. *Die Kabinette Luther*, pp. 216–31, 332–34, 466f., 481, and GcG Vorstand, 11 August 1925, NL Otte/8.

ing to Marx on August 21, 1925, Wirth explained that he believed a schism of the Center Party to be imminent because "capitalism and class egotism" had secured such an influence over party policy that only "political children" among Catholic workers could continue to support it. Wirth concluded that his mission was to serve as leader for the masses that would inevitably stream out of the Center.[8] He indulged in marked exaggeration but nevertheless won great sympathy among Catholic workers. A chagrined Jakob Kaiser reported to DGB headquarters from Cologne that Wirth had persuaded the rank and file of the Christian unions in the west that the coalition policy of the Center Party was somehow to blame for their economic troubles.[9]

A revival of radical nationalism in the DNVP embarrassed Stegerwald in his efforts to defend the Luther cabinet. Ever since the DNVP's divided vote on the Dawes Plan, the Pan-German League had sought to rally party locals against the moderate "yea-sayers." The Luther cabinet's three-shift decree greatly alarmed the league, which feared above all that this coalition would, as Stegerwald predicted, foster a willingness among agrarians and industrialists to compromise with trade union demands. However, the league decided to confine its public attacks on the government to foreign policy issues in order to win the broadest possible support. Its membership had declined from 36,000 in 1918 to 17,000 in 1925, and it clearly did not have the strength by itself to alter the DNVP's course.[10] In August 1925 Stresemann's conclusion of a security pact with the Western powers at Locarno, which involved German recognition of the western borders established by the Treaty of Versailles, provided an excellent target for Pan-German attacks.

The Locarno issue revived divisions between Protestant and Catholic DGB members. Pugnacious leaders of the Nationalist Workers' League who denounced any suggestion that the DNVP should withdraw from the cabinet because of the high cost of social legislation[11] nevertheless felt that they must demonstrate total reliability on patriotic issues in order to retain sympathy in the party for their economic demands. When Alfred Hugenberg committed his newspaper chain to support the Pan-German position on Locarno, the DNAB

8. NL Marx/237/7. See also Josef Becker, "Joseph Wirth und die Krise des Zentrums während des IV. Kabinetts Marx (1927–1928)," *Zeitschrift für die Geschichte des Oberrheins*, 109/2 (1961), pp. 363–66, and Knapp, pp. 114–23.

9. NL Kaiser/217, Kaiser to Vockel, 26 August 1925, and Kaiser to Brüning, 4 September 1925.

10. See Stürmer, pp. 72f., 190f., and "Vorstand des Alldeutschen Verbandes" (Hamburg Forschungsstelle), 31 January 1925, pp. 15f., 1 February, pp. 26f., and 21 March, pp. 23f.

11. See the frank debate between Wilhelm Koch and Bernhard Leopold on 23 September 1925, reprinted in "Unsere Sozialpolitik," DNVP pamphlet no. 233.

joined in the chorus of attacks on the government. Representatives of the Reichslandbund and the Reich Association of Industry found themselves isolated when
they insisted that the Locarno issue must not topple the cabinet, and Westarp
bowed to grassroots pressure on October 22 by announcing that the DNVP
would withdraw its ministers from the government. Franz Behrens made a
feeble effort to persuade Westarp to reconsider, but even he expressed strong
sympathy for the "idealism" of Hugenberg's foreign policy.[12]

The widespread resentment in the Center Party caused by the DNVP's
return to demagogic nationalism encouraged Wirth to attack the Center's coalition policy publicly at the party congress of November 16–17, 1925. Wirth's call
for a united front of all good republicans against monarchists and reactionaries
generated considerable enthusiasm among the delegates of the Catholic workers'
clubs, youth groups, and journalists. Speaking for the party leadership, Stegerwald and Brauns replied that the DNVP was a sick man who must be subjected to
repeated doses of government participation in order to be made well. In the heat
of debate, Wirth launched a frontal assault against the Christian unions. When
Stegerwald claimed that he must display tolerance for the views of monarchist
workers in order to preserve a united DGB as a foundation for the Center Party,
Wirth replied by deploring the division of republican workers between feuding
Christian and socialist unions: "There are tensions and resentments between the
Christian and the other trade unions that seem politically senseless to me. In my
view these reflect organizational rivalries that are meaningless for our historical
development."[13] Thus Wirth echoed the calls for "proletarian unity" often heard
from the younger generation of Christian workers, from the Christian Social
Commonwealth of Rhineland-Westphalia, from Vitus Heller's movement of
Catholic populists in Bavaria, and from the small circle of Catholic socialist
intellectuals around Ernst Michel.[14] He thereby opened a public debate among
German Catholics that the Christian union leaders soon succeeded in suppressing but that was highly important as a symptom of the long-term trend toward
détente between organized religion and the socialist labor movement.

In February 1926 the editor of the *Westdeutsche Arbeiter-Zeitung*, Wilhelm
Elfes, carried Wirth's ideas to their logical conclusion by exhorting German
workers to establish a unified trade union movement as the only realistic response to the growing power and centralization of big business. Elfes predicted

12. Manfred Dörr, "Die Deutschnationale Volkspartei, 1925 bis 1928," Ph.D. diss. (Mar-
burg/Lahn, 1964), pp. 105f., 212–27; Stürmer, pp. 114–25; DNAB circulars of 6 July and 12 August
1925, StA Osnabrück C1/84/73f., 87f.; NL Westarp, Behrens to Westarp, 7 December 1925.
13. Deutsche Zentrumspartei, *Offizieller Bericht des vierten Reichsparteitages* (Berlin, 1925),
pp. 71–76.
14. See Focke, pp. 159–72.

that the rank and file would sweep aside any union leaders who resisted the trend toward unification. [15] The leaders of the Christian unions felt gravely threatened by this initiative. Workers in the Rhine-Ruhr basin, their primary clientele, remained prone to radicalism even in the prosperous mid-1920s because heavy industry's investment of huge sums in labor-saving rationalization programs resulted in a steady stream of layoffs. The Christian metalworkers', miners', and textile workers' unions all revived more slowly than their socialist counterparts from the drastic membership decline of 1923–24. [16] Moreover, a severe recession in the winter of 1925–26 briefly produced an unemployment rate of 25%. Most Christian unions had found themselves forced to implement supplemental unemployment benefits during the preceding year in order to compete with the Free unions, and this recession brought several of the smaller Christian unions to the brink of bankruptcy. [17] All Christian union leaders bitterly resented what they saw as the confused radicalism of Wirth's supporters in the Catholic workers' clubs, which tended to make workers despair of the chances for progress through social legislation and reformist trade unionism. Alarm over Elfes' articles prompted Heinrich Imbusch to make peace with the League of Christian Unions, and an overwhelming majority of the delegates to the eleventh congress of the GcG in April 1926 defied Wirth by resolving to maintain links with monarchist workers and the DHV. At the same time, they emphasized cooperation with the Free unions in the struggle against reactionary employers. [18]

The controversy over a property settlement with Germany's princely families in the spring of 1926 ended experiments with social radicalism by the Catholic workers' clubs. When the SPD joined the Communist Party in support of a referendum to expropriate the princes without compensation, both the Catholic and the Evangelical churches condemned the initiative as a violation of the seventh commandment. [19] Vitus Heller supported the plebiscite vigorously, publicly defying the episcopate in a manner abhorrent to Wirth and his friends in the leadership of the Catholic workers' clubs. The clubs' staunch defense of the

15. *WAZ*, 27 February 1926, pp. 50f.
16. Preller, pp. 336–41; Weisbrod, pp. 52–62, 120–42; Kühr, pp. 30–35; Wilhelm Koch, "Deutschlands Wirtschaftslage und Sozialpolitik," DNAB pamphlet no. 6 (1926), pp. 4–6.
17. Christlicher Fabrikarbeiterverband, *Bericht des Hauptvorstandes für die Jahre 1925–1927*, pp. 3–5; *Der Deutsche Metallarbeiter*, 1 January 1927, pp. 2f.; Gewerkverein christlicher Bergarbeiter, *18. Generalversammlung 1926*, pp. 36f.
18. NL Imbusch/2, Gewerkverein Hauptvorstand, 29 March and 27 May 1926, and GcG, *11. Kongreß 1926*, pp. 243–59, 453–60. Karl Arnold of Düsseldorf advanced a resolution that explicitly endorsed the Republic, but the great majority followed Stegerwald in rejecting this as divisive, endorsing instead the "Volksstaat."
19. Stürmer, pp. 155–59, and Jonathan Wright, "Above Parties": The Political Attitudes of the German Protestant Church Leadership 1918–1933 (London, 1974), pp. 52f.

bishops provoked the worst crisis of discipline in their ranks since 1918.[20] Five million nonsocialist voters, roughly 2 million from the Center Party, supported the unsuccessful referendum in June 1926. This controversy stimulated a modest migration of tens of thousands of workers from the Center Party through one of the radical Catholic splinter parties and usually into the KPD.[21]

This referendum campaign proved a major setback for all the groups seeking to reconcile Christianity and socialism. It also demonstrated that Catholic workers usually did not reject the Christian unions without rejecting the Catholic workers' clubs and Center Party as well. The leaders of all three organizations promptly closed ranks. In June 1926 Wirth condemned the SPD for adopting a Communist-drafted plebiscite text that was calculated to antagonize the Church, and he rejoined the Center Reichstag delegation in July. Jakob Kaiser also arranged a summit conference with the leaders of the Catholic workers' clubs in the Rhineland that achieved a reconciliation, sealed with the discharge of Elfes as editor of the *WAZ*.[22] After the summer of 1926, all leaders of the Catholic workers' clubs agreed with the DGB in exhorting Christian workers to remain separate from socialist workers in their unions as well as their political parties.

Although the Christian unions successfully weathered this storm, Elfes' initiative highlighted enduring and fundamental problems. Before World War I the Christian unions enjoyed the sympathy of many clergymen convinced that membership in the socialist labor movement entailed grave dangers for the worker's soul, but this premise was somewhat old-fashioned in the 1920s. The most conspicuous group seeking to reconcile Christianity and socialism, the Protestant "League of Religious Socialists" in the SPD, merely alienated both the party leadership and the Church authorities by seeking some grand theory that would synthesize their respective doctrines.[23] The trend of the times was toward détente nonetheless. Otto Braun as the head of the Prussian SPD sought tenaciously to subordinate his party's anticlerical tradition to the goal of achieving good relations with the Center Party, and his concessions to Church interests and appointments of Catholics as high officials clearly altered the attitudes of many Catholic priests. In 1924 Monsignor Otto Müller recommended to the archbishop of Cologne that parish priests no longer deny the sacraments to

20. See Heller's *Das neue Volk*, 26 June 1926, pp. 1–4, and *Jahrbuch des Diözesanverbandes der katholischen Arbeitervereine der Erzdiözese Köln* (Cologne, 1929), pp. 9f.
21. Focke, pp. 143–46, and Heinrich Brauns to Otto Geßler, 27 June 1926, NL Geßler/9/1–4.
22. Becker, pp. 368f.; Focke, pp. 142f.; *Zentralblatt*, 12 July 1926, pp. 193–97, and 20 September 1926, p. 276.
23. See Friedrich-Martin Balzer, *Klassengegensätze in der Kirche* (Cologne, 1973), and Renate Breipohl, *Religiöser Sozialismus und bürgerliches Geschichtsbewußtsein zur Zeit der Weimarer Republik* (Zürich, 1971).

members of the Free unions, because the Communist Party was now the only organizer of anticlericalist propaganda.[24] The bishops did not officially revise their antisocialist policy, but enforcement seems to have been lax. Our fragmentary evidence suggests that urban religiosity declined steadily until World War I but that it stabilized or revived slightly thereafter. The realization was spreading in the Catholic clergy that the decline had resulted not from wicked socialist agitation but from problems especially acute during the Wilhelmian period: close ties between the churches and conservative elites, and urbanization so rapid as to create miserable housing conditions, undermine family life, and leave most workers without access to churches.[25]

Many liberal Protestants as well were coming to accept the Free unions as a natural feature of the social order. Reinhard Mumm and the other Christian Socials who lobbied intensively within the Evangelical Church hierarchy for a "social mission" involving close cooperation with the antisocialist Protestant workers' clubs and Christian unions found that many urban pastors preferred a "universal" social mission involving direct dialogue with unchurched Social Democrats.[26] In 1929 the Evangelical Social Congress invited a representative of the Free unions to address it for the first time, and its chairman, Walter Simon, expressed deep sorrow over the fact that the delegates to an earlier congress in 1894 had obstructed dialogue by booing the moderate Social Democrat Eduard David when he tried to address them. Their guest, Fritz Tarnow, admitted to being a "free-thinker" but offered friendly advice in the manner of a Dutch uncle on how the churches could avoid antagonizing socialist workers.[27]

The emergence of such détente was in part the achievement of the Christian unions, which had demonstrated that advocacy of labor interests did not necessarily jeopardize Christian values, and vice versa. But such successes by the Christian unionists undermined the rationale for their organization. Adam Stegerwald and his closest associates clearly perceived the declining importance of the traditional Christian rationale for their unions and sought to give them a new rationale as champions of a program for reconciling the interests of big business, agriculture, and organized labor, a program for welfare legislation

24. Müller to Archbishop Schulte, 2 February 1924, KAB Archiv, and Hagen Schulze, pp. 234–37, 390–92, 534–56.
25. See Joseph Joos, "Geistige Entwicklung in der Arbeiterschaft," *Mitteilungen an die Arbeiterpräsides*, 1926, no. 1, pp. 3–13; Kühr, pp. 52–54; and Graf, pp. 16–27.
26. See the debate over the duties of the *Sozialpfarrer* in *Kirchlich-soziale Blätter*, March–April 1927, pp. 65–68, and at the "Arbeitsgemeinschaft evangelischer Sozialpfarrer," 7–8 August 1929, NL Mumm/636/374–84.
27. *Die Verhandlungen des 36. Evangelisch-sozialen Kongresses, Mai 1929* (Göttingen, 1929), pp. 9–11, 104–18.

combined with tax and tariff measures favoring producers. Thus "corporate pluralism" was replacing religious sentiment as their raison d'être.

THE COMPETITION BETWEEN INDUSTRIALISTS AND AGRARIANS FOR THE SUPPORT OF THE DGB

Throughout 1926 Germany was governed by weak caretaker cabinets. Efforts by industrial and agrarian lobbyists to revive the *Bürgerblock* and the SPD's desire to retain freedom to oppose government measures hindered the formation of a Grand Coalition, which most leaders of the moderate parties, including Brauns and Stegerwald, considered the only logical response to the DNVP's withdrawal from government at the end of 1925.[28] In this situation of prolonged uncertainty, the position of the DGB's Reichstag delegates at the balance point of the parliamentary scales encouraged the Reichslandbund (RLB) to display unprecedented support for their legislative demands. On May 29, 1926, the executive committee of the RLB decided to secure support from the Christian unions for a trade treaty with Sweden that restricted dairy imports by helping to pass Heinrich Imbusch's bill for a reform of the miners' medical insurance and pension system (the Reichsknappschaftsgesetz) that would cost mineowners an estimated RM 10–30 million per year.[29] This support was doubly valuable because the SPD rejected the details of the Imbusch plan, which imposed great responsibility on the miners by assigning them a three-fifths majority on the administrative boards of the new system, purchased through payment of a corresponding share of the contributions to the pension fund. Agrarian support and vigorous agitation by August Winnefeld in the DVP and by the Christian Socials in the DNVP secured enough votes from the bourgeois parties to pass Imbusch's bill in June 1926. The result helped persuade skeptics in the Christian miners' union of the wisdom of Stegerwald's parliamentary tactics.[30]

Passage of the Reichsknappschaftsgesetz infuriated Ruhr industrialists. It outraged Yellow labor leaders as well because the law granted government-recognized trade unions the sole right to nominate labor representatives for the governing boards of the insurance system. Fritz Thyssen and Paul Reusch pro-

28. Stürmer, pp. 133–61; *Die Kabinette Luther,* pp. 942–44; Rudolf Morsey (ed.), *Die Protokolle der Reichstagsfraktion und des Fraktionsvorstands der Deutschen Zentrumspartei, 1926–1933* (Mainz, 1969), pp. 38–40.

29. ZStA/RLB/144/215f. Proponents of compromise with organized labor in the RLB were strengthened early in 1926, when the moderate agricultural employers' association merged with it: see Jens Flemming, *Landwirtschaftliche Interessen und Demokratie* (Bonn, 1978), pp. 318–22.

30. Gewerkverein christlicher Bergarbeiter, *18. Generalversammlung 1926,* pp. 44–46; NL Imbusch/2, Gewerkverein Hauptvorstand, 18 June 1926; NL Diller/8, Lambach circular of June 1926.

tested by withholding substantial contributions promised to the DNVP, but 15 million votes for the Marxist parties' referendum to expropriate the princes had sensitized that party's leadership to the need for a popular social policy. Westarp and his aides replied to the Ruhr industrialists by echoing the DNAB's argument that the Nationalist Party must greatly broaden its blue-collar base before it could gain the power needed to repair the fundamental defects of the Weimar system: "By winning workers for our ideals, we serve the interests of the business community as well."[31] In a triumphant mood, Walther Lambach and Gottfried von Treviranus, a young agrarian friend of Heinrich Brüning, hailed the birth of a firm political alliance between the DGB and Reichslandbund, calling for a "workers' and peasants' government" to protect Germany from the twin threats of Bolshevism and international finance capital. Other party leaders began to imitate their rhetoric.[32]

The emerging alliance between the DGB and the Reichslandbund remained highly unstable, however. Despite the talk about workers and "peasants" joining hands, the RLB was still dominated by wealthy landowners who generally regarded tactical cooperation with trade unions against industrialists as a dangerous experiment. Many leaders of the DNVP and RLB accepted the legislative demands of the Christian unions only because they still hoped to engineer a merger between them and the Yellow unions on an aggressively anti-Marxist platform.[33] The Nationalist Workers' League nourished such hopes by promising DNVP leaders that support for social legislation would dramatically weaken the Marxist parties and cause the Center to renounce permanently any cooperation with the "internationalist" SPD and DDP. The rank and file of the Christian unions, on the other hand, supported schemes for land reform that struck leading agrarians as outright theft. At the congress of the Christian unions in April 1926, Karl Dudey of the metalworkers' union proposed government action to create peasant homesteads by subdividing bankrupt estates east of the Elbe as a long-term measure against urban unemployment. Behrens was booed so badly that he could hardly speak when he tried to defend large estates as an economic necessity in that region.[34] The leaders of the DGB hoped, moreover, that the Labor Ministry's refusal to recognize Yellow unions as collective bargaining agents

31. NL Westarp: von Dryander to Bergassessor Winnacker, 10 July 1926; see also von Dryander to Fritz Thyssen, 24 September 1926, and Johannes Wolf to Westarp, 9 September 1926.
32. Lambach in *Politische Wochenschrift,* 1 July 1926, pp. 628f.; Treviranus in *Berliner Börsen-Zeitung,* 23 July 1926, no. 337; DNVP circular of 6 July 1926, StA Osnabrück C1/15/99–102.
33. See the remarks by Hepp in the RLB Bundesvorstand, 29 May 1926, ZStA/RLB/144/215f., and Lambach's report on confidential talks with leaders of the DNVP, Stahlhelm, and Pomeranian Landbund on the legal status of the Yellow unions, 30 March 1927, NL Lambach/9/87f.
34. GcG, *11. Kongreß 1926,* pp. 346–65, 377–80.

would soon force them to dissolve and thus enable the Christian unions to recruit all working-class supporters of the DNVP.[35] Thus the contracting parties entered this strange alliance with unrealistic and mutually exclusive expectations. Each hoped to weaken or profoundly transform its partner.

Paradoxically, growing support for a Grand Coalition among industrialists in 1926 resulted indirectly in a revival of the *Bürgerblock*. At the annual convention of the Reich Association of Industry on September 4, 1926, the coal and iron magnate Paul Silverberg caused a sensation by proclaiming in the keynote address that German industrialists supported the Weimar Republic and desired the SPD to participate in the government. Silverberg's sincerity has been questioned, and in any case the leaders of heavy industry in the Ruhr promptly organized an anti-Silverberg campaign behind the scenes that prevented effective action by the Reich Association to promote the Grand Coalition.[36] Rudolf Hilferding of the SPD, Stegerwald, and many other observers on both the left and right ascribed tremendous significance to the speech, however, believing that conservative coal, iron, and steel industrialists had at last accepted the progressive political strategies long urged by the dynamic chemical and electrotechnical industries.[37] Agrarian, industrial, and labor representatives in the DNVP all considered Silverberg's speech highly alarming and responded with redoubled efforts to woo the Center Party.

The Reichslandbund in particular displayed real panic in the weeks following the Silverberg speech. For years the economic importance of German agriculture had been declining in comparison to that of industry, and this trend had recently been highlighted by the formation of two of the largest trusts in the history of capitalism, IG Farben and the United Steelworks. Agrarian leaders had nevertheless reassured themselves with the thought that they shared vital interests with protectionist elements in industry and that their ability to turn out a sizable rural vote made them attractive political allies. But when the executive committee of the RLB met on November 5, 1926, this no longer seemed the case. Correctly perceiving that the formation of the international pig iron cartel in 1926 had reduced heavy industry's dependence on protective tariffs, the agrarian leaders mistakenly concluded that even their traditional allies in Ruhr industry supported Silverberg's initiative and planned to espouse free trade in a

35. Heinrich Brauns made affiliation with the DGB the precondition for government recognition of the Yellow farmworkers' league in a conference with von Dewitz of the Pomeranian Landbund on June 8, 1925: ZStA/RAM/6509/172–79. Late in 1926 the Christian unions opened new offices in Hamburg and central Germany specifically to recruit DNAB members: see NL Otte/7/263, GcG Vorstand, 4 November 1926, and *Deutsche Werksgemeinschaft*, 6 March 1927, p. 2.

36. Weisbrod, pp. 246–72.

37. See Hilferding in *Die Gesellschaft*, October 1926, pp. 289–302, and Stegerwald in the *Kölnische Volkszeitung*, 4 October 1926, no. 734.

bid for an alliance with urban workers. The RLB leadership decided that it too must bid for popularity among workers by supporting social legislation as the only way to counteract the enormous economic power of big business.[38] At the end of 1926, prominent agrarians accordingly resurrected the "workers and peasants" slogan of Lambach and Treviranus, notifying the leaders of the Center Party that landowners now agreed wholeheartedly with the DGB that all "populist conservative forces (volkskonservative Kräfte)" must band together in order to prevent the "capitalist trusts" from dominating the state.[39]

Industrialists in the DNVP also stepped up their efforts to woo the Christian unions at this time because they considered Silverberg's speech and the agrarians' reaction to it equally alarming. They polemicized against the Grand Coalition by reminding the Center Party and Christian unions that the supposedly moderate business spokesmen in the DDP and DVP were in fact the most intemperate opponents of Germany's system of social insurance. Passages in Silverberg's speech had criticized the Christian unions for raising extreme demands to compete with the Free unions, implied that employers would prefer to deal with a unified union movement, and expressed the hope that businessmen could cooperate with the SPD against the etatist social policies of Labor Minister Brauns. Nationalist industrialists cited them in a successful effort to foster fears that liberal employers were plotting to revive the Zentralarbeitsgemeinschaft exclusively with the Free unions, banishing the DGB to the outer darkness as they had the Yellow unions in November 1918.[40] However, such arguments could be plausible only as long as Nationalist industrialists supported expensive acts of social legislation in order to demonstrate their reverence for a strong state dedicated to the protection of the economically weak.

In November 1926 the DNVP toppled the minority government of Wilhelm Marx by cooperating with the SPD and KPD to obstruct the workings of the Reichstag. Stegerwald nevertheless resisted overtures from that party. He, Brauns, and Heinrich Imbusch had all responded enthusiastically to Silverberg's speech and believed that the Christian unions should cooperate with moderate industrialists like him to form a Grand Coalition government as the first step in the far more difficult and rewarding task of reviving the ZAG.[41] Frustrating experiences with the first Luther cabinet, to which business lobbyists enjoyed

---

38. ZStA/RLB/144/177–79.

39. Von Kriegsheim to Franz von Papen, 14 January and 11 February 1927, ZStA/RLB/127/1–3.

40. Weisbrod, pp. 250f.; NL Westarp, Walther Rademacher to Kurt Philipp, 7 October 1926; Gustav Hülser, "Republik und Schwarz-weiß-rot," DNVP pamphlet no. 268, pp. 4–6; Wilhelm Koch, "Deutschlands Wirtschaftslage und Sozialpolitik," DNAB pamphlet no. 6, pp. 8–14.

41. *Der Deutsche*, 23 September 1926; *Kölnische Volkszeitung*, 26 September 1926, no. 714, and 4 October 1926, no. 735.

privileged access, had caused a certain radicalization in the outlook of Christian union leaders. They also found to their dismay that many of Germany's largest industrial firms still hoped to undermine or suppress trade unionism.[42] Even Stegerwald came to speak in terms of class struggle when he tried to explain to his colleagues why he had supported a coalition with the DNVP. He contrasted Germany's "botched revolution" of 1918–19, in which only revolutionaries had been shot while monarchist reactionaries continued to dominate the bureaucracy, army, and educational system, with the liquidation of the old elites that had produced genuine social change in the French and Russian revolutions. Stegerwald claimed that he had opposed Wirth's call for an alliance with the SPD only because Wirth underestimated the strength of the reactionaries and their ability to sabotage the policies of any leftist cabinet. The only way to weaken the DNVP was to force it to compromise its unrealistic principles through participation in the government.[43] By the end of 1926 a disillusioned Stegerwald stated frankly that the DNVP contained far too many reactionaries and chauvinists to be a suitable coalition partner: if the Christian Socials and moderate agrarians like Martin Schiele did not soon break away to form their own "Christian conservative party," he argued, the Center would be compelled to cooperate with the left throughout the foreseeable future in a campaign to purge "counter-revolutionary" elements from the army, bureaucracy, and educational system.[44] Brüning opposed Stegerwald's position and worked behind the scenes with Treviranus to bring the DNVP into the government, but the Center Party leadership supported the Grand Coalition consistently throughout the cabinet crisis. It was the SPD that precluded this option in mid-December by returning to a stance of flamboyant opposition in reaction to a series of calculated provocations from the right wing of the DVP. Even then, Center leaders blocked the formation of a rightist government for a month, until President Hindenburg intervened directly to request Wilhelm Marx to form a coalition with the DNVP. The Center Reichstag delegation reluctantly concluded that it had no alternative, but signaled its determination to extract major concessions from the DNVP by placing Joseph Wirth in charge of drafting the guidelines for the new government.[45]

42. See the complaints in BAK R43I/2024/41–43, presidential reception for union leaders, 3 April 1925, and *Zentralblatt*, 13 April 1925, pp. 106f., 6 July, pp. 199f., and 20 July 1925, pp. 204–07.

43. Stegerwald to Jakob Kaiser, 3 November 1925, NL Kaiser/215, partially reprinted in Kosthorst, pp. 110–12.

44. *Tremonia*, 19 November 1926, and *WAZ*, 11 December 1926, pp. 297f. Leftist critics of Stegerwald applauded his change of heart in *Vorwärts*, 18 November 1926, and *Die Deutsche Republik*, 1926–27, no. 8, pp. 8–10.

45. Stürmer, pp. 170–86; Becker, pp. 373–75; *Zentrumsprotokolle 1926–1933*, pp. 80–90; Treviranus to Hugenberg, 20 December 1926, NL Westarp; Heinrich Brauns to Wilhelm Marx, 5 January 1927, NL Marx/73/5.

Wirth designed his government platform to guarantee rejection by the DNVP, including planks that promised strong legislation to protect workers and explicitly acknowledged the legitimacy of the Weimar Constitution as well as existing foreign treaties. Stegerwald encouraged Wirth to sharpen the language of the platform, correctly predicting that the combined pressure of agrarian, industrial, and labor representatives in the DNVP would compel Westarp to accept virtually any terms dictated by the Center. Wirth nevertheless voted against the new Marx cabinet when it took office on January 29, 1927, and resigned from the Center Reichstag delegation again to protest the resurrection of the *Bürgerblock*. But this time, both Imbusch and the Catholic workers' clubs agreed with the strategy of the Center leadership, and Wirth won little support. The DGB enjoyed a very strong position in this government because all coalition partners realized that it was determined to secure dramatic legislative gains for its constituents and could topple the government and seek an understanding with the SPD if its demands were ignored.[46]

The most pressing item on the DGB's legislative agenda was a law to roll back the excessive prolongation of work hours in the winter of 1923–24. Stegerwald had reached agreement with the Free unions on the text of a work hours bill in the fall of 1926 as a foundation for the Grand Coalition. The ADGB was apparently growing impatient with the SPD's hesitation to enter the government and sought to accelerate the process through direct contact with Stegerwald. In January 1927 the Center Party insisted that the DNVP accept this bill in principle as the price for admission into the cabinet.[47] In late February the Center appointed Stegerwald and his colleague Becker-Arnsberg to meet with four industrial spokesmen, Rademacher and Leopold of the DNVP, and Moldenhauer and Pfeffer of the DVP, in order to negotiate the thorny issue of defining permissible exceptions to the eight-hour day in the new law. The talks lasted four weeks, as tensions between industrialists and labor representatives in the DVP and DNVP mounted. The general secretary of the League of Christian Unions, Bernhard Otte, went so far as to warn the bourgeois parties publicly that failure to accommodate the Christian unions on this issue would topple the current government and initiate a process of radicalization in the working class that might culminate in a Bolshevik revolution.[48] The government parties finally accepted a compromise formula drafted by Stegerwald on March 22, despite threats by

46. *Zentrumsprotokolle 1926–1933*, pp. 91–96, and Becker, pp. 376–82. See also Ludwig Heyde's commentary in *Soziale Praxis*, 10 February 1927, columns 138–41.
47. See the cabinet minutes of 25 November and 13 December 1926, BAK R43I/1416/390–92, and 1417/240; *Zentralblatt*, 1 November 1926, p. 305, and 31 January 1927, pp. 25f.; and DVP Zentralvorstand, 19 March 1927, BAK R45II/42/109–11.
48. *Zentralblatt*, 14 March 1927, pp. 61f.

industrialists to terminate all financial contributions. The bill established a 25% bonus as the normal compensation for any work over eight hours and broadened the definition of unhealthy trades where all overtime would be banned. The Reichslandbund agreed to support the bill in exchange for future acceptance by the DGB of higher agricultural tariffs. Intense lobbying by the League of Employers' Associations nearly succeeded in preventing passage, however, by persuading half the DVP Reichstag delegation to boycott the final vote in April and 40 delegates of the DDP and splinter parties to join the SPD and KPD in voting No.[49]

The SPD denounced this Provisional Work Hours Law as a sham because it left enforcement largely to the discretion of the authorities, but the economic incentive to reduce work hours created by the bill clearly improved the trade unions' bargaining position, already strengthened by an economic upswing that reduced unemployment. When reports accumulated that many state labor arbitrators only granted a 10% bonus for overtime, the DGB persuaded Heinrich Brauns to instruct them to close their ears to requests by employers for special treatment. The labor minister also committed himself to imposing the three-shift system for reasons of health and safety in all continuously operating plants of the iron and steel industry over the course of eighteen months.[50] The Free unions' own statistics showed that, whereas more than 60% of the German labor force worked more than 48 hours per week in 1924–26, only 40% did so by 1928.[51] The Provisional Work Hours Law probably represented the most significant legislative gain for workers since 1920. It undoubtedly intensified resentment by industrialists against the state labor arbitration system and the political power of the Christian unions. The industrialists' committees of the DNVP and Center Party were forced to make frantic and only partially successful efforts to dissuade their disgruntled constituents from either defecting to the DVP, the firmest opponent of organized labor, or abandoning party politics altogether.[52]

The political position of the DGB began to deteriorate in June 1927, however, when the leaders of the Reichslandbund discovered that they had exagge-

49. Stürmer, pp. 205–08, 304–06; DVP Reichstagsfraktion, 5 April 1927, BAK R45II/67/49; NL Westarp, J. W. Reichert to Westarp, 9 March 1927; RLB Bundesvorstand, 9 March 1927, ZStA/RLB/144/141f.; *Der Deutsche Metallarbeiter*, 23 April 1927, pp. 260f.

50. GcG circulars of 31 May and 23 June 1927, NL Otte/1/96, 102–04; Weisbrod, pp. 333–43; cabinet minutes of 14 July 1927, BAK R43I/1422/270.

51. Michael Schneider, *Das Arbeitsbeschaffungsprogramm des ADGB* (Bonn/Bad Godesberg, 1975), pp. 47f.

52. See the report on an unusually hostile reception for Heinrich Brauns by Center party industrialists in NL ten Hompel/38, "Mitteilungen der Handels- und Industriebeiräte der Deutschen Zentrumspartei," 1927, no. 1, pp. 1–25; NL Westarp, Fritz Thyssen to Westarp, 23 July 1927; and the circulars of 10 March, 14 March, and 15 September 1927 by the Arbeitsausschuß deutschnationaler Industriellen, StA Osnabrück C1/17:III/128–32, 221f. Contrast Weisbrod, pp. 325–30, who portrays the law as a victory for business lobbyists.

rated the strength of free trade currents among industrialists. To the dismay of
the Christian unions, agrarians in the DNVP demanded substantial increases in
the potato, meat, and lard tariffs that most affected the worker's household
budget. The Reich Association of Industry encouraged Economics Minister Curtius of the DVP to endorse the DNVP's bill, and Brauns and Stegerwald put up
the only real resistance to it. Westarp threatened to dissolve the coalition over
this issue after a heated argument with Stegerwald on July 5, causing the Center
to grant most of the agrarian demands.[53] In mid-July the executive committee of
the RLB concluded that industrialists and the DGB displayed an equally constructive attitude toward food tariffs, but that the unions' demand for unemployment insurance and other social reforms might imperil economic prosperity.[54]
This meeting marked the beginning of a rapprochement between industrialists
and agrarians.

The most ambitious social reform of the Marx cabinet, the Unemployment
Insurance Act of July 1927, initially enjoyed broad support. The Labor Ministry's
bill created a comprehensive national insurance system with dues and benefits
graduated according to income. It was designed to satisfy the workers' desire to
escape the indignity of the means test and the vagaries of local welfare programs,
but was also supported by most employers as a sensible reform that would
eventually decrease the welfare burden by rationalizing its administration. However, many leaders of the Reichslandbund opposed the law from fear that unemployment insurance would encourage farm laborers to flee to the city. Address-
ing the annual congress of the RLB early in 1927, its chairman, Count von
Kalckreuth, termed unemployment insurance a "terribly dangerous experiment" that threatened to "smother our productive economy with a horde of state
pensioners."[55] The bill passed the Reichstag with the support of all parties from
the SPD to the DNVP, but six Nationalist delegates broke party ranks to vote
against it, including five agrarians and the industrialist Bernhard Leopold. Soon
thereafter, East Elbian landowners and the Hugenberg press chain began to
bombard the government and public with reports that unemployment insurance
encouraged fraud, laziness, and labor shortages. These charges made the insurance system controversial long before rising unemployment threatened it with
bankruptcy in 1929.[56]

---

53. Stürmer, pp. 220–24; cabinet minutes of 2 July 1927, BAK R43I/1422/8f.; *Zentrumsprotokolle 1926–1933*, pp. 127–30, 138f.
54. RLB Bundesvorstand, 13 July 1927, ZStA/RLB/144/70–79.
55. *Der Reichslandbund*, 5 February 1927 (ZStA/RLB/4a/457–95), and Preller, pp. 369–73.
56. See Stürmer, pp. 210–12; NL Westarp, Knebel-Doeberitz to Westarp, 15 December
1927; ZStA/RLB/246/5–8, von Oertzen to Knebel-Doeberitz, 9 January 1928; and the discussion of
these charges in BAK R41/299/5 and 300/50, Reichsanstalt für die Arbeitslosenversicherung, circulars of 11 October 1927 and 6 March 1928.

THE DISINTEGRATION OF THE *BÜRGERBLOCK*

The social legislation of the fourth Marx cabinet provoked a backlash within the DNVP that significantly increased class tensions. The chairman of the Pan-German League, Heinrich Class, felt that the willingness of Westarp and other DNVP leaders to purchase entry into the government through concessions on social policy meant that "the so-called right may help to destroy the remnants [of the Empire] that Scheidemann, Erzberger, Rathenau, Wirth and company have left intact."[57] The Pan-German League organized those few industrialists who rejected the Reich Association of Industry as too moderate into the League for Nationalist Economics (Bund zur Nationalwirtschaft und Werksgemeinschaft) under Hugenberg's friend, Paul Bang. This organization was the major patron of the Yellow unions and derived some support from the lignite mines of central Germany, the Berlin metalworking industry, Thuringian cement industry, and Hamburg shipyards.[58] The Pomeranian Landbund came more and more to echo Pan-German attacks on the social institutions of the Weimar Republic, while demanding that the RLB break off all contacts with the Christian farmworkers' union until Franz Behrens publicly accepted RLB discipline by becoming its second vice-president.[59] These reactionaries usually avoided public opposition to popular acts of welfare legislation by relying on the Yellow labor leaders Johannes Wolf and Wilhelm Schmidt to denounce each bill as designed to benefit only the corrupt trade union bureaucracy. In April 1927 the Pan-Germans resolved to devote all their strength to gaining control of the DNVP and identified the DGB as their most dangerous opponent.[60]

Count Westarp made significant concessions to his reactionary critics. In February 1927 he permitted them to pressure Walther Lambach into resigning as the party's chief parliamentary whip.[61] By March Wolf's quarrels with Behrens and Lambach grew so intense that the DNVP Reichstag delegation convened its court of honor to untangle a web of charges and countercharges stretching back over 17 years. The court found Wolf guilty of dishonorable conduct, which normally led to expulsion from the delegation, but when leaders of the Pomeranian Landbund threatened, in effect, to secede from the DNVP if any

57. Hamburg Forschungsstelle, Geschäftsführender Ausschuß des Alldeutschen Verbandes, 5 December 1926, p. 3.

58. See Eduard Stadtler's history of the Bund's parent organization, "'Reichsverband der Deutschen Industrie' und 'Deutsche Industriellen-Vereinigung'" (Berlin, no date, ca. 1926), and Stupperich, *Volksgemeinschaft*, pp. 108–11.

59. NL Westarp, von Rohr-Demmin to Westarp, 22 January 1927, and RLB Bundesvorstand, 14 September 1927, ZStA/RLB/144/46f.

60. Hamburg Forschungsstelle, Geschäftsführender Ausschuß des Alldeutschen Verbandes, 23 April 1927.

61. NL Westarp, Lambach to Westarp, 17 February 1927.

action were taken against Wolf, Westarp intervened to quash the verdict.[62] As more and more party locals came to parrot the slogans of Wolf and Wilhelm Schmidt by denouncing the trade union "monopoly" of labor representation, Westarp called publicly for a brake on proworker social legislation.[63] The right wing of the DNVP was further strengthened in September 1927, when Alfred Hugenberg emerged openly as a frondeur by boycotting a party congress. Hugenberg had long avoided confrontation while propagating patriotic ideals, but he now demanded that the DNVP return to uncompromising struggle against the parliamentary system. Westarp tried to placate Hugenberg by granting him increased control over business contributions to the DNVP and influence over nominations for the next Reichstag election.[64] Hugenberg promptly began to exert his influence in efforts to prevent the renomination of moderate parliamentarians.

Similar class tensions spread to the Center Party in the autumn of 1927, when a controversy over civil service reform undermined the cohesion of the Marx cabinet. The Center Party's ambitious young finance minister, Heinrich Köhler, sought to end the discontent among civil servants stemming from the austere regulation of their salaries during the stabilization crisis of 1923–24. At a civil servants' rally in September 1927 he surprised his party colleagues by committing the government to a 25% salary increase for all lower ranking civil servants and an 18% increase for senior officials.[65] The Christian unions opposed this proposal sharply. Ever since his term as Prussian prime minister in 1921, Stegerwald had advocated replacing civil servants with untenured government employees whenever possible, and such plans enjoyed widespread sympathy among businessmen and farmers concerned over high taxes. When Brüning and Stegerwald criticized Köhler's bill as too expensive, they stood in agreement with an impressive array of economic experts and lobbyists.[66] Nonetheless, this issue took on unusually emotional overtones in the Christian unions because workers in the bourgeois parties were uniquely sensitive to the phenomenon of lingering class prejudice among civil servants. Repeated cases where party col-

62. See the extensive documentation in NL Lambach/9/73–92.

63. Count Westarp, "Deutschnationale Innenpolitik in der Regierungskoalition," DNVP pamphlet no. 292 (1927). In June 1927 the Prussian parliamentary delegations of the DVP and DNVP jointly demanded that Yellow unions be granted government recognition. See the copy of their petition to Chancellor Marx, 7 July 1927, NL Westarp.

64. NL Westarp: Westarp to Hugenberg, 23 May and 8 October 1927, Hugenberg to Westarp, 3–4 June 1927, and Schatzmeister Widenmann to Westarp, 14 November 1927.

65. Heinrich Köhler, *Lebenserinnerungen des Politikers und Staatsmannes 1878–1949* (Stuttgart, 1964), pp. 251f., and Brüning. pp. 126f.

66. See Stegerwald's speech in Deutsche Zentrumspartei, *4. Reichsparteitag 1925*, p. 10, and the similar reasoning in the petition of 7 October 1927 from the Deutsche Industrie- und Handels-Tag to Chancellor Marx, BAK R43I/1157/40–50.

leagues blocked the appointment of trade unionists to government posts because they lacked academic credentials caused great friction in the Center and Bavarian People's parties.[67]

The Christian unions soon isolated themselves, however, by choosing indirect methods to fight Köhler's bill, apparently in deference to pleas from the civil service unions that no faction of organized labor should ever resist pay hikes for any other faction. On September 29, 1927, a DGB delegation to Chancellor Marx demanded that state labor arbitrators decree 25% wage hikes in order to "compensate" workers for the civil service reform. The gambit was designed to frighten the cabinet into slashing Köhler's planned increases, but the DGB should not have abandoned the straightforward argument that Köhler's bill was too expensive if it hoped to attract allies. Westarp promptly denounced the DGB for cynically obstructing a needed reform in order to blackmail the state into filling the workers' pockets.[68] The Christian unions lacked parliamentary leverage because the SPD supported the salary increases, in accord with the program of the Kiel party congress of May 1927 that called for efforts to woo white-collar workers and civil servants. As an opposition party, moreover, the SPD bore no responsibility to display fiscal restraint. The strong civil service lobby guaranteed that the DDP, DVP, and DNVP never wavered in their support for Köhler's bill. No laborites in the Nationalist Party dared oppose the bill openly, even though it was as unpopular among Christian Social workers and DHV members as among Catholic workers.[69]

The Christian unions continued the fight despite their isolation. Indeed, DGB leaders considered this issue ideal for furthering both of their most fundamental aims: to compete effectively with the Free unions by refurbishing their image as a champion of workers' interests, and at the same time to promote revival of the ZAG by focusing attention on a grievance shared by labor and management. One close adviser to Stegerwald compared the civil service controversy to the prewar campaign against the Catholic Integralists as a fight that would galvanize the entire Christian-nationalist labor movement.[70] The Chris-

67. Regarding Peter Schlack's unsuccessful candidacy as *Regierungs-Präsident* of Cologne, for example, see NL Marx/232/5f., memoirs, and WAZ, 29 January 1927, p. 28.

68. NL Otte/7/232f., GcG Vorstand, 17 September 1927, and 1/127–30, GcG circulars of 22 and 29 September 1927; BAK R43I/1157/66–68, chancellor's reception for DGB leaders, 29 September 1927; Kuno von Westarp, "Deutschnationale Innenpolitik in der Regierungskoalition," part II, DNVP pamphlet no. 312, pp. 3f. See also the pleas from the GcG's former colleagues in the Gewerkschaft deutscher Eisenbahner, *Die Deutsche Gewerkschaft*, 8 August and 3 October 1927.

69. *Zentralblatt*, 7 November 1927, pp. 286f.; Paul Rüffer to Reinhard Mumm, 11 October 1927, NL Mumm/140/83–88; conference of DNVP functionaries, 27 March 1928, ZStA/DNVP/58/8–23.

70. Franz Röhr to Stegerwald, 5 November and 16 November 1927, NL Stegerwald/010/"Beamtenfragen"/no. 1143.

tian unions therefore abandoned all concern for the feelings of former friends among the civil servants and openly denounced Köhler's bill as an attempt to restore prewar pay differentials between civil servants and workers, and hence the prewar status hierarchy. Stegerwald told cheering crowds at union and party rallies all over Germany that there must be no increase in salaries without drastic reductions in the number of tenured civil servants, asserting that Germany's bloated bureaucracy represented a relic of the "authoritarian state (Obrigkeits-staat)" that must be dismantled before Germany could establish true democracy. The popularity of this campaign generated considerable support for Stegerwald within the Center Reichstag delegation and persuaded Marx to delay cabinet action on the matter.[71]

In December 1927 the SPD-led Prussian government finally prodded Marx into action by threatening to implement salary hikes for Prussian civil servants even more generous than those of the Köhler bill, which would encourage emulation by the Reichstag parties. The SPD's enthusiastic support for the bill led Marx, understandably enough, to conclude that the Christian unions were irrational for claiming that it harmed workers. The bill passed the Reichstag with overwhelming support on December 14, when Imbusch voted against it and the other laborites in the Center delegation abstained.[72]

Whereas the SPD hoped through its generosity to promote an alliance be-tween civil servants and the labor movement, the DGB was probably more realistic in assessing the implications of this civil service reform. For Stegerwald, Otte, and Imbusch, the crucial development during the controversy was the decision by the Reich Association of Industry to abandon opposition to a fiscally irresponsible bill in order to persuade civil servants to join the ranks of the propertied and the educated in a united political front.[73] Industrialists made no real effort to oppose the civil service lobby. Indeed, the confidential circulars of the civil servants' committee of the DNVP stressed that prominent industrial spokesmen such as Bernhard Leopold and Ludwig Kastl strongly supported the Köhler plan. The committee warned its members that that the SPD's support was merely a tactical maneuver and that the rank and file of the socialist labor movement shared the pathological hatred of Imbusch and Stegerwald for the educated. Nationalist civil servants were told that the business community rep-

---

71. *Zentralblatt*, 17 October 1927, pp. 277–79; *Der Deutsche*, 18 December 1927; *Der Ar-beiter (München)*, 27 October 1927, p. 1, and 17 November, p. 3; *Zentrumsprotokolle 1926–1933*, pp. 145–48, 158f.

72. Cabinet minutes of 3 December 1927, BAK R43I/1426/22f.; NL Marx/72/77–79, memoirs; *Zentrumsprotokolle 1926–1933*, pp. 162f.

73. *Zentralblatt*, 1 January 1928, pp. 1–3, and 1 February 1928, p. 30, and Clemens Lammers to Heinrich Imbusch, 8 December 1927, NL Marx/241/19–22.

resented their natural ally, while "every sort of democracy [i.e., both Christian and socialist] is in principle the enemy of the professional civil service."[74]

The civil service reform unleashed a storm of recriminations among Center Party leaders. In the spring of 1927 Marx had already broken off personal relations with his party's most enthusiastic defenders of cooperation with the SPD, Wirth and the Prussian welfare minister, Heinrich Hirtsiefer, a former vice-chairman of the Christian metalworkers' union. In September 1927 Marx angered the Christian miners' union by refusing to overturn a state artibrator's decree denying wage increases for the lignite mines of central Germany. Now Marx's support for the costly civil service bill made Imbusch regard every sign of opposition to union requests as proof of antiworker prejudice. Imbusch wrote his party chairman an extraordinarily rude letter on November 12, detailing his grievances and concluding that "you have absolutely no feeling for or intellectual grasp of social and economic matters." An indignant Marx refused to have any further dealings with the miners' leader.[75]

Meanwhile, organizations of Catholic civil servants accused Stegerwald and Imbusch of attempting to destroy their profession. When the League of Catholic Teachers threatened Marx that their members would desert the Center Party unless he publicly repudiated Stegerwald's stance, Marx replied privately on December 19 that he considered the agitation by "Stegerwald and a few union secretaries" utterly irresponsible. The recipients of the letter embarrassed Marx by publishing it, which produced a storm of protests from Catholic labor leaders who saw Marx playing the reactionaries' game of denying that unions represented anyone other than their own bureaucracy.[76] By now the conflict had proceeded so far as to generate intense concern among all thoughtful party leaders that class antagonisms might tear the Center to pieces. Stegerwald persuaded Imbusch to terminate his public attacks on Marx, and party leaders achieved a consensus of sorts by blaming Köhler for having ignored the cabinet's duty to avoid raising unrealistic expectations among civil servants.[77] The controversy produced mixed results for the DGB. It clearly improved morale among the membership, but it also permanently alienated politicians like Westarp and Marx, who themselves were jurists or civil servants.

74. Reichsausschuß der deutschnationalen Beamtenschaft, circulars of August and December 1927, StA Osnabrück C1/87/65–70. See also Döhn, pp. 268f.

75. Imbusch to Marx, 12 November 1927, NL Marx/241/8–12, and 241/4, memoirs; Becker, pp. 388–409.

76. See the documentation in NL Marx/241/24–54, and WAZ, 21 January 1928, p. 14, and 28 January, p. 21.

77. See NL Marx/241/32, 55f., Stegerwald to Marx, 12 January 1928, and Prelate Schofer to Marx, 16 January 1928, and *Zentrumsprotokolle 1926–1933*, pp. 171–73.

In the winter of 1927–28, deteriorating labor relations aggravated the class tensions in the bourgeois parties. An economic boom hit Germany early in 1927, pushing real wages up past the levels of 1913, and state labor arbitrators encouraged this trend. By the end of the year, however, the major employers' associations were determined to end the spiral of wage hikes and hours cuts because a chronic trade deficit persuaded them that hard times lay ahead. The Christian unions found it increasingly difficult to defend the system of state labor arbitration as businessmen denounced it for ruinous decrees while the ADGB claimed that workers could secure even greater wage increases without it.[78] In December 1927 Ruhr steel industrialists delayed implementation of a Labor Ministry decree reducing work hours by threatening to shut down their factories. Karl Dudey became involved in a bitter feud with the Duisburg leadership of the DNVP by petitioning the Labor Ministry on behalf of the Nationalist Workers' League to ignore the employers' objections. Count Westarp sternly warned him that the organizational autonomy of the DNAB did not justify such independent policy initiatives.[79] Meanwhile, within the DVP Otto Thiel and Hans Bechly were locked in polemics with the Reichstag delegate Otto Hugo, syndic of the Bochum chamber of commerce, over Hugo's demand that employers be given the right to undercut the wage level guaranteed in collective labor contracts if they faced bankruptcy.[80] Lockouts of tobacco workers and central German metalworkers frayed tempers further, and all of Labor Minister Brauns's moral authority and diplomatic skill were required to avert a massive strike by Ruhr miners in April 1928.[81] The Marx cabinet called for new elections in the spring of 1928 because the DVP, defending liberal principles concerning separation of church and state, could not agree with the Center Party and DNVP on a bill to establish confessional schools. This issue cannot be dismissed as a mere pretext, but it was of course highly significant that party leaders chose to focus attention on what was probably the only major issue on which Marx still agreed with Imbusch, and Hugo with Thiel.

In assessing the demise of the fourth Marx cabinet, the leaders of the GcG concluded glumly that the positive impact of each piece of welfare legislation on

78. See Hans-Hermann Hartwich, *Arbeitsmarkt, Verbände und Staat 1918–1933* (Berlin, 1967), pp. 146f., 292–305, and the petition to Chancellor Marx from the Verein der deutschen Arbeitgeberverbände, February 1928, BAK R43I/1157/130–33.

79. NL Westarp: Dudey to Labor Ministry, 10 December 1927; DNVP Landesverband Niederrhein (Meissner) to Westarp, 15 December 1927; and Westarp to Dudey, 16 December 1927. For background see Gerald Feldman and Irmgard Steinisch, "Notwendigkeit und Grenzen sozialstaatlicher Intervention," *Archiv für Sozialgeschichte*, 20 (1980), pp. 89–97.

80. Documentation in BAK R45II/58/459–501, and 69/43–47.

81. Cabinet minutes of 14 April, 20 April, and 3 May 1928, BAK R43I/1430/21f., 117f., 145f.; Chancellory memoranda on labor disputes, R43I/1157/126f., and 2176/118–20.

the working class had been more than offset by the hostile commentary of the bourgeois press, the confrontation tactics of employers in labor disputes, and the revival of elitism in the bureaucracy.[82] They correctly anticipated substantial gains by the SPD and KPD in the Reichstag election of May 1928 and called in advance for a revival of the Grand Coalition. This demand reflected a real convergence in outlook between the Christian and Free unions. In the years from 1925 to 1927 more and more Christian unionists agreed that no amount of social insurance could in itself guarantee true social equality for German workers. This goal required instead the dismantling of hierarchical structures in the bureaucracy and educational system, and above all greater influence for organized labor over management decisions and public policy. Thus the thinking of Christian workers came more and more to resemble that of the SPD and ADGB, which abandoned all discussion of the nebulous goal of socialism in 1927–28 so as to rally support for immediately attainable reforms designed to promote "economic democracy."[83] Because the DNVP would never support such fundamental reforms, more and more Christian trade unionists concluded that the strategy of encouraging moderation in it through participation in government was bankrupt, that the DNVP leadership had not learned enough since the end of the war to contribute constructively to the tasks of government. Even before the Hugenberg faction gained control of the DNVP late in 1928, the only significant difference over political strategy within the Christian unions pitted enthusiastic partisans of the Grand Coalition against those like Brüning, who hoped to engineer a schism of the DNVP in order to create a populist conservative alternative to the Grand Coalition.[84]

82. GcG circular of 8 March 1928, NL Otte/2/10f., and *Zentralblatt*, 15 March 1928, pp. 73f., and 1 May 1928, p. 126.
83. See Stegerwald's speeches of 25 January and 4 March 1928, NL Stegerwald/004/"1928"/ nos. 518 and 523; GcG Vorstand, 7 February 1928, NL Otte/7/178; Michael Schneider, *Die christlichen Gewerkschaften*, pp. 535–39; and Rudolf Kuda, "Das Konzept der Wirtschaftsdemokratie," in Vetter (ed.), pp. 253–74.
84. These strategic alternatives are discussed in Jakob Kaiser's speeches of December 1927, reprinted in Kosthorst, pp. 238–41, and early 1928, NL Kaiser/219, esp. pp. 16f.

5

The Backlash against Trade Unionism in the Bourgeois Parties

While the Reichstag election of May 1928 made a return to the Grand Coalition inevitable, it also made many leaders of the four major bourgeois parties more reluctant than ever to compromise with organized labor. The Center Party, DDP, DVP, and DNVP all suffered significant losses, but the election did not indicate any clear-cut shift to the left among voters. The SPD's modest gains were more than matched by those of the middle-class special interest parties, which polled 14% of the national vote. Most bourgeois politicians concluded that their support for progressive social legislation had alienated the middle classes without, as the Christian trade unionists had promised, attracting additional labor support. After much hesitation, both the Center Party and the DVP grudgingly consented to send one representative into a cabinet headed by the Social Democrat Hermann Müller, but they refused to draft a joint action program or to participate in the close consultation with partners normal for a coalition government.[1]

Even the leaders of the Christian trade unions initially displayed considerable ambivalence toward the Grand Coalition. They felt that the SPD and ADGB had deliberately fled from government responsibility in the mid-1920s in order to cultivate unrealistic expectations among workers and then defame the DGB leadership as capitalist lackeys when those expectations were not fulfilled. Müller requested Heinrich Brauns to stay on as labor minister, but many Christian union leaders urged him to leave office and compel the SPD to assume direct

1. Thomas Childers, *The Nazi Voter: The Social Foundations of Fascism in Germany, 1919–1933* (Chapel Hill and London, 1983), pp. 124–34, and Ilse Maurer, *Reichsfinanzen und Große Koalition* (Bern and Frankfurt am Main, 1973), pp. 36–39.

responsibility for social policy. They promptly attacked Brauns's successor, the Social Democrat Rudolf Wissell, for allegedly sharing the belief of reactionary industrialists that the state should disengage itself from labor arbitration and permit the "law of the jungle" to prevail.[2] Indeed, for some years the Free unions had sharply criticized state labor arbitration and any government interference in the process of industrial concentration, holding in accord with the teachings of Rudolf Hilferding that the emergence of trusts represented a step toward socialism. Nevertheless, Wissell made extraordinary efforts to encourage cooperation between the Free and Christian unions by defending the social institutions pioneered by Brauns. He persuaded the ADGB to endorse state labor arbitration with unprecedented clarity and won Otte's applause for his firm but tactful response to criticism of the system by employers.[3]

Wissell's conciliatory policy and the growing acceptance of state intervention in the economy by the Free unions encouraged the Christian unions to support the Grand Coalition more enthusiastically. By the fall of 1928 Stegerwald was perhaps its staunchest champion in the bourgeois parties, seconding Hermann Müller's appeal for the Center and DVP to strengthen their ties with his cabinet.[4] But their increasingly close agreement with the Free unions tended to undermine the influence of the Christian unions within the bourgeois parties. While describing the proceedings at the ADGB's national congress of September 1928, the *Zentralblatt* was more or less correct in claiming that Fritz Naphtali's report on economic democracy "basically contained nothing else but what the Christian unions have long been saying about the worker's share of responsibility and ownership in the economy [die Mitverantwortung und den Mitbesitz der Arbeiter in der Wirtschaft]." But the GcG organ became much less plausible when it sought to emphasize the remaining differences between the Free and Christian unions by claiming that the ADGB's "economic democracy" rested on acceptance of the "capitalist spirit," acceptance of the capitalist's claim that economic considerations must override all others, in contrast to the Christian unions' dedication to ethical principles.[5] This strident yet vague claim to be different doubtless reflected anxiety over the backlash against trade unionism that had begun to rock all four of the established bourgeois parties.

2. Mockenhaupt, pp. 245f.; GcG Vorstand, 24 May 1928, NL Otte/7/171f.; *Zentralblatt*, 15 July 1928, pp. 187f.
    3. GcG circular of 16 October 1928, NL Otte/2/52; Hartwich, pp. 340–46; Martiny, pp. 270–72. See also the reception for Wissell in GcG, *12. Kongreß 1929*, pp. 52, 69f.
    4. Chancellor's reception of 27 November 1928, *Akten der Reichskanzlei. Das Kabinett Müller II* (Boppard am Rhein, 1970), pp. 245–50.
    5. *Zentralblatt*, 1 October 1928, pp. 253–55.

THE RISE OF ALFRED HUGENBERG

The backlash against trade unionism had a great deal to do with class tensions and class prejudice, but not necessarily with class conflict in the strict sense. The most striking political defeat for the DGB, the election of Alfred Hugenberg as chairman of the DNVP in October 1928, was not, as many commentators assume, an example of German big business flexing its political muscle. In March 1928 Hugenberg succeeded, to be sure, in exploiting the financial weakness of the party to place his friends Paul Bang and Reinhold Quaatz in secure candidacies for the Reichstag, but his support for these doctrinaire nationalists, who had sought to split the Reich Association of Industry ever since it endorsed the Dawes Plan in 1924, promptly involved Hugenberg in a feud with leaders of big business that ended his control over contributions to the DNVP from Ruhr and Saxon industrialists. In Saxony the industrialist Walther Rademacher made common cause with the Christian trade unionist Georg Hartmann against the ideologue Bang.[6] However, Hugenberg cautiously refrained from direct attacks on the Christian Socials, who went to extraordinary lengths to avoid giving him grounds for complaint. Reinhard Mumm engaged the full weight of his prestige as the guardian of Stoecker's legacy to defend party unity against the many Pietists and Christian Socials who detested Hugenberg as an inflation profiteer, a militarist, and a freethinker who permitted immoral advertisements in his newspapers.[7] Mumm's willingness to offend potential allies for the sake of party unity refutes the claim later advanced by the Pan-Germans that the Christian Socials initiated the schism of the DNVP.

Count Westarp appreciated the Christian Socials' efforts and defended their desire to "preserve their holdings" against attacks from Pan-Germans and the Pomeranian Landbund.[8] Of the 20 leading Christian Socials and prominent moderates allied with them who had sat in the previous chamber, 6 failed to win reelection, a decline proportionate to that of the total delegation from 103 to 73 members. The only embarrassment suffered by the Christian Socials during the nomination process occurred when Emil Hartwig was forced to leave his Hessian

---

6. See Henry A. Turner, "The *Ruhrlade,* Secret Cabinet of Heavy Industry in the Weimar Republic," *Central European History,* 3 (September 1970), pp. 203–08, and NL Westarp, Rademacher to Westarp, 20 March and 3 April 1928.

7. NL Mumm/328/223f., Christian Social leadership conference of 2 December 1927, and Reinhard Mumm, "Christlich-sozial und deutschnational. Ein Wort gegen die Zersplitterungssucht," DNVP pamphlet no. 315. In private correspondence, on the other hand, Mumm admitted having serious policy differences with Hugenberg and questioned his good faith: Mumm to Henrich, 17 February and 19 March 1928, BAK Kleine Erwerbung 365, pp. 3–5.

8. NL Westarp, Westarp to von Rohr-Demmin, 16 March 1928.

electoral district and accept a nomination on the national list instead, a disturbing sign that laborites remained weak in DNVP locals.[9]

The balance of power within the party changed dramatically, however, after its share of the national vote declined from 20.5 to 14.2% in May 1928. A large majority of party activists, it appears, had always sympathized with Hugenberg's clear-cut policies but had held their inclinations in check because of Count Westarp's argument that they must compromise in order to broaden their electoral appeal. Now the Hugenberg press seized upon support for government coalitions and social legislation as the explanation for this defeat, and the bottom was knocked out of the moderates' case.[10] The tiny press enterprises of the DGB hotly denied these claims, asserting that the reactionary positions of the Hugenberg press and continued ties with the Yellow unions had robbed the DNVP of the popularity that its positive legislative record warranted.[11] The DNAB responded more cautiously with detailed statistical analysis. It partially confirmed Hugenberg's case by concluding that more than 1 million Nationalist voters had deserted to the special interest parties, as opposed to a flow of only about 300,000 working-class votes to the SPD. But the DNAB denied that these middle-class voters had repudiated the DNVP's participation in government coalitions—they had simply succumbed to a "materialistic" spirit that led them to exaggerate the economic benefits which they could secure through special interest parties. The DNAB argued that Nationalist workers deserved to be rewarded for their superior loyalty.[12]

The Nationalist Union of Commercial Employees displayed the most aggressive response to the growing influence of Pan-German elements in the DNVP. Relations between the DHV and the Pan-German League resembled in some ways the fratricidal struggle between the SPD and KPD. Closely allied with the league in the 1890s, the DHV leadership had decided after the turn of the century that it merely sought to exploit nationalist ideals in the service of big business. At the DHV's national congress on June 10, 1928, Hans Bechly delivered a scathing attack on "plutocratic" influences in all the bourgeois parties and concluded that trade unions represented a more authentic expression of the popular will. His syndicalist rhetoric and call for a new elite, based solely on

9. NL Westarp, Reichs-Angestellten-Ausschuß to Westarp 1 February 1928, and Emil Hartwig to DNVP Landesverband Hessen-Nassau, 14 March 1928; DNAB circular of 14 April 1928, StA Osnabrück C1/84/189–91.

10. See Karl Dietrich Bracher, *Die Auflösung der Weimarer Republik*, 5th ed. (Villingen, 1971), pp. 276–79, and Reinhard Behrens, pp. 2–4, 358–62.

11. *Zentralblatt*, 1 June 1928, pp. 142–4, and *Der Deutsche*, 5 June 1928, no. 130.

12. NL Westarp, DNAB memorandum of 12 June 1928, and Hannover Angestellten-Ausschuß to Westarp, 22 June 1928.

merit, to wrest control of Germany from the reactionary industrialists, landowners, and bureaucrats alarmed many DNVP leaders. Bechly also attacked Paul Bang by name for claiming that Germany could not continue to pay reparations unless it introduced a 14-hour workday: "If the man believes that, then he is stupid. If he is only saying that, then he is a demagogue!"[13]

Bechly's attitude reflected the fact that the DHV possessed much greater financial strength and above all appeal to youth than did the moribund DNVP party cadre.[14] As his contribution to the debate over the causes of the DNVP's defeat at the polls, Walther Lambach published the article "Monarchism" on June 14, 1928, in the *Politische Wochenschrift*, a magazine founded with financial support from the DHV.[15] All factions in the DNVP agreed that failure to attract youth constituted one of the party's gravest problems. Lambach argued that the election of Field Marshal von Hindenburg as president of the Republic had undermined the popular appeal of monarchism and that the thought of the Hohenzollerns' returning to rule Germany appeared ludicrous to the younger generation. He concluded that the DNVP should open its doors to "conservative republicans" by revising its platform plank on restoration of the monarchy.

The Hugenberg press prompty responded to Lambach's article by demanding his expulsion from the party. On July 24 the right-wing party local of Potsdam II, where Lambach resided, expelled him as a member for repudiating monarchism, for disloyalty to Bang in his dispute with Bechly, and for systematically betraying intimate party secrets to his superiors in the DHV. A DNVP court of honor had exonerated Lambach of the last charge in 1927, and Max Habermann of the DHV argued indignantly that Lambach could not be accused of spying when he maintained the same sort of political connections as any business or agrarian lobbyist, connections that had been most useful to the DNVP in the past.[16] However, Lambach had undoubtedly been tactless in reconciling his duties to the party and the DHV by annoying local leaders with such minor infractions as the use of speaking tours paid for by the party to conduct union business. Many Westarp loyalists also considered him a DHV agent rather than a proper liaison officer, but Westarp received so many threats of resignation from

13. Hans Bechly, "Die Führerfrage im neuen Deutschland" (Hamburg, 1928), esp. pp. 15–20, 23–27, and Bang to Lambach, 16 June 1928, NL Lambach/10/69f.
14. The average age of DHV members declined from 31.6 years in 1927 to 30.2 in 1928: see DHV, *Jahresbericht 1928*, p. 249.
15. Reprinted in Dörr, pp. 554–56.
16. Ibid., pp. 401–09, and Max Habermann, "Querverbindungen," in *Deutsche Handels-Wacht*, 25 July 1928. Regarding Lambach's exoneration in 1927 of charges by his former secretary, Paul Krellmann, see the documentation in NL Lambach/8.

moderate Reichstag delegates who supported Lambach that he decided to suppress the Potsdam verdict.[17]

Lambach later claimed that the furor over his article came as a complete surprise to him, but there can be little doubt that he and other DHV leaders, unlike the Christian Socials, already contemplated splitting the DNVP if that would help weaken the Pan-German League.[18] Public controversy over the Lambach affair raged throughout July and August. The Pan-German *Deutsche Zeitung* escalated the conflict by arguing that Lambach must be expelled even if he retracted his statements on monarchism because the trade unions he represented had for years sought to make the DNVP compromise with the parliamentary system, undermining the party's raison d'être.[19] But Lambach was defended by the organ of the Reichslandbund and other moderately conservative journals such as the *Deutsche Allgemeine Zeitung* and the *Berliner Börsen-Zeitung*. At the end of August the DNVP's court of honor overturned the Potsdam verdict despite a threat from Hugenberg that such action would "kindle a flame of dissension that could no longer be extinguished."[20]

Hugenberg's circle displayed an almost hysterical fear of the DGB in the summer of 1928, grossly exaggerating its political influence.[21] This attitude probably resulted from the disintegration of the Yellow unions. They lost three of their four Reichstag delegates and four of their five Prussian parliamentary delegates in the elections of 1928, losses stemming largely from feuds in which the Yellow leaders destroyed one another's reputations. In November 1927 Wilhelm Schmidt had expelled the treasurer of his Federation of Patriotic Workers' Unions, his colleague in the DNVP Prussian parliamentary delegation, Fritz Wiedemann. Wiedemann founded a rival organization and published exposures of financial corruption in the federation.[22] In the spring of 1928 even Paul Bang was forced to repudiate Schmidt and to announce that his League for Nationalist

17. NL Westarp, Westarp to Treviranus, 30 July 1928.
18. See the contradictory assessments of Lambach's intentions in Dörr, pp. 394–97, Behrens, pp. 113f., and Erasmus Jonas, *Die Volkskonservativen 1928–1933* (Düsseldorf, 1965), pp. 33f. An anonymous memorandum of 10 October 1928, apparently written for Lambach by a DHV colleague, charged that Center Party leaders were seeking to make peace in the DNVP in order to prevent competition from a new conservative republican party, which had from the beginning been "the goal desired by us": "Die Stellung des Zentrums im 'Falle Lambach,' " NL Lambach/10/25–27.
19. "Aufschluß und Ausschluß," clipping from the *Deutsche Zeitung* of 4 August 1928 in NL Lambach/10/49–51.
20. Dörr, pp. 412–25, and NL Westarp, Hugenberg to Westarp, 14 August 1928.
21. See "Der Mann—Die Sache," from the "Schnelldienst" of 26 July 1928, a supplement to the DNVP's official *Korrespondenz* that was controlled by Hugenberg (NL Lambach/10/53–55), and NL Westarp, Freytagh-Loringhoven to Westarp, 12 September 1928.
22. See the contradictory accounts in *Deutsche Werksgemeinschaft* (Schmidt), issues of 27 November 1927, 4 December 1927, and 19 February 1928, and Wiedemann's *Kapital und Arbeit*, 11 December 1927 and 3 September 1928.

Economics would henceforth endorse none of the existing company unions but work instead for the fundamental transformation of society without which the ideal of harmony between management and labor, of the *Werksgemeinschaft*, could never be realized.[23] The breach between Schmidt and Wiedemann hopelessly divided whatever groups of Yellow industrial workers remained in the DNVP.

The Yellow Reich farmworkers' league of Johannes Wolf also fell apart in 1928. The onset of the agricultural depression in Germany at the end of 1927 promoted unrest among East Elbian farmworkers. Even Wolf warned landowners repeatedly that low wages and the harsh treatment of workers were seriously undermining the "solidarity of the rural populace." Moreover, Wolf failed to make any progress in his efforts to win government recognition, and many of his associates felt hampered by their inability to represent members before the increasingly important state labor courts.[24] By the end of 1927 Franz Behrens had established friendly relations with his Reichstag colleague Paul Giese, head of the Yellow farmworkers' league of Brandenburg. Behrens persuaded the Ministry of Agriculture to include the Brandenburg league, but not its Pomeranian associate, in the ministry's program of modest subsidies to farmworkers' unions for educational purposes. In March 1928, at a sensitive stage in the nominations process, Wolf wrote Westarp to report the "possibility" that Giese had embezzled these funds for his personal use. The charge proved groundless but sufficed to sabotage Giese's candidacy.[25] Electoral losses by the DNVP in May then helped persuade landowners in Brandenburg of the political value of the Christian farmworkers' union. In August 1928 Giese signed a merger agreement with the Christian farmworkers' union that left Wolf's organization with almost no followers outside Pomerania.[26] Although the Christian farmworkers' union won only a small fraction of Giese's 15,000 nominal followers as permanent members, these developments marked the demise of Yellow unionism as a nationwide movement that could claim parity with the DGB in the bourgeois parties.

Although Christian Social leaders in the DNVP made concessions on policy matters for the sake of party unity, they quietly reminded all party comrades in

23. *Deutsche Werksgemeinschaft*, 15 April 1928.
24. *Der Reichslandarbeiterbund*, 1 January 1928, p. 5, 15 January, pp. 9–11, and 1 February 1928, pp. 17–19. For background see Dieter Gessner, *Agrarverbände in der Weimarer Republik* (Düsseldorf, 1976), pp. 83–96, and Hildebrandt, pp. 112–18.
25. NL Westarp: Paul Giese to DNVP Ehrenrat, 18 March 1928, Wolf to Westarp, 22 March and 4 April 1928, and Westarp to Wolf, 26 March and 2 April 1928.
26. DNVP Kreisverein Angermünde to DNAB, 28 July 1928, ZStA/DNVP/166/130f.; *Der Deutsche*, 8 August and 11 August 1928; *Der Reichslandarbeiterbund*, 15 August 1928, pp. 121f.; Hildebrandt, pp. 75–77.

the summer and fall of 1928 that wage- and salary-earners represented a growing and ever more influential segment of the electorate, and that the DNVP could influence them only through a long-term alliance with the DGB. Christian Social leaders claimed in particular that the DNVP enjoyed substantially more support from blue-collar workers in the provinces of East Prussia and Lower Silesia, where it cooperated with the Christian unions, than in either Pomerania or Brandenburg, and linear regression analysis of the election results substantiates this claim.[27] The collapse of the Yellow unions made such arguments unanswerable except through rejection of parliamentary politics and rule by the majority. This explains the growing radicalism of Hugenberg, Bang, and Freytagh-Loringhoven, specifically their frequent warnings that the DNVP must be prepared to become a much smaller party for the sake of ideological purity. Many reactionaries who had persuaded themselves that the trade union bureaucracy could someday be discredited in the eyes of ordinary workers were beginning to face the grim fact that their social and economic policies could never win the support of a popular majority.

Westarp's role in suppressing the expulsion verdict against Lambach shifted the focus of Pan-German criticism to the alleged weakness of the DNVP leadership. At the beginning of October 1928 the Pan-Germans began to agitate for separation of the office of party chairman from the leadership of the Reichstag delegation. Following the advice of Treviranus, Walther Lambach requested the Christian Socials to support the reelection of Westarp to both offices as "the

27. Otto Apitz to Wilhelm Lindner, 24 April and 21 May 1928, ZStA/DNVP/210/18–21; DNVP Kreisverein Königsberg to DNAB, 20 July 1928, and reply of 6 August, DNVP/176/89f.; Wilhelm Lindner to DNVP Kreisverein Mansfelder Seekreis, 15 November 1928, DNVP/170/81; NL Mumm/117/315–17, Weiss to Emil Hartwig, 19 November 1928, and reply of 20 November. The following table gives the results of linear regression analysis correlating the census figures in *Statistik des Deutschen Reiches*, vol. 403, with the DNVP vote in vols. 315 and 372, expressed in terms of Pearson's r:

	East Prussia	Lower Silesia	Brandenburg	Pomerania
Dec. 1924				
Farmworkers	.407	.700	.647	.592
Other blue-collar	−.484	−.781	−.888	−.755
1928				
Farmworkers	.584	.773	.745	.646
Other blue-collar	−.613	−.780	−.886	−.997

The figures for Pomerania in particular suggest the strongest possible aversion for the DNVP among all workers not directly under the influence of Nationalist landowners.

strongest opponent of our enemies."[28] Westarp refused to stand for reelection, however, when Hugenberg insisted on campaigning for the party chairmanship, allowing Hugenberg to win an easy victory at the DNVP national committee meeting of October 20. Westarp's resignation has puzzled some commentators but doubtless reflected a realistic assessment of Hugenberg's popularity among the party faithful.[29] Westarp then agreed to serve under Hugenberg as head of the DNVP Reichstag delegation. Hartwig, Lindner, and Rüffer of the DNAB also pledged to follow their new leader as long as he respected the basic principles of the party program. The Christian Socials and the Westarp loyalists in the party resigned themselves to a period of waiting for Hugenberg to be discredited by the sterility of his political program.[30]

THE CRISIS OF POLITICAL CATHOLICISM

Developments within the Bavarian People's Party (Bayerische Volkspartei, BVP) in 1928 spread fears among Catholic workers that the antilabor backlash in the DNVP would spread into the ranks of political Catholicism. The BVP committed itself during the election campaign not to form a coalition with the SPD in the provincial parliament under any circumstances. The harshly antisocialist and antirepublican stance of Cardinal Faulhaber, archbishop of Munich, encouraged the party leadership to treat this policy as a matter of religious principle, although it was prepared under certain conditions to support the Grand Coalition in distant Berlin.[31] The provincial elections greatly strengthened the Bavarian Peasants' League, which demanded the dissolution of the Bavarian Social Ministry in order to reduce government expenses as the condition for a coalition with the BVP. This ministry had been led by the Christian trade unionist Heinrich Oswald ever since its creation in 1920, and Catholic labor leaders in Bavaria had repeatedly promised their followers that the BVP would never permit the "reactionaries" to dismantle it. Monsignor Carl Walterbach and the Bavarian Catholic workers' clubs implored the BVP to consider a provincial coalition with the SPD, but in July 1928 the party capitulated to the demands of the right. Oswald became head of an autonomous department within the Ministry of Agriculture

28. NL Westarp, Lambach to Otto Rippel and Wilhelm Koch, 11 October 1928.
29. See Dörr, pp. 442–64, and Jonas, pp. 40f.
30. DNAB, *Deutsche Angestelltenstimme und Arbeiterstimme*, November 1928, p. 1; *Der Deutsche*, 23 October 1928.
31. Schönhoven, *Die Bayerische Volkspartei*, pp. 203–11, and Ludwig Volk, *Der bayerische Episkopat und der Nationalsozialismus 1930–1934* (Mainz, 1966), pp. 5–7.

and Commerce but lost his vote in the cabinet.[32] This defeat gravely undermined the credibility of Christian labor leaders in Bavaria.

During the election campaign of 1928, Stegerwald, Brüning, and Jakob Kaiser sought above all to reduce the social tensions in the Center Party generated during the controversy over civil service reform. Stegerwald crowned his efforts on behalf of party unity by securing a candidacy on the Reich list for his former adversary, the maverick Joseph Wirth, after the Baden Center refused to renominate him. Stegerwald's quiet efforts behind the scenes gave the Center Reichstag delegation a higher proportion of union officials than that of the SPD, increasing its number of laborites from 13 to 15 despite a decline in its overall size from 69 to 62.[33] Nevertheless, the leaders of the Christian miners' union bitterly resented the fact that several "labor representatives" in the Center Reichstag delegation were relatively docile functionaries of the Catholic workers' clubs, and they believed that Stegerwald should have opposed the renomination of Wilhelm Marx and purged the party of all "reactionary" civil servants. The miners suspected that Stegerwald and his lieutenant Kaiser were so blinded by political ambition that they no longer represented working-class interests.[34] Heinrich Imbusch, much like Hans Bechly, was encouraged to demand a greater leadership role for the Christian unions because they possessed far greater financial strength, appeal to youth, and hence better prospects for the future than did either the Catholic workers' clubs or the Center Party organization. He raised unrealistic demands that would have torn his party to pieces, however, prompting Wirth to label him a "syndicalist."[35]

32. See the commentary in the organ of the Bavarian Catholic workers' clubs, *Der Arbeiter (München)*, 26 July 1928, pp. 1f., 2 August, p. 1, 9 August, pp. 1f., and 20 December 1928, p. 1.
33. WAZ, 17 March 1928; Frey, pp. 108f; Becker, pp. 420–23. According to Michael Schneider, *Die christlichen Gewerkschaften*, p. 630, 24.6% of the Center Reichstag delegates were union functionaries vs. 18.4% of the SPD's.
34. See the typescript protocol, "Geschlossene Sitzung des Gewerkvereins," 14 May 1928, NL Imbusch/4.
35. Joseph Wirth, "Wohin Freund Imbusch?" *Deutsche Republik*, 17 (February 1928). Contrast the figures on age of membership compiled by the Catholic workers' clubs of western Germany with those available for the Christian unions:

	Year	Under 26	26–35	36–45	Over 45
Catholic clubs	1929	7.2%	18.4%	28.5%	45.9%
Construction workers	1927	34.8	23.3	16.8	25.1
	1930	33.8	25.7	15.6	24.9
Woodworkers	1925	39.2	19.5	17.6	23.6
Metalworkers	1921	46.4	18.1	16.0	19.5
	1924	40.7	18.8	17.7	22.8

See Katholische Arbeiter-Bewegung Westdeutschlands, *Bericht über die Jahre 1925–31* (Mönchen-Gladbach, 1931), p. 57; Zentralverband christlicher Bauarbeiter, *Geschäftsbericht des Vorstandes*

The results of the May Reichstag election generated intense fears among Center Party leaders that their party might disintegrate along class lines. Even the relatively modest decline of the Center/BVP vote from 17.4 to 15.2% proved alarming because it marked the resumption of a long-term downward trend that had been interrupted in 1919–24 by the introduction of women's suffrage.[36] The party's losses were concentrated in the large industrial cities of western Germany, where the SPD and KPD made dramatic gains. This coincidence led some die-hard "integralists" to claim that the social doctrines of the Volksverein had finally been proved powerless to inoculate Catholic workers against Marxism, but the available evidence indicates that the Center's losses in these cities came more from the middle classes than from workers.[37]

Stegerwald reacted to the election results by reviving his old project for consolidation of the moderate parties. He argued that an exaggerated stress on confessional bonds had caused the Center's decline, and that the party must devote itself to forging a comprehensive program for economic reform and the stabilization of parliamentary democracy. Serving as interim leader of the Center Reichstag delegation because of Marx's poor health, he announced that the party congress scheduled for the end of the year would commence the process of transforming the Center into a "great Christian people's and state party [grosse christliche Volks- und Staatspartei]."[38] The great majority of Center Party activists apparently agreed with Joseph Joos, however, that the party must redouble its emphasis on confessional bonds and Catholic values in the face of the disturbing trend toward "materialism," toward intensifying class conflict, in society at large. Joos argued that only a religious revival could convince younger Catholic workers that the SPD was unsuitable while regaining for the Center the support of middle-class Catholics who had defected to the DNVP or the splinter parties.[39]

Developments within the Catholic Church soon convinced even Stegerwald that aggressive pursuit of an interconfessional party might cripple the Christian labor movement by strengthening reactionary currents in the Catholic clergy. In

---

für die Jahre 1928–1930, p. 45; *1899–1924. Ein Vierteljahrhundert Zentralverband christlicher Holzarbeiter*, pp. 16f.; and Christlicher Metallarbeiterverband, *Bericht des Verbands-Vorstandes, 1922–1924*, p. 120.

36. See Johannes Schauff, "Die Schicksalskurve der Zentrumspartei. Akute und chronische Krise," memorandum from the summer of 1928 for Center Party leaders, reprinted in Johannes Schauff, *Das Wahlverhalten der deutschen Katholiken im Kaiserreich und in der Weimarer Republik*, Rudolf Morsey, ed. (Mainz, 1975), pp. 191–204.

37. *Der Fels. Monatsschrift für Gebildete aller Stände*, June 1928, pp. 322f. (NL Marx/75); Plum, p. 19; Kühr, pp. 248–50; and Graf, p. 34.

38. *Germania*, 2 July 1928, no. 300. See also Frey, pp. 105f., and Stegerwald's speech of 24 September 1928 in NL Stegerwald/004/"1928"/no. 539.

39. *WAZ*, 22 September 1928, p. 230. See also Johannes Albers, "Zur heutigen Lage des Kölner Katholizismus," speech of 22 June 1928, KAB Archiv, and Stump, pp. 71–73.

the mid-1920s Pope Pius XI had withdrawn Vatican support for the Italian Christian trade unions and Popularist Party, acquiescing to their suppression by the Fascist regime. As these autonomous, lay-administered organizations for Italian Catholics disappeared, the Vatican revived the frankly hierarchical Catholic Action to supervise the participation of Catholics in public life. [40] In 1928 the Vatican discreetly indicated to the German episcopate that it desired to extend Catholic Action north of the Alps, as it prepared for a difficult round of negotiations with the Prussian government over a concordat. The decision apparently reflected discontent with the Prussian Center's long-term coalition with the SPD. [41] At the annual congress of German Catholics in September 1928, the papal nuncio, Cardinal Pacelli, proclaimed the establishment of Catholic Action in Germany as a movement independent of political parties. Even before this development, Joseph Joos and August Pieper, the retired director of the Volksverein, had warned Christian union leaders that a majority of Catholic priests might turn their backs on the Center Party, parliamentary democracy, and social reform, succumbing to nostalgia for the medieval social hierarchy. [42] The harm that such a development might do the Christian labor movement far outweighed the potential gain from an interconfessional party.

Cardinal Pacelli promised German Catholics that Catholic Action would not supplant any of their existing organizations but merely seek to coordinate their activities more effectively. His remarks were hopelessly vague, however, concerning relations between the clergy and laity and between Catholic Action and the existing political parties. [43] While Martin Spahn's Committee of Catholics in the DNVP concluded that Catholic Action meant a quota of leadership posts for them in all Catholic organizations, Wilhelm Marx struck a blow for the Center Party with speeches explaining that Catholic Action, while "nonpartisan" in character, sought above all to "restore the political unity of German Catholics." [44] In the official explanation of Catholic Action for the clerical supervisors of the Catholic workers' clubs of western Germany, Johannes Gickler declared its chief enemy to be the heresy of "laicism," "the steadily growing desire to declare

40. See Richard Webster, *The Cross and the Fasces* (Stanford, 1960).
41. Focke, pp. 151–54. Köhler, *Lebenserinnerungen*, pp. 287–90, reports that the pope received him on the eve of the Reichstag election of 1928 to complain that the Center Party neglected spiritual values in its pursuit of material welfare for the masses. Contrast Stewart Stehlin, *Weimar and the Vatican 1919–1933* (Princeton, 1983), pp. 335–43, who accepts at face value the Vatican's claim never to have interfered in German domestic affairs.
42. Teilnachlaß Pieper, vol. 5, pp. 1014–20, 1139–46, and *WAZ*, 1 September 1928, p. 212, and 22 September, pp. 230f.
43. See Stegerwald to Heinrich Brauns, 11 September 1928, NL Stegerwald/014/Nachtrag no. 11.
44. *Germania*, 1 November 1928, no. 509, and *Kölnische Volkszeitung*, 11 December 1928, no. 895.

the absolute autonomy of all spheres of human social life and to reduce religion and the Church to the role of mere spectator." This statement from the man chosen by the conservative Cardinal Hartmann in the turbulent summer of 1918 to succeed Otto Müller in the club leadership almost sounded like a declaration of war on the Christian unions, but Gickler hastened to add that "laicism" must be combated in a democratic spirit that sought to involve the whole lay populace in the priestly office. Pieper observed sardonically that Catholic Action was "only a slogan imposed by the Pope, which has caught the leaders of German Catholicism by surprise."[45] The leaders and allies of the Christian unions were alarmed, however, because the proclamation of Catholic Action coincided with a financial crisis in the Volksverein, the traditional defender of lay autonomy and ecumenicism among German Catholics. In September 1928 it was compelled to request the Prussian episcopate to authorize a special Church collection on its behalf. DGB leaders had raised nearly RM 1.5 million in an unsuccessful effort to make this request unnecessary. As they had foreseen, it prompted a painful discussion of the Volksverein's disregard for episcopal authority in the past. The bishops insisted on adding representatives of other Catholic organizations to the Volksverein executive committee so that it could function as a clearing house for Catholic Action. In private talks with Center Party leaders, Heinrich Brauns responded by denouncing Catholic Action as dangerously similar to prewar integralism.[46]

The public learned little about the disputes among prominent Catholics over the meaning of Catholic Action, but class tensions within the Catholic populace erupted into open conflict at the Center Party congress of December 8–9, 1928. Wilhelm Marx had announced his imminent retirement as party chairman in October and privately requested the head of the Rhenish Center, Mönnig, to explore sentiment in the provinces concerning the two most serious candidates to replace him, Stegerwald and Joos.[47] After the Center Reichstag delegation privately endorsed Stegerwald in mid-November, Christian union leaders considered his election inevitable, in accord with Center Party traditions of deference to the parliamentary leadership. On November 26 Mönnig reported to Marx, however, that almost all leaders of party locals rejected Stegerwald and

---

45. *Mitteilungen an die Präsides der Arbeitervereine* (Volksverein Bibliothek), January/March 1929, pp. 3f.; Pieper to Stegerwald, 14 January 1929, NL Stegerwald/014/Nachtrag no. 14.

46. Emil Ritter, pp. 447–60; Teilnachlaß Pieper, vol. 5, p. 1108; NL Marx/74/45, memoir on a conference of 22 September 1928 with Brauns, Stegerwald, Giesberts, and Vockel. Stegerwald described his fund-raising activities, which were kept secret in order to avoid charges of "ultramontanism," to "Ew. Hochwürden" (an unnamed prelate), 27 December 1928, NL Stegerwald/014/Nachtrag no. 12.

47. Marx to Mönnig, 24 October 1928, NL Marx/247.

wanted "a man who stands outside all economic and class struggles." Mönnig suggested Monsignor Ludwig Kaas and one other prelate as possibilities.[48] Stegerwald realized that he had many enemies in the party, especially among civil servants. He requested Marx to remain chairman or to permit him to stay home with a "political illness," thus avoiding the embarrassment of rejection by the convention. At the same time, he made it clear that he would not resign from his union offices and devote himself full-time to party work unless he were chosen, like Marx, to head both the party and its Reichstag delegation. The executive committee of the Center Party secured Stegerwald's participation in the convention, where he was scheduled to deliver the main policy address, by endorsing his candidacy for both offices with 15 votes for Stegerwald and 13 abstentions.[49]

An anti-Stegerwald alliance between the Catholic workers' clubs and the leaders of party locals emerged as the Center's larger national committee convened on December 7. Half the committee members were civil servants or academics, and many who rejected Stegerwald were willing to support Joos because of his conciliatory personality and close ties with the episcopate. After a stormy meeting, the committee voted 120 to 40 in favor of a resolution by Monsignor Otto Müller to separate the party chairmanship from that of the Reichstag delegation, contrary to Stegerwald's wishes.[50] The tenor of the proceedings infuriated the Christian trade unionists present. Jakob Kaiser later reported that the head of the Bonn party local stated that "with Stegerwald as chairman, the party would become a workers' party, and we don't want that." The clerical supervisor of the Catholic civil servants' clubs appeared at the meeting, although not a committee member, to claim that Stegerwald's election would prove a hindrance to Catholic Action. When the Center's executive committee reconvened to make a new nomination, this time for the office of party chairman alone, the first candidate discussed was Joseph Joos. The laborites Giesberts, Hirtsiefer, Kloft, Elfes, and Kaiser indignantly rejected this suggestion as a backhanded maneuver against the foremost representative of Christian workers, and they left the meeting in protest. The remaining committee members could not agree on a single candidate and accepted a suggestion by Heinrich Brüning that they request authority from the party congress to appoint a triumvirate.[51]

48. NL Marx/247/18, and Kosthorst, p. 249.
49. NL Marx/247/11, 21/23: Mönnig to Marx, 5 November 1928, Stegerwald to Marx, 30 November 1928, and Marx's memoir, "Mein Rücktritt vom Vorsitz der Partei."
50. Wachtling, pp. 126–29, and *WAZ*, 8 December 1928, pp. 295f.
51. See Kaiser's memorandum of 12 January 1929, reprinted in Kosthorst, pp. 249–53, as well as NL Marx/74/48, autobiographical MS.

Stegerwald ignored this drama behind the scenes when he opened the party congress on December 8, staunchly defending the Grand Coalition while explaining the Center's differences with the SPD concerning the construction of a pocket battleship and the reform of unemployment insurance. He nevertheless suffered a humiliating defeat at the day's end, when the convention rejected the executive committee's triumvirate proposal and conducted instead a secret ballot that returned only 42 votes for Stegerwald as chairman against 92 for Joos and 184 for Kaas, an expert on canon law and foreign affairs not associated with any party faction.[52] Kaas became the first clergyman to head the Center Party. As Joseph Wirth observed, Stegerwald was the victim of a tragic misunderstanding. The middle-class members of the Center Party still viewed him as a partisan laborite despite the fact that he had devoted his political career to forging a balanced economic policy in consultation with industrial and agrarian leaders, even at the risk of seriously alienating his union followers.[53] Indeed, the leading representatives of agricultural and business interests in the Center Party, including Carl Herold of the Christian peasants' leagues, the artisan Thomas Esser, and Rudolf ten Hompel and Clemens Lammers, supported Stegerwald's candidacy,[54] but the uneasy feeling lingered on the floor of the convention that he somehow stood for the dictatorship of the proletariat.[55]

On the morning after the election of Kaas, an angry meeting of labor leaders called by Giesberts announced plans for a mass rally in Essen on December 16 to discuss the future relationship between the Center Party and the Christian labor movement. The *Deutsche* accused Marx and Mönnig of a conspiracy to sabotage Stegerwald's candidacy. The DGB organ linked Stegerwald's defeat with the Lambach affair and the dissolution of the Bavarian Social Ministry as evidence of a bourgeois backlash against trade unionism and warned that the Catholic Church would suffer irreparable damage if it permitted the slogan of Catholic Action to be misused by foes of the labor movement.[56] But the rejection of a trade unionist as party chairman could not be equated with rejection of trade unionism as such. Swallowing his pride, Stegerwald repudiated the *Deutsche's*

52. Deutsche Zentrumspartei, 5. *Reichsparteitag 1928*, pp. 16–44.

53. Joseph Wirth, "'Parteirevolution.' Der Fall Stegerwald," *Deutsche Republik*, 28 December 1928, pp. 385–88.

54. See *Kölnische Volkszeitung*, 12 December 1928, no. 897, and ten Hompel to Lammers, 29 November 1928, NL ten Hompel/29. Ten Hompel wrote that some businessmen in the Center would oppose Stegerwald, but that it was better to have an "energetic chairman with clear goals, even if he sometimes makes mistakes, than a man without initiative."

55. See Carl Bachem to Müller-Fulda, 10 December 1928, and reply of 13 December, in Erich Matthias and Rudolf Morsey (eds.), *Das Ende der Parteien 1933*, Athenäum ed. (Düsseldorf, 1979), pp. 419f. See also Deutz, pp. 118–24.

56. *Der Deutsche*, 11 December and 13 December 1928, and "Arbeiterbeirat der rheinischen Zentrumspartei," circular of 10 December 1928, NL Kaiser/247.

charges and criticized the elitist tendency of followers who claimed that the Center must accept him as chairman just because the leaders of its Reichstag delegation supported him. As the Essen rally convened, Stegerwald insisted that all present accept the election of Kaas as the democratic will of the party.[57]

The rally of December 16 nevertheless signaled a revived militance in the Christian unions. Now Heinrich Imbusch secured an audience for his tough rhetoric that extended well beyond the Christian miners' union. Imbusch declared that workers speaking to party meetings must not imitate academics or deliver sermonettes, so as to avoid offense to middle-class listeners. He exhorted Christian workers in all party locals to display more "will to power."[58] Stegerwald also delivered a speech on sociological trends much sharper in tone than his remarks to the party congress. Since 70% of the German work force had become wage- and salary-earners, he argued, "the 20th century will be formed primarily by the workers." The Center Party had ignored this fact by choosing only 44 workers among the 488 delegates to its congress, one-third of whom could not even attend for financial reasons. Stegerwald warned that if the Center did not reform itself, "nobody can prevent the party I described eight years ago at the Essen Congress of the Christian unions from becoming a reality."[59] Stegerwald nevertheless emphasized that the Christian unions would be happy to cooperate with the predominantly Catholic Center Party if it adopted the appropriate policies. The DGB did not insist on an interconfessional party but demanded only that both Catholic and Protestant workers have a chance to participate in some party with a progressive social program. This speech marked a shift in DGB strategy toward the plan of nurturing a distinctively Protestant party that would cooperate with the Center in the Reichstag, reflecting a new appreciation of the importance of conciliating the Catholic clergy.[60]

The Essen rally alarmed the leaders of the Center Party and Catholic workers' clubs, who at first accused the Christian unions of adopting socialist methods of agitation. Indeed, Joseph Joos embraced the "idealistic" stance of the many bourgeois Catholics who argued that the need to secure the best qualified party leaders outweighed the Christian unions' desire to secure a quota of labor representatives in leadership organs commensurate with the proportion of workers in the rank and file. But tempers soon cooled on both sides. A series of local

---

57. Morsey, *Zentrumsprotokolle 1926–33*, pp. 250f., meeting of 14 December 1928, and Adam Stegerwald, "Zentrumspartei, Arbeiterschaft, Volk und Staat," speech of 16 December 1928 (Berlin, no date), p. 3.

58. Complete text in NL Imbusch/4.

59. Stegerwald, "Zentrumspartei, Arbeiterschaft, Volk und Staat," pp. 7f., 17.

60. Ibid., pp. 9–11. See also Deutz, pp. 113–16.

meetings between representatives of the unions and the workers' clubs culminated on January 5, 1929, in a summit conference, where Joos solemnly promised Jakob Kaiser that the clubs would insist that Catholic Action never be misused to restrict the "autonomy of the labor movement."[61] Ludwig Kaas declared repeatedly that he would follow the political guidelines laid down in Stegerwald's report to the party congress. In a confidential appeal, Kaas even promised that, if Stegerwald accepted the chairmanship of the Center Reichstag delegation for the sake of party unity, "I would strive earnestly to pass the party chairmanship into your hands as soon as the current divisions are overcome or sufficiently reduced." On January 25, 1929, Stegerwald ended the party's leadership crisis to the satisfaction of all by accepting the chairmanship of the Reichstag delegation and announcing that he would resign from his union offices in order to devote himself to party work.[62] In April he entered Hermann Müller's cabinet as transport minister, with Joseph Wirth as minister of occupied territories, and Heinrich Brüning soon succeeded him as head of the Center Reichstag delegation.

THE RUHR LOCKOUT OF NOVEMBER 1928

Stegerwald's reconciliation with the Center Party was encouraged by a major labor dispute that demonstrated the value of the Christian unions' traditional relationship with political Catholicism. Responding with sharply increased militance to the accession of a Social Democratic labor minister, the steel industrialists of the Ruhr locked out more than 200,000 workers on November 1, 1928, rather than accept a binding arbitration decree that imposed wage hikes of 2–3%. The leadership of the Christian metalworkers' union already feared that the moderates in Ruhr industry willing to deal with the trade unions, a group they identified with the Catholics Silverberg and Peter Klöckner, had been eclipsed by the reactionaries who longed for a dictatorship.[63] Now both the Christian and the socialist metalworkers' unions denounced the lockout as an illegal act of defiance against the state. The venerable Franz Wieber drove himself to the point of physical collapse by delivering impassioned speeches against the indus-

61. KAB Archiv, KAB circular of 31 December 1928, and Reichsvorstand, 18 January 1929; *WAZ*, 12 January 1929, pp. 7–9, and 19 January, p. 15.

62. Kaas to Stegerwald, 9 January 1929, NL Stegerwald/014/Nachtrag no. 13, and *Kölnische Volkszeitung*, 7 January 1929, no. 15, and 26 January, no. 65.

63. *Der Deutsche Metallarbeiter*, 15 January 1927, p. 35, and 17 December 1927, p. 801. For background see Weisbrod, pp. 415–24, also suspicious of the Ruhr industrialists, and Feldman and Steinisch, "Notwendigkeit und Grenzen sozialstaatlicher Intervention," esp. pp. 89–91, who stress their moderation.

trialists, charging that they hoped to overthrow the system of collective bargaining and perhaps parliamentary democracy as well.[64]

The speeches by Wieber, a pious Knight of the Order of St. Gregory, the only German trade unionist to receive a papal decoration, made an enormous impression on public opinion. All along the Rhine and Ruhr young priests active in the Catholic workers' clubs embraced Wieber's arguments in the pulpit and the press, provoking indignant but futile protests to their bishops by Catholic businessmen.[65] On November 15 the senior clergy of Essen published a statement flatly condemning the lockout as immoral and unjustified by any legitimate economic interest. Lest there be any further misunderstanding of the Church's position, Cardinal Schulte of Cologne sent his subordinates in Essen a telegram expressing his "gratitude for your conscientious investigation of the true causes of this unfortunate conflict" and promising that the Church would devote itself to raising funds for the victims of the lockout.[66] This stance contrasted sharply with that of the consistory of the Evangelical Church of Rhineland-Westphalia, which rejected a proworker statement drafted by the Christian Socials and declared instead: "It cannot be the task of a Church organ to decide the rights and wrongs of economic policies or the feasibility of economic demands.[67]

The Ruhr lockout resulted in a political debacle for heavy industry despite the fact that the courts partially vindicated its position by striking down the Labor Ministry's practice of declaring arbitration decrees binding even if neither party in the dispute accepted them. The Center Reichstag delegation acted vigorously in conjunction with the SPD to pass a law on November 17 providing welfare payments for the lockout victims, to be administered by the Prussian government. Public feeling ran so high that even the DVP accepted the bill. Prussian Welfare Minister Heinrich Hirtsiefer, a former official of the Christian metalworkers' union, then decreed that the funds would be distributed without a means test, despite demands by industrialists that workers receiving union benefits should have their payments reduced. The industrial associations and their allies in the DVP and DNVP had hoped that welfare payments with a means test would weaken the trade unions, but Hirtsiefer's procedure removed any pres-

---

64. Ursula Hüllbüsch, "Der Ruhreisenstreit in gewerkschaftlicher Sicht," in Mommsen, Petzina, and Weisbrod (eds.), pp. 271–89; *Kölnische Volkszeitung*, 2 November 1928, no. 797, and 5 November, no. 803; telegram from Wieber to the Center Reichstag delegation, 6 November 1928, NL Stegerwald/004/1928/no. 541.

65. NL ten Hompel/29, A. Gilles to ten Hompel, 28 November 1928, and reply of 12 December, and NL ten Hompel/34, Karl Kümpers to the bishop of Münster, 7 December 1928.

66. *Kölnische Volkszeitung*, 15 November 1928, no. 830, and 23 November, no. 848.

67. *Kirchlich-soziale Blätter*, January–February 1929, p. 18, and Stupperich, "Volksgemeinschaft," pp. 260–62.

sure to resume work on the employers' terms. The Ruhr industrialists therefore agreed to reopen their plants and to accept binding arbitration by Interior Minister Carl Severing.[68] Most responsible leaders of Germany's industrial associations apparently concluded from this defeat that confrontation tactics were highly dangerous and that they should revive efforts to reach some sort of consensus with organized labor regarding national economic policy. The Center Party's Committee for Commerce and Industry certainly took this line, promptly arranging a series of monthly conferences with Catholic labor leaders whose outcome will be discussed in chapter 6. However, the crisis atmosphere engendered by the Ruhr lockout intensified the backlash against trade unionism in the bourgeois parties.

An upsurge of animosity toward industrialists among workers in the aftermath of the lockout convinced the Protestant leaders of the Christian unions that they could not long afford to maintain their truce with Alfred Hugenberg. The Nationalist press ignored the DNAB's repeated declarations of solidarity with the Christian metalworkers' union, and the DNVP's official commentary focused attention on the economic difficulties of the employers and the merits of their legal case.[69] Hartwig and Mumm failed to have the labor representative from the Ruhr, Wilhelm Koch, appointed party spokesman in the Reichstag debate on the lockout, and a Ruhr industrialist, Moritz Klönne, represented the DNVP in the hearings of the Reichstag social policy committee, where he denounced the radicalism of the Christian unions. The DNVP Reichstag delegation decided to abstain in the vote on welfare funds, although several probusiness delegates in it voted against them, and the DNVP joined the agitation by the industrial associations for a means test. Such actions tended to destroy the credibility of a labor leader like Karl Dudey, the official of the Christian metalworkers' union who also headed the DNAB provincial association of the Lower Rhine.[70]

These developments encouraged the leading Christian Socials in the DNVP to undertake serious preparations for a schism of the party. At the beginning of December, Gustav Hülser formulated an effective strategy for them in a memorandum entitled "Christian Social *Realpolitik*." Hülser predicted that Hugenberg would consolidate his control over the DNVP but would seek to retain the Christian Socials' allegiance for the sake of his popularity. "We will, however,

68. Weisbrod, pp. 425–42, and *Das Kabinett Müller II*, pp. 250–74.
69. See "Der Arbeitskampf an der Ruhr," DNVP pamphlet no. 332; Gustav Hülser to Lindeiner-Wildau, 3 November 1928, NL Mumm/121/93f.; *Deutsche Angestelltenstimme und Arbeiterstimme*, December 1928, p. 3; *Der Deutsche*, 9 November 1928.
70. NL Mumm/126/43, Mumm to Koch, 8 November 1928, and 117/320, Hartwig to Lindeiner-Wildau, 12 November 1928; *Zentralblatt*, 15 December 1928, p. 330; Stupperich, "Volksgemeinschaft," pp. 263–65.

encounter still more reservations and obstacles wherever Christian Social deeds are called for. If we hold fast to our current methods, we will gradually lose whatever prestige we still have among our closest friends and followers."Hülser urged emulation of the industrialists, agrarians, and Pan-Germans in the DNVP, all of whom maintained an independent press critical of DNVP policies and cleverly cultivated ties with a neighboring party—the DVP, Christian-nationalist Peasants' Party, or the National Socialist Party—so that they could pressure DNVP leaders with a credible threat to secede.[71]

Reinhard Mumm and other elderly Christian Socials worried about Hülser's impetuosity but agreed that his plan represented the only way to secure respect for their principles. They therefore opened a vigorous recruiting drive for a new, "nonpartisan" Christian Social Federation, sharpened their criticism of party policies in two new magazines with a combined circulation of 2,100, and quietly arranged a truce with the Christian People's Service of Baden-Württemberg, a small party of Pietists that had long urged the Christian Socials to leave the DNVP.[72] In a rally on March 18, 1929, leaders of the Protestant workers' clubs and Christian unions prodded the Christian Socials to take an even more militant stance, resolving that Christian workers would "destroy the ossified party system of today" unless the established parties admitted a suitable number of labor leaders to all party organs. The GcG's *Zentralblatt* clarified the meaning of this resolution by stating that the Christian Socials must "pay no more heed to old friendships when these have lost their meaning. With socially reactionary people there can be no common course."[73]

As the Christian Socials pondered the possibility of an open break with Hugenberg, similar class tensions emerged in Germany's two liberal parties. During the election campaign in the spring of 1928, Gustav Stresemann had tried to broaden the DVP's popular appeal by helping the DHV official and youth leader, Frank Glatzel, win the Reichstag seat for the Ruhr formerly held by the Yellow labor leader Otto Adams. The fundamental trend during the campaign, however, was for representatives of big business to consolidate their control of many party locals. Stresemann later complained to a friend: "Everyone accepts the fact that 23 members of the delegation belong directly or indirectly to the business community, but everyone is outraged when a second white-collar work-

71. NL Mumm/121/85–90, with cover letter from Hülser to Mumm, 5 December 1928.
72. See Günter Opitz, *Der Christlich-soziale Volksdienst* (Düsseldorf, 1969), pp. 141f., and the documentation in NL Mumm/283, to which Opitz was denied access, including Christlich-soziale Reichsvereinigung, Vorstandssitzung, 15 September 1929 (283/293) and *Schlesische Warte*, January 1929.
73. *Zentralblatt*, 1 April 1929, p. 95, and Opitz, pp. 142f.

er is to enter the delegation."[74] After the election the DVP held up the formation of a Grand Coalition cabinet for weeks by demanding that it be admitted simultaneously into Otto Braun's Prussian cabinet. In June 1928 Stresemann finally announced on his own authority that he and Julius Curtius would serve in a "cabinet of personalities" under Hermann Müller pending negotiation of the Prussian issue. This action provoked outrage within his Reichstag delegation and public protests from party locals in the Ruhr.[75]

The DVP's approval of welfare payments for workers idled by the Ruhr steel lockout increased the uproar in the party. As the DVP prepared for a national committee meeting on February 26, 1929, right-wing locals in Westphalia and Hanover demanded that Stresemann present the Reich cabinet with an ultimatum calling for "rejection of the current form of state labor arbitration," introduction of the means test for unemployment insurance, massive tax cuts, "rationalization of the social insurance system," and "administrative reform"— which the Christian unions considered a code word for dissolution of the Labor Ministry in the aftermath of the Oswald affair.[76] One could hardly formulate a list of demands more alarming from the standpoint of the DGB. Stresemann's personal authority was not challenged at the committee meeting, and he eventually persuaded the right wing of the party that its ultimatum for economic reform should be postponed until after the Müller cabinet had successfully concluded its efforts to negotiate a reduction in the level of Germany's reparations payments. He nevertheless concluded gloomily that most party activists inwardly opposed his continued participation in the cabinet, while many DVP Reichstag delegates blindly followed marching orders issued by the business associations. Otto Thiel and other close associates promised Stresemann to follow him out of the DVP if the intransigence of its industrial wing led to the fall of the Grand Coalition.[77] However, Stresemann's absorption in foreign affairs and death on October 3, 1929, deprived the DGB of its only powerful liberal ally. The election of the weak Ernst Scholz to replace him as party chairman removed the last effective check on industrial influence in the DVP.

74. Stresemann to Wilhelm Kahl, 13 March 1929, NL Stresemann 3164/104/174722–25.
75. See Turner, *Stresemann*, pp. 241–48.
76. NL Stresemann, 3164/103/174668–70, Ewald Hecker to Stresemann, 24 February 1929. See also 103/174567–71, Schuster to Stresemann, 27 November and 7 December 1928.
77. DVP Zentralvorstand, 26 February 1929, BAK R45II/43/191–383, and NL Stresemann 3164/104/174722–31, 174745–48, Stresemann to Kahl, 13 March 1929, and undated reply. See also Larry Eugene Jones, "'The Dying Middle': Weimar Germany and the Failure of Bourgeois Unity 1924–1930," Ph.D. diss. (University of Wisconsin, 1970), pp. 188–253, and Paul Moldenhauer's account, reprinted in Ilse Maurer and Udo Wengst (eds.), *Politik und Wirtschaft in der Krise 1930–1932. Quellen zur Ära Brüning* (Düsseldorf, 1980), vol. 1, p. 100.

The position of trade unionists in the German Democratic Party was deteriorating as well. Many DDP leaders concluded that their party was no longer viable when it declined to less than 5% of the national vote in May 1928, and they propagated a merger with the DVP in a united liberal party. But the slogan of liberal unity struck the left wing of the DDP as a reactionary call to transform their party from a bridge between the proletariat and the bourgeoisie into a probusiness party. Anton Erkelenz, Ernst Lemmer, and Gertrud Bäumer sharply opposed a merger with the DVP and suggested instead the eventual goal of a fusion with the Center Party, the left wing of the DVP, and Artur Mahraun's Young German Order, a plan close in spirit to Adam Stegerwald's Essen Program of 1920.[78]

In addition to the strains caused by electoral defeat, liberal trade unionists in the DDP suffered when the ADGB appropriated their slogan of "economic democracy" in the summer of 1928. For some years Anton Erkelenz of the Hirsch–Duncker unions had attacked the etatism of Heinrich Brauns and the Christian unions, nourishing hopes among liberal businessmen that organized labor could be persuaded to support efforts to reverse the trend toward increasing state intervention in the economy.[79] The ADGB's newly articulated support for state labor arbitration and governmental regulation of cartels and trusts dashed such hopes, prompting demands by DDP businessmen that the liberal Trade Union Ring repudiate the "socialist" program for economic democracy. In September 1928 the workers' committee of the DDP angrily rejected such demands, and the leading Hirsch–Duncker unionists soon insisted that Erkelenz abandon his liberal anti-interventionism. Party chairman Erich Koch-Weser defended the workers' right to use the slogan of economic democracy but postponed any definition of its meaning until a comprehensive economic program for the party could be drafted.[80] After months of infighting in the party executive, Erkelenz was deposed as vice-chairman of the DDP and head of its organizational committee in August 1929. This was not necessarily proof of an antiunion backlash in the party, since Erkelenz suffered from severe health problems, but it undoubtedly reduced union influence on the party leadership.[81]

78. See the articles by Bäumer and Erkelenz in *Die Hilfe*, 15 June 1928, and Attila Chanady, "The Dissolution of the German Democratic Party in 1930," *American Historical Review*, 73 (June 1968), pp. 1438–43.

79. See Anton Erkelenz, *Moderne deutsche Sozialpolitik* (Berlin, 1926).

80. Werner Schneider, *Die Deutsche Demokratische Partei in der Weimarer Republik 1924–1930* (Munich, 1978), pp. 166–69; Lothar Albertin and Konstanze Wegner (eds.), *Quellen. Linksliberalismus in der Weimarer Republik* (Düsseldorf, 1980), pp. 471–78; Schneider to Erkelenz, 24 November 1928, NL Erkelenz/125.

81. Werner Schneider, pp. 216f. Erkelenz suffered some sort of nervous breakdown in 1928, and even some members of the DDP workers' committee accused him of paranoia when he lashed out

Koch-Weser finally authorized the economist Gustav Stolper to propose a comprehensive economic program for the DDP at its party congress of October 4–6, 1929, but with unfortunate results. The few laborites at the congress denounced Stolper's claim that Germany no longer had an "oppressed proletariat" and that the government should therefore devote itself to helping the peasantry and small businessmen. The congress could not reach agreement on these issues.[82] The workers' committee of the DDP responded to Stolper's proposals by demanding stronger government supervision of cartels and trusts, more power for factory councils, and more labor representation in the various public economic councils, in a program similar to those of the Free and Christian unions. To lend weight to these demands, the executive secretary of the liberal Trade Union Ring, Ernst Lemmer, founded the "Social Republican Circle" in November 1929, a small pressure group of youth leaders and trade unionists in the DDP that resembled the Christian Social Federation in the DNVP.[83]

The Christian unions sought to exert a direct influence on the process of regrouping in the two liberal parties through an alliance with Artur Mahraun's Young German Order, a paramilitary league with nearly 200,000 members. The order had adopted a friendly stance toward the Christian-nationalist labor movement ever since 1920 and displayed intense moral indignation over "plutocratic" influences in the bourgeois parties. In 1928–29 the Young Germans supported the DGB by publicizing the details of Lambach's struggle against Hugenberg, of Stresemann's and Glatzel's campaign against the right wing of the DVP, and of Ernst Lemmer's struggle against businessmen in the DDP. On June 15, 1929, Mahraun staged a mass rally in Dortmund to promote the consolidation of youth groups, idealistic nationalists, and socially progressive forces in the middle of the political spectrum. Baltrusch conveyed Stegerwald's greetings and told the assembled guests that their efforts were loyal to the spirit of the Essen Program. The trade unionists Baltrusch, Karl Dudey, Lemmer, and Gustav Schneider of the liberal white-collar GDA then joined in a discussion with factory owners belonging to the Young German Order. All agreed in condemning efforts to undermine trade unionism and in calling for a revival of the Central Association of 1918.[84]

Baltrusch's position as the economic spokesman for the League of Christian Unions had hindered him from playing an active role in either the DVP or

at antiworker prejudice in the DDP: see Erkelenz to Dr. Rauecker, 21 January 1930, and reply of 22 January, NL Erkelenz/126.

82. Parteitag der DDP, BAK R45III/7/200–235.

83. Reichs-Arbeitnehmer-Ausschuß der DDP, memorandum of 1 February 1930, BAK R45III/43/9–24, and Werner Schneider, pp. 170–74, 220f.

84. Hornung, pp. 52–68; Alexander Keßler, *Der Jungdeutsche Orden in den Jahren der Entscheidung* (Munich, 1974), vol. 1, pp. 7–53; *Der Deutsche*, 19 June 1929.

DNVP, but the Young German Order proved willing to grant him considerable influence on formulating its social program. Erich Glimm, the GcG's expert on labor law, and Arthur Adolf, head of a small union of communal officials affiliated with the DGB, soon joined Baltrusch as regular speakers at Young German rallies. On November 10, 1929, Glimm published an article arguing that the Young German Order had the best chance of achieving the aim also pursued by the Christian People's Service of Baden-Württemberg and the Christian Social Federation: the creation of a socially progressive party for German Protestants resembling the Center Party for Catholics.[85] This apparently represented the first explicit discussion of the plan hinted at by Stegerwald ever since the beginning of 1928.

THE SCHISM OF THE DNVP AND THE FALL OF THE GRAND COALITION

These maneuvers by the Protestant leaders of the Christian-nationalist labor movement were intended to stabilize parliamentary government by isolating its enemies on the right, by denying Alfred Hugenberg the support of idealistic nationalists and Protestant churchmen. Unfortunately, they also tended to undermine parliamentary government by encouraging hasty action on the part of influential personages who resented the SPD's opposition to naval rearmament, agrarian protectionism, and tax reductions. Beginning early in 1929, many DVP politicians, army generals, and presidential advisers urged Hindenburg to appoint a purely "bourgeois" cabinet even though the Grand Coalition was the only parliamentary combination capable of commanding a stable majority.[86] Any terrain won by the DGB in its campaign against Hugenberg would be cited by General Kurt von Schleicher and other intriguers as evidence that the president could afford to turn the SPD out of office, even if this meant a brief period of government through presidential emergency decrees, in the hope that a moderately conservative Reichstag majority would soon coalesce.

The most difficult immediate problem facing the Müller cabinet in 1929 was how to finance the new system of national unemployment insurance in the face of steadily increasing rates of unemployment. In May 1929 this issue led to a major clash between the SPD, which insisted on covering any shortfall by increasing contributions to the system or from general revenue, and the DVP, which insisted on reduction of benefits. The two parties agreed to postpone resolution

85. "Politische Neuordnung," *Der Jungdeutsche*, 10 November 1929.
86. See Gerhard Schulz's introduction to Maurer and Wengst, eds., *Quellen. Politik und Wirtschaft*, pp. xxxii–liv.

of their conflict only because they shared an interest in ratification of the Young Plan for refinancing reparations, which they knew would be subjected to withering attacks from Hugenberg's propaganda machine.[87]

The issue of unemployment insurance generated even more pressure on Christian trade unionists in the DNVP to distance themselves from Hugenberg. Their party chairman encouraged discussion of a scheme to replace unemployment insurance with a system of compulsory savings that would divert a percentage of each worker's paycheck into an individual savings account to which the worker had access only in case of disability or loss of job. Although indignant attacks on the plan by the DHV and DNAB caused Hugenberg to retreat for the moment,[88] his attitude toward unemployment insurance exposed Christian trade unionists to attacks from their socialist competitors. Behrens and Hülser therefore declared publicly that they would never abandon the principles of the unemployment insurance act of 1927: abolition of the means test, a single insurance chest for all workers so that risks would be shared, and acceptance by the national government of the responsibility to subsidize the system during recessions.[89]

However, Hugenberg's crusade against the Young Plan proved highly effective in countering efforts by the DGB to isolate him on the right. He succeeded by July 1929 in forging an alliance with Germany's largest organization of combat veterans, the Stahlhelm, the Reichslandbund, and the still tiny Nazi Party in a referendum campaign against the plan. The popularity of this campaign among party members helped Hugenberg win sole control over party policy at a meeting of the DNVP's national committee on June 15. Here Emil Hartwig found himself alone in speaking out against a Hugenberg dictatorship. Hartwig later complained bitterly to the ailing Mumm of the cowardice of the Westarp loyalists, who opposed Hugenberg secretly.[90] Hugenberg's cooperation with the Stahlhelm represented a special disappointment for the DGB. Roughly one-quarter of that organization's members were manual workers, and the DGB had competed fiercely with the Yellow unions for its endorsement since 1924. The Stahlhelm drifted rightward during 1928, however, as the faction following Theodor Duesterberg toyed with the idea of creating a mass movement for the

87. Maurer, *Reichsfinanzen und Große Koalition*.
88. See Hartwig to DNVP Parteivorstand, 14 May 1929, NL Mumm/117/309, and DNVP, "Mitteilung Nr. 16," 7 May 1929.
89. *Zentralblatt*, 1 May 1929, p. 117; *Die Rundschau*, 19 May 1929, p. 43, and 8 September 1929, pp. 75f.
90. DNVP, "Mitteilung Nr. 27," 22 June 1929, and Hartwig to Mumm, 16 July 1929, NL Mumm/283/156. See also Elisabeth Friedenthal, "Volksbegehren und Volksentscheid über den Young-Plan und die Deutschnationale Sezession," Ph.D. diss. (Tübingen, 1957), pp. 38–52.

overthrow of the Republic modeled on the Italian Fascist Party. In October 1928 Duesterberg announced that the Stahlhelm would create its own "Self-Help" organizations for workers as ersatz unions, "since a large segment of the Christian unions has drawn so close to the Marxist unions in practice that a distinction between them can hardly be discerned any longer."[91] The Stahlhelm Self-Help never attracted many members, but it undermined the credibility of the DGB among unorganized Protestant workers. Moreover, Hugenberg's alliance with the Stahlhelm enabled him to divide the ranks of the Christian Social leadership. Wilhelm Koch, the only Christian Social to have held cabinet office, and Paul Rüffer belonged to the veterans' organization and supported the referendum campaign enthusiastically, denouncing pacifist currents in the Christian unions. On August 3, 1929, they boycotted a meeting of the Christian Social Federation because they doubted its loyalty to the DNVP.[92]

Seeking to restore unity among the Christian Socials, Reinhard Mumm insisted that the impetuous Hülser undertake no offensive action that might split the DNVP. He also acknowledged, however, that the disciples of Adolf Stoecker could never sacrifice their fundamental social principles for the sake of party unity, and he declared that the expulsion of any individual Christian Social leader from the DNVP must be met by the resignation of all the rest.[93] Many DNVP party locals soon began to purge trade unionists during the selection of nominees for the Prussian communal elections of November 1929. On October 22 Karl Dudey issued an ultimatum to the party in Duisburg, threatening to run a separate DNAB ticket. Mumm implored Dudey to rescind the ultimatum, but Hartwig warned Mumm that a breach was inevitable, appealing to Mumm to lead the Christian Socials in the decisive struggle.[94] On October 29, 1929, the central committee of the Christian Social Federation endorsed Dudey's action and resolved to inform Hugenberg privately that it could not remain loyal to the DNVP unless he resigned as party chairman.[95] The die was cast.

The Christian Socials delayed overt action, however, hoping to link their cause to that of the mighty Reichslandbund. Hugenberg had indulged in such

91. *Der Deutsche*, 31 October 1928; Alois Klotzbücher, "Der politische Weg des Stahlhelm, Bund der Frontsoldaten, in der Weimarer Republik," Ph.D. diss. (Erlangen, 1964), pp. 41–46; Volker Berghahn, *Der Stahlhelm* (Düsseldorf, 1966), pp. 103–16.

92. Rüffer to Mumm, 18 July, 26 July, and 4 November 1929, NL Mumm/140/54–58; 283/246; Koch to Mumm, 15 July 1929; 283/267–74, CSRV Vorstand. Baltrusch defended the Young Plan halfheartedly in *Zentralblatt*, 15 August 1929, pp. 214f.

93. "Wir Christlich-sozialen und die Parteikrisis der Gegenwart," speech of June–July 1929, NL Mumm/224/8–11.

94. NL Mumm/282/328–37, Dudey to DNVP Landesverband Niederrhein, 22 October 1929, and Mumm to Dudey, 25 October 1929; 117/291, Hartwig to Mumm, 23 October 1929.

95. CSRV Vorstand, NL Mumm/283/339–43. The Duisburg DNVP capitulated to Dudey's ultimatum but too late to affect events in Berlin: see Dudey's circular of 14 November 1929, NL Mumm/110/54f.

rhetorical excesses during his anti-Young campaign as to preclude any possibility that the leaders of the DVP and Center Party would form a cabinet with him, and his agreement to Nazi demands that the referendum include a paragraph threatening President Hindenburg with imprisonment if he signed the law proved offensive to leading agrarians. As the DNVP prepared for its annual congress on November 21–23, 1929, Gottfried von Treviranus informed Count Westarp that he had organized a faction of 25–30 anti-Hugenberg Reichstag delegates willing to secede from the party, discussed formation of a nonsocialist government with the leaders of the moderate parties, and received pledges of massive financial support from industrialists and the Defense Ministry. But Westarp opposed the project and persuaded Treviranus to wait for the failure of Hugenberg's referendum to alter the mood of the DNVP's rank and file.[96]

The Christian Socials were bitterly disappointed to find no hint of opposition to Hugenberg from the Westarp group when the party congress convened. Hugenberg utterly dominated the proceedings, parroting again and again his slogans that the Young Plan meant slavery for Germany and the triumph of Bolshevism. Representatives of the *Mittelstand* and Yellow unionists also rose to denounce collective bargaining, consumers' cooperatives, and all other "restrictions on free enterprise." Once again, an impassioned Emil Hartwig stood alone as he sought to defend the Christian Social tradition.

> If we want to combat Marxism, combat it successfully, you cannot do that by defending all your privileges against the legitimate demands of the workers, and you cannot do that without letting workers themselves lead the struggle to win back their colleagues from the movement dominated by Marxist ideas. That must be achieved primarily by the workers, and we have achieved many successes in this struggle over the last 40 to 50 years. . . . I don't see where the bourgeois movement [for social reform], our other friends who are non-workers, have achieved successes in this regard. . . . If the Christian and nationalist labor movement has maintained its position against Marxism, it has done that by gathering its colleagues together in collective organizations wherever they require aid.

Hartwig portrayed collective bargaining, consumers' cooperatives, and savings banks for workers in particular as innovations by the Christian labor movement that had spread to the socialist, influencing it in a conservative direction.[97]

96. Friedenthal, pp. 65–72, 127f., and NL Westarp: "Niederschrift des Grafen Westarp über Entstehung und Verlauf der Parteikrise Ende November/Anfang Dezember 1929," pp. 1f.

97. See the typescript of the party's own protocol of the proceedings in ZStA/DNVP/55/47f., and the report on the congress for the Reich Chancellory in BAK R43I/2654/288–96.

Despite the reticence of the Westarp loyalists, Hugenberg initiated expulsion proceedings against Treviranus at the end of November, after receiving a copy of a letter in which he explained his plans for a secession, since abandoned. The Christian Social leaders publicly declared their solidarity with Treviranus. Hülser, Lambach, and Hartwig went further on December 2, when the Reichstag majority rejected Hugenberg's law against the Young Plan. Hugenberg had granted Martin Schiele, as president of the Reichslandbund, the exclusive right to publicly express reservations about the referendum text, but the three most militant Christian Social leaders announced to the press that they shared Schiele's views. Schiele ignored this unsolicited declaration of support, and Hugenberg announced to the national committee of the DNVP on December 3 that the three Christian Socials would be expelled from the party. Mumm, Behrens, and Wilhelm Lindner promptly joined their colleagues by resigning from the party. Westarp condemned their action, but Treviranus also resigned and persuaded six friends in the Reichstag delegation to join him.[98]

Westarp's refusal to criticize Hugenberg publicly destroyed whatever chance the secessionists had of winning support from DNVP party locals. Wilhelm Koch and Paul Rüffer remained loyal to Hugenberg, and even the Christian Social bastions of Düsseldorf-East and Southern Westphalia repudiated the secession while urging reconciliation.[99] Hartwig and Lindner hoped for valuable support from the network of DNAB locals, but this organization apparently melted away as soon as the friendship of Nationalist employers and party officials was lost.[100] Nevertheless, the Christian People's Service of Baden-Württemberg welcomed a merger with the experienced Christian Social politicians as soon as they severed all links with the DNVP, and a rally in Berlin on December 28, 1929, proclaimed the birth of the Christian Social People's Service (Christlich-soziale Volksdienst, CSVD). Soon thereafter Walther Lambach and most DHV activists in the DNVP joined with Treviranus to form the Popular Conservative Federation, hoping for eventual union with the Westarp loyalists in the DNVP.[101] The political situation was further complicated in January 1930, when the Young

98. Jonas, pp. 52–55. See also Hartwig's transcript of his farewell speech in NL Diller/9, and the abridged official party account of the debate in DNVP, "Mitteilung Nr. 51," 5 December 1929 (also in NL Diller/9).

99. Gemein, pp. 59f., 117. Estimates of the number of resignations from the DNVP at this time ranged from Hugenberg's 1,000 to the SPD's 45,000: Friedenthal, pp. 134f.

100. Both Rüffer and Hartwig mustered an impressive array of declarations of loyalty from DNAB locals, but most of Rüffer's were dispatched by local leaders of the DNVP rather than workers: see *Deutsche Angestelltenstimme und Arbeiterstimme*, January 1930, and DNVP, "Mitteilung Nr. 3," 25 January 1930 (NL Diller/10), as well as the reports on the DNAB from DNVP locals in ZStA/DNVP/17.

101. Opitz, pp. 149–57; *Der Deutsche*, 30 January 1930; Jonas, pp. 19–22.

German Order, encouraged by the schism of the DNVP, proceeded to form the People's National Federation (Volksnationale Reichsvereinigung). Artur Mahraun was determined to compete aggressively for the allegiance of Christian workers and secured the participation of a dozen GcG functionaries, led by Baltrusch, in the formation of his party.[102]

DGB leaders hoped that the three new parties in the middle of the political spectrum, the People's National Federation, the CSVD, and Treviranus' Popular Conservative Federation, would form a close alliance, joining if possible with the Christian-nationalist Peasants' Party. They recognized that it would be difficult to fuse these four organizations but hoped that they could cooperate in a sort of corporatist cartel for German Protestants, where the representatives of each class would preserve organizational autonomy while forming a unified Reichstag delegation.[103] Both Lambach and Baltrusch maintained membership in the CSVD and assured its leaders that their respective parties shared Christian Social ideals.[104] However, the DGB ran a risk by dispatching its agents into three parties, where they were allied with mutually antagonistic groups. Instead of consolidating those parties into a single bloc, this strategy might simply dissipate the energies of the Christian-nationalist labor movement. Above all, the new parties required patient cultivation. Given time, they might enable Germany to achieve, not the classic two-party parliamentary system, but at least an orderly alternation between left-of-center and right-of-center majority coalitions. DGB leaders realized, however, that they remained far removed from this goal at the end of 1929. Despite the schism of the DNVP, DGB leaders were still gripped by the fears expressed at the national congress of the Christian unions in September 1929, where Adam Stegerwald declared publicly that, if the Grand Coalition fell, the most likely result would be a return to "the privilege-state of 1914," or worse.[105]

However, one DGB leader, Hermann Müller's successor Heinrich Brüning, was widely suspected of complicity in the intrigues that toppled the Grand Coalition in March 1930. This was probably not true. Brüning himself consistently maintained that all his efforts in the first three months of 1930 were dedicated to preserving the Grand Coalition by arranging a fiscal compromise

102. See the list of 650 charter members and their occupations in *Der Jungdeutsche*, 30 January 1930; Mahraun to Baltrusch, 2 April 1930, BAK NS 26/858; Keßler, pp. 66–83.
103. Lambach to Wilhelm Classen, 23 January 1930, NL Lambach/2, and *Der Deutsche*, 30 January 1930.
104. Lambach to Mumm, 17 June 1930, NL Mumm/129/143, and Baltrusch to the editors of the Christian Social *Aufwärts* (Bielefeld), 30 January 1930, NL Mumm/101/114f.
105. GcG, *12. Kongreß 1929*, pp. 102f. In a conference of DVP leaders, Otto Thiel angrily denied Otto Hugo's claim that a "bourgeois majority" would soon emerge in the Reichstag: DVP Zentralvorstand, 14 December 1929, BAK R45II/44/293–99, 385–89.

between the SPD and DVP, and that he strongly discouraged President Hindenburg from pursuing Schleicher's plan for a "bourgeois government."[106] Brüning
undoubtedly encouraged the intriguers, however, by advocating reform of proportional suffrage and perhaps even a restoration of the monarchy, and by expressing eagerness to form a right-of-center government if Hugenberg could be
removed as chairman of the DNVP. The stance of Stegerwald and the other blue-
collar Christian union leaders, on the other hand, was unambiguous. In December 1929 they vigorously supported the SPD's resistance to demands for
massive increases in agricultural tariffs.[107] In February 1930 the DGB signed a
joint declaration with the Free and Hirsch–Duncker unions insisting that any
deficit in the unemployment insurance system be covered from general revenue,
recommending an "emergency contribution" (*Notopfer*) from the well-to-do for
this purpose. Stegerwald supported this plan in the cabinet with a memorandum
of February 11 that blamed Germany's recession primarily on the massive salary
ircreases for civil servants in 1927. The transport minister demanded an emergency contribution for unemployment insurance from the civil servants because
they suffered no threat of unemployment and enjoyed generous pension benefits.[108] Brüning and other leaders of the Center Reichstag delegation rebuked
Stegerwald for strengthening the SPD's resistance to a compromise with the
DVP, but his position was enormously popular among Christian workers, as a
mass rally in Essen soon demonstrated.[109]

By March 1930, however, the Christian unions had become isolated in their
support for the Grand Coalition. In 1929 Joseph Joos and Otto Müller devoted
themselves entirely to anti-Marxist apologetics. Their campaign against the
"spirit of class conflict," which they saw reflected in the confrontation tactics of
the Christian unions, did help revive support for the Center Party among the
Catholic clergy, and thus in a sense it slowed the drift rightward in the Catholic
camp.[110] But Joos and his associates also displayed a growing contempt for
liberals and Social Democrats as flotsam on the sea of history, whose "materialistic" world view rendered them incapable of sustaining effective resistance

106. See Brüning's memorandum on his audience of 1 March 1930 with Hindenburg in Rudolf
Morsey, "Neue Quellen zur Vorgeschichte der Reichskanzlerschaft Brünings," in Hermens and
Schieder (eds.), pp. 213–15, and Brüning, pp. 145–49.

107. *Zentrumsprotokolle 1926–1933*, pp. 360–69.

108. *Zentralblatt*, 15 February 1930, p. 49, and *Das Kabinett Müller II*, pp. 1449–52.

109. *Zentrumsprotokolle 1926–1933*, pp. 387f., 406–08, and *Kölnische Volkszeitung*, 10 March
1930, no. 126.

110. See "Weltanschauliches und Klassenmässiges in der deutschen Arbeiterbewegung," *Der
Arbeiterführer. Zeitschrift für die katholischen Arbeitervereine Westdeutschlands*, Herbst 1929,
pp. 25–30; KAB Archiv, Reichsvorstand, 12 November 1929; and Heinrich Teipel, "Die Parteipolitik des katholischen Klerus," *Deutsche Republik*, 28 December 1929, pp. 393–98.

to Bolshevism. In March 1930, as the Müller cabinet entered its death throes, the *Westdeutsche Arbeiter-Zeitung* ignored the parliamentary crisis in order to devote an entire issue to religious persecution in the Soviet Union, explaining that the "struggle between Moscow and Rome" represented the decisive conflict of the twentieth century.[111] In chapter 2, I suggested that Joos and Erzberger had supported the Weimar Coalition so enthusiastically in 1919 because they considered it the only way to maintain the unity of German Catholicism, which seemed threatened above all by the prospect that conflict with the SPD might provoke wholesale defections by industrial workers. By 1929, however, Joos was gravely concerned by the defection of middle-class Catholics to the DNVP and splinter parties, a problem that obviously could not be solved through cooperation with the SPD.

Support for the Grand Coalition was weakening within the Social Democratic Reichstag delegation as well. The same exasperation with party politics, the same refusal to make any more compromises already noted for Hans Bechly and Heinrich Imbusch could be observed among the ADGB representatives in it. On March 26, 1930, Free union leaders mobilized a majority in the SPD delegation to reject out of hand a compromise plan by Brüning for financing unemployment insurance that had been accepted by all the other government parties.[112] Their action came as a considerable shock to the leaders of the Christian unions, who had always regarded the DVP as the main source of difficulties for the cabinet. DGB leaders, including Brüning, considered the Social Democrats basically well intentioned although sometimes misguided, but they felt that the DVP deliberately sought to engineer a political crisis that would undermine parliamentary democracy. Now the SPD appeared guilty of toppling the Grand Coalition.[113] On March 27 Brüning made the fateful decision to accept Hindenburg's offer to head a nonsocialist cabinet, after Hindenburg promised him the power to issue presidential emergency decrees on the basis of Article 48 of the Weimar Constitution in case he failed to win a Reichstag majority. Filled with forebodings of a radicalization of the working class,[114] the Christian trade unionists were plunged into a premature campaign to forge a parliamentary majority that would be progressive in social issues, conservative in cultural issues, and realistic in dealing with worldwide economic trends.

111. *WAZ*, 29 March 1930. See also the remarkably conservative, even authoritarian argumentation in Joseph Joos, "Chaos oder Ordnung?" (speech of 24 May 1930, Volksverein-Bibliothek), and Knapp, pp. 245–50.
112. Maurer, pp. 108–39, and Ursula Hüllbüsch, "Die deutschen Gewerkschaften in der Weltwirtschaftskrise," in Werner Conze and Hans Raupach (eds.), *Die Staats- und Wirtschaftskrise des Deutschen Reichs, 1929–1933* (Stuttgart, 1967), pp. 135–54.
113. *Zentrumsprotokolle 1926–1933*, pp. 334, 353, 423f.
114. See Stegerwald's remarks, ibid., pp. 427f.

Studies of politics in Great Britain and the Federal Republic of Germany have pointed to the presence of a large minority of blue-collar workers among the supporters of the conservative parties as a crucial factor explaining the stability of parliamentary government. Both union leaders and conservative politicians have been deterred from adopting extremist policies by the fear of alienating workers whose loyalties were divided between them.[115] As we have seen, a similar mechanism operated in the Weimar Republic during the mid-1920s. The mechanism remained imperfect, however, because of the ongoing rivalry between the separate labor federations for socialist and Christian workers. Conservatives were sometimes encouraged to adopt a confrontation course by the hope that they could avoid paying the price through exploiting tensions between the Free and Christian unions. But by 1928, electoral trends suggested to bourgeois politicians that their efforts to cultivate a trade union constituency were causing mass defections. Even before the onset of the Great Depression, trade unionists in the DNVP and DVP, and to a lesser extent in the Center and Democratic parties, came to be treated as interlopers, while each party's leadership strove to reinforce the shared values that held their mostly middle-class corps of activists together.

---

115. See Wolfgang Hirsch-Weber, *Gewerkschaften in der Politik* (Cologne and Opladen, 1959), and Robert McKenzie and Allen Silver, *Angels in Marble* (Chicago, 1968).

6

Deflationary Economics and Trade Unionism under Heinrich Brüning

When Brüning entered office on March 30, 1930, with Adam Stegerwald as his labor minister, he undoubtedly intended to reduce public expenditure so as to eliminate budget deficits, and to encourage the reduction of wages and prices so as to help German exports compete more successfully on the world market. Historians remain deeply divided concerning his goals, however. Some portray Brüning as sincerely dedicated to employing the best economic theory available at the time in order to end the economic crisis as quickly as possible,[1] whereas others argue that Brüning sought to aggravate the crisis, deliberately impoverishing the German people in order to attain the political goals of constitutional reform and abolition of reparations.[2] The unpublished memoirs of Brüning's confidant Max Habermann, written in 1934, lend support to the latter interpretation. Brüning apparently visited the DHV official shortly before assuming office to say that "as a trade unionist" he should reject President Hindenburg's offer of the chancellorship. Brüning warned that his primary goal would be to build a trade surplus big enough to mobilize business interests in the West to

1. See Horst Sanmann, "Daten und Alternativen der deutschen Wirtschafts- und Finanzpolitik in der Ära Brüning," *Hamburger Jahrbuch für Wirtschafts- und Gesellschaftspolitik*, 10 (1965), pp. 118–20, 127–31, and Knut Borchardt, "Zwangslagen und Handlungsspielräume in der großen Weltwirtschaftskrise der frühen dreißiger Jahre," in *Wachstum, Krisen, Handlungsspielräume der Wirtschaftspolitik* (Göttingen, 1982), pp. 167–74.
2. Contrast the sympathetic accounts by Wolfgang Helbich, *Die Reparationen in der Ära Brüning* (Berlin 1962), and Werner Conze, "Die Reichsverfassungsreform als Ziel der Politik Brünings," in Michael Stürmer (ed.), *Die Weimarer Republik. Belagerte Civitas* (Königstein, 1980), pp. 340–48, with the highly critical Hans Mommsen, "Heinrich Brünings Politik als Reichskanzler. Das Scheitern eines politischen Alleinganges," in Karl Holl (ed.), *Wirtschaftskrise und liberale Demokratie* (Göttingen, 1978), esp. pp. 23–32.

pressure their governments into abandoning reparations claims, and that this goal would require tight credit, high levels of unemployment, and vigorous action to reduce wages and prices. Habermann replied that he must follow the president's call if he perceived a real chance to revise the Treaty of Versailles, and that all patriotic trade unionists would support him as long as he divided the material burdens of the liberation struggle fairly among all classes. According to Habermann, Brüning made the same speech to his (unnamed) friends among the leaders of the blue-collar Christian unions and received the same answer.[3] Thus key DGB leaders apparently pledged in private to support a program that went well beyond the government's publicly announced goal of balancing the budget.

One should not present an exaggerated picture of Brüning and his supporters in the DGB as nationalist ideologues, however. They sincerely believed, with considerable justification, that Germany's chronic trade deficit indicated a fundamentally sick economy, and that the campaign against reparations through deflation was also necessary for restoring the ability of German industry to compete on the world market. Catholic labor leaders became acquainted with the gloomy assessment of economic trends that underlay Brüning's thinking during a series of monthly conferences in 1929 with Center Party industrialists, arranged by Stegerwald and Rudolf ten Hompel to alleviate the class tensions resulting from the Ruhr steel lockout. The negotiators soon agreed that the civil service salary reform of 1927 had caused a dangerous inflationary spiral, that management and labor should cooperate to eliminate Germany's chronic balance of payments deficit, that high taxes and wages hampered industry's ability to export, and that further increases in agricultural tariffs should be opposed.[4] The negotiators could not reach full agreement, however, and Joos and Otto Müller were disappointed in their hope to issue a joint economic program that would demonstrate the power of the Catholic faith to transcend class conflict. GcG representatives rejected claims by employers that wage reductions were necessary, although they did agree to renounce further wage hikes and agitate instead for price reductions. Ten Hompel and Albert Hackelsberger, on the other hand, rejected labor's demand for a loosening of cartel price agreements.[5] Delivering the official report on economic policy to the twelfth congress of the Christian unions in September 1929, the vice-chairman of the metalworkers' union, Karl Schmitz, focused public attention on the trade deficit, the disturbing persistence

3. Max Habermann, "Der DHV im Kampf um das Reich," unpublished MS, DHV-Archiv (Hamburg), pp. 70f.
4. NL ten Hompel/33, conference protocols of 21 January and 26 February 1929, and vol. 35, memorandum for conference of 18 June 1929.
5. NL ten Hompel/33, conference protocols of 27 March, 29 April, and 19 December 1929, and GcG Vorstand, 26 April 1929, NL Otte/7/140.

of unemployment throughout the recent boom years, and the disastrous world-wide decline in agricultural prices, concluding that workers must confine all efforts to increase their real income to the task of reducing the cost of living. This unprecedented plea to abandon all demands for wage hikes reflected a more penetrating assessment of Germany's economic problems than any offered by the Free unions.[6]

The Christian labor press greeted Brüning's appointment enthusiastically and argued that if the squabbling Reichstag parties could not reach agreement, he should impose urgently needed measures to balance the budget through presidential decree.[7] Yet all DGB leaders realized that they would be utterly discredited if the government displayed any hint of favoritism for the propertied while implementing its austerity program. Heinrich Imbusch, although intensely patriotic, still believed that trade unions were basically supposed to fight for their membership rather than formulate objectively correct economic policies, and he became chairman of the DGB as well as the Christian miners' union after Stegerwald departed from union office in 1929, while Bernhard Otte advanced to the chairmanship of the League of Christian Unions.[8] Imbusch and Otte sought in all subsequent dealings with the Brüning cabinet to function as a barometer of the mood of the working class as a whole, to guarantee that government policy did not diverge too greatly from the views of the SPD and Free unions. Brüning's rise to power had returned the Christian unions to the center of the political stage as the only faction of organized labor with direct access to government leaders, but Brüning's determination to adopt unpopular austerity measures could make this association extremely dangerous.

THE FAILURE OF EFFORTS TO FORGE A DEFLATIONARY CONSENSUS

Brüning and Stegerwald were forced to rely on efforts to forge a consensus between management and labor in favor of deflation because of a dismal situation in the Reichstag. Brüning apparently preferred to head a centrist cabinet that could seek support from either the left or the right. Indeed, he considered the

---

6. GcG, *12. Kongreß 1929*, pp. 233–45, and Knut Borchardt, "Wirtschaftliche Ursachen des Scheiterns der Weimarer Republik," in *Wachstum, Krisen, Handlungsspielräume*, pp. 194–205. Contrast Michael Schneider, *Die christlichen Gewerkschaften*, pp. 690–92, who derides the Christian unions for economic confusion. Borchardt's judgement is not entirely balanced either, however. He doubtless exaggerates both the role of state labor arbitration in pushing wage levels upward and the importance of wage levels as causes of the Great Depression.

7. *Zentralblatt*, 15 April 1930, pp. 113f., and WAZ, 19 April 1930, p. 92.

8. Michael Schneider, *Die christlichen Gewerkschaften*, pp. 477–79.

SPD more reasonable on fiscal policy than many of his supposed allies in the DVP.[9] But President Hindenburg desired him to form an aggressively anti-socialist government and insisted that he appoint Martin Schiele as agriculture minister to implement protectionist measures for East Elbian agriculture (*Ost-hilfe*) that would forge a new, right-of-center majority bloc in the Reichstag. The political goals of the presidential circle distorted Brüning's original economic plan and soon aroused opposition even from the Christian unions. On April 7 Schiele presented his first tariff bill to the cabinet and promptly collided with Stegerwald, who claimed that it would cripple export industry and expose the government parties to lethal attacks from the SPD. Brüning cut short the debate to insist on acceptance of most of the agrarian demands.[10] The government program became even less consistent when Brüning acceded to demands by representatives of small shopkeepers that his tax increases include an increase in the sales tax on consumers' cooperatives and department stores from 0.85 to 1.35%. On April 12 Peter Schlack, head of the consumers' cooperatives associated with the Christian unions, denounced this proposal on the floor of the Reichstag and termed the new cabinet the "most reactionary" in the history of the Republic. Peter Tremmel, highly sensitive to Communist agitation as leader of the mostly unskilled and semiskilled members of the Christian factory workers' union, supported Schlack in the Center Reichstag delegation and asked how the government could expect workers to make sacrifices when it proposed taxes and tariffs designed to increase their cost of living. In the first of many confrontations between moderates and militants within the Christian labor movement, Wieber, Joos, and Ersing insisted that all Christian trade unionists must support Brüning.[11]

The balance of forces in the Reichstag remained unclear throughout the spring of 1930, as the supporters of Westarp in the DNVP Reichstag delegation struggled with Hugenberg for control of party policy. Gottfried von Treviranus, appointed a minister without portfolio, continued to urge the cabinet to rely on agricultural protectionists and the anti-Hugenberg Nationalists for a Reichstag majority. Brüning and Stegerwald obviously remained skeptical of these claims, however. In May 1930 they joined forces with Economics Minister Dietrich of

9. See *Zentrumsprotokolle 1926–1933*, pp. 428–30, and Breitscheid's memorandum on a conference with Brüning on 29 March 1930 in Morsey, "Neue Quellen zur Vorgeschichte der Reichskanzlerschaft Brünings," pp. 227f.

10. Tilman Koops, "Zielkonflikte der Agrar- und Wirtschaftspolitik in der Ära Brüning," in Mommsen, Petzina, and Weisbrod (eds.), pp. 852f., and *Akten der Reichskanzlei. Die Kabinette Brüning I und II* (Boppard am Rhein, 1982), pp. 23–33.

11. *Zentrumsprotokolle 1926–33*, pp. 439–43, meetings of 11–14 April 1930, and WAZ, 3 May 1930, p. 106.

the DDP and Finance Minister Moldenhauer of the DVP to insist that Schiele modify his *Osthilfe* program, which provided RM 50 million in credits for bankrupt East Elbian estates, so as to placate the SPD and trade unions. *Osthilfe* was linked to the expenditure of 50 million to support peasant settlements and 25 million to improve housing for farmworkers. Far from agreeing to conservatives' demands that he pressure the Prussian Center into toppling Otto Braun's cabinet of the Weimar Coalition, Brüning compelled Schiele to accept joint administration of *Osthilfe* by the Prussian authorities so as to keep bridges open to the SPD.[12]

Brüning and Stegerwald attached primary political importance to the talks between leaders of the ADGB and Reich Association of Industry that began soon after the fall of the Grand Coalition in an effort to draft a joint statement on economic policy. Since the beginning of 1930 Stegerwald had been publicly appealing for a revival of the old ZAG as the best way to deal with unemployment and trade deficits, and Brüning told his cabinet that the success of these confidential talks was "absolutely essential" for the success of his plan to balance the budget.[13] In mid-May Stegerwald and Moldenhauer achieved their first concrete success in consensus building when they persuaded the industrialists on the governing board of the unemployment insurance system to repudiate the DVP's opposition to any increase in contributions and to endorse a hike from 3.5 to 4% of the hourly wage.[14] This success encouraged them to believe that the Grand Coalition had fallen only because the politicians of the DVP and SPD had dogmatized issues of relatively small financial gain or loss in a spirit alien to that of the practitioners of collective bargaining. In their talks with ADGB leaders during late May and early June, moderate business lobbyists like Hans von Raumer and Ludwig Kastl again repudiated the DVP's rigid opposition to all tax increases. The negotiators agreed to support Brüning's efforts to balance the budget, a special levy on the salaries of civil servants to help finance unemployment insurance, and some sort of reduction in both wages and prices. The representatives of management and labor disagreed about the timing and relative size of the wage and price cuts, and they lacked any authority to determine the actual course of collective bargaining. But they apparently reached tentative agreement on June 5–6 to issue a joint declaration of principles on June 13. The

---

12. *Die Kabinette Brüning*, pp. 106–14, 128–31; Hermann Pünder, *Politik in der Reichskanzlei. Aufzeichnungen aus den Jahren 1929–1932*, Thilo Vogelsang, ed. (Stuttgart, 1961), pp. 51–53, entry of 25 May 1930; Hagen Schulze, pp. 627–33, 681f.

13. See *Die Kabinette Brüning*, p. 183, meeting of 3 June 1930, and Udo Wengst, "Unternehmerverbände und Gewerkschaften in Deutschland im Jahre 1930," *Vierteljahrshefte für Zeitgeschichte*, 25 (January 1977), p. 102.

14. See Michael Schneider, *Das Arbeitsbeschaffungsprogramm des ADGB*, p. 114.

cabinet rejoiced in the progress of these talks because it believed that they would eliminate serious parliamentary opposition to its budget.[15]

The conciliatory stance of business leaders encouraged Labor Minister Stegerwald to follow their requests and the dictates of classical economic theory by employing the state labor arbitration system to promote deflation. On June 10 the labor minister issued a binding arbitration decree that reduced wages in the Ruhr steel industry by 7–8% after employers pledged to cut their prices by the same proportion. Stegerwald announced that state arbitrators would henceforth seek to lower the level of both wages and prices. The Christian metalworkers' union defended this action by arguing that wages would have dropped by 20% without a state-guaranteed collective labor contract, but the Free unions and SPD attacked the labor minister sharply.[16] Stegerwald's decision was probably unavoidable because the state arbitration system could survive only if it followed the trend of the business cycle in setting wage levels. For years, however, the Free unions had been telling their members that, because the maldistribution of income was the major barrier to economic growth, wage increases were always good for the economy as a whole, and since 1924 the Christian union press had often echoed this highly dubious but popular argument.[17]

Christian labor leaders hoped to make deflationary economics palatable to workers with vigorous action to impose sacrifices on civil servants. When Catholic unionists and industrialists held another conference on May 22, 1930, Peter Tremmel warned that an economic policy based on high unemployment and wage reductions would drive workers to Bolshevism. The government must begin, he argued, by reducing civil service salaries and administrative overhead so that workers would understand the need for wage reductions. Ten Hompel and the other industrialists agreed, even endorsing legislation to prohibit civil servants from running for elective office so as to break the power of their lobby. In return, Otte and Fahrenbrach agreed to oppose calls by the ADGB for the imposition of a mandatory 40-hour week as a measure against unemployment.[18] The reports of priests active in the Catholic workers' clubs underscored the depth of feeling among the poorest elements of the working class against the civil

---

15. Wengst, "Unternehmerverbände und Gewerkschaften," pp. 102–04, and Maurer and Wengst (eds.), *Quellen. Politik und Wirtschaft,* pp. 190–96.

16. Hartwich, pp. 160–62; *Zentralblatt,* 1 July 1930, p. 205; Schorr, pp. 174f. The government protocol of Stegerwald's decisive conference with Ernst Poensgen of the Ruhr steel employers' association on 6 June 1930 is reprinted in Maurer and Wengst (eds.), *Quellen. Politik und Wirtschaft,* pp. 197–202.

17. Michael Schneider, *Das Arbeitsbeschaffungsprogramm des ADGB,* pp. 34–65, and *Die christlichen Gewerkschaften,* pp. 584–87.

18. See the protocol in NL ten Hompel/36.

servants. Clergymen also encountered intense hostility in working-class neighborhoods because of their own financial security and decided, after some gentle prodding by their bishops, to sacrifice 10% of their salaries for the unemployed in a voluntary _Notopfer_. The Protestant pastors in the Christian Social People's Service also believed in the need for material sacrifices by those on fixed incomes for the sake of national solidarity.[19]

In June 1930 the civil service lobby countered this threat effectively by joining forces with hard-line industrialists to sabotage the first effort to revive the ZAG. Within the councils of industry, von Raumer succeeded in mustering a majority against demands by Ernst von Borsig and Fritz Thyssen for an assault on the state labor arbitration system that would have made agreement with the ADGB impossible. Extreme statements in the probusiness press made union leaders fearful of publicly associating themselves with the Reich Association of Industry, however, and on June 13 they agreed with Kastl and von Raumer that it would be better to continue their contacts on a confidential basis.[20] The DVP Reichstag delegation then adopted on June 16 the sort of provocative position that the industrial associations had renounced by resolving that the government must "loosen" collective labor contracts, that is, require the renegotiation of long-term contracts guaranteeing wage levels set under conditions of prosperity, before the DVP would accept a _Notopfer_ from civil servants in the budget. This resolution climaxed a series of bitter attacks against Moldenhauer in the liberal press for weakly following Stegerwald's policies, and Moldenhauer felt compelled to resign from the cabinet. The DHV leaders Bechly, Thiel, and Glatzel denounced the reactionaries in their party who had toppled him.[21] On June 24 the ADGB publicly announced the failure of efforts to revive the Zentralarbeitsgemeinschaft, declaring that Stegerwald's wage cuts and the resolutions of the DVP Reichstag delegation had destroyed the "psychological preconditions" for cooperation between management and labor. Bernhard Otte deplored this step, reasoning that only continued negotiations could encourage moderate industrialists to restrain the excesses of their intransigent colleagues, but even the Christian unions feared that a majority of industrialists hoped to exploit the economic crisis in order to abolish collective bargaining.[22] A furious Brüning

---

19. Cologne Archdiocese, "Arbeitervereine," vol. 6, KAB to Cardinal Schulte, 5 June 1930, and Schulte to Cardinal Bertram, 7 June 1930; WAZ, 28 June 1930, p. 156; Georg Ammer to Reinhard Mumm, 15 August 1930, and reply of 16 August, NL Mumm/99/279f.
20. Maurer and Wengst (eds.), _Quellen_, pp. 212–34.
21. Döhn, pp. 261–65; DVP Zentralvorstand, 4 July 1930, BAK R45II/46/119–39, 177–87; Maurer and Wengst (eds.), _Quellen. Politik und Wirtschaft_, pp. 243–46.
22. Maurer and Wengst (eds.), _Quellen. Politik und Wirtschaft_, pp. 257–60, and _Zentralblatt_, 15 June 1930, p. 177.

informed Center Party leaders that the same reactionary industrialists in the
DVP who had toppled the Grand Coalition now thwarted the revival of the ZAG
and sabotaged his efforts to balance the budget.[23]

The failure of this effort to revive the ZAG compelled Brüning to rely on the
political strategy of Treviranus for passing his budget. In July 1930 Count Westarp finally broke with Hugenberg in order to support the government, but he
brought only 25 Reichstag delegates with him instead of the 40 Treviranus had
expected. Brüning therefore suffered a narrow defeat in the Reichstag and ordered new elections.[24] The SPD and the Free unions promptly launched an
exuberant campaign against Brüning's austerity measures. Christian union leaders, fearing that many young workers would abandon their movement, considered this agitation very dangerous and attacked the SPD bitterly for fleeing from
government responsibility as soon as the economic outlook worsened. Although
defending Brüning's policies in general terms, the Christian union leadership
pledged during the campaign to combat any government measures that would
reduce the real income of workers.[25] A revival of close cooperation with the
Catholic clergy helped the Center Party to avoid losses during the Reichstag
election of September 1930,[26] but Brüning could not "win" the election unless
his conservative supporters and the Protestants in the DGB succeeded in dramatically strengthening the new parties of the moderate right.

Brüning's electoral hopes hinged in large measure on the Conservative People's Party (Konservative Volkspartei, KVP), founded in July 1930 through a
merger of the Westarp loyalists from the DNVP with the Popular Conservatives
led by Treviranus and Lambach. This party remained deeply divided, however.
Lambach and Treviranus proclaimed that their new party endorsed trade unionism and would cooperate closely with the DGB, but industrialists like Walther
Rademacher and Bernhard Leopold still demanded equal treatment for the
Yellow unions, warning Westarp that Lambach's position ruined the KVP's
chances of obtaining financial support from the Berlin banks and Ruhr industrialists.[27] Count Westarp felt compelled to respond to reproaches from the

---

23. *Zentrumsprotokolle 1926–1933*, pp. 456 f., 20–24 June 1930.
24. Bracher, *Auflösung*, pp. 299–303, and Jonas, pp. 71–77.
25. See GcG circular of 20 August 1930, NL Otte/2/108–10; Zentralverband christlicher
Textilarbeiter, *10. Generalversammlung 1930*, pp. 112f., 152–63; *Zentralblatt*, 15 June 1930, pp.
178f., and 15 August 1930, p. 241.
26. Alfred Milatz, "Das Ende der Parteien im Spiegel der Wahlen, 1930 bis 1933," in Matthias
and Morsey (eds.), pp. 745f.
27. NL Westarp: Leopold to Westarp, 27 July and 14 August 1930, reply of 16 August, and von
Maltzahn to Westarp, 22 August 1930. Treviranus later stated that big business provided only 25% of
the KVP's campaign funds, compared with 40% from the DHV and 35% from membership dues:
Jonas, pp. 137f.

DNVP by pledging that his party would pursue the traditional goals of the political right, would pressure Brüning to break once and for all with the SPD and adopt measures that favored agriculture and industry against organized labor.[28] Thus the KVP remained deeply divided between "Tory democrats" and traditional conservatives. In September 1930 it suffered a humiliating defeat at the polls, winning only three Reichstag seats. The Christian unions were especially disappointed that their acceptance of highly unpopular food tariffs failed to strengthen the government politically. Martin Schiele failed to rally significant support for the pro-Brüning KVP or Christian-nationalist Peasant's Party among farmers.[29]

The merger in July 1930 between the DDP and the People's National Federation led by Artur Mahraun and Friedrich Baltrusch represented the second initiative supported by the Christian unions to strengthen moderate forces in the Reichstag. The decision by a small team of negotiators to form a united State Party surprised the members of both the DDP and the Young German Order. Anton Erkelenz responded by joining the SPD and urging the Hirsch–Duncker unions to merge with the ADGB, but most of his liberal union colleagues rejected this course, welcoming at first the influx of Christian trade unionists into the State Party.[30] DDP members soon grew resentful, however, of the Young Germans' genteel anti-Semitism and efforts to purge the State Party of all "plutocrats" and "pacifists." The Hirsch–Duncker unions were outraged when the final nomination lists for the State Party denied them any parliamentary representation, while guaranteeing Reichstag seats for Baltrusch and Adolf of the DGB.[31] During the election campaign, DGB leaders in the State Party failed utterly to attract Christian Social voters from the DNVP or white-collar workers from the DVP. In September the State Party won only 3.8% of the national vote, compared with 4.9% for the DDP in 1928. It promptly dissolved in a welter of recriminations, and its Reichstag delegation split between 6 followers of Mahraun and 14 DDP veterans.[32]

For the Christian unions the only positive result of the election was the success of the Christian Social People's Service, the CSVD, which won almost

---

28. Jonas, pp. 105–09, and NL Westarp, Westarp to Rademacher, 16 September 1930.
29. Jonas, pp. 84–86, and Gessner, pp. 226–38.
30. Jones, " 'The Dying Middle'," pp. 480–542, and Erkelenz to A. Lange, 13 August 1930, NL Erkelenz/59/162f.
31. DDP Vorstand, 12 August 1930, BAK R45III/22/88–96; DDP Reichs-Arbeitnehmer-Ausschuß, circular of 12 August 1930, R45III/44/58–60; Young German circular of 16 August 1930, reprinted in Maurer and Wengst (eds.), *Quellen. Politik und Wirtschaft*, pp. 367–75.
32. Albertin and Wegner (eds.), *Quellen. Linksliberalismus*, pp. 581–97, DDP Vorstand, 27 September 1930; and *Der Deutsche*, 9 October 1930.

900,000 votes and 14 Reichstag seats. The CSVD displayed a strong consensus on social issues, embracing the program of the Christian unions wholeheartedly. Theocratic currents in the traditionally Calvinist regions of western and southwestern Germany that were the party's strongholds made it the only party besides the Center to argue that all Christians stood under a moral obligation to support the state social insurance system, independent trade unions, participation by workers in management decisions, and government intervention to alleviate the suffering caused by recessions.[33] CSVD leaders responded to attacks from the DNVP in a manner very different from Count Westarp, rejecting appeals to join a united bourgeois front and denouncing the bourgeois parties for being every bit as "materialistic" as the SPD: "We are not of the left, we are not of the right, we are servants of Christ!"[34] The League of Christian Unions donated office space, logistical support, and small sums of money, and the great majority of its Protestant members voted for the CSVD in September. The CSVD developed such a strong esprit de corps that, in December 1930, the Christian unions accepted without protest a disappointing decision by party headquarters to award a Reichstag seat promised Behrens to the leader of the Bavarian provincial party instead, as a reward for unexpectedly successful campaign performance.[35]

Despite the CSVD's relative success, the September election was a disastrous defeat for Brüning and his supporters. The most important result of the election was the shocking growth of the Nazi Party, which attained 18.3% of the vote and 107 Reichstag seats, becoming the second strongest party behind the SPD. Hugenberg's DNVP emerged somewhat weakened but still defiant with 41 seats. Even among the parties of the moderate right that nominally supported Brüning, the uncompromising special interest parties, which by this time included the DVP as well as splinter parties for small businessmen and farmers, far outnumbered his genuine supporters in tbe KVP, the State Party, and the CSVD.[36]

BRÜNING'S ANTAGONISTIC ALLIANCE WITH ORGANIZED LABOR

Brüning's response to the electoral defeat of September 19, 1930, was profoundly ambiguous. On the one hand, he decided to implement his austerity

33. See the speech by Paul Bausch at the party congress of April 1930 in NL Mumm/334/105–18; *Der Christliche Volksdienst* (Stuttgart), 25 January 1930, p. 4, 12 April, pp. 3f., and 7 June 1930; and Reinhard Mumm, "Aus der Arbeit des CSVD im Reichstag" (August, 1930), in NL Mumm/334/15–22.

34. Paul Bausch, "Zweifrontenkampf," in *Der Christliche Volksdienst* (Stuttgart), 12 July and 19 July 1930.

35. Opitz, pp. 214f.; *Der Christliche Volksdienst* (Stuttgart), 24 January 1931; Karl Dudey to Gustav Hülser, 28 January 1931, NL Mumm/110/6–9.

36. Milatz, pp. 748–58.

measures without giving the SPD any voice in formulating policy. On September 30 the cabinet issued a comprehensive economic program that called for new tax increases, reductions in social insurance benefits, and a 6% reduction in civil service salaries, while declaring that the private sector should imitate these austerity measures. Labor Minister Stegerwald explained to the press that Germany's wage policy had been "lost in a maze" ever since 1927, and employers seized eagerly on this statement while arguing successfully for wage reductions before state labor arbitrators all over the country.[37] On the other hand, Brüning decided to seek the SPD's support in the Reichstag. He carefully refrained from any sort of attack on Otto Braun's Prussian government, despite the urgings of many of his conservative supporters, and sought earnestly to persuade SPD leaders that the only alternative to him was a reactionary or fascist dictatorship. In October 1930 the SPD Reichstag delegation adopted the equally ambiguous policy of "tolerating" Brüning. The SPD refused to accept direct responsibility for government measures, forcing Brüning to implement them through presidential decree, but it also obstructed parliamentary maneuvers to rescind those decrees or topple the cabinet.[38]

The Christian unions responded to the election result by pressuring Brüning to establish a more genuine partnership with the socialist labor movement. The GcG's *Zentralblatt* sniped at Treviranus in its commentary on the election by observing that "the Reich Chancellor has fallen victim to the hopes raised by his Popular Conservative political advisers, who did not have the strength to fulfill their promises."[39] The election outcome also discredited or chastened right-wingers within the GcG. The only prominent blue-collar unionist in the Conservative People's Party, Georg Hartmann, narrowly failed to win reelection to the Reichstag from Saxony. As provincial leader of the Christian farmworkers' union, Hartmann had already alienated his GcG colleagues by opposing all strikes. The Christian unions discharged him soon after his political defeat.[40] Franz Behrens, angered by the conduct of landowners during the election, apparently made no effort thereafter to discourage his union colleagues from seeking to subdivide large estates into peasant homesteads.[41]

37. *Kölnische Volkszeitung*, 1 October 1930, no. 501B; *Der Deutsche*, 3 October 1930; BAK R43I/1158/185f., petition of 13 October 1930 from the Zentralverband christlicher Textilarbeiter to Chancellor Brüning.
38. Erich Matthias, "Die Sozialdemokratische Partei Deutschlands," in Matthias and Morsey (eds.), pp. 103–12, and Hagen Schulze, pp. 634–45.
39. *Zentralblatt*, 1 October 1930, p. 290.
40. NL Westarp: von Maltzahn to Westarp, 11 October 1930, Hartmann to Westarp, 29 July 1932, and Westarp to State Secretary Planck, 3 August 1932.
41. Stegerwald noted in a Reich Chancellory memorandum of 5 November 1930 (BAK R43I/1447/320–23) that Behrens had begun to oppose the demands of agrarian lobbyists more sharply than his socialist counterpart.

The publication of Brüning's economic program on September 30 caused divisions within the Christian labor movement. The Catholic workers' clubs of western Germany promptly endorsed it, and Joos, Giesberts, and Bernhard Letterhaus appealed privately to GcG leaders not to attack the government in public because that would merely accelerate the radicalization of Christian workers.[42] Otte concluded that Brüning's deflationary program would be a disaster for the working class, however, because the government was unwilling to reduce food prices and rents, which accounted for 75% of the worker's budget.[43] On October 9 Imbusch led the executive committee of the DGB in publicly condemning the government's program, demanding guarantees that the cost of living would decline as much as wages. The Christian unions also echoed Free union demands that the government act promptly to reduce unemployment through public works, although they still refrained from endorsing the ADGB's call for a mandatory 40-hour week.[44] In an unusual effort to defend their program before a public forum, Brüning and Stegerwald attended the DGB's national committee meeting of November 20–21, but their speeches apparently did not have much impact. Imbusch emphasized that the DGB retained complete independence even when its friends sat in government, and he concluded the meeting by exhorting all workers to remember the heroic days of May 1924, when 450,000 miners had halted the advance of "social reaction" by sustaining a lengthy strike despite their poverty.[45] Thus it was made clear to the cabinet that it must undertake vigorous action to reduce the cost of living if it desired a truce with the trade unions that would establish a firm foundation for the SPD's new policy of toleration.

Union opposition to the government's economic program proved especially distressing to Stegerwald, who responded with a new initiative to bring the leading representatives of management and labor together. In the last two weeks of October 1930, a massive strike by the socialist metalworkers' union of Berlin, undertaken despite unfavorable conditions on the job market, underscored the depth of anger among workers against wage reductions. ADGB leaders themselves were alarmed by the decision of both the Communist and Nazi parties to support the strike. Brüning and Stegerwald thereafter enjoyed considerable success in persuading both industrialists and union leaders that attacks on the

42. *WAZ,* 18 October 1930, p. 252; Giesberts to Otte, 7 October 1930, NL Otte/6/132; KAB Archiv, Reichsvorstand, 9–10 October 1930.

43. GcG circular of 2 October 1930, NL Otte/2/119–21.

44. *Zentralblatt,* 15 October 1930, p. 305, 1 November, pp. 333f., and 15 November 1930, pp. 351f.

45. *Der Deutsche,* 22 November 1930.

government worsened unemployment by strengthening radical movements and persuading foreign investors to withdraw their capital from Germany.[46] Stegerwald realized that labor relations were now so tense as to make a formal revival of the old ZAG virtually impossible, but he hoped that management and labor could reach voluntary agreement in most branches of industry on measures to lower the cost of living and to stretch out employment opportunities by shortening the work week.[47] The first serious round of negotiations took place in the Labor Ministry on November 12, involving Otte, Graßmann and two other ADGB leaders, and a delegation of industrialists led by Silverberg, Kastl, and von Borsig. On December 9 they agreed tentatively on a joint program that demanded elimination of the sales tax on department stores, while declaring that government measures to protect agriculture "should not conflict with price reductions" and "must take account of Germany's position in the world market, which requires expansion of exports." Employers promised to implement the 40-hour week wherever possible, giving part-time work priority over layoffs. They also endorsed collective bargaining and state labor arbitration, while labor leaders agreed that existing collective labor contracts should be altered through negotiation where plants were threatened by bankruptcy. The program contained remarkable concessions by business leaders, who faced bitter opposition to their moderate policies that was centered in the Ruhr mine operators' association.[48] The executive committee of the ADGB endorsed this agreement but was overruled on December 15 by the delegates of its member unions, who feared that the primary objective of the employers was to discredit the unions by associating them with wage cuts. Pleas by Otto Wels, Fritz Husemann, Tarnow, and Graßmann to accept the agreement for the sake of political stability were ignored. Otte deplored this decision, arguing that the Free unions failed to realize that further wage reductions were inevitable but that the proposed agreement would exert a restraining influence on employers. He also warned Christian union leaders that a large faction in the industrial associations had opposed talks with the trade unions from the beginning, rejoiced at the intransigence of the ADGB, and would now launch a general offensive against state labor arbitration and collective bargaining.[49] As Otte and some socialist labor leaders recog-

46. Eisner, pp. 239–45, and Pünder, pp. 71f., entry of 8 November 1930. See also the Chancellory memorandum of December 1930, reprinted in Matthias and Morsey (eds.), pp. 203–05.
47. See Otte's account of conversations with Stegerwald in the GcG circular of 16 October 1930, NL Otte/2/126f., and Fonk to ten Hompel, 11 November 1930, NL ten Hompel/35.
48. Wengst, "Unternehmerverbände und Gewerkschaften," pp. 109–12, and Maurer and Wengst (eds.), *Quellen. Politik und Wirtschaft*, pp. 478, 496–98.
49. Maurer and Wengst (eds.), *Quellen*, pp. 498–507, 518f., and NL Otte/2/148, GcG circular of 15 December 1930.

nized, this probably represented the last chance to revive a healthy form of "corporate pluralism" in the Weimar Republic.

The fear of an assault on the social institutions of the Republic helped persuade Otte and other Christian union leaders that they should strengthen Brüning and Stegerwald against the "true reactionaries" in the business community, in the Agriculture and Economics ministries, and in the president's camarilla. At the end of 1930 the Christian union press began to display a markedly more favorable attitude toward the government, and Otte resumed meetings with Center Party industrialists in order to support Stegerwald's ongoing efforts to revive the ZAG. Seeking to facilitate these talks and to defend Stegerwald against socialist attacks, *Der Deutsche* even conceded that wage reductions in vital export industries might be necessary to revive the economy and that the "purchasing power" economics long propagated by both the Free and Christian unions displayed "certain gaps and over-simplifications."[50] Stegerwald sought to nourish this rapprochement with the unions by leading the struggle against new tariffs demanded by Martin Schiele. On February 17, 1931, he threatened to resign from the cabinet if it accepted Schiele's counterdeflationary program after the Labor Ministry had "implemented wage reductions in order to undermine the system of reparations."[51] This clash initiated a two-month political battle in which Stegerwald's position won support from the Reich Association of Industry and the Economics, Finance, and Foreign ministries. Brüning took Stegerwald's threats quite seriously, confiding to State Secretary Pünder that he could easily dispense with the services of Wirth or von Guerard but that Stegerwald's resignation would almost undoubtedly topple the cabinet.[52] In April Schiele nevertheless secured tariff hikes for grain and livestock through the influence of President Hindenburg, but Stegerwald succeeded in vetoing the butter tariff he considered most objectionable. This was Schiele's last political victory. Brüning decided thereafter to abandon efforts to woo the radicalized agrarian organizations, and the cabinet returned to a more consistent pursuit of deflation in all sectors of the economy.[53]

Brüning and Stegerwald may have deliberately exaggerated the strength of reactionary or pro-Nazi currents in big business so as to make organized labor more pliant, but there was some foundation for the trade unionists' fears. Within

50. NL Otte/7/83, GcG Vorstand, 17 January 1931, and 3/3–6, GcG circular of 22 January 1931; NL ten Hompel/38, "Mitteilung des Handels- und Industriebeirates der Deutschen Zentrumspartei," 2 April 1931; *Zentralblatt*, 1 February 1931, pp. 34–39; *Der Deutsche*, 11 March 1931.
51. *Die Kabinette Brüning*, pp. 874–76.
52. Ibid., pp. 884–96, 905–09, and Pünder, pp. 90f., entry of 25 February 1931.
53. *Zentrumsprotokolle 1926–33*, pp. 524–26, 21–24 March 1931; *Die Kabinette Brüning*, pp. 1023–30, 25 April 1931; Koops, pp. 860–64.

the DVP, Hans Bechly and Otto Thiel sought desperately at the beginning of 1931 to win public endorsement of collective bargaining from the representatives of Ruhr industry by offering to support drastic restrictions in the Labor Ministry's arbitration powers and cutbacks in the social insurance system. The concessions they offered in negotiations with the prominent lobbyist Max Schlenker went far beyond those acceptable to the blue-collar Christian unions. However, in mid-February Schlenker refused to sign any joint declaration on DVP social policy, explaining that Ruhr industrialists could not reach any agreement on these issues and that most of them inclined to the view that "the importance of trade unions may diminish greatly in the not too distant future."[54] Gustav Krupp and Albert Vögler began at this time to repudiate the moderate stance of the Reich Association of Industry by demanding that the government abolish state arbitration and permit employers faced by bankruptcy to insist on renegotiation of their collective labor contracts.[55] At the end of February the United Steelworks shut down its mill in Ruhrort-Meiderich after local workers, following the exhortations of their union leaders, rejected an ultimatum to accept 20% wage cuts. Employers exploited this event to launch a strident press campaign that cast the trade unions in the role of the Pharisees before Pontius Pilate: "We have a law, and by that law he must die." The Christian unions found to their dismay that shopkeepers, communal officials, and even many priests active in the Catholic workers' clubs were swayed by such articles, blaming trade unionism for the depression. GcG leaders concluded that the Ruhr industrialists were determined to revive the Yellow unions.[56] In April, when Free and Christian union leaders visited the Labor Ministry to protest government plans for further reductions in social insurance benefits, Stegerwald leaked documents to them showing that the League of Employers' Associations, although it refrained from making such demands in public, privately pressured the government to abolish unemployment insurance altogether and return to welfare payments with a means test. This revelation placed a further strain on relations between management and labor but helped again to persuade Free and Christian union leaders that Stegerwald was doing the best job possible of resisting reactionary demands.[57]

---

54. Bechly to Dingeldey, 16 February 1931, NL Dingeldey/35/15f. See also Dingeldey to Schlenker, 30 October 1930, and reply of 14 January 1931 (NL Dingeldey/35/5–10), and Thiel to Dingeldey, 26 January 1931 (NL Dingeldey/92/11–14).

55. Michael Grübler, *Die Spitzenverbände der Wirtschaft und das erste Kabinett Brüning* (Düsseldorf, 1982), pp. 349–52.

56. *Zentralblatt*, 1 March 1931, pp. 78f., and 15 March 1931, pp. 84–87; *WAZ*, 7 March 1931, pp. 56f.; GcG circulars of 4–9 March 1931, NL Otte/3/36–43; Heinrich Fahrenbrach to Stegerwald, 16 April 1931, NL Stegerwald/008/1931-II/no. 905.

57. NL Otte/3/49–71, circular of 28 April 1931.

Thus Stegerwald persuaded the unions to moderate their position, but organized labor also exerted somewhat more influence on the Brüning cabinet than most commentators recognize. Much like the other chancellors from the Center Party who headed nonsocialist governments, Fehrenbach and Marx, Brüning was inclined to dismiss petitions submitted by the SPD or ADGB alone as expressions of doctrinaire socialism but grew extremely nervous when the Christian unions endorsed them. This became clear after the government issued its complex emergency decree of June 1931. The Christian unions' initial response was mixed. Otte defended the measures halfheartedly, while the organ of the Christian miners' union condemned them. The leaders of the Catholic workers' clubs charged in private that Imbusch's tough rhetoric merely encouraged Ruhr workers to join the Communist factory cells.[58] Imbusch's stance received vigorous support from most member unions of the GcG, however, and on June 15 it decided to sign a joint protest declaration with the ADGB and Hirsch–Duncker unions. On June 18 Imbusch persuaded the national committee of the DGB to agitate in public against the decree provisions cutting unemployment insurance benefits, miners' pensions, and the wages of city-employed manual workers.[59] Repeated private warnings to Stegerwald, who often attended meetings of the GcG executive committee, that the Christian unions would continue this agitation and cooperate more closely with the ADGB in issuing joint petitions obviously impressed the chancellor and labor minister. In August 1931 they won the Christian unions' gratitude by persuading the cabinet to rescind the decree provisions concerning the wages of communal workers and to restore some of the cuts in unemployment insurance benefits. This decision provoked sharp attacks in the press, even including Center Party newspapers, against the government's willingness to knuckle under to union demands. Some Center Party politicians also attacked the new tendency in the Christian unions to heed calls for "proletarian solidarity."[60]

Deteriorating labor relations in the Ruhr coal mines induced the Christian unions to increase their pressure on the government. In July 1931 Stegerwald incurred the wrath of the mine operators by prolonging for three months the wage levels established in January. Employers considered this decree an

---

58. *Zentralblatt,* 15 June 1931, p. 177; *Der Bergknappe,* 20 July 1931; KAB Archiv, Reichsvorstand, 17–18 June 1931.
    59. *Zentralblatt,* 15 July 1931, pp. 209–11, and *Kölnische Volkszeitung,* 26 June 1931, no. 931.
    60. NL Otte/7/59, GcG Vorstand, 23 July 1931, and 3/90–95, 127, GcG circulars of 7 August, 12 August, and 13 October 1931; *Die Kabinette Brüning,* pp. 1591–98, 1611f., 19–21 August 1931; *Zentralblatt,* 15 August 1931, pp. 253f., 1 September, pp. 271f., and 1 October 1931, pp. 289f.; *Kölnische Volkszeitung,* 25 August 1931, no. 400B, 31 August, no. 410, and 5 November 1931, no. 524B.

egregious example of how the government's desire for popularity resulted in disastrous "political wages," and they threatened to discharge tens of thousands of workers if the Labor Ministry did not decree 12% wage reductions at the end of September.[61] In the late summer the public statements of the national industrial associations, although they still avoided direct attacks on Brüning, began to endorse the Ruhr industrialists' radical criticism of the social institutions of the Weimar Republic, which allegedly represented an unviable mixture of socialism and capitalism.[62] Even Brüning's staunch supporters in the Center Party Committee for Commerce and Industry petitioned the government to reduce all collective contract wages by 25%, and Walther Rademacher of the Conservative People's Party, one of the architects of the compromise social legislation of the mid-1920s, urged Count Westarp to help topple Brüning because of the chancellor's stubborn defense of collective bargaining.[63] Stegerwald implored the leaders of the Christian unions in September 1931 to volunteer suggestions for making collective bargaining and state arbitration more elastic in order to save them, but Imbusch persuaded his colleagues to reject any concessions. Moreover, a conference of GcG functionaries in Rhineland-Westphalia resolved at the end of the month to support the Christian miners' refusal to accept any wage cuts.[64]

Stegerwald suffered from a tremendous nervous strain as he entered this cross fire between the industrial associations and the trade unions. In private correspondence he sharply condemned the refusal by his former colleagues to accept economic realities. "Since the Christian labor movement lacks any clear social theory, you often demand things that cannot be carried out during a crisis within a capitalist system. Many in the camp of Christian workers view the capitalist system as a moneybag from which one takes whatever one wants." Stegerwald warned that the Ruhr mine operators had long pressured the national industrial associations to support Hugenberg and Hitler in their efforts to overthrow parliamentary government, and that the Labor Ministry would play into their hands if it again rejected any reduction in miners' wages.[65] On September 30 Brüning and Stegerwald persuaded the cabinet to resolve the labor dispute

---

61. BAK R43I/2178/306–15, Zechenverband to Labor Ministry, 14 September 1931. See also Turner, *"Ruhrlade,"* pp. 134f.

62. See *Die Kabinette Brüning*, pp. 1764–69, joint petition by all the major business associations of 29 September 1931.

63. NL ten Hompel/32, Fonk to ten Hompel, 12 August 1931, and NL Westarp, Rademacher to Westarp, two letters of 15 October 1931.

64. NL Otte/3/117–20, GcG circular of 29 September 1931, and 7/32, GcG Vorstand, 3 October 1931. See also NL Imbusch/2, Gewerkverein Hauptvorstand, 10 October 1931.

65. Stegerwald to Jakob Kaiser et al., 23 September 1931, NL Stegerwald/104/Nachtrag no. 17.

with a special presidential decree mandating 7% wage cuts, which were made painless by government subsidies releasing miners and their employers from the duty to contribute to the unemployment insurance system. Industrialists outside the Ruhr protested sharply against this act of favoritism, however.[66] Stegerwald wrote his union friends on October 2 that he had come to understand the dilemma faced by the ex-socialists Pierre Laval and Ramsay MacDonald. He asked them whether he should follow his inclinations, resign from the cabinet, and reap popularity, even if that meant toppling Brüning and handing the government over to Hitler and Hugenberg, or whether he should imitate the French and British labor leaders, who pursued the economic policies they considered objectively correct, even at the cost of a breach with their former comrades.[67] Heinrich Fahrenbrach, chairman of the Christian textile workers' union, replied tactfully that Stegerwald could reconcile his duties to the state and to workers by stressing at every opportunity that "any weakening of the trade unions strengthens Communism." The Christian unions asked nothing more than that the labor minister defend them in the same way that Schiele defended agriculture, State Secretary Trendelenburg business, and Finance Minister Dietrich the civil service. Fahrenbrach concluded by referring to Stegerwald's bid for the chairmanship of the Center Party in December 1928, promising that if Stegerwald followed his advice, "then you will always have the organized Christian workers behind you, even if false friends again treat you as shabbily as they did at the Cologne Party Congress."[68]

Stegerwald's fears reflected the success of Alfred Hugenberg in persuading the Reichslandbund, the Stahlhelm, and the Nazi Party to join the DNVP at a joint rally of the national opposition in Bad Harzburg, scheduled for October 11. This development demonstrated that Brüning had made no progress toward broadening his base of support on the right, as President Hindenburg desired. According to Brüning, some industrialists also sought to persuade the president's advisers that he would never implement the wage reductions needed to save the economy because of his background as a trade union secretary, and the president urged him at the beginning of October to dismiss all cabinet ministers suspected of leftist sympathies, including Stegerwald, Wirth, and Dietrich.[69] Brüning salvaged his position on the eve of the Harzburg rally by making what he considered minor sacrifices, dismissing Wirth and Foreign Minister Curtius. Steger-

---

66. *Die Kabinette Brüning*, pp. 1772f., and Gewerkverein christlicher Bergarbeiter, *Geschäftsbericht des Hauptvorstandes für die Jahre 1930/32*, pp. 105–07.
67. NL Stegerwald/104/Nachtrag no. 18.
68. Ibid., Fahrenbrach to Stegerwald, 3 October 1931.
69. *Zentrumsprotokolle 1926–33*, pp. 545f., 12 October 1931, and Brüning, p. 386.

wald also persuaded the cabinet to retain compulsory state labor arbitration and refuse to authorize the undercutting of wage levels set by collective labor contracts. A joyous Fahrenbrach reported to his union colleagues that, although Brüning had wavered in the face of the industrialists' onslaught, the firm stand by the Christian unions had stiffened the resistance of Stegerwald, who had then won Brüning over.[70] Hindenburg remained disappointed, however, by Brüning's failure to persuade prominent industrialists or agrarians to enter his cabinet. Brüning won only the services of Hans von Schlange-Schöningen, a former head of the Pomeranian DNVP who had already lost the confidence of most agrarians, as Reich commissar for *Osthilfe,* and of Hermann Warmbold, a relatively obscure expert on chemical products for agriculture, as economics minister.[71]

Although Brüning turned back the campaign by industrialists for an economic policy of untrammeled free enterprise, his own concept of deflation through balanced sacrifices produced a new emergency decree in December 1931 that placed great strains on the patience of trade unionists. Brüning ordered a 10% reduction in the prices of all cartels and syndicates, and a return to the wage level of January 1, 1927, in all collective labor contracts. This unprecedented interference with contract rights proved equally offensive to management and labor. Nevertheless, the ADGB leadership was now so thoroughly convinced that a fascist dictatorship would result if Brüning fell that it considered public opposition to the decree futile.[72] Christian union leaders reacted to the decree with an unprecedented display of confusion. Their *Zentralblatt* alternately exhorted Christian workers to resist the government's measures, to display understanding for its difficulties, and to accept its decisions as Germany's tragic fate. When Brüning defended his decree before the Center Reichstag delegation with a lengthy speech on foreign affairs and the world economic system, however, Heinrich Imbusch replied that "it is pointless to preach reason to hungry men."[73] Although Imbusch apparently did not realize it, this was also the least reasonable of Brüning's major policy decisions from the standpoint of the economist. Soaring unemployment, the devaluation of the English pound, and the imposition of foreign exchange controls in the summer of 1931, which

---

70. *Die Kabinette Brüning,* pp. 1788f., 2 October 1931, and Fahrenbrach to Kaiser, 10 October 1931, NL Kaiser/220.

71. See Bracher, *Auflösung,* pp. 385–90, and Pünder, p. 108, entry of 23 November 1931.

72. See "Leipart und Breitscheid über die Notverordnung" (Berlin, 1931, speeches of 16 December), and Otte's report on a conference with ADGB leaders of 11 December 1931 in NL Otte/3/155.

73. *Zentralblatt,* 15 December 1931, pp. 369–73, and 1 January 1932, pp. 1f.; Morsey, *Zentrumsprotokolle 1926–33,* p. 557, 15 December 1931.

increased the maneuvering room for monetary policy, all rendered Brüning's stubborn adherence to the program of deflation highly questionable. At this point his obsession with abolishing reparations doubtless clouded Brüning's judgment.[74]

Imbusch's gruff response reflected an organizational crisis within the Christian unions that threatened to rob the Brüning cabinet of one of its last sources of popular support. The Christian unions lost only 2% of their membership in 1930, compared with 5% for the ADGB, but in the first six months of 1931 they began to suffer as much as their socialist rivals, losing 6.5%.[75] By the end of 1931, Christian union members, who were clustered in the centers of heavy industry on the Rhine and Ruhr, suffered more heavily from unemployment than did Free unionists. Surveys by the Catholic workers' clubs of western Germany in 1931 found that as many as 70% of their members were unemployed in some industrial districts, while no district reported a majority working full time.[76] The Christian unions kept pace with the ADGB in providing unemployment benefits to members throughout 1931, but by December some of the smaller Christian unions stood on the verge of bankruptcy. All Christian unions would be forced to curtail unemployment benefits drastically if the economy did not revive soon, which would ease the task of antiunion agitators in the Communist Party and the NSDAP. The DGB and clerical press emphasized, moreover, that unemployment struck most directly at the roots of the Christian labor movement by undermining family values, destroying pride in one's trade, and in general replacing cultural with material concerns.[77] By the beginning of 1932 the very survival of the Christian unions depended on prompt action by the government to reduce unemployment.

THE REVIVAL OF CHRISTIAN SOCIALISM

In 1919–20 many figures in the Christian labor movement had adopted the slogans of "Christian socialism" or the *Gemeinwirtschaft* in order to press for fundamental reforms of the capitalist economy. Such socialist currents had been

74. Contrast Borchardt, "Zwangslagen," pp. 167–74, with Carl-Ludwig Holtfrerich, *Alternativen zu Brünings Wirtschaftspolitik in der Weltwirtschaftskrise* (Wiesbaden, 1982), pp. 16–22, and Sanmann, pp. 133–36.

75. GcG, *Jarhbuch 1931*, pp. 50f., and NL Otte/7/41–56, questionnaires to member unions on their problems in the summer of 1931.

76. Katholische Arbeiter-Bewegung Westdeutschlands, *Bericht über die Jahre 1925–31*, pp. 75–79, and WAZ, 1 October 1932, p. 240.

77. NL Imbusch/2, "Generalversammlung 1933," pp. 2f.; Christlicher Metallarbeiterverband, *Generalversammlung 1932*, pp. 42–44; *Zentralblatt*, 15 June 1930, p. 188, 15 October, pp. 309f., and 15 November 1930, pp. 337f.; *Kirchlich-soziale Blätter*, Jan–Feb. 1931, pp. 1–8.

driven underground during the 1920s but emerged with redoubled force during the Great Depression. The drift toward socialism in the Christian unions can be said, with some precision, to have begun with the banking crisis of July 1931, when the leaders of several investment banks in Berlin appealed to the Reich for massive subsidies in order to stave off collapse. The public experienced sensational revelations at this time of mismanagement and corruption in big business. The DGB press agreed at first with Chancellor Brüning's assessment that the government should resist calls for interference with free enterprise, but repeated warnings against experiments with a planned economy merely underscored the concept's growing popularity.[78]

Brüning soon imposed some restrictions on free enterprise by creating a Bank Oversight Office and insisting that government officials join the supervisory boards of all banks receiving government loans. These innovations enabled the government to exert significant influence over major investment decisions in the private sector, if it chose to do so.[79] The Christian unions applauded this step. On November 1, 1931, the *Zentralblatt* went further by arguing that the banking crisis proved that the misguided investments of private businessmen rather than collectivist social policies were to blame for the Great Depression. The trade unions should insist that the new government banking controls serve as the "beginnings of an orderly planned economy" in which the world would never again see mountains of wheat, cotton, and coffee burned while millions suffered privation.[80] Two months later the paper even adopted a view formerly denounced as Marxist: that historical progress depended on the replacement of one dominant class by another.

> All true revolutions have their historical origins not in the wickedness of the lower orders but in the failure of the old leadership. One can even say that this thought has something profoundly Christian about it. . . . We need not engage in a partisan interpretation of history in order to proclaim the thesis that workers are now summoned to leadership. Everything points in this direction.

78. Stegerwald explained the government's policy to the GcG executive committee on 23 July 1931 (NL Otte/7/58f.). Their consensus was reflected in *Der Deutsche*, 22 July 1931; *Zentralblatt*, 1 August 1931, pp. 227f., and 15 August, pp. 241–44; and in Walther Lambach, "Planwirtschaft?" *Hamburgischer Corrrespondent*, 21 August 1931 (NL Lambach/15).

79. Karl Erich Born, *Die deutsche Bankenkrise 1931* (Munich, 1967), pp. 153–71; Henning Köhler, "Das Verhältnis von Reichsregierung und Großbanken 1931," in Mommsen, Petzina, and Weisbrod (eds.), pp. 870–73.

80. Heinrich Körner, "Um die Neuordnung des wirtschaftlichen und sozialen Lebens," *Zentralblatt*, 1 November 1931, pp. 322f.

Nonetheless, this editorial described the new order that German workers would soon establish in exceedingly vague terms. Its essential principles would be "freedom in the workplace and the economy," fervent patriotism, and "reward according to achievement [das Leistungsprinzip]," all of which might be considered the essential principles of the nineteenth-century bourgeoisie.[81]

Such rhetorical tacking between revolutionary and conservative slogans reflected a growing conflict between Catholic social theory and the economic views prevalent in the Christian unions. In 1930–31 the social theorists of the Volksverein and the Catholic workers' clubs participated in the international discussions that led to the promulgation of the papal encyclical *Quadragesimo anno* on the fortieth anniversary of Pope Leo XIII's *Rerum novarum*. The corporatist ideal expressed in this document avoided hierarchical overtones by endorsing the existing voluntary associations of workers and employers as the foundation for the cooperative society of the future, but the pope, insisting that the state not infringe on the rights of the independent entrepreneur, also instructed all Catholics to oppose socialism and communism.[82] On the other hand, several member unions of the GcG adopted essentially socialist positions because of the economic problems they encountered. The Christian construction workers' union had always advocated government action to flatten the erratic business cycle in their trade, while seeking to build a network of producers' cooperatives that might someday supplant the private entrepreneur. Uniquely high unemployment rates during the Great Depression caused it to demand that the government assume primary responsibility for raising mortgage capital and planning housing starts.[83] More significant was the drift leftward by the Christian miners' union, which argued that its employers did not perform a significant economic function because the Rhenish-Westphalian Coal Syndicate was so bureaucratized as to make the concept of entrepreneurial risk-taking meaningless.[84] As labor relations deteriorated in 1931, mine operators sought to discredit the unions by publishing stories about mismanagement and corruption in the miners' pension fund, while the Christian miners' union responded by exposing the blunders of management. At year's end, the *Bergknappe* even compared the

81. *Zentralblatt*, 15 January 1932, pp. 18–20.
82. See Oswald Nell-Breuning, "Der Königswinterer Kreis und sein Anteil an 'Quadragesimo anno,'" in *Wie sozial ist die Kirche?* (Düsseldorf, 1972), pp. 99–136; *WAZ*, 3 October 1931, pp. 237–40; *Zentralblatt*, 1 September 1931, pp. 259–61.
83. Zentralverband christlicher Bauarbeiter, *15. Generalversammlung 1928*, p. 129, and *Geschäftsbericht des Vorstandes für die Jahre 1928–30*, pp. 44f., 63–65; BAK R43I/2045/143–45, Friedrich Baltrusch to Chancellor Brüning, 25 May 1932.
84. Gewerkverein christlicher Bergarbeiter, *20. Generalversammlung 1930*, pp. 40f., and "Die 'Verbeamtung' der Wirtschaft," by Prof. A. Streller, *Der Bergknappe*, 18 July 1931, pp. 3f.

mine operators' stance in collective bargaining with England's "hunger block-ade" during World War I, perhaps the most deadly insult that a patriotic German could direct at a fellow countryman.[85]

In January 1932 Heinrich Imbusch launched a campaign to nationalize the coal mines by organizing two mass rallies in the Ruhr. He and his lieutentants presented a strong case that could not be dismissed as Marxist. They observed that the state-owned coal mines reported modest profits in 1931 while the private mines complained of massive losses. For years the coal syndicate had, they argued, extracted monopoly profits from the entire economy, which were then invested in enormous labor-saving machines that deprived miners of work, pro-duced far more coal than anyone needed, and deprived other industries of much needed capital. The only solution, they argued, was to reverse the unfortunate trend toward selfish individualism embodied in the reform of the Prussian min-ing laws in 1865 and return to the fine old Prussian tradition of public ownership of the nation's mineral wealth. Although the attacks on technological innovation revealed that Imbusch was no economist, his concern that growth sectors of industry were being starved of investment funds because of the uniquely strong market position of the coal syndicate was shared by many contemporary ex-perts.[86]

It might seem that Imbusch's new program would cause a collision with that noted defender of private enterprise, Heinrich Brüning, but it appears to have been designed to deflect the wrath of the miners away from the government. In the rallies demanding socialization, Imbusch also praised Brüning's impressive diplomatic success in persuading the Entente powers to accept at least a tempo-rary moratorium on reparations, and he toned down his criticism of the govern-ment's emergency decrees. Indeed, Imbusch sought to reinforce Brüning's au-thority by arguing that the mine operators deserved to be expropriated, in part, because they abused their economic power to support the "national opposition," sabotaging all efforts to revive parliamentary government. The mine operators represented a "state within the state" and disrupted national unity during the most sensitive phase of Brüning's campaign to liberate Germany from the chains of the Treaty of Versailles: "Therefore we must extract this thorn from the flesh of the German people." Imbusch said nothing about immediate steps to pressure the government to adopt his program, merely observing: "I have confidence in

85. *Der Bergknappe*, 28 November 1931, p. 2. See also the outraged comments on the Chris-tian miners' propaganda in the "Stimmungsbericht" of the *Bergbauverein* in Essen, 1 January 1932, ZStA/RAM/288/324f.

86. *Der Bergknappe*, 30 January 1932, p. 2, and 13 February 1932, p. 1. See also Weisbrod, pp. 63–92, and Ottfried Dascher, "Probleme der Konzernorganisation," in Mommsen, Petzina, and Weisbrod (eds.), pp. 128–34.

the ability of the operators of the Ruhr mines to compel through their recklessness even the most reluctant of governments to take this step."[87]

Indeed, Brüning and Stegerwald were not unreceptive to Imbusch's arguments. Stegerwald had written the Christian union leaders on October 2, 1931, that he and Brüning fully shared their anger against the Ruhr mine operators: "only an idiot" could advocate nationalization before the state put its own finances in order, but afterward the government would seriously consider the idea. On the same day, Brüning observed within the cabinet that he was "no friend of a planned economy, but the public demands it. The world is moving in this direction."[88] Years later Brüning wrote that Imbusch had thoroughly understood the economic rationale for deflation (to Brüning the highest possible compliment) and had given the government valuable political support with his attacks on the Ruhr industrialists.[89] Imbusch had some reason to expect the government to adopt his program if he succeeded in bringing public opinion behind it.

Imbusch's campaign for nationalization of the mines caused some confusion among DGB leaders but proved popular with the rank and file. He promptly won enthusiastic support from the Christian textile workers' union, the Young German Order, the Bavarian Catholic workers' clubs, and the economics experts in the Berlin headquarters of the Christian unions, Baltrusch and Heinrich Körner. All the Christian unions formally endorsed his plan by the end of April.[90] The Christian Social People's Service also backed Imbusch when it denounced the "hegemony of the trusts and syndicates" and declared its preference for "socialization by the state rather than socialization by the sinister forces of the banks and stock exchanges" wherever the truly independent entrepreneur could not maintain himself.[91] However, suggestions by the Christian miners that their industry was only one of several needing radical reform prompted leading Catholic social theorists to dig in their heels. Theodor Brauer and the leaders of the Catholic workers' clubs of western Germany conceded that a state coal monopoly was permissible under some circumstances, but they sharply opposed a planned economy or socialization of other industries. The Christian metalworkers' union

87. *Der Bergknappe*, 20 February 1932, p. 1, and Heinrich Imbusch, "Für Freiheit, Gerechtigkeit und Fortschritt," speech of 10 January 1932 (Essen, 1932), p. 26.
88. Stegerwald to Kaiser et al., 2 October 1931, NL Stegerwald/014/Nachtrag no. 18; *Die Kabinette Brüning*, p. 1793.
89. Brüning to Frau Imbusch, 17 December 1948, NL Imbusch/4.
90. *Textilarbeiter-Zeitung*, 5 March 1932, p. 32; *Der Arbeiter (München)*, 4 February 1932, p. 2; NL Imbusch/1, Carl Schirmer to Rütten, 20 February 1932; NL Imbusch/2, Gewerkverein Hauptvorstand, 30 April 1932, p. 11.
91. See the campaign poster from the spring of 1932 in StA Osnabrück C1/15/11.

adopted the same stance, and the last congress of the Christian unions in September 1932 was dominated by a heated debate over the feasibility of a planned economy.[92] But there could be no doubt about the sympathies of the membership. Although Franz Wieber was compelled in rallies of the Christian metal workers to rebuke delegates who rose to demand expropriation of the capitalists,[93] there is no evidence of complaints from coal miners against the course of Imbusch. His polemics with employers apparently increased his popularity greatly.

Imbusch's response to the Great Depression resembled that of the SPD Reichstag delegation, which introduced several bills for nationalizing key industries or increasing the government's power for economic planning. On the the other hand, the Christian unions displayed little interest in the ADGB's more practical proposal for dealing with the immediate problem of unemployment, the Woytinsky–Tarnow–Baade plan for financing public works through expansion of the money supply. After the summer of 1931 the Free unions agitated vigorously on behalf of deficit spending.[94] Stegerwald was at first receptive to the idea but grew discouraged when his industrialist friends in the Center Party condemned it as inflationary. Pointing out that the advocates of deficit spending also included the Nazi Party, Hugenberg, and Hjalmar Schacht, Stegerwald then sought to persuade Christian workers that the W-T-B Plan would benefit only selfish landowners and industrialists who hoped for a return of hyperinflation that would free them from debt.[95] Stegerwald succeeded because the proposition that deficit spending could help revive the economy seemed mere wishful thinking to most leaders of the Christian unions, although they remained convinced that the government must undertake some sort of public works program, regardless of the threat to the currency.[96] Although some authorities condemn this stance as tragically shortsighted, hailing the W-T-B Plan as an exciting anticipation of Keynesian solutions to Germany's economic problems, many economic historians have recently argued that the Weimar Republic's total lack of credit and social stability made Keynesian formulas irrelevant.[97]

92. *Zentralblatt*, 15 March 1932, pp. 82–85, and 1 August 1932, p. 203; GcG, *13. Kongreß 1932*, esp. pp. 308–14.
93. Christlicher Metallarbeiterverband, *13. Generalversammlung 1932*, pp. 111–15.
94. Michael Schneider, *Das Arbeitsbeschaffungsprogramm des ADGB*, esp. pp. 83–87.
95. NL ten Hompel/32, Fonk to ten Hompel, 6 August and 22 August 1931; *WAZ*, 8 August 1931, p. 187, and 15 August 1931, p. 194.
96. GcG Vorstand, 16 March 1932, NL Otte/7/5f; *Zentralblatt*, 1 April 1932, p. 100.
97. Contrast Michael Schneider, *Die christlichen Gewerkschaften*, pp. 693f., with Harold James, "Gab es eine Alternative zur Wirtschaftspolitik Brünings?" *Vierteljahrschrift für Sozial- und Wirtschaftsgeschichte*, 70, no. 4 (1983), pp. 532–41, and Theodore Balderston, "The Origins of Economic Instability in Germany 1924–1930: Market Forces versus Economic Policy," *Vierteljahrschrift für Sozial- und Wirtschaftgechichte*, 69, no. 4 (1982), pp. 495–513.

One proposal for combating unemployment did enjoy great popularity among Christian workers, government action to create small farms in sparsely populated East Elbia. Even before the onset of the Great Depression, social activists in both the Catholic and Protestant churches, concerned over the gradual erosion of religious values in the big cities, advocated settlement programs in order to reverse the trend toward "excessive" industrialization and urbanization. Official Catholic teaching sanctioned compulsory land redistribution if "monopolists" denied small farmers any hope of owning the soil that they tilled, and many patriotic leagues also favored colonizing the "eastern march" in order to strengthen its defenses against Poland.[98] By January 1932 the press was filled with stories of favoritism for big landowners in the government's *Osthilfe* program, and Junkers rivaled the Ruhr mine operators as targets of popular resentment. In a cabinet meeting of February 5, Reich Commissar Schlange-Schöningen requested additional appropriations for *Osthilfe,* but Stegerwald rejected any more subsidies unless Schlange gave equal priority to subdividing bankrupt estates among settlers. Stegerwald realized that settlement programs could not solve the unemplyment problem but hoped to prevent any further influx of farmworkers into the cities while creating some jobs in housing and highway construction.[99] Above all, Stegerwald was responding to the increasingly radical mood of union members in a way that threatened the cohesion of the cabinet. Schlange-Schöningen endorsed settlement in principle but demanded that control over it be transferred from the Labor Ministry to his office. He wrote the Chancellory at the beginning of March: "I cannot condemn 25% of my fellow agrarians [Berufsgenossen] to walk the plank without having sufficient influence to guarantee that my eastern homeland is placed on an economically secure footing by true experts." Such remarks by the Pomeranian nobleman made Stegerwald and other government leaders suspect that he intended to sabotage their settlement program. Stegerwald confided to State Secretary Schäffer that Schlange's demand to control the program "would in practice mean its subordination to the large landowners," adding that this could be achieved only over Stegerwald's "political corpse."[100] This dispute delayed action on settlements for several weeks.

In February 1932 the ADGB announced plans for a Crisis Congress of the

---

98. See *Mitteilungen an die Arbeiterpräsides,* January/March 1929, pp. 21f. (Volksverein Bibliothek); *Kirchlich-soziale Blätter,* March/April 1929, pp. 31f.; and Hornung, pp. 111–15.

99. See Schorr, pp. 230–32, and Heinrich Muth, "Agrarpolitik und Parteipolitik im Frühjahr 1932," in Hermens and Schieder (eds.), pp. 319–27.

100. Udo Wengst, "Schlange-Schöningen, Ostsiedlung, und die Demission der Regierung Brüning," *Geschichte in Wissenchaft und Unterricht,* September 1979, p. 541.

Free unions to support demands for expansion of the money supply in order to create at least 1 million jobs in the public sector. Stegerwald cited this announcement in a memorandum of March 3 to argue that the government must act energetically. He submitted for consideration by the cabinet a plan for public works that would employ 200,000 workers directly and generate perhaps 400,000 additional jobs indirectly, at a cost of RM 1.2 billion. Stegerwald acknowledged that his program would require some form of deficit spending but argued: "The political dangers in this matter appear to me so great that we must not shrink from financial measures that would seem objectionable in other circumstances."[101] News of the Labor Ministry plan leaked to the press on March 7, and angry officials in the Economics Ministry and Chancellory concluded that Stegerwald was diverging from established policy in a bid for personal popularity. Conferences by senior bureaucrats in late March and early April yielded agreement that Stegerwald's plan could not possibly be financed without jeopardizing the currency.[102] On April 13 Stegerwald appeared before the Crisis Congress with the highly unpopular message that no government could stimulate economic recovery "artificially." He nevertheless gave his word to satisfy two secondary demands of the trade unions: implementation of the 40-hour week in order to "stretch out" job opportunities and vigorous promotion of farm settlements.[103] Stegerwald did not believe that these measures would significantly reduce unemployment, but he was convinced that the unions must have some proof of their ability to influence government policy if they were to continue to resist radical agitation.[104]

On April 20 Stegerwald submitted to the Chancellory a proposal to impose the 40-hour week in the mining, chemical, paper, food, and construction industries. Most of these already observed the 40-hour week in practice. However, the length of the work week varied greatly in the coal industry, with some mines demanding overtime shifts and others on half-time. The miners' unions felt that their employers sought in this way to reward deferential miners with extra work while impoverishing militant union members. The mine operators nevertheless persuaded the Economics Ministry that they must retain their freedom because

101. BAK R43I/2045/12–14.
102. BAK R43I/2045/15, Chancellory memrandum of 7 March 1932, and 2045/26–31, "Ressortbesprechungen," 1 and 5 April 1932. See also Henning Köhler, "Arbeitsbeschaffung, Siedlung und Reparationen in der Schlussphase der Regierung Brüning," *Vierteljahrshefte für Zeitgeschichte*, 17 (June 1969), pp. 280–85.
103. See the SPD's press report on the congress, reprinted in Wolfgang Luthardt (ed.), *Sozialdemokratische Arbeiterbewegung und Weimarer Republik* (Frankfurt am Main, 1978), vol. 1, pp. 252–60, and BAK R43I/2024/323–27, Chancellory memorandum of 13 April 1932.
104. GcG Vorstand, 28 April 1932, NL Otte/7/1–4, and *Zentrumsprotokolle 1926–33*, pp. 567–69, 9 May 1932.

of complex fluctuations in the demand for different types of coal, but Stegerwald flatly rejected Warmbold's arguments and demanded at the beginning of May that the cabinet reach a quick decision on his proposed decree.[105] The mine operators and the national industrial associations responded with a barrage of protests, denouncing any bureaucratic regulation of the economy. Warmbold announced his resignation from the cabinet on May 6, citing differences with Stegerwald and Dietrich.[106] The episode caused a significant change in the stance of the probusiness press. In April 1932 the *Berliner Börsen-Zeitung* still displayed great restraint in criticizing the government, but on May 14 it denounced the "Stegerwaldian spirit, i.e., the spirit of theoretical economic planners" as the major cause of the Great Depression, adding that Stegerwald's insistence on retaining state labor arbitration was in itself sufficient to ruin the prospects for economic recovery even if he did not implement further etatist reforms.[107] Brüning retained the support of the Reich Association of Industry's leadership and of Germany's mammoth petrochemical and electro-technical combines, but the radical mood of the Ruhr industrialists matched that of many other businessmen.

The conflict over the 40-hour week coincided with a revival of Stegerwald's dispute with Schlange-Schöningen. On April 19 Stegerwald acted to fulfill his second pledge to the ADGB by proposing a detailed settlement program to the cabinet that would guarantee Labor Ministry control and empower the government, in the absence of private buyers, to purchase bankrupt estates at whatever price it considered fair and subdivide them for settlers. Brüning realized, however, that he had entered another crisis in his relations with President Hindenburg, who disapproved of the cabinet's recent decision to ban the Nazi SA. Brüning anxiously sought to persuade Stegerwald in private that it was politically necessary to have an East Elbian landowner administer his settlement program, and on May 20 the labor minister formally agreed to withdraw his plan and surrender control over settlement to Schlange-Schöningen.[108] But Stegerwald would not yield in the issue of the 40-hour week. On May 23 the cabinet finally debated the Labor Ministry's proposed decree, and a majority expressed opposition. A defiant Stegerwald announced that he would not withdraw his bill unless

105. BAK R43I/1456/47–55, Stegerwald to Chancellory, 20 April 1932, and 2043/90–102, Stegerwald to Chancellory, 13 May 1932; ZStA/RAM/288/338–53, memorandum of May 1932.

106. BAK R43I/2043/18–22, 45f., 52–55: petitions to Brüning from the VDAV on 2 May 1932, the RDI on 3 May, and the RDI "Fachgruppe Bergbau" on 4 May. There are also numerous protest letters in ZStA/RAM/288/355–72. For Warmbold's resignation see Bracher, *Auflösung*, p. 444.

107. Contrast *Berliner Börsen-Zeitung*, 29 April 1932, no. 200, and 14 May, no. 224. See also Schorr, pp. 241–45.

108. Muth, pp. 331–38; Wengst, "Schlange-Schöningen," pp. 543–45; Brüning, p. 583.

the cabinet significantly altered its next emergency decree so as to satisfy his views on financing settlements, reducing the sales tax, and protecting social insurance. Brüning postponed any formal vote on the issue.[109] Stegerwald was apparently seeking grounds to resign from the cabinet before the next round of budget cuts took place.

President Hindenburg dismissed the Brüning cabinet at the end of May. Although it would be misleading to claim that the old field marshal paid much attention to the views of industrialists, the campaign by Brüning and Stegerwald to defend collective bargaining and state labor arbitration certainly constituted a major cause of their fall. President Hindenburg and General Schleicher had always assumed that Brüning's fundamental aim was to isolate Hugenberg, win support from conservatives, and persuade the Center Party to break decisively with the SPD in both Prussia and the Reich. The polemics against the cabinet by the industrial associations and the Reichslandbund in May 1932 doubtless played a crucial role in convincing them that the chancellor's support on the right was dwindling and that they had been mistaken regarding his character. We know that the president's son and adviser Oskar von Hindenburg began in May to refer derisively to Brüning and Stegerwald as the "trade unionists," and the president himself agreed that Stegerwald displayed "Bolshevik" tendencies in the settlement issue.[110] Petitions to the president in May 1932 from prominent East Elbian agrarians, whose views Hindenburg undoubtedly respected, did not confine themselves to the specific problems of agriculture but also attacked Brüning's policies on industrial wage levels and social insurance.[111] When the president received Count Westarp to discuss the political situation after Brüning's resignation, his aide Meißner explained that "the change was necessary in order to make possible a more firmly and clearly nationalist policy and to liberate the cabinet from the influence of the trade unions." Meißner later reiterated as Westarp was leaving that Brüning's economic policy had been confused, and that "the influence of the tradè unions and Stegerwald hindered thoroughgoing measures."[112]

Brüning's fall benefited the Christian labor movement in the short run. Economic pressures had pushed the Christian unions so far to the left in the spring of 1932 that they could no longer afford any association with the govern-

109. Cabinet minutes, 23 May 1932, BAK R43I/1456/269–71.
110. See Pünder, pp. 127–29, entry of 29 May 1932; Wengst, "Schlange-Schöningen," pp. 545f.; Brüning, pp. 590–600; and the president's memorandum of 10 June 1932, reprinted in Thilo Vogelsang, *Reichswehr, Staat und NSDAP* (Stuttgart, 1962), pp. 459–66.
111. For example, Graf Kalckreuth to Hindenburg, 12 May 1932, ZStA/RLB/54/50–53.
112. See Westarp's memorandum of 1 June 1932 in Werner Conze, "Zum Sturz Brünings. Dokumentation," *Vierteljahrshefte für Zeitgeschichte*, 1 (June 1953), pp. 287f.

ment. The extent to which Imbusch succeeded in altering the economic outlook of Christian workers, despite the rearguard action fought by Wieber and Theodor Brauer on behalf of private enterprise, became clear when the public learned in July 1932 that the Reich had acquired a controlling interest in the United Steelworks from Friedrich Flick. The GcG promptly joined the SPD in demanding that this new financial bailout lead to effective government control of heavy industry as a whole.[113] Both the Christian unions and the CSVD, doubtless the last organizations outside the Center Party that sought to rally popular support for Brüning, would probably have turned against him if he had implemented the austerity measures planned for his fifth major emergency decree.[114] Hindenburg's appointment of the arch-conservative Catholic agrarian, Franz von Papen, to form a cabinet of aristocrats and bureaucrats enabled the Christian labor movement to go into flamboyant opposition with no qualms of conscience. When Papen implemented in June virtually the same measures that Brüning had planned in May, ex-minister Stegerwald could join his old friends in denouncing the "reactionary" government.[115]

In a deeper sense, of course, Brüning's fall represented a decisive defeat for the Christian-nationalist labor movement. The attacks on Brüning and Stegerwald in the presidential entourage reflected a widespread trend during the Great Depression for the Christian unions to lose all contact with moderate industrialists and agrarians who desired to strengthen moderate elements in organized labor. As DGB leaders frequently complained, public opinion had come to brand trade unionism itself as Marxist.[116] The same development had taken place among left liberals. In February 1930 Anton Erkelenz wrote the prominent Stuttgart industrialist Robert Bosch, a champion of the Weimar Coalition in 1919 and disciple of Friedrich Naumann, that "if things have come so far that such a generous and reasonable entrepreneur as yourself can no longer reach any understanding with such a passionately objective [leidenschaftlich sachlich urteilender] labor leader as myself, then indeed the time would have come where open conflict between the two camps must break out." Angered by high wage

---

113. *Zentralblatt*, 1 August 1932, pp. 194f., and GcG, *13. Kongreß 1932*, p. 345. For background see Henning Köhler, "Zum Verhältnis Friedrich Flicks zur Reichsregierung am Ende der Weimarer Republik," in Mommsen, Petzina, and Weisbrod (eds.), pp. 879–83.

114. The protocols of two conferences suggest an imminent breach: CSVD Reichsleitung, 8 May 1932, NL Mumm/330/392–97, and cabinet reception for union leaders, 18 May 1932, BAK R43I/2045/147–50.

115. See Reichsarbeiterbeirat der Deutschen Zentrumspartei, "Um den sozialen Volksstaat," speeches at a rally in Essen on June 29, 1932, Volksverein Bibliothek.

116. *Der Deutsche*, 29 May 1932; *WAZ*, 11 June 1932, pp. 139f.; *Zentralblatt*, 15 June 1932, pp. 158–60, and 15 July, pp. 190–92.

levels and years of friction with his factory council over technological innovations, Bosch nevertheless continued his march into the antidemocratic camp.[117] The DGB pursued two basic goals throughout the Weimar period: to forge a consensus between the trade unions and moderate employers concerning social and economic policy, and to win acceptance for trade unionism within nationalist circles so that resentment against the Treaty of Versailles did not fuel socially reactionary, antipluralist movements. The first battle was lost when Brüning fell. The second then entered its most desperate phase, when the National Socialist German Workers' Party (Nationalsozialistische Deutsche Arbeiterpartei, NSDAP) emerged as the strongest political movement in the country.

117. Bosch to Erkelenz, 20 January 1930, and reply of 3 February, NL Erkelenz/126. See also the correspondence in vol. 136: when Erkelenz appealed to Bosch in the fall of 1932 to defend the Weimar constitution in public, he did not even receive a direct reply. Bosch's aide responded with a rambling attack on "French-style" parliamentarism and called for a "neo-aristocracy" to govern Germany (Debatin to Erkelenz, 12 October 1932).

7

The Rise of National Socialism

Christian trade unionists realized from the early 1920s that they faced dangerous competition from numerous movements of the radical right that espoused the goal of weaning workers from Marxism. According to a hostile but well-informed witness, Adam Stegerwald told his lieutenants after the occupation of the Ruhr in 1923: "In the last decade the trade union tide swept through Germany. In the next ten years Germany will be dominated by the nationalist movement. This speeding locomotive will run over us unless we manage to climb aboard."[1] Many of these movements advocated a corporatist reform of society superficially similar to that urged by Christian labor leaders. The DGB membership displayed a lively interest in the most successful of these movements, Italian Fascism, and in the groups that sought to imitate it north of the Alps. However, assessments of fascism within the Christian-nationalist labor movement fell into three distinct categories. Despite claims by the DGB to have forged a unified movement, responses to fascism revealed that the value systems prevalent among white-collar workers in the DHV, Protestant blue-collar workers in the Nationalist Workers' League, and Catholic workers remained very different.

ATTITUDES TOWARD FASCISM IN THE DGB

As we have seen, Adam Stegerwald's efforts to build a centrist political movement encountered resistance throughout the 1920s from workers in the DNVP who identified with the right. This resistance was strongest among the thousands

1. Wilhelm Schmidt in *Deutsche Werksgemeinschaft*, 16 March 1924, p. 6.

of members of the Nationalist Union of Commercial Employees who had supported the anti-Semitic German Social Party before 1914, men such as Georg
Brost and Alfred Diller, senior DHV officials who had been skeptical from the
start about allying with the blue-collar Christian unions. They found to their
consternation, however, that the leading spokesmen for "racial purity" in the
DNVP were thoroughly hostile toward trade unionism. The *völkisch* publicists
Axel von Freytagh-Loringhoven and Max Maurenbrecher counted among the
most extreme opponents of social legislation and collective bargaining, and the
racist Major Henning led the opposition in the DNVP Reichstag delegation to
the DHV's proposals for profit sharing.[2] The issue of anti-Semitism became
acutely embarrassing for these DHV activists after the assassination of Walther
Rathenau in 1922, when the Christian Socials joined other party moderates to
demand the expulsion of Henning and his racist colleagues Wulle and von
Graefe. They later announced that the DHV, although it was the oldest and most
dedicated guardian of *völkisch* ideals, approved the expulsion because "a certain
faction in the *völkisch* movement . . . feels justified in treating union members
as second-class citizens."[3] This press release set the tone for numerous attacks on
the Racial Freedom Party founded by the expellees.

The DHV's chairman, Hans Bechly, encouraged his followers to support
parliamentary democracy, although he avoided any debate over racial ideology.
At the national congress of the DHV in June 1924, Bechly stressed that his union
had been "German nationalist" and *völkisch* long before any parties gave themselves these names. "*Völkisch* ideals should not be a partisan issue but should,
like Christian ideals, permeate all of public life. . . . No party will ever grow
strong enough—even if it grew very large it would never be cohesive enough—
to bring about the unity of the German people through political means."[4] Bechly
also opposed directly a common thesis among antidemocratic ideologues by
exhorting his followers not to blame parliamentary institutions for the divisions
in German society, but rather to help overcome the spirit of class hatred that
prevented the Reichstag from functioning properly. The congress adopted a
resolution along these lines by endorsing efforts to permeate all non-Marxist
parties and exert immediate influence on the national, state, and local governments.[5] In 1926 Walther Lambach supported Bechly's moderate position by
publishing a highly informative and even entertaining handbook on the workings

2. NL Diller/6, "Der Wiesenbund," circular of 10 November 1921.
3. "Wir und die Völkischen," in "Mitteilung des Reichs-Angestellten-Ausschusses der
DNVP," December 1922, NL Diller/7.
4. Hans Bechly, "Volk, Staat, und Wirtschaft," speech of 29 June 1924 (Hamburg, 1924), pp.
20f.
5. Ibid., pp. 16, 63.

of the Reichstag, *The Regime of the 500*. Lambach also attacked the shibboleths of the antiparliamentary right, explaining for example that it was necessary for parliamentarians to be grouped in rival party delegations because "an unformed mob of 500 independents would be every bit as unable to work and fight as a mob of 500 armed men unaccustomed to cooperation and discipline."[6] Lambach then offered an insightful analysis of the interaction between parties and economic interest groups, of committee work, of the steps involved in passing a law. He concluded that he would not satisfy the curiosity of those DHV colleagues who kept asking him for plans to reform parliamentary government, because "at this time it seems to me that the best chance for improvement lies in the widest possible dissemination of accurate information." This was probably the only political treatise published in the Weimar Republic to win the applause of all parties from the SPD to the DNVP.[7]

A very different language was spoken by two Reichstag delegates elected in May 1924, the DHV district leaders of Brandenburg and Bremen, Franz Stöhr and Gustav Hartz. Stöhr, a Sudeten German and veteran of the prewar anti-Semitic movement, accepted a seat for the Racial Freedom Party in Thuringia, while Hartz sat for the right-wing DNVP local of Weser-Ems. Both candidacies occurred at the initiative of party locals rather than the DHV leadership, which exerted all its efforts to win a seat in the Center Reichstag delegation for Otto Gerig. Bechly nevertheless authorized his employees to accept these invitations because "the *völkisch* movement must not be led into reactionary channels."[8] Both Hartz and Stöhr soon claimed space in the DHV organ to inform its membership that the antics of Marxist Jews transformed the proceedings of the Reichstag into a nauseating farce.[9] Such statements conflicted with the political intent of the DHV leadership but reflected sentiments quite common among members. Max Habermann, who was in charge of the DHV's extensive educational programs, therefore decided that the DHV must give equal exposure to the critics and defenders of the Weimar Republic. In 1925 he hired a young National Socialist, Albert Krebs, the recent recipient of a doctorate in German philology, to assist the DHV with "civic education." Habermann promised Krebs that the DHV would tolerate all shades of anti-Marxist opinion, including the National Socialist, and would encourage open debate over fundamental political principles. Under Habermann's guidance the DHV actively dissemi-

6. Walther Lambach, *Die Herrschaft der Fünfhundert* (Hamburg and Berlin, 1926), p. 12.
7. Ibid., p. 150, and book reviews in NL Lambach/18.
8. DHV circular of 29 February 1924, NL Diller/7, and Hamel, p. 239.
9. *Deutsche Handelswacht*, 9 July 1924, p. 300, and 16 July 1924, p. 309.
10. See Albert Krebs, *Tendenzen und Gestalten der NSDAP* (Stuttgart, 1959), pp. 13–15, and Hamel, pp. 123–66.

nated the writings of several "conservative revolutionary" intellectuals who raised precisely those charges against parliamentary democracy that Bechly and Lambach sought to refute.[10] This curious situation arose in part from differences within the inner circle of DHV leaders, but all DHV leaders seem to have endorsed Habermann's cultural activities. The DHV of the Weimar Republic resembled in some ways the Wilhelmian SPD, where radical rhetoric, in accord with hallowed traditions, served to legitimize reformist practice.

The DHV redoubled its efforts after 1924 to discredit the radical right, despite the tone of Habermann's publications. It strove with considerable success to brand the Racial Freedom Party as a "bourgeois" and "reactionary" movement by exposing its ties to the Yellow unions. These ties ran through the United Patriotic Leagues (Vereinigte vaterländische Verbände), a loose umbrella organization embracing the Pan-German League, Yellow unions, and the remnants of many Free Corps. Fritz Geisler served as chairman of this organization, and Wilhelm Schmidt, Johannes Wolf, Paul Bang, and Freytagh-Loringhoven sat on its executive committee.[11] Geisler was reviled by the entire Christian-nationalist labor movement, but the DHV took the lead in the campaign against him with press attacks that elicited a libel suit, during which the DHV persuaded the court of Geisler's financial dependence on employers. In 1925 Geisler lost his position in the United Patriotic Leagues, and his loose umbrella organization of Yellow unions fell to pieces.[12] Wilhelm Schmidt promptly took his place as an agitator for Yellow unionism in the patriotic leagues and the Protestant church. His slogans exercised a fatal attraction even for a relatively enlightened conservative such as Count Westarp.[13]

The agitation of the Yellow unions again began to disturb the DHV in 1927–28, when they seized upon Benito Mussolini's decision to suppress the last remnants of independent trade unionism as a model for all who wished to combat Marxism successfully. The Pan-German League, Pomeranian Landbund, and Yellow unions devoted themselves to publicizing the features of the "syndicalist" social order created by Mussolini's Charter of Labor in 1927. This agitation,

11. Amrei Stupperich, *Volksgemeinschaft*, pp. 45–52, and Hertzman, pp. 141–63.
12. Contrast the accounts in the *Zentralblatt*, 2 March 1925, pp. 69f., and DHV, *Jahresbericht 1925*, p. 234, with that of the *Deutsche Werksgemeinschaft*, 26 July 1925. Interestingly, in view of the rivalry between the NSDAP and other organizations on the radical right, the testimony of a Nazi named Fahrenhorst formerly employed by Geisler played a major role in his downfall.
13. In his unpublished memoirs, written under the Hitler regime, Westarp spoke in the following terms of his troubled relations with the Christian trade unionists: "I personally considered a vertical organization [of workers] by factories, based on solidarity between, as people say today, the leader and his followers, more valuable than the union, whose horizontal organization on the basis of trades encourages conflicts of interest and class struggle between employers and workers" (NL Westarp, "Konservative Politik in der Republik," pp. 124f.).

linked to the claim that Germany's trade unions were the true source of class division and class hatred, evidently proved highly popular among members of the DNVP and Stahlhelm. [14] In December 1927 Walther Lambach responded with a speech that sought to cast all the would-be imitators of Mussolini north of the Alps in Fritz Geisler's mold. Lambach praised Mussolini enthusiastically as a true populist but asserted that Franz Seldte of the Stahlhelm, Adolf Hitler, and Artur Mahraun, the men he considered the most likely imitators, possessed none of Mussolini's spirit and freedom of action.

> The Italian example proves that a paramilitary league, if it enjoys good fortune, . . . can band together with blue- and white-collar workers, intellectuals, and rural tenant farmers in the spirit of fascism, conquer political power, and then use that power to impose its will on the captains of industry and finance. That this success could be imitated in Germany, where we observe the interpenetration [Verquickung] of paramilitary organizations and capitalist reaction, appears increasingly improbable the more one studies Italian developments. [15]

Lambach could detect no social policy among the potential fascist leaders in Germany beyond that of exiling the heads of the socialist labor movement. The implementation of this policy, he argued, would merely cause German workers to return to the stance of sullen hostility toward the state that had prevailed under Bismarck. Lambach emphasized the differences in social structure that made it almost impossible to impose unity on Germans from above: "What Mussolini found in Italy was not a heap of ruins created by liberalism, containing huge and thoroughly solid boulders, but rather a road paved with fine gravel." Lambach was pleading, in effect, for a system of corporate pluralism instead of totalitarian dictatorship. [16] His speech was admirably suited to discredit those unimaginative propagandists who praised Mussolini with the obvious hope of restoring patriarchal labor relations, but the "reactionary" label could not readily be pinned on the NSDAP after social radicals like Joseph Goebbels and the

14. *Deutsche Werksgemeinschaft*, 8 May 1927, and *Der Reichslandarbeiterbund*, 5 December 1928, p. 177. For background see Klaus-Peter Hoepke, *Die deutsche Rechte und der italienische Faschismus* (Düsseldorf, 1968).
15. Walther Lambach, "Faschismus in Italien und in Deutschland?" DNVP pamphlet no. 319, p. 11.
16. Ibid., pp. 15f. Compare Maier, p. 592: "Italian fascism substituted for prior organization in the political arena or marketplace; German Nazism arose in resentment against the organization that seemed to dominate."

Strasser brothers reestablished that party in the cities of central and northern Germany after 1924. These skillful demagogues praised the social gains made by workers during the revolution, expressed admiration for Lenin, and avoided identification with conservative elites.[17]

Protestant blue-collar workers in the DNVP frowned upon blatant anti-Semitism. The infrequent anti-Semitic remarks in their speeches and private correspondence were generally defensive in character, references to the hypocrisy of those who sought to discredit trade unionism in the name of racial purity, although they (like Stegerwald) sometimes jeered at the "Jewish democratic press" when attacked by the *Frankfurter Zeitung* or *Berliner Tageblatt.*[18] All knowledgeable commentators agreed that the blue- and white-collar workers in the DGB could not see eye to eye on the issue of race.[19] Christian Social leaders had no disciplinary problems comparable to those of the DHV, where Nazi sympathizers in the rank and file were always suspicious of cooperation with the moderate Reichstag parties. Thus it seems that susceptibility to racist propaganda depended more on class than confession.

But the Nationalist Workers' League in the DNVP displayed an obsession with national unity that had certain fascistoid features. The Christian Social Paul Rüffer established a widely imitated propaganda line with the following cry in a rally of 1920: "Of what use is the republican constitution to the German worker, how can a worker as Reich President help him, if the Treaty of Versailles remains in force?"[20] DNAB propoganda consistently advocated monarchism and remilitarization, while denouncing the SPD for weakly or treacherously supporting the "Versailles system." The DNAB's confidential commentary for activists on the heady electoral victories of 1924, the formation of the first Luther cabinet in January 1925, and the even more gratifying election of field marshal von Hindenburg as president of the Republic betrayed a powerful yearning to make both the SPD and KPD disappear from the political landscape.[21] For most of the

17. See Dietrich Orlow, *The History of the Nazi Party, 1919–1933* (Pittsburgh, 1969), pp. 55–104; Max Kele, *Nazis and Workers* (Chapel Hill, 1972), pp. 81–99; and Wilfried Böhnke, *Die NSDAP im Ruhrgebiet 1920–1933* (Bonn/Bad Godesberg, 1974), pp. 74–100.

18. See, for example, Franz Behrens, "Unser nationales Wollen," in GcG, *25 Jahre christlicher Gewerkschaftsbewegung*, pp. 75f.

19. "Der Wiesenbund," circular of 10 November 1921, NL Diller/6; *Soziale Praxis*, 29 April 1926, column 411 (ludwigy Heyde); Bernhard Otte to Hans Bartei, 26 November 1928, NL Otte/4/143f. See also the numerous monitory letters to Hans Bechly from Nazi DHV members in BAK NS 26/836.

20. "Deutschnationale Arbeitertagung in Hannover, am 26. Oktober 1920," DNVP pamphlet no. 88, p. 12.

21. See Emil Hartwig, "Aufbau und Tätigkeit des Deutschnationalen Arbeiterbund," DNVP pamphlet no. 213 (1925) pp. 17f., and the DNAB circulars of 25 February, 7 April, and 5 June 1925 in StA Osnabrück C1/84/34–63.

Christian Socials, however, the quarrel with Hugenberg in 1928–29 put an end to this emphatically rightist orientation, this obsesssion with weakening the SPD.

Many Christian Socials might also be considered fascistoid for their admiration of the Free Corps. As mentioned in chapter 3, some elements in the DGB enthusiastically supported "active" resistance in the Ruhr in 1923. The links forged at that time involved the Christian farmworkers' union in a major scandal in January 1926, after the Prussian police discovered a fugitive from justice, Paul Schulz, on the payroll of a marketing firm owned by it. Schulz was soon convicted of organizing the vigilante executions of "traitors" (*Fememord*), and the scandal deepened when it was revealed that he had been hired at the urging of a functionary of the League of German Employers' Associations. The socialist press speculated that the GcG helped reactionary industrialists to organize rings of assassins. Behrens denied that the low-level union functionaries who had hired Schulz knew of his crimes, dissolved the business enterprise in question, and found employment outside the farmworkers' union for his longtime friend and vice-chairman, Karl Meyer. The significance of this curious episode remains unclear, but after Schulz's release from prison he became the trusted aide of the prominent Nazi Gregor Strasser and established contacts between him and the DGB leadership.[22]

Attitudes toward fascism among the core membership of the Christian unions, the Catholic workers of western and southern Germany, were unambiguously negative, however. Whereas even those DHV leaders most opposed to the radical right felt compelled to express sympathy for Mussolini and *völkisch* ideals, Catholic labor leaders characterized the NSDAP as part of an international fascist movement rivaling the Comintern as a threat to democracy and trade unionism. When the Catholic workers' clubs of Bavaria and western Germany first took notice of the Nazi Party in 1923, they resolved to expel any member who joined it, denouncing it as a tool of reactionary industrialists and counterrevolutionary Free Corps veterans.[23] For Joseph Joos and his colleagues, Mussolini's suppression of parliamentary democracy was sufficient to warrant categorical rejection of Italian Fascism, and they considered Hitler an even more extreme representative of such dictatorial tendencies.

The press of the Christian unions avoided direct discussion of the Weimar

22. See the refutation of charges in GcG, *11. Kongreß 1926*, pp. 168–71, and *Zentralblatt*, 25 January 1926, p. 25, and 25 April 1927, p. 112, and Peter Stachura, *Gregor Strasser and the Rise of Nazism* (London, 1983), pp. 90f.

23. *WAZ*, 21 April 1923, p. 54, and Jürgen Aretz, *Katholische Arbeiterbewegung und Nationalsozialismus* (Mainz, 1978), pp. 45–47.

Constitution so as not to deepen divisions between Catholic and Protestant members, but in May 1923 the *Zentralblatt* reprinted an article in which the chairman of the Italian league of Christian unions reported that he had made a terrible mistake by not resisting Mussolini's rise to power because the Duce had decided to destroy trade unionism.[24] In the mid-1920s the GcG organ differed with Lambach's portrayal of Mussolini as a true populist by advancing the more accurate argument that the new syndicalist order in Italy merely robbed workers of the right to strike without providing them any effective protection against employers.[25] Heinrich Imbusch and other Christian union leaders believed that many reactionary industrialists in Germany longed to imitate Mussolini's measures. Reinforcing the DHV's campaign to expose links between the Yellow unions and the Racial Freedom Party, Imbusch brought an unemployed lignite miner from the Halle-Merseburg district to Essen in August 1924 to tell the national congress of the Christian miners' union that the Racial Freedom Party was a dangerous "parasite," eating its way into the body of the German people. He told a frightening story of a well-financed party organization working hand in glove with the local paramilitary leagues to employ physical intimidation against trade unionists and to guarantee that agents of the mineowners won all factory council elections.[26]

Developments in Austria intensified the GcG leaders' fear of fascism by suggesting that conservative Catholics sympathized with the movement. In the late 1920s frequent street battles between the militia of the Austrian Social Democratic Party, which was more militantly anticlerical than its German counterpart, and the rightist Home Guards poisoned Austria's political atmosphere. In 1929 Bernhard Otte wrote his counterpart in Vienna to express concern over reports that the Austrian Christian unions sometimes collaborated with the Home Guards. Johann Staudt replied that years of "red terror" had so embittered his followers that "they would sometimes ally with the devil against the Social Democrats."[27] The Austrian league of Christian unions nevertheless broke with the Home Guards in May 1930, when they publicly endorsed the ideal of the "fascist state" and adopted an ambiguous corporatist program with hierarchical overtones. Staudt informed Otte that the "half-fascist" university professors like Othmar Spann who drafted this program "aimed among other things

---

24. *Zentralblatt*, 15 May 1923, pp. 78f.
25. *Zentralblatt*, 15 September 1924, pp. 191f., 31 May 1926, pp. 163f., and 23 May 1927, p. 137.
26. Gewerkverein christlicher Bergarbeiter, *17. Generalversammlung 1924*, pp. 97f.
27. Staudt to Otte, 13 November 1929, NL Otte/4/229. For background see Anton Pelinka, *Stand oder Klasse?* (Vienna, 1972), pp. 21–34.

at the destruction of the Christian and nationalist trade unions." Both Staudt and Otte were disturbed to see that the Catholic clergy and the influential Christian Social Party did not oppose the Home Guards' rightist pronouncements.[28]

Within Germany itself Mussolini's negotiation of the Lateran Treaties with the Vatican in 1929 produced a distinctly more favorable attitude toward him in the Catholic press. The extent of sympathy for Italian Fascism in the Vatican and the German Catholic Church hierarchy remains a highly controversial subject, although it was clearly less pronounced than in Austria.[29] German press commentaries on the Lateran Treaties nevertheless appear to have generated great anxiety among Catholic labor leaders. In the Reichstag election campaign of September 1930, when most politicians still failed to take the Nazis seriously, the Catholic workers' clubs upgraded the NSDAP into the second most heavily criticized political opponent after the KPD.[30] Their resistance to the Nazis was doubtless reinforced by the desire to weed out authoritarian strains in German Catholicism. This background made it inevitable that the GcG and DHV would adopt very different responses to the Nazi electoral victory of September 1930. The former dedicated itself to weakening the NSDAP, while the latter sought primarily to strengthen the left wing of the party sympathetic to trade unionism.

EFFORTS BY THE DHV TO STRENGTHEN THE "NAZI LEFT"

Just as the various groups in the DGB found it difficult to adopt a common stance toward National Socialism, the problem of trade unionism posed a threat to the unity of the NSDAP. Hitler, like many party activists, hated the Free unions for crippling Germany's war effort and exploiting Germany's defeat in order to gain political power.[31] Hitler knew well, on the other hand, that overt opposition to trade unionism had prevented other *völkisch* organizations from winning over the working class. In his autobiography he adopted a subtler position by embracing, in effect, many of the complaints of the Christian unions against their Marxist rivals. Hitler spoke at length of his youthful days as a construction worker in Vienna, when colleagues pressured him to join their union and portrayed "the fatherland as an instrument of the bourgeoisie for the exploitation of the working class, . . . religion as a means for stultifying the people and making them easier to exploit, morality as a symptom of stupid, sheeplike patience, etc." When Hitler argued with them, the reader is told, they threatened physical

28. Staudt to Otte, 25 June 1930, NL Otte/5/73f., and *Zentralblatt*, 1 August 1930, pp. 231f.
29. Contrast Plum, pp. 171–211, with Hoepke, pp. 79–89, 101–21, and Stehlin, pp. 348–64.
30. Aretz, pp. 49–52.
31. See Tim Mason, *Sozialpolitik im Dritten Reich* (Opladen, 1977), pp. 15–41.

violence and drove him from the work site. Such experiences convinced him that the existing unions sought to compel ignorant workers to join their ranks in order to spread Marxist ideology, not to improve their material welfare.[32] Hitler nevertheless praised trade unions in the abstract as one of the "most important institutions of the nation's economic life," through which a people could be "tremendously strengthened in its power of resistance in the struggle for existence." "Above all, the trade unions are necessary as foundation stones of the future economic parliament or chambers of estates." Hitler nevertheless repeatedly cited practical difficulties in order to veto suggestions that he establish National Socialist trade unions, fearing that they would endanger his control of the movement.[33]

Some Nazis sought to give a definite content to Hitler's abstract endorsement of trade unionism in principle. The most influential was Gregor Strasser, who rebuilt the party organization north of the river Main after 1924 and rose by 1928 to the post of chief propagandist and Reich Organization Leader in the Munich party headquarters. Franz Stöhr was a friend of Strasser, and in 1927 the two men adopted the arguments of the DHV as they broke with the Racial Freedom Party. In March Strasser persuaded the handful of Nazi Reichstag delegates to dissolve their parliamentary association with it, citing its endorsement of the "reactionary" company union program of Paul Bang. Shortly thereafter, the Reichstag delegates Stöhr, Wilhelm Kube, an alumnus of the DHV, and the "national Bolshevik" Ernst zu Reventlow defected from the Racial Freedom Party to the NSDAP, announcing that they desired a socially revolutionary rather than a reactionary *völkisch* movement. The official Nazi organ, the *Völkische Beobachter*, also began in 1927 to endorse the workers' cause in specific strikes for the first time.[34]

In October 1927 Stöhr published an article in one of Strasser's magazines calling attention to the fact that the Christian-nationalist trade unions could not be held responsible in any way for Germany's defeat in World War I. He observed regretfully, however, that the need to compete with the ADGB had recently brought a Marxist taint to them: "Thus we saw in the postrevolutionary period that the union leaders of all factions sought less to improve the material

---

32. Adolf Hitler, *Mein Kampf*, trans. Ralph Mannheim (Boston, 1943), pp. 40–51, quotation on p. 40.
33. Ibid., pp. 596–606, quotation on p. 598, and Henry Turner, "Hitlers Einstellung zur Wirtschaft und Gesellschaft vor 1933," *Geschichte und Gesellschaft*, 2 (1976) pp. 89–117.
34. Kele, pp. 122–24, and Jeremy Noakes, *The Nazi Party in Lower Saxony 1921–1933* (London, 1971), pp. 59–61, 101–04. The importance of Paul Bang's program in this controversy, ignored by most recent commentators, is discussed in Friedrich Kass, "Nationalsozialismus und Gewerkschaftsgedanke," Ph.D. diss. (Munich, 1934), pp. 20–22.

conditions of their followers than to preserve, stabilize, and extend the parliamentary regime." For Stöhr the fact that the other Reichstag delegates of the DGB had voted for the Dawes Plan in 1924 proved the extent of Marxist corruption. He concluded that the NSDAP should decide in the near future whether to infiltrate and seek control of the DGB or establish its own unions.[35] Hitler continued to postpone any decision in this matter, but in August 1928 the pleas of Stöhr, Joseph Goebbels as *Gauleiter* of Berlin, and Albert Krebs, all of whom presented overwhelming evidence that the NSDAP was not winning over industrial workers, persuaded Hitler to authorize the formation of separate National Socialist factory cells, the first subdivision of the party organization along vocational lines.[36]

Stöhr's statements suggested that he was unwilling to absolve from the charge of Marxism any union that differed with Nazi party policy. However, the DHV found a man willing to serve as an honest broker between it and the NSDAP in Albert Krebs. Krebs attained some influence in the party by serving as *Gauleiter* of Hamburg from 1926 to 1928 and then as district leader of the factory cells organization and chief editor of the Hamburg party organ. Hoping to promote cooperation between the two organizations, he began in 1928 to organize a network of comrades throughout Germany who belonged to both the DHV and the NSDAP. In November 1928 he published an article that represented the most generous stance toward the trade unions taken by any prominent Nazi. Krebs argued that all unions must compromise with the existing government because they were charged with the essentially "maternal" task of improving social welfare, a task that had nothing to do with the manly revolutionary struggle of the NSDAP. All Nazis should therefore seek friendly coexistence with the Christian-nationalist union leaders so that their valuable skills and experience could be devoted to reconstructing the social order after the NSDAP had conquered the state.[37]

Krebs enjoyed little influence in 1929 because the DHV and NSDAP came onto a collision course over the Young Plan. Although the DHV was officially neutral toward the Young Plan, the Reichstag delegates Thiel, Glatzel, and Gerig were committed to its support. In the summer of 1929 some Nazi DHV activists began to demand that their union sever all ties with the DVP and Center Party. Stöhr warned the DHV leadership that he would air complaints against them at a special conference on trade unionism scheduled for the Nuremberg

35. "Der Nationalsozialismus und die Gewerkschaftsfrage," *Nationalsozialistische Briefe*, October 1927, pp. 104–07.
36. Kele, pp. 131, 149f., and Krebs, pp. 69f.
37. "Partei und Gewerkschaft," *Nationalsozialistische Briefe*, November 1928, pp. 149–52.

party congress in September, but the DHV refused to send a representative to the rally or permit DHV locals to join the local anti-Young referendum committees organized by Hugenberg and Hitler.[38] At the Nuremberg conference, which included factory cell organizers as well as DHV members, Stöhr attacked the unions as "drum-beaters for the Dawes Plan." He vetoed a proposed resolution condemning the Yellow unions on the grounds that "it would not be consistent to boycott the 'Yellows' while resolving complete toleration for the trade unions, some of which have in their own way harmed the interests of workers every bit as much as have the company unions." The conference eventually resolved that the Nazi factory cells represented the foundation for future Nazi trade unions, and the League of Christian Unions responded by demanding that the DHV expel Stöhr.[39]

The utter failure of Nazi efforts to "conquer" the DHV helped restore the influence of Krebs, however. During the winter of 1929–30 the *Völkische Beobachter* sounded charge by publishing stinging attacks on Thiel and Lambach. The DHV's youth auxiliary demanded that Thiel lay down his honorary membership in it, and Nazi activists disrupted several union meetings to demand the election of new leaders.[40] But the uprising soon subsided when the DHV leadership expelled a number of Nazi rowdies. This proved an effective deterrent because expulsion entailed the loss of substantial pension and insurance benefits. In February 1930 Krebs wrote Hitler to warn that the DHV could not be taken by storm and that, even if it could, the new Nazi union leadership would soon be forced to divert its attention from the political struggle and make compromises with the existing social system. This argument was well suited to appeal to Hitler's fears concerning the possible spread of a "trade union mentality" among his followers. The party leadership made use of Krebs's good offices to limit the number of expulsions, and the party never again encouraged its followers to stage an uprising in the union.[41]

The Reichstag election of September 1930 revealed nonetheless that the NSDAP enjoyed great popularity among DHV members. The DHV leadership violated its pledges of nonpartisanship during the campaign by bankrolling the Conservative People's Party and directing union functionaries to distribute its propaganda, while it expelled Nazis who attempted to defend their party in

38. NL Krebs/8/93, Konrad Rössler to DHV headquarters, 9 August 1929, and "DHV Verwaltung: Auszüge," entry of 23 August 1929, p. 152.

39. Kele, p. 151, and *Zentralblatt*, 1 November 1929, p. 295.

40. Interview with Mr. Hermann Schumacher, the former head of the Fahrende Gesellen, in Hamburg on 12 October 1979, and NL Krebs/5/5f., Krebs to Carl Kaufmann, 1 February 1930.

41. NL Krebs/7/54–58, Krebs to Hitler, 6 February 1930, and 3/54, report on a conference with Nazi leaders of 8–9 March 1930.

union meetings.[42] These measures backfired, however. The DHV's own criticism of Hugenberg and industrialist influence in the DVP encouraged union
members to embrace the "conservative revolutionary" thesis, long discussed in
DHV publications, that parliamentary government was hopelessly corrupt and
dominated by plutocrats. Moreover, the fear of unemployment was driving a
wedge between the DHV and Christian unions. Throughout 1929–30 the DHV
sought without success to remove the ceiling on unemployment insurance benefits that prevented commercial employees from receiving higher payments than
skilled factory workers, to establish separate insurance chests for white-collar
workers, or to lengthen the term of notice an employer must give before firing a
white-collar worker. The blue-collar Christian unions firmly opposed this pursuit of "special privileges," and DHV publications began to reflect Nazi rhetoric
by comparing Germany's crusade for liberation from the Treaty of Versailles to
the struggle of white-collar workers to avoid sinking into the morass of the
proletariat.[43] Although recent research has sharply questioned the received
wisdom that white-collar workers in general stampeded to the NSDAP, DHV
members certainly did. Max Habermann later estimated that 50% of them voted
Nazi in 1930. Sixteen of the 107 members of the new Nazi Reichstag delegation
belonged to the DHV, including two future *Gauleiter* and the future premier of
Thuringia.[44]

The leaders of the DHV responded to the election by resolving to cooperate
with the growing pool of Nazi union members in order to promote the acceptance of a progressive social program by the NSDAP. In its official commentary
the DHV expressed gratification that "there are now sufficient elements within
National Socialism that emphatically resist its development into an instrument of
social reaction."[45] Habermann in particular, judging that Hitler was a sincere if
sometimes misguided patriot, hoped to persuade him that he could best serve
the crusade against the Versailles treaty by cooperating with Chancellor Brüning, covertly coordinating his activities as leader of the "national opposition"
with the government. With the support of Treviranus, Habermann dispatched
Albert Krebs to Munich on September 19, 1930, in order to convey an invitation
for Hitler to meet with Brüning and an attractive proposal for financial coopera-

42. Larry Eugene Jones, "Between the Fronts: The German National Union of Commercial
Employees from 1928 to 1933," *Journal of Modern History*, 48 (September 1976), pp. 470–74.
43. NL Otte/6/108, Otte to Ersing, 21 February 1930; DHV, *Jahresbericht 1929*, pp. 105–07,
153–63, and *Jahresbericht 1930*, pp. 8–17.
44. Habermann MS, "Der DHV im Kampf um das Reich," p. 77, and Kosthorst, p. 145. See
also Childers, pp. 169–75, and Richard Hamilton, *Who Voted for Hitler?* (Princeton, 1982), pp. 16–
30, 391–93.
45. DHV, *Jahresbericht 1930*, p. 8.

tion between the DHV and NSDAP in providing medical insurance to Storm Troopers (members of the *Sturmabteilung*, SA). Hitler accepted both suggestions but grew angry when Krebs insinuated that it was more appropriate for him to deal with a man like Brüning than with the "reactionary" Hugenberg. Hitler denounced "social reactionary" as a Marxist slogan and offered the following definition of his own social program: "What is socialism then? When people have enough to eat and a little fun then they have their socialism. That's just what Hugenberg thinks too!"[46] Brüning's two meetings with Hitler had no practical results because Hitler was unwilling to moderate his antigovernment propaganda, but the DHV continued to seek financial influence over the NSDAP. Substantial loans to the Nazi press helped guarantee a favorable attitude toward the DHV in the *Völkische Beobachter* while reinforcing the position of Krebs against his rivals in the Hamburg party organization.[47]

Whereas Habermann remained optimistic about the chances for influencing Hitler, Albert Krebs came to fear that an influx of technocrats and careerists into the NSDAP after its electoral triumph would reinforce all the worst tendencies of the Munich party leadership. During 1930 many of the NSDAP's agrarian experts came to embrace the autarchic economic policies and hierarchical, anti-union brand of corporatism long propagated by the Pomeranian Landbund, as they sought with considerable success to infiltrate the agrarian leagues.[48] Most alarming for the trade unionist were the activities of Otto Wagener, the former businessman and SA chief of staff appointed late in 1930 to head a new Department for Economic Policy in the Munich party headquarters. Wagener formulated an original set of economic policies based on social Darwinist principles in confidential talks with Hitler and succeeded in recruiting many middle echelon industrial managers and owners of small factories for the NSDAP. At least one of his recruits, Walter Funk, had openly supported the Yellow unions in the past.[49]

Returning from the interview where Hitler offered his curious new definition of socialism, Albert Krebs found in his mailbox a confidential draft by Wagener for a new economic program for the NSDAP. This document embraced the ideal of the "company union" (*Werksgemeinschaft*) and described the employer as the

46. Krebs, pp. 26–29, 143f., and the Krebs diary, entries of 19 and 21 September 1930, NL Krebs/1/61f.

47. Brüning, pp. 191–97; Krebs, p. 26; diary entries in NL Krebs/1/68–75, 119f.; Benno Ziegler to Krebs, 18 November 1930, and reply of 22 November in NL Krebs/10/112–16.

48. See Gerhard Schultz, *Aufstieg des Nationalsozialismus* (Frankfurt am Main, 1975), pp. 619–22.

49. Ibid., pp. 622–28. See also Henry Turner's introduction to Wagener's memoirs, *Hitler aus nächster Nähe* (Frankfurt am Main, 1978), pp. i–xvii, and the praise for Wagener in the Yellow unions' *Deutsche Werksgemeinschaft*, 20 December 1930.

"Führer" within his factory. All disputes over wages and working conditions would be settled within the "family" of the individual company in the National Socialist state of the future. Trade unions would be responsible merely for vocational training. Wagener also adopted the arguments of the Pan-German League in favor of replacing social insurance with compulsory savings plans.[50] Krebs dispatched an impassioned rebuttal to the party headquarters in Munich and to many of his Nazi DHV contacts. Krebs argued that, whereas Wagener sought merely to guarantee absolute security for small businessmen, the National Socialist ideal of natural selection demanded an element of healthy struggle between capital and labor, as well as the existence of powerful unions to encourage the emergence of talented leaders from the working class. Nazi ideals therefore required a corporatist order in which democratically controlled trade unions formed parity boards with the employers' associations that would oversee wages and working conditions. Krebs angrily denied Wagener's assertion that the party's decision to organize factory cells already implied the rejection of trade unionism. All factory cell leaders, Krebs warned, were determined to combat Yellow unionism at all costs.[51]

Krebs won enthusiastic support from the participants in his weekend seminars for Nazi DHV members, many of whom wrote to Munich to support his program,[52] but this group did not have much influence by itself. Krebs found it easy to win powerful allies within the party for negative attacks on the Yellow unions and "bourgeois reactionaries," but not for positive cooperation with any existing unions. Krebs hoped for support from Joseph Goebbels, whose propaganda adopted many of the slogans and symbols of the labor movement. When Goebbels came under fire from other Nazis in November 1930 for supporting the Berlin metalworkers' strike, Krebs leaped to his defense in the Hamburg party organ, denouncing those Nazis who opposed strikes so as not to offend businessmen. But Goebbels refused to make common cause with Krebs or to cooperate in drafting a constructive social program. Krebs concluded glumly that Goebbels' propaganda merely sought to "kill thought" and "deliberately exclude any consideration of reality."[53]

Krebs found it equally difficult to cooperate with the earnest social revolutionaries on the left fringe of the NSDAP. Gregor Strasser's brother Otto shared Krebs's sense of outrage when Hitler reduced the ideal of socialism to bread and

50. Otto Wagener, "National-Sozialistische Wirtschaftsaufgaben," memorandum of September 1930 (Hamburg Forschungsstelle).
51. Krebs to NS Reichsleitung, Organisations-Abteilung II, 15 October 1930, NL Krebs/7/105–41.
52. NL Krebs/2/27f., 73, and 5/37–39, 94f.
53. NL Krebs/7/153–55, Krebs to Goebbels, 25 October 1930, and reply by Goebbels' secretary, 28 October 1930, and 1/97f., diary entry of 27 January 1931.

circuses, but Otto Strasser despised trade unionism as much as capitalism.[54] Krebs made no effort to support Otto's small circle of intellectuals when Hitler expelled them from the party in July 1930. Discontented Storm Troopers constituted a much more powerful but equally unpredictable force on the left wing of the Nazi Party. Manual workers apparently comprised about 45% of the SA membership, as opposed to only 25% of the party cadre. Many SA units proudly called themselves "proletarian" and denounced the "bourgeois" party cadre, agreeing with Krebs that the NSDAP should compete actively with the Marxist parties in working-class neighborhoods and eschew efforts to cultivate respectability.[55] However, these currents in the SA stood closer in spirit to revolutionary syndicalism than to trade unionism. Activist Storm Troopers called for direct action, a march on Berlin, and simultaneous attacks on Jewish/reactionary businesses and Marxist union offices. Some grew so discontented with Hitler's policy of seeking power legally that they resigned from the NSDAP in order to join Otto Strasser's National Socialist Fighting Front. But such SA activists condemned ties with the DHV or Christian unions for being every bit as corrupting an influence as financial dependence on the business community.[56]

The only promising ally for Krebs within the party was the National Socialist Factory Cells Organization (Nationalsozialistische Betriebszellen-Organisation, NSBO) established by Gregor Strasser at the end of 1930. Goebbels had attacked all existing trade unions indiscriminately while organizing his early factory cells in Berlin, but the first cells in Hamburg and the Ruhr followed the advice of Krebs by seeking friendly relations with the DGB. Gregor Strasser inclined toward the position of Krebs when he appointed Reinhold Muchow, a former DHV activist, and Walter Schuhmann to organize a nationwide cell network. The party circular announcing the formation of the NSBO condemned Yellow unions sharply while expressing the desire for peaceful coexistence with the trade unions. The NSBO pledged not to form its own unions and to confine its activities to the struggle against Marxist political ideology. Muchow went even further in a pamphlet of January 1931 by pledging to support the trade unions in all strikes over economic issues.[57] Muchow, Krebs, and Franz Stöhr succeeded in encouraging DHV locals and Nazi cells to agree on candidates in most white-

54. NL Krebs/7/45f., 68, Krebs to Otto Strasser, 29 January 1930, and reply of 19 March.
55. See Michael Kater, "Sozialer Wandel in der NSDAP im Zuge der nationalsozialistischen Machtergreifung," in Wolfgang Schieder (ed.), *Faschismus als soziale Bewegung. Deutschland und Italien im Vergleich* (Hamburg, 1976), pp. 30–38; Orlow, pp. 210–19; and Eberhart Schön, *Die Entstehung des Nationalsozialismus in Hessen* (Meisenheim am Glan, 1972), pp. 128–32, 185f.
56. See the circular of 27 September 1931 by SA malcontents in Hamburg, NL Krebs/6/94–100.
57. NL Krebs/7/183–86, circular from Strasser to the Nazi Gauleiter, 23 December 1930, and 7/196f., "Organisation der Nationalsozialistischen Betriebszellen. Ziel und Systematik ihrer Arbeit," by Reinhold Muchow.

collar factory council elections in 1931. Muchow also screened Krebs from attacks by the Hamburg party bosses when he sought to negotiate alliances with Protestant officials of the blue-collar Christian unions.[58] Many factory cell organizers trained under Goebbels nevertheless continued to reflect his hostility toward the unions. At the end of 1930 the Hessian NSBO adopted guidelines that diverged from the Strasser–Muchow line by portraying Nazi factory cells as the first step toward the formation of Nazi trade unions. Party comrades belonging to unions were instructed to remain in them for the present but to establish separate National Socialist lists in all factory council elections. Both the Free and the Christian unions seized on these guidelines as a revelation of the true purpose of the NSBO and resolved to expel any union member who supported it in factory council elections.[59] Thus even the NSBO remained deeply divided over its stance toward the trade unions.

A proliferation of rival spokesmen for the NSDAP in 1931–32 makes it difficult to assess the extent of DHV influence on the party's economic policy. At the very least the DHV succeeded, with the help of shrewd samplers of public opinion like Goebbels, in persuading Hitler that support for Yellow unionism would be suicidal. The DHV may also have succeeded in undermining Otto Wagener's influence. In December 1930, after reading Krebs's rebuttal of Wagener's program, Gregor Strasser assured him that "the position of Dr. Wagener is insecure and insignificant. Hitler does not like him any more."[60] Wagener remained a party spokesman until 1933, but he appears to have modified his views in order to placate the DHV. According to Wagener's memoirs, his confidential position papers for Hitler in 1931 assigned trade unions a role going well beyond mere vocational training and scrupulously avoided the terminology of company unionism.[61] In one of his few definite pronouncements on social policy, Hitler eventually endorsed the DHV's stand favoring social insurance against compulsory savings, although he also took extraordinary precautions to keep any financial dealings with the DHV a secret so as not to offend party activists who detested the labor movement in all its forms.[62] It seems that the DHV succeeded

58. NL Krebs/1/100–14, diary entries of 6 February–21 March 1931; 12/83, Muchow to Krebs, 28 February 1931; 12/102–09, Uschla affidavit, 9 April 1931; 10/118, Krebs to Benno Ziegler, 23 May 1931. Krebs forged alliances with the local representatives of the nationalist railroad workers' union (Gewerkschaft deutscher Eisenbahner) and a tiny union of canal workers affiliated with the GcG, but such cooperation between the NSBO and any union other than the DHV seems to have been unique to the Hamburg region.

59. *Zentralblatt,* 15 February 1931, pp. 59f.; NL Otte/7/83f., GcG Vorstand, 17 January 1931; ADGB circular of 9 January 1931, DGB Bibliothek-Düsseldorf.

60. NL Krebs/1/83f., diary entry of 5 December 1930, and 7/187, 203–06, Strasser to Krebs, 24 December 1930, and reply of 3 January 1931.

61. Turner (ed.), *Hitler aus nächster Nähe,* pp. 123–28.

62. Schulz, pp. 627–31, and Krebs, pp. 100f.

by and large in neutralizing the influence of the fellow travelers who began to desert to the NSDAP from the DVP and DNVP after September 1930, without, however, achieving any positive clarification of the Nazi social program.

In October 1931 the DHV leadership was deeply distressed by Hitler's decision to join the Harzburg Front with Hugenberg against Chancellor Brüning. Alarmed by the prospect of a permanent coalition between the DNVP and NSDAP, Max Habermann responded with a public call for an alliance between Brüning and Hitler. Neither the Nazi nor the Center Party appears to have given the proposal serious consideration, but Gregor Strasser took the opportunity to praise Habermann's idealism and initiate a conciliatory press exchange with him. Hitler also sought to mollify the DHV by encouraging his lieutenants to intensify their attacks on the Yellow unions, including, for the first time, the Yellow farmworkers' league of Johannes Wolf.[63] On November 6, 1931, Strasser brought Habermann and Bechly to Munich, where Hitler promised them that the Third Reich would retain trade unions, collective bargaining, and state labor arbitration in much their present form. Hitler's rambling monologue made a bad impression on the DHV leaders, but after he left they enjoyed a spirited discussion with Strasser. Habermann felt that he had persuaded Strasser that, with all other political forces in the process of dissolution, a partnership between Brüning and Hitler was the last alternative to a destructive absolute dictatorship by either the army or Hitler.[64]

In February 1932 the DHV leadership nevertheless abandoned all hope of influencing Hitler after he decided to challenge Hindenburg directly for the presidency. Hitler's decision seemed to signal a determination to seek total power. Hans Bechly and Bernhard Otte signed the founding declaration of the nonpartisan committee formed to reelect Hindenburg, and the DHV expelled all Nazi sympathizers who sought to persuade union locals to condemn Bechly's stand or who insulted the field marshal, even including the Reichstag delegate Albert Forster. Thereafter the DHV terminated all forms of financial cooperation with the NSDAP.[65] In May 1932, after losing the election, Hitler expelled Albert Krebs from the party. Krebs responded with a circular to Nazi DHV members warning against the tendency toward "Asiatic despotism" in Hitler's court.[66] The DHV leaders retained a certain bond of personal sympathy with Gregor Strasser, but no other means of influencing the Nazi Party.

63. Stachura, pp. 96f.; *Der Deutsche*, 1 and 11 November 1931; *Arbeit und Recht* (Wilhelm Schmidt's renamed journal), 12 December 1931 and 16 January 1932. However, Stachura exaggerates Strasser's sympathy for the Christian unions.

64. Krebs, pp. 32f., and NL Krebs/1/193f., diary entries of 27 November–3 December 1931.

65. Jones, "Between the Fronts," pp. 478f.

66. Krebs/13/2, Hitler to Krebs, 20 May 1932, and 13/43f., Krebs circular of 31 May 1932.

THE CHRISTIAN UNIONS' CAMPAIGN AGAINST
NATIONAL SOCIALISM

Whereas the DHV leadership responded to the Nazi electoral victory of September 1930 by seeking influence within the party, the blue-collar Christian unions maintained a stance of militant opposition. The *Zentralblatt* denounced those who urged that the NSDAP now be drawn into the national government, arguing that "such participation would mean the dismantling of the democratic state [Volksstaat], especially since this conforms with the wish of other delegates from the so-called bourgeois parties to restore the old hierarchical conditions."[67] Although Brüning sometimes considered the possibility of a coalition with Hitler, Labor Minister Stegerwald opposed such suggestions uncompromisingly, insisting that no declared enemies of parliamentary democracy be given power. He claimed among party colleagues to have confidential information that Hitler had promised his financial backers in Ruhr industry to suppress the trade unions and impose drastic wage reductions.[68] The GcG chairman Bernhard Otte also opposed the NSDAP firmly. In a closed meeting of January 1931 he persuaded the leaders of the blue-collar Christian unions that it was their duty, both "as citizens and as trade unionists," to "tolerate no National Socialist agitation in union locals and, moreover, to combat National Socialist ideas with all their strength." He advised, however, that this could best be done not by direct attacks but by "sharply delineating Christian-nationalist principles and the will of our movement."[69] As Otte acknowledged with this last piece of advice, it was very difficult to combat Nazi propaganda without seeming to confirm its claim that the trade unions were merely front organizations for the SPD and Center Party.

Disciplinary action against union members who agitated for the NSBO represented the earliest and most successful form of anti-Nazi activity in the Christian unions. The GcG agreed wholeheartedly with the firm attitude of the Free unions in such matters and condemned the efforts by the DHV to cooperate with Nazi cells in factory council elections. Union discipline greatly impeded the growth of the NSBO, which attained only 39,000 members by the end of 1931. Although its membership increased to 290,000 during the following year, a large proportion of them, and the great majority of cell leaders, were either white-collar or handicraft workers.[70]

67. *Zentralblatt*, 1 October 1930, p. 291.

68. *Zentrumsprotokolle 1926–33*, p. 504 (12 January 1931). See also Stegerwald's speeches in *Kölnische Volkszeitung*, 6 November 1931, no. 525, and Reichsarbeiterbeirat der Deutschen Zentrumspartei, "Um den sozialen Volksstaat" (1932), pp. 21–25.

69. NL Otte/7/83f., GcG Vorstand, 17 January 1931.

70. Hans-Gerd Schumann, *Nationalsozialismus und Gewerkschaftsbewegung* (Hanover and Frankfurt am Main, 1958), pp. 38f., and Krebs, pp. 73–75.

Efforts to establish the patriotic credentials of the existing trade unions represented a second form of anti-Nazi activity in the Christian unions. GcG leaders believed that the German electorate would never have endorsed the absurd mixture of "Marxist" and "reactionary" planks in the Nazi platform if their judgment had not been clouded by legitimate anger against the Treaty of Versailles. Much like Chancellor Brüning, they responded with intensified agitation for the abolition of reparations, union with Austria, and the return of the Saar to the Reich.[71] The combat veteran Jakob Kaiser took the lead in efforts to demonstrate that the program of the Christian unions alone offered a true synthesis of "national" and "social" values. In January 1931 he published an anonymous article in the *Zentralblatt* that even defended efforts by the SA to prevent the screening of the movie version of Remarque's antiwar novel, *All Quiet on the Western Front*. Kaiser professed to admire the novel but to despise its treatment by Hollywood, which made the sacrifices by the gallant German troops seem utterly meaningless. He granted that the radical right committed distasteful excesses but argued that this was "no longer any reason for thinking workers to reject national pride, for they have become the nation." The article denounced the "Jewish-liberal press" for insulting the German national character and predicted that "in the future the fate of the nation will be determined by that segment of the working class which properly understands the newly awakened national consciousness and knows how to represent it in a dignified fashion."[72] This position clashed with that of the Catholic workers' clubs, which consistently sought to promote reconciliation with France. Many Catholic union members apparently found this effort to "climb aboard" the nationalist locomotive highly distasteful, indeed, unchristian.[73] Kaiser toned down his rhetoric thereafter, although Bernhard Otte halfheartedly demanded the return of Germany's colonial empire early in 1932, hoping that this would create 500,000 jobs.[74]

The Christian unions hoped above all that their patriotic declarations would encourage the ADGB to renounce the vestiges of Marxist internationalism. In the spring of 1931 Otte made it known that the Christian unions would find it much easier to support petitions by the Free unions to the government on social policy if the ADGB would firmly and publicly condemn reparations.[75] Later that year the *Zentralblatt* endorsed for the first time the writings of August Winnig,

71. See the electoral analysis in *Zentralblatt*, 1 October 1930, pp. 290f., and 1 January 1931, pp. 4f., as well as Jakob Kaiser's circular of July 1931 to union locals, NL Kaiser/220.

72. *Zentralblatt*, 15 January 1931, pp. 17–19. Kosthorst, pp. 62–64, argues unconvincingly that this standpoint was not "nationalistic."

73. See the protest letter, GcG Ortskartell Lindlar to GcG headquarters, 5 February 1931, NL Kaiser/220.

74. *Zentralblatt*, 15 February 1932, pp. 62f.

75. NL Otte/3/72, GcG circular of 1 June 1931.

who had denounced the "uprooted" Marxist intelligentsia for distorting the true spirit of German workers ever since his expulsion from the SPD in 1920. This probably represented a bid by the DGB leadership for an alliance with right-wing dissidents in the Free unions.[76] After Chancellor Brüning also demanded a public gesture of support for his foreign policy, the ADGB's chairman Theodor Leipart began in December 1931 to agitate for the abolition of all reparations. Condemning those idealists willing to risk the ruin of Germany's economy for the sake of international understanding, he quarreled publicly with Rudolf Breit-scheid, the SPD's official spokesman on foreign policy.[77] This was probably the most serious disagreement between the ADGB and SPD since the time of the Kapp Putsch in 1920, when the unions stood to the left of the party.

In the autumn of 1931 the Christian unions were encouraged to undertake direct attacks on the NSDAP by Hitler's decision to participate in the Harzburg Front with the DNVP and Stahlhelm. The Christian union press reported sarcastically and at length on the efforts by Hugenberg's industrial and agrarian supporters to influence the Nazi program.[78] Heinrich Imbusch, although he observed shrewdly that any industrialist who thought he could "buy" the self-willed Hitler was making a terrible mistake, considered it self-evident that "the National Socialist German Workers' Party is at the present time the great hope of the reactionaries."[79] The Christian unions saw their worst fears confirmed when the NSBO, far from opposing Hitler's alliance with Hugenberg, devoted itself to preparations for civil war against organized labor. The Nazi factory cells in the Ruhr, for example, began training members to operate public utilities so that there could be no repetition of the general strike that had defeated the Kapp Putsch. This development prompted the SPD and Free unions to expand and reorganize their militia in the Iron Front.[80] In January 1932 the Christian unions, Catholic workers' clubs, and Catholic youth groups imitated the Social Democrats by forming the Popular Front (Volksfront). Christian workers were instructed not to join the socialist militia, but local leaders of the Popular Front were advised to establish close ties with their socialist counterparts and with the police in order to formulate contingency plans for resisting an uprising by the

76. See the review of *Vom Proletariat zum Arbeitertum* in *Zentralblatt*, 1 December 1931, pp. 367f., and Wilhelm Ribhegge, *August Winnig* (Bonn/Bad Godesberg, 1973), esp. pp. 259–67. In 1930 Winnig agitated for the Conservative People's Party and praised the Christian unions, but he switched his allegiance to Hitler in 1932.
77. Brüning, p. 471; Michael Schneider, *Das Arbeitsbeschaffungsprogramm des ADGB*, pp. 116–18.
78. See, for example, *Der Deutsche*, 11 February 1932, and *Der Bergknappe*, 13 February 1932, p. 3.
79. Imbusch, "Für Freiheit, Gerechtigkeit und Fortschritt" (Essen, 1932), pp. 7–9.
80. Böhnke, pp. 175f., and Matthias, "Die Sozialdemokratische Partei," pp. 122–27.

Communists or Nazis. The Popular Front provided effective protection for union and Center Party rallies in western Germany during the turbulent months that followed.[81]

The campaign to reelect President Hindenburg in 1932 offered the Christian union leaders a chance to oppose the Nazi electoral juggernaut without, they hoped, appearing to engage in "partisan" politics. Christian unionists were thrilled by Chancellor Brüning's success in persuading the SPD to back the field marshal, further evidence that the Marxist heritage in the socialist labor movement was being liquidated. Otte and Hans Bechly counted among the first public figures to declare for Hindenburg. Although all senior Christian union leaders, Protestant as well as Catholic, endorsed Otte's stand, it came to seem more partisan when the Hugenberg loyalist Wilhelm Koch persuaded the national association of the Protestant workers' clubs to condemn the formation of the Popular Front and refuse to endorse Hindenburg.[82] The Protestant workers' clubs were weak and internally fragmented, but their criticism remained dangerous because of renewed efforts in the Hugenberg and Nazi press to portray the Christian unions as "ultramontane." By 1932 many of the isolated Protestant Christian union activists in the large cities of central and northern Germany despaired of ever shaking off this label, and a few of them came to pin their hopes on the NSDAP.[83] Moreover, by this time the threat of unemployment could easily make Chancellor Brüning's defense of collective bargaining rights seem insignificant. Many white-collar and a few blue-collar members of the DGB complained bitterly of their leaders' pro-Hindenburg stance, explaining that Adolf Hitler was the most effective champion of the nationalist causes long espoused by the DGB, and that he should not be branded as "socially reactionary" because no government could adopt economic measures more harmful to workers than the emergency decrees of Heinrich Brüning.[84] Hindenburg won an absolute majority in the second round of voting on April 10, but Hitler scored surprising local successes among Christian miners in economically backward regions threatened by shutdowns, in both Catholic Upper Silesia and the Protestant ore-mining regions of Clausthal-Zellerfeld, upper Hesse, and the

81. KAB Archiv: Reichsvorstand, 14–15 January 1932, and KAB circulars of 27 February and 1 March 1932. See also NL Otte/7/19–22, GcG Vorstand, 11 February 1932, and Aretz, pp. 60–62.
82. *Textilarbeiter-Zeitung*, 12 March 1932, p. 34, and *Zentralblatt*, 15 May 1932, pp. 143f.
83. See the proposal for an alliance between the Christian canal workers' union of Hamburg and the NSDAP in Bernd to Krebs, 21 October 1930, NL Krebs/2/33–36, and BAK NS 26/827, Klein (Hamburg) to Otte, 4 March 1932, and reply of 5 March.
84. Compare NSDAP Ortsgruppe Blankensee to Hans Bechly, 27 February 1932, NL Krebs/10/50–52, and Tobias Beck (Weissenburg-Bayern) to Bernhard Otte, 9 March 1932, BAK NS 26/827.

Siegerland. The Christian metalworkers' union also noted significant Nazi in-roads among its Protestant members.[85]

The Christian unions were not the only organization to find that Hitler exerted an unusually strong attraction among Protestant members. Indeed, most of the NSDAP's dramatic electoral breakthroughs occurred in predominantly Protestant towns and villages. Thus the Christian unions' best hope for combating it lay in close cooperation with the Christian Social People's Service, which competed directly with the Nazis for the votes of the hundreds of thousands of Protestant peasants, workers, and petits bourgeois who felt politically homeless. Some figures in the CSVD shared the extreme hostility toward Social Democracy that prevented so many German conservatives from effectively opposing Hitler's rise to power. However, Christian trade unionists, led by the party's vice-chairman Gustav Hülser, promoted the spread of a more balanced viewpoint in the movement, as did the strongly humanitarian Pietists led by the party chairman Wilhelm Simpfendörfer. Even Reinhard Mumm, one of the most conservative Christian Socials, renounced his earlier attacks on the SPD as fundamentally antichristian in 1931, hoping to promote cooperation among all pro-Brüning moderates.[86] Alarming reports of Nazi propaganda successes in their strongholds during the next few months apparently persuaded CSVD leaders, nonetheless, that they must consider Max Habermann's idea for a coalition between Brüning and Hitler. On March 22, 1932, Hülser and Simpfendörfer met with Hitler in Berlin to discuss the possibility of supporting him in the second round of the presidential election. They were horrified, however, by Hitler's unusually frank declaration that Germany must choose between Russian Bolshevism and Italian Fascism, and that settlement programs were futile until Germany acquired more *Lebensraum*. Hitler evaded all questions on social policy, and his assurance that he considered Christianity "indispensable for disciplining the nation spiritually and for supporting state authority" did not comfort his listeners. Hülser concluded his account of the meeting for party comrades with the following solemn prayer: "May God preserve our Fatherland from ever having this man as lord of its fate."[87] Thereafter the CSVD consistently opposed the Nazis.

85. NL Imbusch/2, Gewerkverein Hauptvorstand, 19 March 1932, pp. 7–9, and 13 June 1932, pp. 6–8; Christlicher Metallarbeiterverband, *13. Generalversammlung 1932*, pp. 94f. See also Sigurd Plesse, *Die nationalsozialistische Machtergreifung im Oberharz* (Clausthal-Zellerfeld, 1970), pp. 30–36, 65–70, and Graf, pp. 35–40.
86. Contrast Mumm's articles in *Das Volk. Siegerländer Tageblatt*, 6 January 1930 (NL Mumm/198/24), with *Kirchlich-soziale Blätter*, 1931, no. 7/8, pp. 105–08. See also Hülser's speech in *Der Christliche Volksdienst* (Stuttgart), 3 October 1931.
87. See the confidential report by Simpfendörfer and Hülser in NL Mumm/330/387–89, as well as the accounts written by both men many years later in the Splitternachlaß Hülser, DGB Bibliothek, Düsseldorf.

After provincial elections confirmed fears that the Nazi tide was rising, the Christian unions rallied all their Protestant leaders behind the CSVD in the Reichstag election campaign of July 1932. Simpfendörfer granted Franz Behrens the second place on his national nominations list, and the Christian farmworkers' union abandoned all pretense of nonpartisanship. Although Friedrich Baltrusch and Walther Lambach did not receive Reichstag seats, they shepherded the DGB activists who had supported the Young German People's National Federation or the Conservative People's Party into the Christian Social movement.[88]

The election results proved disheartening, however. The Center Party held its ground, but the NSDAP gained a plurality of 37% and commanded, together with the KPD, an obstructionist majority dedicated to the overthrow of parliamentary government. The Nazis swept aside the opposition of the Christian Socials, reducing their strength from 870,000 votes in 1930 to only 365,000. Moveover, CSVD losses were heaviest in those districts where the support of Christian workers was most important, in East Prussia, Lower Silesia, and Rhineland-Westphalia. The East Prussian Christian Social vote, 12,000, was only about one-half as large as the membership of the Christian farmworkers' union in that province. As conservative landowners in the DNVP complained, farmworkers who had faithfully resisted all Marxist propaganda now succumbed en masse to the pseudosocialism of the NSDAP.[89] Indeed, all the groups that Adam Stegerwald had hoped to incorporate into the labor movement by founding the DGB—Protestant "Tory workers" inculcated with habits of deference toward elites, manual workers employed by the government, lower ranking civil servants, and white-collar workers—constituted prime sources of support for the Nazi movement. They had been outraged by the bourgeois parties' decision to ignore the interests of working-class constituents since 1928, but they could find no home in the Marxist parties.[90] The anti-Nazi agitation of the Christian unions was not entirely futile, to be sure. Hitler's popularity in working-class neighborhoods apparently peaked in the spring of 1932 and declined slowly but steadily after Brüning's fall, when the SPD and the Free and Christian unions all adopted a stance of uncompromising opposition to the Papen government.[91] But

88. Otte to Wilhelm Simpfendörfer, 14 June 1932, NL Otte/6/4; *Die Rundschau* (Reichsverband ländlicher Arbeitnehmer), 17 July 1932, p. 51; *Tägliche Rundschau*, issues of 13, 20, and 30 July 1932.

89. Opitz, pp. 269–79, 345–47, and "Der Nationalsozialismus: Eine Gefahr," undated memorandum of 1932 by von Kleist-Schmenzin, BAK NS 26/837.

90. See Mason, *Sozialpolitik,* pp. 56–68; Hamilton, esp. pp. 170f., 386–90; and Childers, pp. 185–88, 240–57. It is striking that Hamilton, who has apparently never even heard of the Christian unions, church-affiliated workers' clubs, or the DNAB, concluded again and again in his incomparably detailed analysis of urban voting patterns that "Tory workers" must have contributed a far greater proportion of voters for the bourgeois parties than has hitherto been recognized, and that their defection to the NSDAP was a crucial cause of those parties' decline after 1928.

91. Böhnke, pp. 189–92.

the collapse of the CSVD caused many Christian trade unionists to despair of party politics altogether. The only thing they judged certain in this time of crisis was that all workers must rally around their trade unions as the last bulwark against anarchy or tyranny.[92]

The only Christian labor leaders with clear-cut programs for coping with the crisis were Joseph Joos and Heinrich Imbusch, but unfortunately their ideas conflicted. Joos decided by the beginning of August that the Center Party should sacrifice all other considerations to the goal of restoring constitutional government through a parliamentary majority as quickly as possible. The only feasible combination for such a majority was a coalition between the Center/BVP and the NSDAP, and by late August Joos persuaded the Center leadership to conduct serious negotiations with the Nazi Reichstag delegation. Joos displayed a curious and unshakable optimism concerning the chances for persuading Hitler to head a genuine coalition government without the authority to issue presidential emergency decrees, that is, bound to the will of the Reichstag. Brüning and most Christian union leaders agreed that this solution would be desirable, but they soon perceived that Hitler had no intention of reviving the parliamentary system.[93] Heinrich Imbusch was apparently the first of them to conclude that the parliamentary system could not function until the economic crisis had been overcome. He was drawn toward a solution propagated by the DHV leadership and the circle of corporatist intellectuals who wrote for Hans Zehrer's magazine *Die Tat*, an alliance of the army, paramilitary leagues, trade unions, and other organizations willing to combat unemployment energetically.

Both Joos and Imbusch pinned their hopes in large measure on the reasonableness of Gregor Strasser, which they, like Max Habermann, exaggerated. Strasser certainly opposed Goebbels within the Nazi hierarchy by emphasizing the need for tactical alliances with existing organizations, be they economic interest groups or political parties, but he probably cultivated such contacts merely in order to gain total power for Adolf Hitler as quickly as possible.[94] In February 1932 Strasser sharply opposed the counsels of Goebbels and Göring when they persuaded Hitler to contest the presidential election. Strasser predicted correctly that this course would merely alienate all potential allies without

---

92. See the anguished speech by Franz Wieber in Christlicher Metallarbeiterverband, *13. Generalversammlung 1932*, pp. 28–31.

93. Rudolf Morsey, *Der Untergang des politischen Katholizismus* (Stuttgart, 1977), pp. 56–69. Contrast the optimistic *WAZ*, 31 December 1932, p. 317, with the realistic *Zentralblatt*, 15 December 1932, p. 309.

94. Peter Stachura's recent biography is highly sympathetic, but Udo Kissenkoetter, *Gregor Strasser und die NSDAP* (Stuttgart, 1978), is far more convincing with his portrait of Strasser as a loyal soldier of the Führer who quarreled with Goebbels over means rather than ends.

offering any chance of victory. Aggravated by these internal party conflicts, in April he published an anonymous article in *Die Tat* that condemned the self-ishness of all political parties and called for the future political order to be based on the economic associations and paramilitary leagues. Some observers saw this as a veiled attack on Hitler's policy, but Hindenburg's electoral victory left Hitler dependent on Strasser's unrivaled managerial talent and contacts with promi-nent figures outside the NSDAP.[95] Strasser's bitterness against the political parties was shared to varying degrees by Bechly, Habermann, and Imbusch, and this represented a starting point of sorts for the formulation of a joint program.

A more important area of convergence was shared support for increased government intervention in the economy. The *Tat* circle, Strasser, General Kurt von Schleicher, and the advocates of a planned economy in the Christian unions all shared a lofty conception of state sovereignty that set them apart from both the rigid defenders of the free market and the Marxist economists in the SPD who believed that the rules of capitalist orthodoxy must be either scrupulously obeyed or entirely abolished. The leaders of the Free unions were coming to share this faith in state intervention as they promoted the W-T-B Plan for public works through deficit spending, and in May 1932 Gregor Strasser caused a sensation by praising that plan on the floor of the Reichstag.[96] ADGB leaders did not comment publicly on this development, nor did they, despite reports to the contrary in the Communist press, seek to forge an alliance with Strasser. Howev-er, some of them wanted to distance themselves from the "evolutionary" think-ing of the SPD with a "revolutionary" program for immediate government action in order to regain the support of disgruntled workers who had joined the KPD and NSDAP.[97] Christian union leaders were less reserved. The Christian

95. Kissenkoetter, pp. 127–29; Orlow, pp. 246–65; Klaus Fritzsche, *Politische Romantik und Gegenrevolution* (Frankfurt am Main, 1976), pp. 249–59.

96. See Avraham Barkai, *Das Wirtschaftssystem des Nationalsozialismus* (Cologne, 1977), pp. 37–57, and Michael Schneider, *Das Arbeitsbeschaffungsprogramm des ADGB*, pp. 146–54.

97. Reinhard Neebe, "Unternehmerverbände und Gewerkschaften in den Jahren der Großen Krise 1929–33," *Geschichte und Gesellschaft*, 9 (1983), pp. 321f. In September 1932 the *Rote Fahne* published what purported to be an official government protocol of a meeting on September 9, where General Schleicher allegedly brought Graßmann and Eggert of the ADGB together with Strasser and Otto Wagener. There Graßmann allegedly agreed in principle to support a military dictatorship and to make the unions state organs in exchange for a law making union membership mandatory for all workers. The document is clearly a forgery, and the meeting almost certainly never took place: see Henryk Skrzypczak, "Fälscher machen Zeitgeschichte. Ein quellenkristischer Beitrag zur Gewerk-schaftspolitik in der Ära Papen und Schleicher," *Internationale wissenschaftliche Korrespondenz*, 11 (December 1975), pp. 452–66, and Heinrich Muth, "Schleicher und die Gewerkschaften 1932. Ein Quellenproblem," *Vierteljahrshefte für Zeitgeschichte*, 29 (April 1981), pp. 189–215. Stachura, p. 101, cites the forged protocol, exaggerating Strasser's contacts with union leaders, and it plays a central role in Hannes Heer's misleading indictment of the ADGB leadership, *Bürgfrieden oder Klassenkampf* (Neuwied and Berlin, 1971), esp. pp. 87–89, which remains useful nonetheless for describing the seepage of Christian-nationalist arguments into the Free union press in 1932.

miners' union and the GcG economists Baltrusch and Heinrich Körner all praised Strasser's program warmly, applauding in particular his plan for massive electrification projects and his denunciation of the Ruhr steel industry for condemning German ore mines to extinction by purchasing cheaper Swedish iron ore.[98]

During the second half of 1932, Habermann and Imbusch strove to bring Strasser and General Schleicher together in an alliance to topple Chancellor von Papen. The motives and calculations of the various parties in this alliance remain obscure. Although Kurt von Schleicher had raised Papen to power and assumed office under him as defense minister, he soon distanced himself from the unpopular chancellor. When ADGB leaders asked about the purchase of Friedrich Flick's controlling interest in the United Steelworks at a government reception on July 30, Schleicher declared himself "in complete agreement with the trade unions" that the government must secure control over management wherever its money was invested, implicitly criticizing von Papen's efforts to reprivatize the firm. Leipart and Grassmann came away convinced that Schleicher held the real power in the government and that he was a "wise and decent" fellow.[99] The meeting's tone was remarkably friendly in view of the fact that Schleicher and Papen had used armed force just ten days before to remove Otto Braun as prime minister of Prussia, thus destroying the SPD's most important bastion. In August Hans Zehrer purchased the daily newspaper of the CSVD, the *Tägliche Rundschau*, apparently with modest subsidies from the Defense Ministry and more substantial backing from the DHV. Zehrer then intensified his agitation for an anticapitalist Schleicher government that would more or less ignore the Reichstag but would reflect the "popular will" by cooperating closely with all those unions and leagues that expressed it most directly.[100] Heinrich Imbusch, who like Habermann apparently conferred repeatedly with Strasser or his aides in these months, also held a private conference with Schleicher in mid-August that became the subject of many rumors. A conservative Catholic well acquainted with the Christian labor leaders warned Papen on August 19 that Imbusch was his firmest opponent in the GcG because the Christian miners "hope for the fulfillment of certain wishes with regard to nationalization of the mines through a Hitler-Schleicher-Stegerwald combination," adding that this plan was being discussed with Schleicher's aides.[101] The extent to which Schleicher nourished such hopes remains unclear.

98. GcG, *13. Kongreß 1932*, pp. 277, 315–17, 343–53.

99. See the ADGB's protocol in Dieter Emig and Rüdiger Zimmermann, "Das Ende einer Legende. Gewerkschaften, Papen und Schleicher. Gefälschte und echte Protokolle," *Internationale wissenschaftliche Korrespondenz*, 12 (March 1976) pp. 34–37.

100. Fritzsche, pp. 272–77.

General Schleicher finally decided to wrest the chancellorship from Papen at the end of November, after a new Reichstage election had weakened the NSDAP somewhat without resolving the constitutional impasse. Schleicher sought to overcome the government's isolation by reaching out to Strasser and the union leaders. On December 3 he offered Strasser the vice-chancellorship, probably because he expected a Hitler chastened by electoral defeat to accept a modest share of power, or perhaps because he hoped to provoke a schism between moderates and extremists in the NSDAP.[102] Hitler flatly rejected the offer, and a despairing Strasser resigned from all his party offices on December 8 without seeking to rally support against the intransigents, a decision that shocked and dismayed his sympathizers in the DGB.[103] Although Schleicher now had no chance of securing a parliamentary majority, the Christian unions urged him to perservere in a presidial government along corporatist lines. Schleicher rescinded the most offensive of Papen's social measures on taking office and publicly declared that the creation of jobs would be his top priority, and that he sought a "middle path" between capitalism and socialism. The DGB press praised Schleicher's program warmly, citing it as proof that the unions retained more vitality than the political parties. Even Jakob Kaiser, like Stegerwald more a politician than a union organizer, imitated the syndicalist rhetoric of Imbusch by arguing that the Christian unions' demand for a government "corresponding to the popular will" could be satisfied either in a parliamentary or a corporatist form. "The popular will is not expressed *only* in the parties. The social will of the people in particular is expressed above all by the unions."[104]

Such statements by the Christian unionists doubtless encouraged Schleicher's last political experiment in January 1933, when he solicited public declarations by the leaders of big business and organized labor in favor of dissolving the Reichstag and postponing new elections for nine months in violation of the constitution. Schleicher, hoping to retain the support of the DNVP, had kept most of Papen's cabinet ministers, but his ties with the unions and ambiguous rhetoric concerning the future of capitalism outraged many conservatives and Ruhr industrialists. On the left the SPD opposed Schleicher bitterly, blaming him correctly for the July coup against Otto Braun's Prussian cabinet. Leipart

101. Henseler (the German delegate to the ILO) to Papen, in Vogelsang, p. 268. The *Kölnische Volks-Zeitung* noted nervously on the same day (19 August, no. 227) that Imbusch was conferring with Schleicher but denied that he represented the Center Party.

102. See Peter Hayes, "'A Question Mark with Epaulettes'? Kurt von Schleicher and Weimar Politics," *Journal of Modern History*, 52 (March 1980), pp. 35–65.

103. Kissenkoetter, pp. 147–77; Stachura, pp. 103–20; Karl Hahn, "Max Habermann und der 20. Juli," deposition of 21 February 1946, DHV Archiv; *Der Deutsche*, 24 December 1932.

104. "Christliche Gewerkschaften und Staatsführung," speech of 12 December 1932, pp. 10f., NL Kaiser/221. See also *Zentralblatt*, 15 December 1932, p. 309.

and his associates at ADGB headquarters apparently agreed with the Christian unions that Schleicher should be supported as the only alternative to a dictatorship by Hugenberg or Hitler, but the SPD exerted considerable pressure on them not to discuss political issues with the new cabinet. On January 26 Schleicher appealed personally to Graßmann and Eggert of the ADGB for support, but they refused to endorse any unconstitutional "state of emergency."[105] Schleicher's utter isolation enabled Papen to persuade President Hindenburg at the end of January to appoint Hitler as head of a cabinet in which he would supposedly be supervised and restrained by Papen as vice-chancellor and Alfred Hugenberg as minister of both economics and agriculture. With this cabinet there emerged the political combination that had long been the nightmare of Christian trade unionists, the alliance of Nazis and reactionaries. Although this development is often described as the result of the machinations of big business, the leadership of the Reich Association of Industry had spoken out unambiguously for the retention of Schleicher, attracted in particular by his repudiation of Papen's agrarian protectionism. Both big business and organized labor were in fact internally divided to the point of political paralysis at this juncture.[106] The Weimar Republic received the coup de grace, not because big business had decided to install Hitler in power, but because the failure of the Christian unions' efforts to create a social foundation for parliamentary democracy through a system of "corporate pluralism" left a chaotic situation. The paralysis of parliamentary government nurtured the growth of the NSDAP and created a power vacuum in which the clique of reactionary politicians around Hindenburg enjoyed decisive influence over the nation's destiny.

CORPORATIST REFORM OR TOTALITARIAN DICTATORSHIP?

In retrospect it seems clear that all leading Nazis agreed on the need for destroying the trade unions after Gregor Strasser resigned his party offices in December 1932, and they undoubtedly intended to suppress all rival political parties. Such plans were kept secret, however, when Hitler became chancellor. Many DGB

---

105. Michael Schneider, *Das Arbeitsbeschaffungsprogramm des ADGB*, pp. 156f., 199–202; Bracher, *Auflösung*, pp. 607–31; Emig and Zimmermann, pp. 41–43.

106. See Tim Mason, "The Primacy of Politics," in Henry A. Turner (ed.), *Nazism and the Third Reich* (New York, 1972), pp. 176–80; Neebe, "Unternehmerverbände und Gewerkschaften," pp. 324–26, and *Großindustrie, Staat und NSDAP 1930–1933* (Göttingen, 1981), pp. 140–76; and Henry A. Turner, Jr., *German Big Business and the Rise of Hitler* (Oxford and New York, 1985). Contrast Dirk Stegmann, "Zum Verhältnis von Großindustrie und Nationalsozialismus 1930–1933," *Archiv für Sozialgeschichte*, 13 (1973), pp. 399–482, and "Antiquierte Personalisierung oder sozialökonomische Faschismus-Analyse?" *AfS* 17 (1977), pp. 275–96.

leaders initially persuaded themselves that Alfred Hugenberg was their only real enemy in the new cabinet. Stegerwald expressed this fallacy in its starkest form when he told party colleagues that "Hitler recognizes that a dictatorship [is] impossible, Hugenberg is of the opposite opinion."[107] The illusion that Hitler intended to restore parliamentary government was soon dispelled. The suppression of the Communist Party after the Reichstag fire, the campaign for the Reichstag election of March 5, in which the Nazis employed state censorship and physical intimidation against all opponents, and finally the Enabling Act of March 23 demonstrated Hitler's determination to govern without consulting the other political parties. Leaders of the Free, Christian, and Hirsch–Duncker unions all continued to hope nonetheless that they might be able to save their organizations by severing all ties with the political parties. NSBO officials cleverly nurtured such hopes by telling union functionaries of the second and third echelons that the Führer merely intended to achieve the unification of the trade union movement that had long been desired by all insightful labor leaders but that had been thwarted by party divisions. Such conversations usually culminated in the suggestion that the union functionary could save his job in the unified union of the future by joining the NSDAP now.[108]

Christian trade unionists assumed that they enjoyed special sympathy in government circles because of their nationalist and corporatist traditions. Hitler had led his followers to believe that one of his first goals as ruler would be to create a new "economic parliament," and Fritz Thyssen led a faction of enthusiastic corporatists within the NSDAP who subscribed to the "Universalism" of the Viennese professor Othmar Spann.[109] Christian union leaders understood quite well that the corporatist theories popular among the middle classes often had a dangerously antidemocratic and antilabor thrust, but they had enjoyed considerable success in combating such tendencies among the Catholic clergy. In 1932 Catholic labor leaders and the prominent social theorists in the Königswinter Circle reached agreement that the ideal social order free of class hatred described in the papal encyclical *Quadragesimo anno* could be achieved only by the existing, purely voluntary organizations of workers and employers, in the context

---

107. *Zentrumsprotokolle 1926–1933*, p. 616, 2 February 1933.

108. The most complete account of such blandishments is the published diary of the ADGB turncoat, Hermann Seelbach, *Das Ende der Gewerkschaften* (Berlin, 1934). See also the similar account by an official of the Hirsch–Duncker metalworkers' union, Stocksinger (Breslau), in his letters of 27 and 30 March 1933, NL Erkelenz/136, and Karl Bracher, Wolfgang Sauer, and Gerhard Schulz, *Die nationalsozialistische Machtergreifung. Studien zur Errichtung des totalitären Herrschaftssystems in Deutschland 1933/34* (Cologne and Opladen, 1960), pp. 178–82.

109. Heinrich A. Winkler, *Mittelstand, Demokratie und Nationalsozialismus* (Cologne, 1972), pp. 111–20, 178f., and Bracher, Sauer, and Schulz, pp. 644–55.

of parliamentary government, through a gradual evolutionary process.[110] Theodor Brauer was the most enthusiastic drafter of blueprints for a future social order among them, but even he proposed only one immediate reform of fundamental significance, the transfer of unemployment insurance to the control of the unions. Brauer argued vigorously that the paralysis of parliament resulted from excessive state intervention in the economy, which tended to politicize every conflict of economic interest. Thus his brand of Catholic corporatism sounded remarkably similar to "Manchester liberalism."[111] For Bernhard Otte even this proposal went too far, however, because he did not see how it could be combined with the principle of voluntary union membership. Otte's brand of corporatist social theory boiled down to the suggestion that the state should give the existing parties in collective bargaining certain tasks of mutual interest to perform, such as vocational training, in the hope that this would improve the tenor of labor relations to the point where the Zentralarbeitsgemeinschaft of 1918 could be revived.[112]

Brauer had no formal connection with the GcG since his appointment to a chair in economics at Karlsruhe, and he had quarreled with the advocates of state economic planning. After Hitler came to power, however, Brauer's call for decentralization took on new significance, and he became the pivotal figure in efforts by the Christian unions to preserve a sphere of freedom in social and economic matters under the Third Reich. On March 8, 1933, the executive committee of the League of Christian Unions resolved that the time had come to create an "organic corporatist social order based on the desire for self-administration," stressing that this order must be the "free work of free men" under a state that guaranteed legal rights, the "freiheitliche Rechtsordnung."[113] On March 17 the Christian unions staged a mass rally in Essen that ratified a new program in which Brauer and Otte sought to adapt their corporatism to the changed political circumstances. The "Essen Guidelines" maintained a discreet silence about the future of parliamentary government but urged the "genuine fulfillment of the popular will" in political affairs. The crux of the message was that corporatist self-administration should free the state to fulfill its "specifically political tasks."

110. See Josef van der Velden (ed.), *Die berufsständische Ordnung. Idee und praktische Möglichkeiten* (Cologne, 1932), printing papers from a conference of 12–13 May 1932, esp. pp. 5–7; NL Otte/7/1f., GcG Vorstand, 28 April 1932; and Heinrich Bußhoff, "Berufsständisches Gedankengut zu Beginn der 30er Jahre in Österreich und Deutschland," *Zeitschrift für Politik*, November 1966, pp. 452–62.
111. Van der Velden, pp. 54f. Compare Borchardt, "Wirtschaftliche Ursachen," pp. 186–90.
112. Van der Velden, pp. 89–97.
113. *Zentralblatt*, 15 March 1933, p. 61.

Regarding the future economic order, voluntary organization, decentralization, and above all freedom were described as the most truly "German" values.[114]

The Free unions soon began to follow the course pioneered by the GcG. The ADGB leadership issued public statements in late March that abjured all contacts with the SPD, argued that the social tasks of trade unions remained the same regardless of the political regime, and pledged to cooperate with employers for the sake of economic revival.[115] Noting this convergence, Anton Erkelenz, who had propagated a fusion of the rival union leagues more consistently than any other labor leader, appealed to Leipart and Stegerwald on April 1 to merge voluntarily and thus present Germany's new rulers with a fait accompli. Erkelenz predicted that the only alternative was a compulsory state union.[116] NSBO representatives essentially confirmed this prediction when they met with ADGB leaders on April 5. The Nazis claimed at first that they wanted to retain the Free unions intact and sought the cooperation of union officials for an orderly transition, in which only those guilty of "corruption" would be discharged. Sharp questioning by Leipart revealed, however, that their plan was for a union based on compulsory membership, with all leaders appointed from above, which would accept wage levels dictated by the state. It also revealed, more encouragingly, that the NSBO had no specific commission from Hitler for this proposal.[117] The government still seemed undecided, an impression confirmed by sharp disputes within the cabinet between Hugenberg and Labor Minister Franz Seldte, who wanted to involve Theodor Brauer in a commission to draft detailed proposals for corporatist social reform.[118] During the last two weeks of April, Erkelenz's suggestion bore fruit as a small group of union leaders, which included Stegerwald, Brauer, Kaiser, Otte, Leipart, Graßmann, Leuschner, and Ernst Lemmer, conferred repeatedly in order to draft a charter for a unified federation of labor.

Brauer and Kaiser apparently dominated these discussions, doubtless because the Free and Hirsch–Duncker unionists realized that they had the best contacts in government circles and spoke the language most likely to influence

---

114. GcG, *Die Essener Richtlinien der christlich-nationalen Gewerkschaften 1933* (Berlin, 1933), pp. 6, 22. See also Kosthorst, pp. 167–73.

115. See Gerhard Beier, "Einheitsgewerkschaft. Zur Geschichte eines organisatorischen Prinzips der deutschen Arbeiterbewegung," *Archiv für Sozialgeschichte*, 13 (1973), pp. 226–29, and Neebe, "Unternehmerverbände und Gewerkschaften," pp. 327–29.

116. Erkelenz to Leipart, 1 April 1932, NL Erkelenz/136, and Erkelenz to Stegerwald, 1 April 1932, NL Stegerwald/014/Nachtrag no. 1.

117. Three-page typescript protocol in NL Erkelenz/136.

118. Gerhard Beier, "Zur Entstehung des Führerkreises der vereinigten Gewerkschaften Ende April 1933," *Archiv für Sozialgeschichte*, 15 (1975), pp. 366–73.

Hitler. To the joy of the Christian unionists, the negotiators promptly agreed that the future union league would "recognize and respect the constructive value of religious forces for the political and social order" and seek to serve national strength as well as the interests of workers. ADGB leaders rejected a passage proposed by Brauer implying that the political parties had never represented the will of the people, but the Free unionists reluctantly accepted a passage declaring that "the people's desire for unity and power will no longer tolerate class division or uprooted internationalism."[119] Kaiser and other Christian unionists would later cite this unification charter, drafted primarily by them, as the foundation for the united German Labor Federation of the Federal Republic, but it was a document accepted under duress. It diverged so sharply from the traditions of the Free unions that an ADGB congress or national committee meeting might well have rejected it. However, the point became moot on May 2, when Adolf Hitler, after staging a lavish May Day celebration in order to assure German workers of his benevolence, launched a carefully planned paramilitary operation by the SA and NSBO to seize control of all Free union offices.[120]

Many commentators have been quick to criticize the trade unions' efforts to curry favor with Hitler in the spring of 1933. Such criticism often ignores the grim circumstances of the time, which left union leaders little alternative. The alacrity and apparent enthusiasm with which they adjusted their rhetoric to that of the new government are striking nonetheless. In a sober critique of the ADGB leadership, Hans Mommsen has suggested that their virulent anti-Communism, strengthened by the tendency to attribute all uncomfortable criticism from the rank and file to the KPD, served as a "catalyst" for misguided efforts to imitate fascist sloganeering. In an observation even more applicable to the Christian unions, Mommsen also notes that the willingness of Leipart to support corporatist social reform reflected an exaggeration of the importance of trade unions, which cannot effectively defend the pluralist social order in the absence of a functioning parliament.[121] Their old dream of purging the Free unions from all Marxist influence appears to have played a similar catalytic role in the thinking of Christian union leaders. Many Christian trade unionists rejoiced in the suppression of the KPD, and some approved of the harassment of the SPD, perceiving a vindication of their own struggle against Marxism in the victory of the Nazi Party, despite its excesses and perversions. In a closed meeting of the Christian miners' union, Heinrich Imbusch commented in the following terms on the aftermath of

119. Ibid., pp. 385–92, reprinting the various drafts of the charter.
120. Schumann, pp. 67–70.
121. Hans Mommsen, "Die deutschen Gewerkschaften zwischen Anpassung und Widerstand 1930–1944," in Vetter (ed.), pp. 281–90.

the Reichstag fire: "Today the Social Democrats and Communists are being badly treated. Well, they have earned this bad treatment by their own conduct. In the past they treated us the same way." He then recapitulated old grievances against the unfair competitive practices of Free union organizers before the war and the Old Union's decision to launch a strike in 1912 despite the opposition of the Christian miners' union. Such remarks betrayed a serious distortion of judgment. Imbusch remained true to his principles, however, by warning the delegates that the time might soon come when they would need to "fight for their rights" again because nobody could tell whether the socially reactionary or progressive faction would win the upper hand within the NSDAP.[122]

But despite their harsh words for Marxists the Christian trade unionists displayed a sense of solidarity with the Free unions that contrasted sharply with efforts by the white-collar DHV and GDA to cultivate a special relationship with the Nazis. In March 1933 Max Habermann pressured the anti-Nazis Lambach and Otto Gerig out of the DHV leadership, hoping, he later explained, to establish a "bond of vassalage [eine Art Lehensverhältnis]" between the DHV and NSDAP. The large faction of card-carrying Nazis in the union nevertheless compelled Habermann and Hans Bechly to resign on April 10 in favor of Franz Stöhr and Hermann Miltzow. On April 29 the DHV formally withdrew from the DGB and declared itself National Socialist. Events in the formerly liberal GDA followed much the same course.[123] However, far from severing all ties with organizations likely to displease Hitler, the Christian unions sought to strengthen their links with the ADGB, to "win the Free unions for the nation." The Christian union press emphasized repeatedly that the Free unions represented the healthiest elements in the working class and that the Third Reich would be acting in a self-destructive fashion if it failed to secure their voluntary cooperation.[124]

The new German Labor Front (Deutsche Arbeitsfront, DAF), created in May 1933, nevertheless sought to drive a wedge between the Free and Christian unions. The SA left the offices of the Christian and Hirsch–Duncker unions untouched when it occupied those of the ADGB. The cynical leader of the DAF, Robert Ley, declared that the non-Marxist unions must submit to him "voluntarily," but he also encouraged workers to believe that the DAF was a unified union league, a more effective representative of their interests than they had

122. Typescript minutes, "Gewerkverein Generalversammlung," 12 March 1933, pp. 102–04, NL Imbusch/1.
123. Schumann, pp. 57f.; Hamel, pp. 259–66; "Ostern 1933," circular from Habermann to DHV activists, BAK NS 26/836 (source of quotation).
124. Kosthorst, p. 277, speech of 12 April 1933; *Die Rundschau*, 10 April 1933, p. 27; *Textilarbeiter-Zeitung*, 6 May 1933, p. 1.

ever known. On May 3 the executive committee of the Hirsch–Duncker unions placed itself under Ley's control, and he summoned four GcG leaders to demand submission, repeating assurances that most Christian union functionaries could keep their jobs in the DAF. Otte, Baltrusch, and Behrens signed the declaration required of them, but Jakob Kaiser refused and went into hiding the next day after an arrest warrant was issued against him.[125] Stegerwald, Imbusch, Brauer, and the three signers of Ley's declaration nevertheless agreed to enter the new senate of the DAF, and the Christian union press offered the most optimistic interpretation possible of this "reorganization" of the trade unions.[126] These Christian labor leaders acted from lofty motives, hoping to protect Free union colleagues from persecution and to save a kernel of trade unionism in the DAF, but they doubtless aided the Nazis by encouraging workers to accept the new order.

Hitler's desire for an amicable relationship with the Catholic Church encouraged these Christian union leaders to hope that they could still influence Nazi social policy. Vice-chancellor von Papen apparently sought reconciliation with the Center Party laborites in order to present a united Catholic front during the impending negotiations between Hitler and the Vatican over a concordat. Remarkable amity prevailed between Papen and Joseph Joos at a closed meeting of Catholic journalists on April 1, where Joos accepted not only the thesis that all Catholics must close ranks to defend Church interests, but also that they should avoid political uproar, because toppling the current government would most likely result in a Communist dictatorship. On April 3, moreover, Theodor Brauer joined Papen's new League of the Cross and Eagle.[127]

Most of Papen's conservative Catholic supporters were interested in anything but defense of the Christian unions, however. The isolation of the Christian unions already became apparent during the debate in the Center Party Reichstag delegation on March 23 over the Enabling Act. The laborite wing of the party formed the core of the group of 12–14 delegates opposed to the act in the name of democratic principle. The party chairman, Ludwig Kaas, urged acceptance as the lesser of two evils, but many other delegates in the pro-Hitler majority, led by the industrialist from Baden, Albert Hackelsberger, displayed real enthusiasm for the "national revolution." Hackelsberger served in the Reichstag until

125. Kosthorst, pp. 180–82, and Schumann, pp. 76–78, 169–73.

126. *Zentralblatt*, 15 May 1933, pp. 117f.; *Die Rundschau*, 10 May 1933, p. 35; *Der Arbeiter* (Munich), 18 May 1933, p. 10.

127. "Augustinusverein," meeting of 1 April 1933, NL Emil Ritter/C2/15, and Kosthorst, p. 173.

1938 as a "guest" of the National Socialist Delegation.[128] He represented the dominant school of thought within the Center Party Committee for Commerce and Industry, which had decided in the summer of 1932 to repudiate the Center's stance of opposition to Papen precisely because it approved his efforts to curb the pernicious influence of the trade unions. Many of these owners of small and medium-sized factories later applauded von Papen's coalition with Hitler for the same reason.[129] Moreover, many Catholic civil servants joined the NSDAP in March 1933, and Nazi fellow travelers gained control of the Christian peasants' clubs. Even Catholic agrarians who remained aloof from the NSDAP took advantage of the altered circumstances to denounce Stegerwald and Imbusch as the demagogues primarily responsible for Germany's economic problems.[130] The Catholic laborites' isolation was most dramatic in Bavaria, where Monsignor Carl Walterbach fought a lonely battle against Nazi fellow travelers in the BVP. In early May Walterbach was arrested after the business enterprises owned by his Catholic workers' clubs declared bankruptcy. The Munich Archdiocese did not defend him although he was eventually acquitted of all criminal charges. The club leaders appointed by the conservative Cardinal Faulhaber introduced a new tone of enthusiastic support for the government.[131] Thus, although many Catholic bishops apparently continued to wish the Christian unions well, there was no consensus supporting them within the Catholic community. When the negotiations for a concordat intensified in June, the Church hierarchy spread its sheltering wing over the Catholic workers' clubs but declared itself disinterested in the

128. See Morsey, *Untergang*, pp. 134–41, which minimizes tensions within the party, and the more objective earlier account by Detlef Junker, *Die Deutsche Zentrumspartei und Hitler* (Stuttgart, 1969), pp. 171–97. Brüning, Joos, Wirth, Imbusch, Kaiser, Fahrenbrach, and Ersing opposed the law. Stegerwald's position is not known.

129. This development is ignored by Morsey but emerges quite clearly from the correspondence in NL ten Hompel, vols. 21 and 24. Years later, after he had ample opportunity to know the Third Reich for what it was, ten Hompel wrote the following in his unpublished memoirs (NL ten Hompel/1, "Erzberger," p. 10):

> Unfortunately the Christian unions too [like the Free] deliberately strove to intrude themselves between the workers and the management of a plant in all issues, even purely internal company matters. The thicker this wedge, the more influence one could exert on management and the workers. The formation of a true partnership [Arbeits- und Vertrauensgemeinschaft] between management and labor, like that implemented so brilliantly by National Socialism, did not fit in at all with the trade union program.

130. Kosthorst, p. 175; Morsey, *Untergang*, pp. 117–21. Joos and Carl Walterbach offered an exceedingly gloomy assessment of currents in the Catholic populace in a meeting of the KAB Reichsverbandsvorstand, 28–29 March 1933 (KAB Archiv), concluding that workers and the Volksverein clergy alone remained immune to Nazi agitation.

131. See Karl Schwend, "Die Bayerische Volkspartei," in Matthias and Morsey (eds.), p. 503, and *Der Arbeiter (München)*, 18 May 1933, pp. 1f, 10. The numerous show trials of political opponents staged by the Nazis in 1933–34 remain an unexplored topic.

fate of the Center Party and the Christian unions. However, the bishops did seek to protect individual Christian union leaders from persecution.[132]

The Christian trade unionists retained some influence as a potential source of international respectability. In June 1933 Robert Ley dispatched Otte and the ADGB's Wilhelm Leuschner to a congress of the International Labor Organization in Geneva to seek recognition for the DAF. But Leuschner described Nazi terror quite frankly to his foreign colleagues, and Otte was not persuasive. A furious Ley had Leuschner arrested on his return from Geneva and denounced the Christian union leaders for treason, expelling them from the DAF on June 23–24. Heinrich Imbusch concluded that the reactionary faction had finally won the upper hand in the NSDAP, and he fled to the League of Nations mandate territory in the Saar with the liquid assets of the Christian miners' union.[133] Adam Stegerwald also transferred the assets of the GcG's insurance firm to its Saar affiliate. He reminded Chancellor Hitler of the Christian unions' strong influence in that region, where they matched the Free unions in size, and argued that the DAF's arbitrary actions harmed Germany's chances in the upcoming Saar plebiscite. This argument persuaded Hitler to order more lenient treatment of former union officials by the DAF and the Gestapo.[134] During the summer of 1933 each Christian trade union signed a treaty with the DAF, surrendering a combined total of RM 24 million in assets in exchange for assumption by the DAF of their legal liabilities, including pension claims. DAF negotiators sought to sweeten the pill by repeating assurances that most Christian union secretaries could keep their jobs, but by September roughly 500 of them, 90% of the total, had resigned or been fired. Disillusionment with the Third Reich spread quickly.[135]

The Christian trade unionists of the Saar, swamped by their socialist competitors in the years from 1919 to 1922, had regained numerical parity after the Ruhr Struggle of 1923 precisely because they championed the ideas of patriotic resistance to the French authorties and reunification with the Reich.[136] The

132. Aretz, pp. 72–111.
133. Schumann, pp. 80f.; Elfriede Nebgen, *Jakob Kaiser* (Stuttgart and Berlin, 1967) p. 11; NL Imbusch/6, memoir by "Kollege Paul," pp. 6f.
134. Stegerwald to Hitler, 12 July 1933, NL Stegerwald/014/Nachtrag no. 21, and NL Kaiser/10, copies of letters from Peter Kiefer to Hitler, 5 July 1934 and November 1934.
135. NL Stegerwald/014/Nachtrag no. 25, Jakob Kaiser, "Zur Situation in der früheren deutschen Arbeiterbewegung," memorandum of November 1933; NL Kaiser/10, affidavit of 13 September 1958; NL Fahrenbrach/2 (DGB Bibliothek), circular from Bernhard Otte, 30 May 1933; Wolfgang Wittig folder (DGB Bibliothek), memoir of 10 March 1948. A Christian union secretary who made a career in the DAF later complained of being boycotted by all his former colleagues: memorandum of 15 September 1945 by Adolf Schaar, NL Kaiser/246.
136. See Patrik von zur Mühlen, *"Schlagt Hitler an der Saar!"* (Bonn, 1979), pp. 26f., 64, and Gewerkverein christlicher Bergarbeiter, *17. Generalversammlung 1924*, pp. 55f.

plebiscite campaign of 1933–34 therefore exposed them to a cruel dilemma. In May 1933 the number two man in the Christian miners' union of the Saar, Peter Kiefer, sought a personal audience with Hitler and agreed to become co-leader of the German referendum campaign. In October of that year Kiefer became chairman of his union with Nazi support.[137] Heinrich Imbusch caused considerable confusion among Christian workers in the spring of 1934 when he sided with the remnants of the SPD and KPD, which opposed reunification, and contested the validity of Kiefer's election. The overwhelming majority of Saar residents, and many of Imbusch's former colleagues in Germany, believed that reunification must come regardless of political conditions in the Reich, that a vote for Germany did not imply endorsement of National Socialism.[138]

The Blood Purge of June 1934 nevertheless convinced even those DGB leaders sympathetic to National Socialism in the past, such as Max Habermann, that the Third Reich was fundamentally evil. The murder of Gregor Strasser, Kurt von Schleicher, and two priests prominent in Catholic Action, along with the SA leadership, demonstrated that Hitler was indeed something like an "Asiatic despot." Habermann and Jakob Kaiser joined Wilhelm Leuschner as the leaders of the trade union wing of the German Resistance. Kaiser maintained close contact with hundreds of former colleagues as their legal representative in protracted court battles with the DAF over pension claims.[139] These activities masked the recruitment of a nationwide network of former union functionaries prepared to establish a unified and democratic union federation after Hitler's fall. The shared experience of persecution by the Nazis convinced Free and Christian trade unionists that their differences in the past were insignificant.[140] The Catholic workers' clubs represented another focal point of opposition to the Third Reich. The clubs were forced to confine themselves to religious activities after 1933, but old democrats like Joseph Joos, Otto Müller, and Bernhard Letterhaus continued to lead them. Their retreats and pilgrimages preserved the traditions of the Christian labor movement. In 1944 Habermann, Letterhaus, Müller, and several other Christian labor leaders paid with their lives for complicity in the Stauffenberg plot to assassinate Hitler.[141] Shattered by the destruction of their movement, Otte and Franz Wieber died soon after the Nazi seizure of power,

137. Von zur Mühlen, pp. 70–73.
138. Ibid., pp. 126–38, and Nebgen, pp. 18–22. In January 1935, 91% of the Saar electorate approved reunification with the Reich.
139. Karl Hahn, "Max Habermann und der 20. Juli" (DHV Archiv) p. 2, and Nebgen , pp. 23–25. Stegerwald won his pension claims in 1941 through the direct intervention of the Führer: see Finance Minister Schwerin von Krosigk to Syrup, 21 November 1941, NL Stegerwald/018.
140. Mommsen, "Die deutschen Gewerkschaften zwischen Anpassung und Widerstand," pp. 291–99, and Nebgen, pp. 31–214.
141. Aretz, pp. 150–237, and Focke, pp. 175–93.

and Heinrich Imbusch was taken by pneumonia in the last year of World War II, after returning from exile incognito to live in his hometown of Essen. But Kaiser, Karl Arnold, Gustav Hülser, and enough of their associates survived to guarantee that there would be no division of the trade unions along religious lines in the Federal Republic.

The rise of the NSDAP revealed the futility of the DGB's efforts to synthesize militant nationalism with the values of the labor movement. The parties that resisted Nazi propaganda most successfully during the Great Depression, the SPD and Center, had for years inculcated their followers with a moral repugnance for militarism and racism. They did not, like DGB leaders, rely on the dubious thesis that Hitler was the tool of Ruhr industrialists while praising his nationalist ideals. Within the Catholic community, however, by far the strongest opposition to Nazism emerged where religious and trade union values overlapped. The core membership of the Christian unions counted among the most energetic opponents of Hitler's rise to power.[142] There was, to be sure, some resemblance between the rhetoric of the Christian-nationalist labor movement and that of the NSDAP, but Michael Schneider seriously distorts the record when he claims that the Christian trade unionists greeted the advent of the Third Reich more enthusiastically than they had the Weimar Republic. Schneider's conclusion reflects more anxiety over the influence of Christian Democrats in the leadership of today's German Labor Federation than scholarly acumen: "Enthusiastic support for the monarchy, emphatic nationalist pathos and support for imperialist policies, an initially reserved response to the Weimar democracy with marked anti-parliamentary resentments, and finally the offer to participate actively in the construction of the 'Third Reich': these are deficits which hardly permit any uncritical connection with the tradition of the Christian trade unions."[143] It is unreasonable to compare the largely coerced acclamations observable throughout the German press in the months after Hitler came to power with the honest expression of hopes and fears in the Christian union press of 1918–19. This book should have demonstrated that the Christian trade unionists were, for the most part, dedicated and unusually skillful defenders of parliamentary democracy, whose efforts to organize and enlighten the millions of German workers reared with the ideas that Schneider finds so objectionable were crucial to the survival of the Weimer Republic. Nobody who refused to have dealings with people who were not already good democrats could have saved that "republic without republicans."

---

142. This point is made repeatedly in the local and regional studies by Kühr, Stump, Plum, and Schönhoven.

143. Michael Schneider, *Die christlichen Gewerkschaften*, pp. 727f., and quotation on p. 766.

Part of the reason for the similarity between the rhetoric of the Christian unions and that of the NSDAP was that Hitler shrewdly exploited legitimate resentment against real abuses that had first been criticized by the Christian unions. In a detached and reflective mood, Adam Stegerwald told his followers that the ultimate cause of Hitler's triumph had been their failure to implement the program for party reform adopted at the Essen Congress of 1920.[144] The idea might appear fanciful, but Stegerwald's speech at Essen retains great significance as the first detailed argument that all the established political parties of the Weimar Republic were living in the past. Stegerwald attacked the SPD and liberal parties for adhering to traditional views on the irreconcilability of class interests that should be modified in the light of the impressive successes achieved through direct negotiations between business and union leaders, the Center Party for assuming that Catholicism could continue to serve as a substitute for a political program even after the abolition of discrimination against Catholics, the DNVP for refusing to acknowledge that the masses had attained a level of education and political experience warranting their participation in government. His arguments would receive striking confirmation in the decade to follow, as each party's cadre became increasingly overaged and unrepresentative of the electorate. This ossification of the party system was a necessary condition for the triumph of National Socialism.

144. GcG, *Die Essener Richtlinien*, pp. 68f.

members respond in the affirmative just as often as nonmembers when asked if they believe in God. They are less likely to attend church services, but the differential is certainly smaller than it was at the turn of the century. About 80% of the salaried functionaries of the German Labor Federation today are church members.[7] Thus Christian trade unionists cannot be dismissed as a historical curiosity. The question remains of whether their program contained important insights missing from that of the socialist labor movement.

The sociologist Theodor Geiger felt that shared economic interests had compelled Christian and socialist workers alike to modify the ideologies inherited from the nineteenth century: "One need only disregard a little conventional phraseology to make a Christian trade unionist and an Amsterdamer [Free unionist] resemble each other like two peas in a pod."[8] Both Free and Christian union leaders agreed during the 1920s that their programs were converging, but each side claimed that it had not changed at all, that the other was abandoning unrealistic principles as a result of practical experience. The two movements doubtless influenced each other. The Christian unions came increasingly to embrace Social Democratic positions when they campaigned for worker participation in factory management, for state ownership of heavy industry, for egalitarian reform of the educational system, and for a purge of reactionaries from the bureaucracy. These were matters of intense concern to the great majority of "class-conscious," that is, well-informed and self-respecting workers, regardless of their party affiliation. At the same time, the existence of the Christian labor movement promoted self-criticism within the SPD concerning attitudes toward religion, national security, and participation in coalition governments. In these matters the traditional Social Democratic positions resulted more from nineteenth-century circumstances than from the fundamental desires of German workers.

In a major policy address to the Kiel Party Congress of the SPD in 1927, Rudolf Hilferding sought earnestly to define the lessons that could be learned from the existence of the Christian labor movement. Hilferding believed that the SPD's most urgent task was to win the allegiance of the misguided but class-conscious workers who voted for the Center Party and DNVP. Far from assuming that such workers were a vanishing breed, he noted that German conservatives had achieved spectacular success in broadening their electoral base since

---

7. Horst W. Schmollinger, "Zur politisch-gesellschaftlichen Beteiligung von Gewerkschafts-mitgliedern: Gewerkschafter in Parteien, Kirchen und Vereinen," in Ulrich Borsdorf et al. (eds.), *Gewerkschaftliche Politik: Reform aus Solidarität. Zum 60. Geburtstag von Heinz O. Vetter* (Cologne, 1977), pp. 148–52.

8. Geiger, pp. 14f.

1918 "because thousands of proletarians, real workers confused by inflation and the other postwar developments, have voted for it," adding that "the whole power of the Center is based on . . . the schism of the trade union movement."[9] Hilferding concluded that the SPD must demonstrate to Christian workers that it was no longer the enemy of organized religion, that all its legislative demands in this regard had been satisfied in 1919. With specific reference to the thorny issue of the confessional school, Hilferding argued that the SPD must abandon efforts to eliminate the influence of the clergy on the curriculum and cooperate instead with Christian workers in the campaign to secure equal access to higher education for the disadvantaged. This represented a major departure from the tradition of August Bebel. Significantly, Hilferding urged détente with the churches, not because he was impressed by the theoretical arguments of the League of Religious Socialists, but because the example of the English trade unions and the Catholic workers of western Germany convinced him that the Christian faith need not hinder workers from participating effectively in class struggle.[10]

Hilferding also argued that the SPD must abandon its old stance of hostility toward the military establishment. Two months earlier, in December 1926, Philipp Scheidemann had made spectacular revelations concerning illegal rearmament on the floor of the Reichstag. His speech served to nip negotiations for the formation of a Grand Coalition in the bud and nurtured fears in the officer corps that national security required the exclusion of the SPD from government office. Adam Stegerwald had denounced Scheidemann's initiative as proof that a doctrinaire outlook prevented the SPD from participating fruitfully in the government of the Republic, and Hilferding essentially endorsed this position. The SPD must support the Reichswehr in principle, Hilferding argued, and it must participate in coalition governments so as to encourage the promotion of reliable republican officers.[11]

Indeed, Hilferding urged policies similar to those of Stegerwald in many respects, and he was the Social Democrat whose realism and responsible attitude the DGB leadership most admired. However, his argumentation demonstrated the continuing influence of Kautsky's thinking on the SPD leadership. Hilferding urged participating in coalitions as essential for preserving parliamentary democracy, but he defended parliamentary democracy as the best platform for proletarian class struggle. The SPD's goal remained that of the Communist

9. The entire speech is reprinted in Luthardt (ed.), vol. 1, pp. 369–93, quotation on p. 392.
10. Ibid., pp. 382f.
11. Ibid., pp. 390f. For background see Stürmer, pp. 170–80, and Hayes, pp. 41f.

Manifesto, to "elevate the working class to a political party." When it had thereby achieved an absolute electoral majority, the SPD would accomplish the "overthrow of the capitalist system (Sturz des kapitalistischen Systems)." Social Democrats would never initiate a civil war, Hilferding maintained, because the Soviet example demonstrated that such strife was terribly wasteful. But he predicted that the proletariat's inexorable march toward political power would prompt the middle classes to rally behind the fascist banner in an effort to overthrow the Weimar Constitution.[12] His thinking rested on the premise that the working class enjoyed a monopoloy of political virtue. His model of economic democracy sounded very much like the dictatorship of the proletariat. Hilferding's prophecy was self-fulfilling to the extent that, despite his commitment to parliamentary democracy in principle, he espoused goals that could never be achieved through the politics of compromise between organized labor and other interest groups.

Writing in 1924, Ludwig Heyde argued that the Christian unions had taught Social Democrats that one could combine effective trade unionism with commitment to the principle that "in all zeal for social reform, regard for the interests of the nation as a whole must establish some boundaries for the advocacy of class interests."[13] Social Democratic leaders made enormous sacrifices for the sake of the nation from 1914 to 1923, compromising their principles and ignoring tactical considerations from a sense of patriotic duty. But a reaction against this policy of concessions had set in by the time Heyde wrote, and Social Democrats were striving to recover their sense of identity as a movement dedicated to proletarian class struggle. Christian labor leaders recognized more clearly than the Weimar Social Democrats that parliamentary democracy must rest on an element of consensus, some sense of shared identity common to the entire electorate. Workers had to learn to regard farmers and businessmen as something more than class enemies. Trade unions had to show landowners and industrialists that they understood the structure of the existing economy and would not ruin it. Organized labor had to show small businessmen and farmers that they could cooperate fruitfully against monopolies and class privilege, to show big business that they could cooperate against agrarian protectionism and the top-heavy bureaucracy. It was easy to ridicule Adam Stegerwald, this diminutive peasant's son, with his clean-shaven skull and large nose, who spoke endlessly about the Volksgemeinschaft. However, despite all the mistakes and limitations of Stegerwald and his colleagues, their efforts to win sympathy and negotiating partners for the

---

12. Luthardt (ed.), pp. 369, 379, 391.
13. *Soziale Praxis,* 30 October 1924, columns 914f.

unions within the bourgeois parties of the Weimar Republic represented the decisive battlefront in the campaign for democracy.

As we have seen, these efforts by the Christian unionists failed because of a backlash against progressive social legislation among middle-class party activists after 1927. Hard-line industrialists who could not reconcile themselves with collective bargaining, much less economic democracy, shopkeepers who blamed consumers' cooperatives for their economic problems, fanatical nationalists who blamed unions for Germany's defeat, conservative landowners, and elitist bureaucrats succeeded in eliminating union influence over the policies of the DNVP and DVP. The rejection of the DGB in these parties went hand in hand with rejection of parliamentary government. The Center Party responded to fears of disintegration by cultivating such close ties with the Catholic Church that it could not rally a broad coalition in defense of parliamentary democracy. Throughout the depression years the Reich Association of Industry displayed a more conciliatory attitude than did either the DVP or DNVP, and this crucial fact suggests that Carl Legien and Adam Stegerwald were not misguided when they sought in November 1918 to forge an agreement with Hugo Stinnes as a foundation for parliamentary government. In 1931–32 the calmly calculating leadership of the Reich Association became increasingly unrepresentative of the business community, however, and the Christian unions could do nothing to halt the explosive growth of the NSDAP or the turn against the Republic by President Hindenburg and the army leadership.

The widespread acceptance in the Federal Republic of strong unions, factory councils, and some sort of worker participation in management (*Mitbestimmung*) suggests nonetheless that the efforts of the Christian trade unionists were not in vain. Veterans of the Christian unions, most notably Jakob Kaiser and Karl Arnold, played an important role in the formation of both the Christian Democratic Union (CDU) and the German Labor Federation. Unionists who cooperated in the Resistance agreed that their past divisions had eased the way for Hitler's rise and that they should establish a unified union organization observing strict religious and political neutrality. The DGB founded by them in 1949 has adhered to their program by refraining from overt support of the SPD and guaranteeing a quota of leadership posts to Christian Democrats.[14] Within the

14. See Hirsch-Weber, pp. 49–59. An official history of the German unions recently published by the DGB devotes flattering attention to the contributions of the Christian labor movement. Its biographical appendix discusses the careers of four Free union leaders and seven Social Democrats as opposed to nine leaders of the Catholic workers' clubs, eleven Christian trade unionists, and four Hirsch–Duncker labor leaders: Ludwig Rosenberg and Bernhard Tacke, *DGB. Der Weg zur Einheitsgewerkschaft* (Düsseldorf, 1978).

CDU the veterans of the Christian unions organized a network of Social Committees to defend labor interests, which represent a significant voting bloc.[15]

These Christian trade unionists found it difficult to agree on a program in the immediate postwar period. Kaiser led a group of enthusiastic "Christian socialists" who advocated state ownership of Ruhr heavy industry, but Konrad Adenauer and Ludwig Erhard rallied the support of a number of Christian labor leaders behind their alternate model of the "social market economy."[16] The Social Committees have nonetheless tenaciously supported the position of the DGB on the issue of *Mitbestimmung* and have won acceptance in the CDU for significant labor representation on the supervisory boards of large industrial firms. The Christian workers' mediating role was symbolized in the close personal friendship of Arnold, the head of the GcG in Düsseldorf during the 1920s who rose to become prime minister of Northrhine-Westphalia, and Hans Böckler, the Social Democratic chairman of the DGB. Their relationship promoted the politics of compromise during the most turbulent debates of the 1950s.[17]

Their Christian faith did not contribute any specific ideas to the program of the Christian trade unionists more realistic or forward-looking than those of the ADGB. Indeed, one central feature of their program, enthusiastic support for state labor arbitration, has been rejected by all factions in the Federal Republic. Christian unionists wanted to involve the state because they believed fervently that ethical considerations should determine wage levels, not the "law of the jungle" on the labor market, but there is a consensus in the Federal Republic today that the smooth functioning of collective bargaining depends on the "autonomy of the contracting parties." Some commentators harshly condemn the Weimar system of arbitration for transforming every conflict of economic interest into a political crisis, while driving wages up to levels that starved industry of investment funds. These charges can be disputed, but even the system's defenders argue only that it played a valuable role for promoting acceptance of collective bargaining within a reluctant business community, not that it should be reintroduced today.[18] The true contribution of the Christian trade unionists to

15. Of 260 Christian Democrats elected to the Bundestag in 1953, 54 were trade unionists, although this proportion has since declined somewhat. A poll conducted in 1976 showed that 57.8% of all DGB members voted for the SPD, 28.4% for the CDU/CSU, and 8% for the FDP: Hirsch-Weber, pp. 68–70, and Schmollinger, p. 137.

16. Focke, pp. 220–60.

17. Detlev Hüwel, *Karl Arnold* (Wuppertal, 1980), pp. 84–90; Hirsch-Weber, pp. 134–39; Wolfgang Rudzio, "Das Ringen um die Sozialisierung der Kohlewirtschaft nach dem Zweiten Weltkrieg," and Martiny, "Die Durchsetzung der Mitbestimmung im deutschen Bergbau," in Mommsen and Borsdorf (eds.).

18. Contrast Borchardt, "Zwangslagen," pp. 176–81, and "Wirtschaftliche Ursachen," pp. 186–90, with the more persuasive arguments by Hartwich, pp. 301–26, 363–88, and Balderston, pp. 500–05.

the German labor movement lay in their unusual sensitivity to the corrosive effect of class egotism. Christian workers knew that no class had a monopoly on political virtue because they knew that no class was immune to the sin of pride. The ancient wisdom of the Christian churches in diagnosing the many and devious ways in which pride could seize hold of the human heart offered them valuable guidance at a time when so many people identified themselves so passionately with conflicting ideologies and causes.

Veterans of the Christian unions exerted no direct influence on the SPD in the Federal Republic, but their example probably encouraged the triumph of the Revisionist position in that party. The SPD's postwar leader, Kurt Schumacher, argued consistently that the rejection of civil war in favor of parliamentary politics implied the rejection of "class struggle" as the foundation for the party program. He insisted that the SPD define itself according to political principles rather than class interests and embrace all who supported those principles, regardless of their class situation. When the Godesberg Party Congress of the SPD finally adopted a comprehensive new program in 1959, it not only dropped the demand for state ownership of the means of production, it also rejected a Marxist preamble concerning the socialist world view in favor of a terse declaration: "Democratic socialism . . . is rooted in Christian ethics, in humanism, and in classical philosophy."[19] This might be considered the sweetest triumph for the League of Christian Unions.

19. See Harold Schellenger, *The SPD in the Bonn Republic: A Socialist Party Modernizes* (The Hague, 1968), pp. 32–48.

BIBLIOGRAPHY

UNPUBLISHED SOURCES

BAK: BUNDESARCHIV, KOBLENZ
BAK R43I: Records of the Reich Chancellory of the Weimar Republic.
BAK R45II: Records of the German People's Party (DVP).
BAK R45III: Records of the German Democratic Party (DDP).
BAK NS 26: Historical archive of the NSDAP.
NL Otte (BAK Kleine Erwerbung 461): Fragmentary records of the League of Christian
    Unions.
Kleine Erwerbung 497: Fragmentary records of the Hirsch–Duncker unions.
Personal papers: NL Eduard Dingeldey, NL Erkelenz, NL Kaiser, NL Krebs, NL Lam-
    bach, NL ten Hompel.

ZStA: ZENTRALES STAATSARCHIV DER DDR, POTSDAM

ZStA/DNVP: Records of the German Nationalist People's Party and the Nationalist
    Workers' League.
ZStA/RAM: Records of the Reich Labor Ministry.
ZStA/RLB: Records of the Reich Agrarian League (Reichslandbund).
ZStA/ZAG: Records of the Central Association of Industrial Employers and Employees
    (Zentralarbeitsgemeinschaft).
NL Mumm: Personal papers of Reinhard Mumm.

VOLKSVEREIN BIBLIOTHEK:

The municipal library of Mönchen-Gladbach houses the most extensive collection of the
    relevant pamphlets, periodicals, and published transcripts as well as the Teil-
    nachlaß Pieper, a typescript history of the Volksverein, including transcripts of the
    proceedings of its executive committee.

DGB BIBLIOTHEK:

The headquarters of today's German Labor Federation in Düsseldorf houses an excellent
    collection of union publications (including a nearly complete run of Der Deutsche),
    the Imbusch papers (NL Imbusch), and a few papers for Heinrich Fahrenbrach,
    Gustav Hülser, and Wolfgang Wittig.

KAB ARCHIV AND NL DESSAUER:

Records of the Reich executive committee of the Catholic workers' clubs and the papers of
    Friedrich Dessauer and Emil Ritter are tended by the Kommission für
    Zeitgeschichte, Bonn.

NL STEGERWALD:

Stegerwald Papers, Konrad-Adenauer-Stiftung, Bonn.

COLOGNE ARCHDIOCESE:

Historisches Archiv des Erzbistums Köln.

NL MARX AND NL BACHEM:

Papers of Wilhelm Marx and Carl Bachem, Stadtarchiv Köln.

IGBE BIBLIOTHEK:

The library of the Industriegewerkschaft Bergbau und Energie in Bochum houses publications of the various miners' unions and a handwritten "Protokoll- und Copier-
buch" recording the decisions of the executive committee of the Christian miners'
union from 1895 through 1920.

STA OSNABRÜCK:

Nidersächsisches Staatsarchiv, Osnabrück, with complete records of a DNVP party local.

NL WESTARP:

Westarp papers, tended by and used with the kind permission of his grandson, Friedrich
Freiherr Hiller von Gaertringen.

NL DILLER AND "GESCHÄFTSFÜHRENDER AUSSCHUß DES ALLDEUTSCHEN VERBANDS":

Alfred Diller Papers and records of the Pan-German League, Forschungsstelle zur
Geschichte des Nationalsozialismus, Hamburg.

DHV ARCHIV:

Deutscher Handels- und Industrieangestellten Verband, Hamburg, including the digest
of the decisions taken by the DHV's executive committee, cited as "DHV Verwaltung: Auszüge," and Max Habermann's unpublished memoirs, cited as
"Habermann MS."

NL STRESEMANN AND THE HOLBORN PAPERS:

Manuscripts and Archives, Sterling Memorial Library, Yale University.

PUBLICATIONS OF THE ORGANIZATIONS STUDIED

CHRISTIAN-NATIONALIST UNIONS

Gesamtverband der christlichen Gewerkschaften Deutschlands (League of Christian
Unions)

Zentralblatt der christlichen Gewerkschaften (biweekly).
*Bericht über die Verhandlungen des 4. Deutschen Arbeiter-Kongresses, 28–30 October
1917*, Cologne, 1918.
*Niederschrift der Verhandlungen des 10. Kongresses der christlichen Gewerkschaften
Deutschlands, 20–23 November 1920*, Cologne, 1920.
25 Jahre christlicher Gewerkschaftsbewegung 1899–1924. Festschrift, Berlin, 1924.

Niederschrift der Verhandlungen des 11. Kongresses der christlichen Gewerkschaften Deutschlands, 17–20 April 1926, Berlin, 1926.
Niederschrift der Verhandlungen des 12. Kongresses der christlichen Gewerkschaften Deutschlands, 15–18 September 1929, Berlin, 1929.
Niederschrift der Verhandlungen des 13. Kongresses der christlichen Gewerkschaften Deutschlands, 18–20 September 1932, Berlin, 1932.
Die Essener Richtlinien 1933 der christlich-nationalen Gewerkschaften, Berlin, 1933.
Jahrbuch der christlichen Gewerkschaften 1925, Berlin, 1925.
Jahrbuch der christlichen Gewerkschaften 1930. Bericht über das Jahr 1929, Berlin, 1930.
Jahrbuch 1931. Bericht über das Jahr 1930, Berlin, 1931.
Jahrbuch 1932. Bericht über das Jahr 1931, Berlin, 1932.

Zentralverband christlicher Bauarbeiter (Christian Construction Workers' Union)

Geschäftsbericht des Vorstandes, 1918–19, und Niederschrift der Verhandlungen der 11. Generalversammlung, 30. Mai bis 1. Juni 1920, Berlin, no date.
Geschäftsbericht des Vorstandes 1920–21, und Niederschrift der Verhandlungen der 12. General-Versammlung, 14–18 Mai 1922, Berlin, no date.
Geschäftsbericht des Vorstandes, 1922–24, und Niederschrift der Verhandlungen der 13. Generalversammlung, 10–13 Mai 1925, Berlin, no date.
Geschäftsbericht des Vorstandes, 1925–27, und Bericht über die Verhandlungen der 15. Generalversammlung, 13–16 August 1928, Berlin, no date.
Geschäftsbericht des Vorstandes für die Jahre 1928–30, Berlin, no date.

Gewerkverein christlicher Bergarbeiter (Christian Miners' Union)

Der Bergknappe (weekly).
Protokoll der 15. Generalversammlung, 24–27 August 1919, Essen, no date.
Protokoll der Außerordentlichen Generalversammlung, 22–23 Februar 1920, Essen, no date.
Protokoll der 16. Generalversammlung, 3–7 Juli 1921, Essen, no date.
Protokoll der 17. Generalversammlung, 24–26 August 1924, Essen, no date.
Protokoll der 18. Generalversammlung, 13–15 Mai 1926, Essen, no date.
Bericht des Hauptvorstandes über die Jahre 1926/27, Essen, 1928.
Geschäftsbericht des Hauptvorstandes für die Jahre 1928/29, Essen, 1930.
Protokoll der 20. Generalversammlung, 3–6 August 1930, Essen, no date.
Geschäftsbericht des Hauptvorstandes des Gewerkvereins für die Jahre 1930/32, Essen, 1933.

Zentralverband christlicher Fabrik- und Transportarbeiter (Christian Factory and Transport Workers' Union), *Bericht des Hauptvorstandes für die Jahre 1925–1927*, Berlin, no date.

Zentralverband der Gemeindearbeiter und Straßenbahner, Sitz Köln (Union of Municipal Employees), *Geschäftsbericht des Vorstandes, 1913–1919*, Cologne, no date.

Zentralverband christlicher Holzarbeiter (Christian Woodworkers' Union), *1899/1924. Ein Vierteljahrhundert Zentralverband christlicher Holzarbeiter*, no place or date.

Zentralverband der Landarbeiter, renamed Reichsverband ländlicher Arbeitnehmer in 1929 (Christian Farmworkers' Union)

Die Rundschau. Zeitung für das schaffende Landvolk (biweekly).
Verhandlungs-Bericht über den 1. Verbandstag, 16–19 Mai 1920, Berlin, no date.

Verhandlungsbericht über den 3. Verbandstag, 18–20 Juli 1926, Berlin, no date.
Geschäftsbericht erstattet von der Hauptverwaltung zum 4. Verbandstag 1929, Berlin, 1929.

Zentralverband christlicher Lederarbeiter (Christian Leatherworkers' Union), *Bericht für die Jahre 1925–26, und Niederschrift über die Verhandlungen der 11. Verbandsgeneralversammlung, 21–24 August 1927*, Frankfurt am Main, 1927.

Christlicher Metallarbeiterverband (Christian Metalworkers' Union)

Der deutsche Metallarbeiter (biweekly).
Bericht des Verbands-Vorstandes, 1918–19, Duisburg, no date.
Protokoll über die Verhandlungen der 9. Generalversammlung, 15–19 August 1920, no place or date.
Bericht des Verbands-Vorstandes, 1922–1924, no place or date.
Protokoll über die Verhandlungen der 11. General-Versammlung, 16–20 August 1925, no place or date.
Protokoll über die Verhandlungen der 12. General-Versammlung, 16–20 September 1928, no place or date.
Protokoll über die Verhandlungen der 13. General-Versammlung, 26–28 September 1932, no place or date.

Zentralverband christlicher Textilarbeiter (Christian Textile Workers' Union), *Protokoll über die Verhandlungen der 11. Generalversammlung, 3–7 August 1930*, no place or date.

Deutschnationaler Handlungsgehilfen-Verband (German Nationalist Union of Commercial Employees)

Deutsche Handels-Wacht (biweekly).
Der Deutschnationale Handlungsgehilfen-Verband im Jahre 1924. Rechenschaftsbericht erstattet von seiner Verwaltung, Hamburg, 1925.
Der DHV im Jahre 1925, Hamburg, 1926.
Der DHV im Jahre 1926, Hamburg, 1927.
Der DHV im Jahre 1927, Hamburg, 1928.
Der DHV im Jahre 1928, Hamburg, 1929.
Der DHV im Jahre 1929, Hamburg, 1930.
Der DHV im Jahre 1930, Hamburg, 1931.

Gewerkschaft deutscher Eisenbahner und Staatsbediensteter (Union of German Railroad Workers and State Employees), *Die deutsche Gewerkschaft*, biweekly, title varies, housed in the Staatsbibliothek preußischer Kulturbesitz, Berlin.

Deutscher Gewerkschaftsbund. *Der Deutsche*, daily.

CATHOLIC WORKERS' CLUBS AND THE VOLKSVEREIN

Westdeutsche Arbeiter-Zeitung (weekly).
Der Arbeiter (München). Organ des Verbandes süddeutscher katholischer Arbeiter-Vereine (weekly).
Mitteilungen an die Präsides der katholischen Arbeitervereine der Erzdiözese Köln (quarterly).
Bericht des 12. Verbandstages der kath. Arbeiter- und Knappenvereine Westdeutschlands, 14.–15. September 1919, Mönchen-Gladbach, 1919.

Bericht des zweiten Kongresses des Kartellverbandes der katholischen Arbeiter- und Arbeiterinnenvereine Deutschlands, 5–8 Mai 1921, Mönchen-Gladbach, no date.
Otto Müller, "Die kath. Arbeitervereine Westdeutschlands in ihren Verbandsorganisationen und Arbeitersekretariaten," 2d ed., Mönchen-Gladbach, 1926.
Jahrbuch des Diözesanverbandes der katholischen Arbeiter- und Knappenvereine der Erzdiözese Köln, Cologne, 1929.
Soziallehre der Kirche und Arbeiterbewegung. Roms Stellung zu wichtigen sozialen Gegenwartsfragen, Gladbach-Rheydt, 1930.
Die katholische Arbeiter-Bewegung Westdeutschlands. Bericht über die Jahre 1925– 1931, Mönchen-Gladbach, 1931.
Josef van der Velden (ed.), *Die berufsständische Ordnung. Idee und praktische Möglichkeiten*, Cologne, 1932.

YELLOW UNIONS

Deutsche Werksgemeinschaft. Wochenschrift der vaterländischen Arbeitnehmerbewegung Groß-Deutschlands in Stadt und Land, biweekly, August Scherl Verlag, Wilhelm Schmidt (ed.), renamed *Arbeit und Recht* in 1930. Housed in the Staatsbibliothek preußischer Kulturbesitz, Berlin.
Der Reichslandarbeiterbund, biweekly, Johannes Wolf (ed.), housed in the Berlin Staatsbibliothek (DDR).
Die nationalen Berufsverbände. Denkschrift zur 2. Reichstagung des Nationalverbandes Deutscher Berufsverbände, 11–15 November 1921, Berlin, no date.

POLITICAL PARTIES

Deutsche Volkspartei (DVP)

Bericht über den Ersten Parteitag, 13. April 1919, Berlin, 1919.
Bericht über den zweiten Parteitag, 18–20 Oktober 1919, Berlin, 1920.

Deutsche Zentrumspartei (Center Party)

Germania, daily, Berlin.
Kölnische Volkszeitung, daily, Cologne.
"Bericht über die erste Tagung der Arbeiter-Zentrumswähler Westdeutschlands in Bochum am 23. Juni 1918," Mönchen-Gladbach, no date.
Erster Reichsparteitag des Zentrums! 19–22 January 1920, Berlin, no date.
Offizieller Bericht des zweiten Reichsparteitages der Deutschen Zentrumspartei, 15–17 January 1922, Berlin, no date.
Offizieller Bericht des vierten Reichsparteitages der Deutschen Zentrumspartei, 16–17 November 1925, Berlin, no date.
Offizieller Bericht des fünften Reichsparteitages der Deutschen Zentrumspartei, 8–9 Dezember 1928, Trier, no date.
"Um den sozialen Volksstaat. Vorträge gehalten auf der außerordentlichen Tagung des Reichsarbeiterbeirats der Deutschen Zentrumspartei am 29. Juni 1932 in Essen," no place or date.

Deutschnationale Volkspartei (DNVP) and Christian Social Movement

Deutsche Arbeiterstimme, biweekly of the Deutschnationale Arbeiter-Bund, most complete collection in NL Diller. Renamed *Deutsche Angestelltenstimme und Arbeiterstimme* in 1928.

"Aufbau und Tätigkeit des Deutschnationalen Arbeiterbundes," DNVP pamphlet no. 213 (1925).
Die deutschnationale Arbeiter-Bewegung, ihr Werden und Wachsen, published by the Deutschnationale Arbeiter-Bund, Berlin, no date (ca. 1926).
DNVP Korrespondenz, biweekly for party functionaries.
New York Public Library, collection of DNVP pamplets on microfilm.
Kirchlich-soziale Blätter, monthly of the Kirchlich-soziale Bund.
Der Christliche Volksdienst (Stuttgart), biweekly.
Tägliche Rundschau, daily of the CSVD, 1930–32.

MEMOIRS AND PUBLISHED DOCUMENTS

Akten der Reichskanzlei der Weimarer Republik

Das Kabinett Bauer, 21. Juni 1919 bis 27. März 1920, edited by Anton Golecki, Boppard am Rhein, 1980.
Das Kabinett Müller I, 27. März bis 21. Juni 1920, edited by Martin Vogt, Boppard am Rhein, 1971.
Das Kabinett Fehrenbach, 25. Juni 1920 bis 4. März 1921, edited by Peter Wulf, Boppard am Rhein, 1972.
Die Kabinette Wirth I und II, 10. Mai 1921 bis 22. November 1922, edited by Ingrid Schulze-Bidlingmaier, 2 vols., Boppard am Rhein, 1973.
Das Kabinett Cuno, 22. November 1922 bis 12. August 1923, edited by Karl-Heinz Harbeck, Boppard am Rhein, 1968.
Die Kabinette Stresemann I. und II., 13. August 1923 bis 23. November 1923, edited by Karl Dietrich Erdmann and Martin Vogt, 2 vols., Boppard am Rhein, 1978.
Die Kabinette Marx I und II, 30. November 1923 bis 15. Januar 1925, edited by Günter Abramowski, 2 vols., Boppard am Rhein, 1973.
Die Kabinette Luther I und II, 15. January 1925 bis 17. Mai 1926, edited by Karl-Heinz Minuth, 2 vols., Boppard am Rhein, 1977.
Das Kabinett Müller II, 28. Juni 1928 bis 27. März 1930, edited by Martin Vogt, 2 vols., Boppard am Rhein, 1970.
Die Kabinette Brüning I und II, 30. März 1930 bis 10. Oktober 1931, edited by Tilman Koops, 2 vols. (still incomplete), Boppard am Rhein, 1982.

Gerhard Beier, "Zur Entstehung des Führerkreises der vereinigten Gewerkschaften Ende April 1933. Dokumentation aus dem Leuschner-Nachlaß," *Archiv für Sozialgeschichte,* 15 (1975).
Heinrich Brüning, *Memoiren 1918–1934,* Stuttgart, 1970.
Werner Conze, "Zum Sturz Brünings (Dokumentation)," *Vierteljahrshefte für Zeitgeschichte,* 1 (June 1953).
Dieter Emig and Rüdiger Zimmermann, "Das Ende einer Legende. Gewerkschaften, Papen und Schleicher. Gefälschte und echte Protokolle," *Internationale wissenschaftliche Korrespondenz,* 12 (March 1976).
Gerald Feldman and Irmgard Steinisch, "The Origins of the Stinnes–Legien Agreement: A Documentation," *Internationale wissenschaftliche Korrespondenz,* 9 (December 1973).
Heinrich Köhler, *Lebenserinnerungen des Politikers und Staatsmannes 1878–1949,* edited by Josef Becker, Stuttgart, 1964.

Albert Krebs, *Tendenzen und Gestalten der NSDAP. Erinnerungen an die Frühzeit der Partei*, Stuttgart, 1959.

Ernst Lemmer, *Manches war doch anders. Erinnerungen eines deutschen Demokraten*, Frankfurt am Main, 1968.

Rudolf Morsey, "Neue Quellen zur Vorgeschichte der Reichskanzlerschaft Brünings," in Hermens and Schieder (eds.), *Staat, Wirtschaft und Politik in der Weimarer Republik.*

———— *(ed.), Die Protokolle der Reichstagsfraktion und des Fraktionsvorstands der Deutschen Zentrumspartei 1926–1933*, Mainz, 1969.

Rudolf Morsey and Karsten Ruppert (eds.), *Die Protokolle der Reichstagsfraktion der Deutschen Zentrumspartei 1920–1925*, Mainz, 1981.

Reinhard Mumm, *Der christlich-soziale Gedanke. Bericht über eine Lebensarbeit in schwerer Zeit*, Berlin, 1933.

Hermann Pünder, *Politik in der Reichskanzlei. Aufzeichnungen aus den Jahren 1929– 1932*, edited by Thilo Vogelsang, Stuttgart, 1961.

Quellen zur Geschichte des Parlamentarismus und der politischen Parteien Linksliberalismus in der Weimarer Republik. Die Führungsgremien der Deutschen Demokratischen Partei und der Deutschen Staatspartei 1918–1933, edited by Lothar Albertin and Konstanze Wegner, Düsseldorf, 1980.
Politik und Wirtschaft in der Krise, 1930–1932. Quellen zur Ära Brüning, edited by Ilse Maurer and Udo Wengst, Düsseldorf, 1980.

Gerhard A. Ritter and Susanne Miller (eds.), *Die Deutsche Revolution 1918–1919. Dokumente*, 2d ed., Hamburg, 1975.

Hermann Seelbach, *Das Ende der Gewerkschaften. Aufzeichnungen über den geistigen Zusammenbruch eines Systems*, Berlin, 1934.

Statistisches Reichsamt, *Statistische Jahrbücher des Deutschen Reiches*, Berlin, 1920– 33.

Gottfried von Treviranus, *Das Ende von Weimar. Heinrich Brüning und seine Zeit*, Düsseldorf and Vienna, 1968.

Henry A. Turner (ed.), *Hitler aus nächster Nähe. Aufzeichnungen eines Vertrauten 1929–1932*, Frankfurt am Main, 1978.

SECONDARY SOURCES CITED MORE THAN ONCE

Lothar Albertin, *Liberalismus und Demokratie am Anfang der Weimarer Republik. Eine vergleichende Analyse der Deutschen Demokratischen und der Deutschen Volkspartei*, Düsseldorf, 1972.

Jürgen Aretz, *Katholische Arbeiterbewegung und Nationalsozialismus. Der Verband katholischer Arbeiter- und Knappenvereine Westdeutschlands 1923–1945*, Mainz, 1978.

Günter Arns, "Die Krise des Weimarer Parlamentarismus im Frühherbst 1923," *Der Staat*, 8 (1969).

Theodore Balderston, "The Origins of Economic Instability in Germany 1924–30: Market Forces versus Economic Policy," *Vierteljahrschrift für Sozial- und Wirtschaftsgechichte*, 69, no. 4 (1982).

Friedrich-Martin Balzer, *Klassengegensätze in der Kirche. Erwin Eckert und der Bund der Religiösen Sozialisten Deutschlands*, Cologne, 1973.

Avraham Barkai, *Das Wirtschaftssystem des Nationalsozialismus. Der historische und ideologische Hintergrund 1933–1936*, Cologne, 1977.

Josef Becker, "Joseph Wirth und die Krise des Zentrums während des IV. Kabinetts Marx (1927–1928). Darstellung und Dokumente," *Zeitschrift für die Geschichte des Oberrheins*, 109, no. 2 (1961).

Reinhard Behrens, "Die Deutschnationalen in Hamburg 1918–1933," Ph. D. diss., Hamburg, 1973.

Gerhard Beier, "Einheitsgewerkschaft. Zur Geschichte eines organisatorischen Prinzips der deutschen Arbeiterbewegung," *Archiv für Sozialgeschichte*, 13 (1973).

Volker Berghahn, *Der Stahlhelm. Bund der Frontsoldaten 1918–1935*, Düsseldorf, 1966.

Johann Baptist Beßler, "Die Streikbewegung in der deutschen Landwirtschaft, unter besonderer Berücksichtigung Ostelbiens und Mitteldeutschlands," Ph. D. diss., Erlangen, 1927.

Hans-Joachim Bieber, *Gewerkschaften im Krieg und Revolution. Arbeiterbewegung, Industrie, Staat und Militär in Deutschland 1914–1920*, 2 vols., Hamburg, 1981.

Theodor Böhme, *Die christlich-nationale Gewerkschaft*, Stuttgart, 1930.

Wilfried Böhnke, *Die NSDAP im Ruhrgebiet 1920–1933*, Bonn-Bad Godesberg, 1974.

Knut Borchardt, "Zwangslagen und Handlungsspielräume in der großen Weltwirtschaftskrise der frühen dreißiger Jahre. Zur Revision des überlieferten Geschichtsbildes," and "Wirtschaftliche Ursachen des Scheiterns der Weimarer Republik," in *Wachstum, Krisen, Handlungsspielräume der Wirtschaftspolitik. Studien zur Wirtschaftsgeschichte des 19. und 20. Jahrhunderts*, Göttingen, 1982.

Karl Erich Born, *Die deutsche Bankenkrise 1931. Finanzen und Politik*, Munich, 1967.

————, *Staat und Sozialpolitik seit Bismarcks Sturz. Ein Beitrag zur Geschichte der innenpolitischen Entwicklung des Deutschen Reiches 1890–1914*, Wiesbaden, 1957.

Ralph Bowen, *German Theories of the Corporative State*, New York and London, 1947.

Karl Dietrich Bracher, *Die Auflösung der Weimarer Republik. Eine Studie zum Problem des Machtverfalls in der Demokratie*, 5th ed., Villingen, 1971.

Karl Dietrich Bracher, Wolfgang Sauer, and Gerhard Schulz, *Die nationalsozialistische Machtergreifung. Studien zur Errichtung des totalitären Herrschaftssystems in Deutschland 1933/34*, Cologne and Opladen, 1960.

Rudolf Brack, *Deutscher Episkopat und Gewerkschaftsstreit 1900–1914*, Cologne and Vienna, 1976.

Günter Brakelmann, "Evangelische Pfarrer im Konfliktfeld des Ruhrbergarbeiterstreiks von 1905," in Reulecke and Weber (eds.), *Fabrik, Familie, Feierabend*.

Rennie Brantz, "Anton Erkelenz, the Hirsch–Duncker Trade Unions, and the German Democratic Party," Ph. D. diss., Ohio State University, 1973.

Theodor Brauer, *Krisis der Gewerkschaften*, 2d ed., Jena, 1924.

Eric Dorn Brose, "Christian Labor and the Politics of Frustration in Imperial Germany," Ph. D. diss., Ohio State University, 1978.

Rüdiger vom Bruch, "Bürgerliche Sozialreform und Gewerkschaften im späten deutschen Kaiserreich. Die Gessellschaft für soziale Reform 1901–1914," *Internationale wissenschaftliche Korrespondenz*, 15 (December 1979).

Annemarie Burger, *Religionszugehörigkeit und soziales Verhalten*, Göttingen, 1964.

Heinrich Bußhoff, "Berufsständisches Gedankengut zu Beginn der 30er Jahre in Österreich und Deutschland," *Zeitschrift für Politik*, November 1966.

Theodor Cassau, *Die Gewerkschaftsbewegung. Ihre Soziologie und ihr Kampf*, Halberstadt, 1925.

Attila Chanady, "The Disintegration of the German Democratic Party in 1930," *American Historical Review*, 73 (June 1968).

————. "The Disintegration of the German National People's Party 1924–1930," *Journal of Modern History*, 39 (March 1967).

Thomas Childers, *The Nazi Voter: The Social Foundations of Fascism in Germany, 1919–1933*, Chapel Hill and London, 1983.

Herbert Christ, "Der politische Protestantismus in der Weimarer Republik," Ph.D. diss., Bonn, 1967.

Richard A. Comfort, *Revolutionary Hamburg: Labor Politics in the early Weimar Republic*, Stanford, 1966.

Werner Conze, "Die Reichsverfassungsreform als Ziel der Politik Brünings," in Michael Stürmer (ed.), *Die Weimarer Republik. Belagerte Civitas*, Königstein, 1980.

Werner Conze and Hans Raupach (eds.), *Die Staats- und Wirtschaftskrise des Deutschen Reichs 1929–1933* (Stuttgart, 1967).

Hans Dieter Denk, *Die christliche Arbeiterbewegung in Bayern bis zum Ersten Weltkrieg*, Mainz, 1980.

Ernst Deuerlein, "Heinrich Brauns. Schattenriß eines Sozialpolitikers," in Hermens and Schieder (eds.), *Staat, Wirtschaft und Politik in der Weimarer Republik*.

Josef Deutz, *Adam Stegerwald, Gewerkschafter—Politiker—Minister 1874–1945. Ein Beitrag zur Geschichte der christlichen Gewerkschaften in Deutschland*, Cologne, 1952.

Lothar Döhn, *Politik und Interesse. Die Interessenstruktur der Deutschen Volkspartei*, Meisenheim am Glan, 1970.

Manfred Dörr, "Die Deutschnationale Volkspartei, 1925–1928," Ph.D. diss., Marburg an der Lahn, 1964.

Dieter Düding, *Der nationalsoziale Verein 1896–1903. Der gescheiterte Versuch einer parteipolitischen Synthese von Nationalismus, Sozialismus und Liberalismus*, Munich and Vienna, 1972.

Freya Eisner, *Das Verhältnis der KPD zu den Gewerkschaften in der Weimarer Republik*, Cologne and Frankfurt am Main, 1977.

Ulrich Engelhardt, *"Nur vereinigt sind wir stark." Die Anfänge der deutschen Gewerkschaftsbewegung 1862/63 bis 1869/70*, 2 vols., Stuttgart, 1977.

Klaus Epstein, *Matthias Erzberger und das Dilemma der deutschen Demokratie*, Ullstein ed., 1976.

August Erdmann, *Die christliche Arbeiterbewegung in Deutschland*, Stuttgart, 1908.

————, *Die christlichen Gewerkschaften. Insbesondere ihr Verhältnis zu Zentrum und Kirche*, Stuttgart, 1914.

Lothar Erdmann, *Die Gewerkschaften im Ruhrkampf*, Berlin, 1924.

Wilhelm Ersil, "Über die finanzielle Unterstützung der rechtssozialistischen und bürgerlichen Gewerkschaftsführer durch die Reichsregierung im Jahre 1923," *Zeitschrift für Geschichtswissenschaft*, 6 (1958).

Ellen Evans, "Adam Stegerwald and the Role of the Christian Trade Unions in the Weimar Republic," *Catholic Historical Review*, 54 (1974).

Richard J. Evans, *The Feminist Movement in Germany 1894–1933*, London, 1976.

Ernst Faber, "Die evangelischen Arbeitervereine und ihre Stellungnahme zu sozialpolitischen Problemen," Ph.D. diss., Würzberg, 1927.

Gerald Feldman, "Arbeitskonflikte im Ruhrbergbau 1919–22. Zur Politik von Zechenverband und Gewerkschaften in der Überschichtenfrage," *Vierteljahrshefte für Zeitgeschichte*, 28 (April 1980).

————, *Army, Industry, and Labor in Germany 1914–1918*, Princeton, 1966.

————, "Economic and Social Problems of the German Demobilization 1918–19," *Journal of Modern History*, 47 (March 1975).

————, "Die freien Gewerkschaften und die Zentralarbeitsgemeinschaft 1918–1924," in Heinz Oskar Vetter, *Vom Sozialistengesetz zur Mitbestimmung*.

————, "German Business between War and Revolution: The Origins of the Stinnes–

Legien Agreement," in Gerhard A. Ritter (ed.), *Entstehung und Wandel der modernen Gesellschaft. Festschrift für Hans Rosenberg,* Berlin, 1970.
———, *Iron and Steel in the German Inflation, 1916–1923,* Princeton, 1977.
———, "Die wirtschaftspolitischen Vorstellungen des 'Alten Verbandes' in der Weimarer Republik," in Mommsen and Borsdorf (eds.), *Glück auf, Kameraden!*.
Gerald Feldman and Irmgard Steinisch, "Notwendigkeit und Grenzen sozialstaatlicher Intervention. Eine vergleichende Fallstudie des Ruhreisenstreits in Deutschland und des Generalstreiks in England," *Archiv für Sozialgeschichte,* 20 (1980).
———, "Die Weimarer Republik zwischen Sozial- und Wirtschaftsstaat. Die Entscheidung gegen den Achtstundentag," *Archiv für Sozialgeschichte,* 18 (1978).
Jens Flemming, "Grossagrarische Interessen und Landarbeiterbewegung. Überlegungen zur Arbeiterpolitik des Bundes der Landwirte und des Reichslandbundes in der Anfangsphase der Weimarer Republik," in Mommsen, Petzina, and Weisbrod (eds.), *Industrielles System.*
———. *Landwirtschaftliche Interessen und Demokratie. Ländliche Gesellschaft, Agrarverbände und Staat 1890–1925,* Bonn, 1978.
Franz Focke, *Sozialismus aus christlicher Verantwortung. Die Idee eines christlichen Sozialismus in der katholisch-sozialen Bewegung und in der CDU,* Wuppertal, 1978.
Walter Frank, *Hofprediger Adolf Stoecker und die christlichsoziale Bewegung,* 2d ed., Hamburg, 1935.
Ludwig Frey, *Die Stellung der christlichen Gewerkschaften Deutschlands zu den politischen Parteien,* Berlin, 1931.
Dieter Fricke, "Zur Förderung der christlichen Gewerkschaften durch die nichtmonopolistische Bourgeoisie," *Zeitschrift für Geschichtswissenschaft,* 29 (1981).
——— (ed.), *Die bürgerlichen Parteien in Deutschland. Handbuch,* 2 vols., Berlin, 1970.
Elisabeth Friedenthal, "Volksbegehren und Volksentscheid über den Young-Plan und die Deutschnationale Sezession," Ph.D. diss., Tübingen, 1957.
Klaus Fritzsche, *Politische Romantik und Gegenrevolution. Fluchtwege in der Krise der bürgerlichen Gesellschaft: Das Beispiel des 'Tat'-Kreises,* Frankfurt am Main, 1976.
Theodor Geiger, *Die soziale Schichtung des deutschen Volkes. Soziographischer Versuch auf statistischer Grundlage,* Stuttgart, 1932.
Gisbert Gemein, "Die DNVP in Düsseldorf 1918–1933," Ph.D. diss., Cologne, 1969.
Dieter Gessner, *Agrarverbände in der Weimarer Republik. Wirtschaftliche und soziale Voraussetzungen agrarkonservativer Politik vor 1933,* Düsseldorf, 1976.
Albin Gladen, "Die Streiks der Bergarbeiter im Ruhrgebiet in den Jahren 1889, 1905 und 1912," in Reulecke (ed.), *Arbeiterbewegung an Rhein und Ruhr.*
Herbert Gottwald, "Gesamtverband der christlichen Gewerkschaften Deutschlands 1901–1933," in Dieter Fricke (ed.), *Die bürgerlichen Parteien in Deutschland. Handbuch,* Leipzig, 1968.
Hans Graf, *Die Entwicklung der Wahlen und politischen Parteien in Groß-Dortmund,* Hannover and Frankfurt am Main, 1958.
Helga Grebing, "Zentrum und katholische Arbeiterschaft 1918–1933. Ein Beitrag zur Geschichte des Zentrums in der Weimarer Republik," Ph.D. diss., Berlin, 1953.
Heiner Grote, *Sozialdemokratie und Religion. Eine Dokumentation für die Jahre 1863 bis 1875,* Tübingen, 1968.
Michael Grübler, *Die Spitzenverbände der Wirtschaft und das erste Kabinett Brüning,* Düsseldorf, 1982.
Iris Hamel, *Völkischer Verband und nationale Gewekschaft. Der Deutschnationale Handlungsgehilfen-Verband 1893–1933,* Frankfurt am Main, 1967.
Richard Hamilton, *Who Voted for Hitler?* Princeton, 1982.

Hans-Hermann Hartwich, *Arbeitsmarkt, Verbände und Staat 1918–1933. Die öffentliche Bindung unternehmerischer Funktionen in der Weimarer Republik*, Berlin, 1967.

Peter Hayes, "'A Question Mark with Epaulettes'? Kurt von Schleicher and Weimar Politics," *Journal of Modern History*, 52 (March 1980).

Hannes Heer, *Bürgfrieden oder Klassenkampf. Zur Politik der sozialdemokratischen Gewerkschaften 1930–1933*, Neuwied and Berlin, 1931.

Horstwalter Heitzer, *Der Volksverein für das katholische Deutschland im Kaiserreich 1890–1918*, Mainz, 1979.

Wolfgang Helbich, *Die Reparationen in der Ära Brüning. Zur Bedeutung des Young-Plans für die deutsche Politik 1930 bis 1932*, Berlin, 1962.

Ferdinand Hermens and Theodor Schieder (eds.), *Staat, Wirtschaft, und Politik in der Weimarer Republik. Festschrift für Heinrich Brüning*, Berlin, 1967.

Lewis Hertzman, *DNVP: Right-Wing Opposition in the Weimar Republic, 1918–1924*, Lincoln, Nebraska, 1963.

Horst Hildebrandt, "Die Rolle der sogenannten 'wirtschaftsfriedlichen' Landarbeiterbewegung in Ostelbien während der Weimarer Republik," Ph.D. diss., Rostock, 1969.

Wolfgang Hirsch-Weber, *Gewerkschaften in der Politik. Von der Massenstreikdebatte zum Kampf um das Mitbestimmungsrecht*, Cologne and Opladen, 1959.

Franz Hitze, *Kapital und Arbeit und die Reorganisation der Gesellschaft*, Paderborn, 1880.

Klaus-Peter Hoepke, *Die deutsche Rechte und der italienische Faschismus. Ein Beitrag zum Selbstverständnis und zur Politik von Gruppen und Verbänden der deutschen Rechten*, Düsseldorf, 1968.

Carl-Ludwig Holtfrerich, *Alternativen zu Brünings Wirtschaftspolitik in der Weltwirtschaftskrise*, Wiesbaden, 1982.

Klaus Hornung, *Der Jungdeutsche Orden*, Düsseldorf, 1958.

Ursula Hüllbüsch, "Die deutschen Gewerkschaften in der Weltwirtschaftskrise," in Conze and Raupach (eds.), *Die Staats- und Wirtschaftskrise*.

———, "Der Ruhreisenstreit in gewerkschaftlicher Sicht," in Mommsen, Petzina, and Weisbrod (eds.), *Industrielles System*.

Detlev Hüwel, *Karl Arnold. Eine politische Biographie*, Wuppertal, 1980.

Richard Hunt, *German Social Democracy 1918–1933*, New Haven, 1964.

Harold James, "Gab es eine Alternative zur Wirtschaftspolitik Brünings?" *Vierteljahrschrift für Sozial- und Wirtschaftsgeschichte*, 70, no. 4 (1983).

Erasmus Jonas, *Die Volkskonservativen 1928–1933. Entwicklung, Struktur, Standort und staatspolitische Zielsetzung*, Düsseldorf, 1965.

Larry Eugene Jones, "Adam Stegerwald und die Krise des Deutschen Parteiensystems. Ein Beitrag zur Deutung des 'Essener Programms' vom November 1920," *Vierteljahrshefte für Zeitgeschichte*, 27 (January 1979).

———, "Between the Fronts: The German National Union of Commercial Employees 1928 to 1933," *Journal of Modern History*, 48 (September 1976).

———, "'The Dying Middle': Weimar Germany and the Failure of Bourgeois Unity 1924–1930," Ph.D. diss., University of Wisconsin, 1970.

Detlef Junker, *Die Deutsche Zentrumspartei und Hitler. Ein Beitrag zur Problematik des politischen Katholizismus in Deutschland*, Stuttgart, 1969.

Hartmut Kaelble and Heinrich Volkmann, "Konjunktur und Streik während des Übergangs zum Organisierten Kapitalismus in Deutschland," *Zeitschrift für Wirtschafts- und Sozialwissenschaften*, 92, no. 5 (1972).

Friedrich Kass, "Nationalsozialismus und Gewerkschaftsgedanke," Ph.D. diss., Munich, 1934.

Michael Kater, "Sozialer Wandel in der NSDAP im Zuge der nationalsozialistischen

Machtergreifung," in Wolfgang Schieder (ed.), *Faschismus als soziale Bewegung. Deutschland und Italien im Vergleich*, Hamburg, 1976.

Max Kele, *Nazis and Workers: National Socialist Appeals to German Labor, 1919–1933*, Chapel Hill, North Carolina, 1972.

Alexander Keßler, *Der Jungdeutsche Orden in den Jahren der Entscheidung. Band I, 1928–1930*, Munich, 1974.

Udo Kissenkoetter, *Gregor Strasser und die NSDAP*, Stuttgart, 1978.

Klemens von Klemperer, *Germany's New Conservatism: Its History and Dilemma in the Twentieth Century*, Princeton, 1968.

Alois Klotzbücher, "Der politische Weg des Stahlhelm, Bund der Frontsoldaten, in der Weimarer Republik. Ein Beitrag zur Geschichte der 'Nationalen Opposition' 1918–1933," Ph.D. diss., Erlangen, 1964.

Thomas Knapp, "Joseph Wirth and the Democratic Left in the German Center Party 1918–1928," Ph.D. diss., Catholic University of America, 1967.

Max Jürgen Koch, *Die Bergarbeiterbewegung im Ruhrgebiet zur Zeit Wilhelms II. (1889–1914)*, Düsseldorf, 1954.

Jürgen Kocka, *Klassengesellschaft im Krieg. Deutsche Sozialgeschichte 1914–1918*, Göttingen, 1973.

Henning Köhler, "Arbeitsbeschaffung, Siedlung und Reparationen in der Schlußphase der Regierung Brüning," *Vierteljahrshefte für Zeitgeschichte*, 17 (July 1969).

———, "Das Verhältnis von Reichsregierung und Großbanken 1931," and "Zum Verhältnis Friedrich Flicks zur Reichsregierung am Ende der Weimarer Republik," in Mommsen, Petzina, and Weisbrod (eds.), *Industrielles System*.

Tilman Koops, "Zielkonflikte der Agrar- und Wirtschaftspolitik in der Ära Brüning," in Mommsen, Petzina, and Weisbrod (eds.), *Industrielles System*.

Erich Kosthorst, *Jakob Kaiser. Der Arbeiterführer*, Stuttgart and Berlin, 1967.

Antje Kraus, "Gemeindeleben und Industrialisierung. Das Beispiel des evangelischen Kirchenkreises Bochum," in Reulecke and Weber (eds.), *Fabrik, Familie, Feierabend*.

Klaus Kreppel, *Entscheidung für den Sozialismus. Die politische Biographie Pastor Wilhelm Hohoffs 1848–1923*, Bonn-Bad Godesberg, 1974.

Herbert Kühr, *Parteien und Wahlen im Stadt- und Landkreis Essen in der Zeit der Weimarer Republik*, Düsseldorf, 1973.

Karl Kupisch, *Adolf Stoecker. Hofprediger und Volkstribun*, Berlin, 1970.

Walther Lambach, *Die Herrschaft der Fünfhundert. Ein Bild des parlamentarischen Lebens im neuen Deutschland*, Hamburg and Berlin, 1926.

Heinz Landmann, "Die Entwicklung der Hirsch–Dunckerschen Gewerkvereine nach dem Kriege," Ph.D. diss., Freiburg, 1924.

Vernon L. Lidtke, "August Bebel and German Social Democracy's Relation to the Christian Churches," *Journal of the History of Ideas*, 27 (1966).

Werner Liebe, *Die Deutschnationale Volkspartei, 1918–1924*, Düsseldorf, 1956.

Wolfgang Luthardt (ed.), *Sozialdemokratische Arbeiterbewegung und Weimarer Republik. Materialien zur gesellschaftlichen Entwicklung 1927–1933*, 2 vols., Frankfurt am Main, 1978.

Robert McKenzie and Allen Silver, *Angels in Marble: Working Class Conservatives in Urban England*, Chicago, 1968.

Charles Maier, *Recasting Bourgeois Europe: Stabilization in France, Germany, and Italy in the Decade after World War I*, Princeton, 1975.

Martin Martiny, "Arbeiterbewegung an Rhein und Ruhr vom Scheitern der Räte- und Sozialisierungsbewegung bis zum Ende der letzten parlamentarischen Regierung der Weimarer Republik (1920–1930)," in Reulecke (ed.), *Arbeiterbewegung an Rhein und Ruhr.*

Tim Mason, "The Primacy of Politics," in Henry A. Turner (ed.), *Nazism and the Third Reich,* New York, 1972.

——, *Sozialpolitik im Dritten Reich. Arbeiterklasse und Volksgemeinschaft,* Opladen, 1977.

Klaus Mattheier, *Die Gelben. Nationale Arbeiter zwischen Wirtschaftsfrieden und Streik,* Düsseldorf, 1973.

——, "Werkvereine und wirtschaftsfriedlich-nationale (gelbe) Arbeiterbewegung im Ruhrgebiet," in Reulecke (ed.), *Arbeiterbewegung an Rhein und Ruhr.*

Erich Matthias and Rudolf Morsey (eds.), *Das Ende der Parteien 1933,* Athenäum ed., Düsseldorf, 1979.

Erich Matthias, "Die Sozialdemokratische Partei Deutschlands," in Matthias and Morsey (eds.), *Das Ende der Parteien.*

Ilse Maurer, *Reichsfinanzen und Große Koalition. Zur Geschichte des Reichskabinetts Müller (1928–1930),* Bern and Frankfurt am Main, 1973.

Hans Meier-Welcker, *Seeckt,* Frankfurt am Main, 1967.

Alfred Milatz, "Das Ende der Parteien im Spiegel der Wahlen 1930 bis 1933," in Matthias and Morsey (eds.), *Das Ende der Parteien.*

Susanne Miller, *Burgfrieden und Klassenkampf. Die deutsche Sozialdemokratie im Ersten Weltkrieg,* Düsseldorf, 1974.

Hubert Mockenhaupt, *Weg und Wirken des geistlichen Sozialpolitikers Heinrich Brauns,* Munich, 1978.

Hans Mommsen, "Die Bergarbeiterbewegung an der Ruhr 1918–1933," in Reulecke (ed.), *Arbeiterbewegung an Rhein un Ruhr.*

——, "Die deutschen Gewerkschaften zwischen Anpassung und Widerstand 1930–1944," in Heinz Oskar Vetter (ed.), *Vom Sozialistengesetz zur Mitbestimmung.*

——, "Heinrich Brünings Politik als Reichskanzler. Das Scheitern eines politischen Alleinganges," in Karl Holl (ed.), *Wirtschaftskrise und liberale Demokratie,* Göttingen, 1978.

——, "Die Sozialdemokratie in der Defensive. Der Immobilismus der SPD und der Aufstieg des Nationalsozialismus," in Hans Mommsen (ed.), *Sozialdemokratie zwischen Klassenbewegung und Volkspartei,* Frankfurt am Main, 1974.

——, "Soziale Kämpfe im Ruhrbergbau nach der Jahrhundertwende," in Mommsen and Borsdorf (eds.), *Glück auf, Kameraden!.*

Hans Mommsen and Ulrich Borsdorf (eds.), *Glück auf, Kameraden! Die Bergarbeiter und ihre Organisationen in Deutschland,* Cologne, 1979.

Hans Mommsen, Dietmar Petzina, and Bernd Weisbrod (eds.), *Industrielles System und politische Entwicklung in der Weimarer Republik,* Athenäum ed., Düsseldorf, 1977.

Rudolf Morsey, *Die Deutsche Zentrumspartei 1917–1923,* Düsseldorf, 1966.

——, *Der Untergang des politischen Katholizismus. Die Zentrumspartei zwischen christlichem Selbstverständnis und "Nationaler Erhebung" 1932/33,* Stuttgart, 1977.

John A. Moses, *Trade Unionism in Germany from Bismarck to Hitler, 1869–1933,* 2 vols., Totowa, New Jersey, 1982.

Patrik von zur Mühlen, *"Schlagt Hitler an der Saar!" Abstimmungskampf, Emigration und Widerstand im Saargebiet 1933–1935,* Bonn, 1979.

Otto Müller, *Die christliche Gewerkschaftsbewegung Deutschlands,* Karlsruhe, 1905.

Heinrich Muth, "Agrarpolitik und Parteipolitik im Frühjahr 1932," in Hermens and
    Schieder (eds.), *Staat, Wirtschaft und Politik.*
_____, "Schleicher und die Gewerkschaften 1932. Ein Quellenproblem," *Viertel-*
    jahrshefte für Zeitgeschichte, 29 (April 1981).
Elfriede Nebgen, *Jakob Kaiser. Der Widerstandskämpfer,* Stuttgart and Berlin, 1967.
Reinhard Neebe, *Großindustrie, Staat und NSDAP 1930–1933. Paul Silverberg und der*
    Reichsverband der Deutschen Industrie in der Krise der Weimarer Republik,
    Göttingen, 1981.
_____, "Unternehmerverbände und Gewerkschaften in den Jahren der Großen Krise
    1929–33," *Geschichte und Gesellschaft,* 9 (1983).
Oswald Nell-Breuning, "Der Königswinter Kreis und sein Anteil an 'Quadragesimo
    anno,'" in Oswald Nell-Breuning, *Wie sozial ist die Kirche? Leistung und Ver-*
    sagen der katholischen Soziallehre, Düsseldorf, 1972.
Jeremy Noakes, *The Nazi Party in Lower Saxony 1921–1933,* London, 1971.
Ulrich Nocken, "Corporatism and Pluralism in Modern German History," in Dirk Steg-
    mann et al. (eds.), *Industrielle Gesellschaft und politisches System. Festschrift für*
    Fritz Fischer, Bonn, 1978.
Uwe Oltmann, "Reichsarbeitsminister Heinrich Brauns in der Staats- und Währungs-
    krise 1923/24. Die Bedeutung der Sozialpolitik für die Inflation, den Ruhrkampf
    und die Stabilisierung," Ph.D. diss., Kiel, 1968.
Günter Opitz, *Der Christlich-soziale Volksdienst. Versuch einer protestantischen Partei*
    in der Weimarer Republik, Düsseldorf, 1969.
Dietrich Orlow, *The History of the Nazi Party: 1919–1933,* Pittsburgh, 1969.
Reinhard Patemann, "Der deutsche Episkopat und das preußische Wahlrechtsproblem
    1917/18," *Vierteljahrshefte für Zeitgeschichte,* 13 (October 1965).
_____, *Der Kampf um die preußische Wahlreform im Ersten Weltkrieg,* Düsseldorf,
    1964.
Anton Pelinka, *Stand oder Klasse? Die christliche Arbeiterbewegung Österreichs 1933*
    bis 1938, Vienna, 1972.
Brian Peterson, "The Politics of Working-Class Women in the Weimar Republic," *Cen-*
    tral European History, 10 (1977).
_____, "The Social Bases of Working-class Politics in the Weimar Republic: The
    Reichstag Election of December 1924," Ph.D. diss., University of Wisconsin—
    Madison, 1976.
Sigurd Plesse, *Die nationalsozialistische Machtergreifung im Oberharz. Clausthal-*
    Zellerfeld 1929–1933, Clausthal-Zellerfeld, 1970.
Günter Plum, *Gesellschaftsstruktur und politisches Bewußtsein in einer katholischen*
    Region 1928–1933. Untersuchung am Beispiel des Regierungsbezirks Aachen,
    Stuttgart, 1972.
Klaus Pollmann, *Landesherrliches Kirchenregiment und soziale Frage. Der evangelische*
    Oberkirchenrat der altpreußischen Landeskirche und die sozialpolitische Be-
    wegung der Geistlichen nach 1890, Berlin and New York, 1973.
Heinrich Potthoff, *Gewerkschaften und Politik zwischen Revolution und Inflation,* Düs-
    seldorf, 1979.
Ludwig Preller, *Sozialpolitik in der Weimarer Republik,* Düsseldorf, 1978 (first pub-
    lished 1949).
Nathan Reich, *Labour Relations in Republican Germany: An Experiment in Industrial*
    Democracy 1918–1933, New York, 1938.
Jürgen Reulecke (ed.), *Arbeiterbewegung an Rhein und Ruhr. Beiträge zur Geschichte*
    der Arbeiterbewegung in Rhineland-Westfalen, Wuppertal, 1974.

Jürgen Reulecke and Wolfhard Weber (eds.), *Fabrik, Familie, Feierabend. Beiträge zur Sozialgeschichte des Alltags im Industriezeitalter*, Wuppertal, 1978.
Wilhelm Ribhegge, *August Winnig. Eine historische Persönlichkeitsanalyse*, Bonn-Bad Godesberg, 1973.
Emil Ritter, *Die katholisch-soziale Bewegung Deutschlands im neunzehnten Jahrhundert und der Volksverein*, Cologne, 1954.
Gerhard A. Ritter, *Die Arbeiterbewegung im Wilhelminischen Reich. Die Sozialdemokratische Partei und die freien Gewerkschaften 1890–1900*, Berlin, 1959.
Gerhard A. Ritter and Klaus Tenfelde, "Der Durchbruch der Freien Gewerkschaften Deutschlands zur Massenbewegung im letzten Viertel des 19. Jahrhunderts," in Gerhard A. Ritter, *Arbeiterbewegung, Parteien und Parlamentarismus*, Göttingen, 1976.
Ludwig Rosenberg and Bernhard Tacke, *DGB. Der Weg zur Einheitsgewerkschaft*, Düsseldorf, 1978.
Ronald Ross, *Beleaguered Tower: The Dilemma of Political Catholicism in Wilhelmine Germany*, Notre Dame, 1976.
Horst Sanmann, "Daten und Alternativen der deutschen Wirtschafts- und Finanzpolitik in der Äa Brüning," *Hamburger Jahrbuch für Wirtschafts- und Gesellschaftspolitik*, 10 (1965).
Klaus Saul, *Staat, Industrie, Arbeiterbewegung im Kaiserreich*, Düsseldorf, 1974.
Johannes Schauff, *Das Wahlverhalten der deutschen Katholiken im Kaiserreich und in der Weimarer Republik*, edited by Rudolf Morsey, Mainz, 1975.
Harold Schellenger, Jr., *The SPD in the Bonn Republic: A Socialist Party Modernizes*, The Hague, 1968.
Manfred Schick, *Kulturprotestantismus und soziale Frage 1890–1914*, Tübingen, 1970.
Erich Schmidt-Volkmar, *Der Kulturkampf in Deutschland 1871–1890*, Göttingen, 1962.
Horst W. Schmollinger, "Zur politisch-gesellschaftlichen Beteiligung von Gewerkschaftsmitgliedern: Gewerkschafter in Parteien, Kirchen und Vereinen," in Ulrich Borsdorf et al. (eds.), *Gewerkschaftliche Politik: Reform aus Solidarität. Zum 60. Geburtstag von Heinz O. Vetter*, Cologne, 1977.
Michael Schneider, *Das Arbeitsbeschaffungsprogramm des ADGB. Zur gewerkschaftlichen Politik in der Endphase der Weimarer Republik*, Bonn-Bad Godesberg, 1975.
———, *Die Christlichen Gewerkschaften 1894–1933*, Bonn, 1982.
Werner Schneider, *Die Deutsche Demokratische Partei in der Weimarer Republik 1924–1930*, Munich, 1978.
Eberhart Schön, *Die Entstehung des Nationalsozialismus in Hessen*, Meisenheim am Glan, 1972.
Klaus Schönhoven, *Die Bayerische Volkspartei 1924–1932*, Düsseldorf, 1972.
———, *Expansion und Konzentration. Studien zur Entwicklung der Freien Gewerkschaften im Wilhelminischen Deutschland 1890 bis 1914*, Stuttgart, 1980.
Helmut Schorr, *Adam Stegerwald. Politiker der 1. deutschen Republik*, Recklinghausen, 1966.
Gerhard Schulz, *Aufstieg des Nationalsozialismus. Krise und Revolution in Deutschland*, Frankfurt am Main, 1975.
Hagen Schulze, *Otto Braun oder Preussens demokratische Sendung*, Frankfurt am Main, 1977.
Hans-Gerd Schumann, *Nationalsozialismus und Gewerkschaftsbewegung. Die Vernichtung der deutschen Gewerkschaften und der Aufbau der "Deutschen Arbeitsfront,"* Hannover and Frankfurt am Main, 1958.

Max Schwarz, *MdR. Biographisches Handbuch des Reichstags*, Hannover, 1965.

William O. Shanahan, *German Protestants Face the Social Question: The Conservative Phase*, Notre Dame, 1954.

James Sheehan, "Conflict and Cohesion among German Elites in the Nineteenth Century," in James Sheehan (ed.), *Imperial Germany*, New York, 1976.

Henryk Skrzypczak, "Fälscher machen Zeitgeschichte. Ein quellenkristischer Beitrag zur Gewerkschaftpolitik in der Ära Papen und Schleicher," *Internationale wissenschaftliche Korrespondenz*, 11 (December 1975).

Hans Speier, *Die Angestellten vor dem Nationalsozialismus. Ein Beitrag zum Verständnis der deutschen Sozialstruktur 1918–1933*, Göttingen, 1977.

Peter Stachura, *Gregor Strasser and the Rise of Nazism*, London, 1983.

Dirk Stegmann, "Antiquierte Personalisierung oder sozialökonomische Faschismus-Analyse?" *Archiv für Sozialgeschichte*, 17 (1977).

———, "Hugenberg contra Stresemann. Die Politik der Industrieverbände am Ende des Kaiserreichs," *Vierteljahrshefte für Zeitgeschichte*, 24 (October 1976).

———, "Zum Verhältnis von Großindustrie und Nationalsozialismus 1930–1933. Ein Beitrag zur Geschichte der sog. Machtergreifung," *Archiv für Sozialgeschichte*, 13 (1973).

———, "Zwischen Repression und Manipulation: Konservative Machteliten und Arbeiter- und Angestelltenbewegung 1910–1918," *Archiv für Sozialgeschichte*, 12 (1972).

Stewart A. Stehlin, *Weimar and the Vatican 1919–1933: German-Vatican Diplomatic Relations in the Interwar Years*, Princeton, 1983.

Hans-Josef Steinberg, *Sozialismus und deutsche Sozialdemokratie. Zur Ideologie der Partei vor dem 1. Weltkrieg*, Hannover, 1967.

Irmgard Steinisch, "Der Gewerkverein Christlicher Bergarbeiter," in Mommsen and Borsdorf (eds.), *Glück auf, Kameraden!*.

Michael Stürmer, *Koalition und Opposition in der Weimarer Republik 1924–1928*, Düsseldorf, 1967.

Wolfgang Stump, *Geschichte und Organisation der Zentrumspartei in Düsseldorf 1917–1933*, Düsseldorf, 1971.

Amrei Stupperich, *Volksgemeinschaft oder Arbeitersolidarität. Studien zur Arbeitnehmerpolitik in der Deutschnationalen Volkspartei, 1918–1933*, Göttingen, 1982.

———, "Volksgemeinschaft oder Arbeitersolidarität. Studien zur Stellung von Arbeitern und Angestellten in der Deutschnationalen Volkspartei (1918–1933)," Ph.D. diss., Göttingen, 1978.

Klaus Tenfelde, "Linksradikale Strömungen in der Ruhrbergarbeiterschaft 1905 bis 1919," in Mommsen and Borsdorf (eds.), *Glück auf, Kameraden!*.

———, *Sozialgeschichte der Bergarbeiterschaft an der Ruhr im 19. Jahrhundert*, Bonn-Bad Godesberg, 1977.

Rolf Thieringer, "Das Verhältnis der Gewerkschaften zu Staat und Parteien in der Weimarer Republik," Ph.D. diss., Tübingen, 1954.

Charles Tilly, Louise Tilly, and Richard Tilly, *The Rebellious Century 1830–1930*, Cambridge, Massachusetts, 1975.

Henry Ashby Turner, Jr., *German Big Business and the Rise of Hitler*, Oxford and New York, 1985.

———, "Hitlers Einstellung zur Wirtschaft und Gesellschaft vor 1933," *Geschichte und Gesellschaft*, 2 (1976).

———, "The *Ruhrlade*, Secret Cabinet of Heavy Industry in the Weimar Republic," *Central European History*, 3 (September 1970).

—————, *Stresemann and the Politics of the Weimar Republic*, Princeton, 1963.

Hans-Peter Ullmann, *Der Bund der Industriellen, 1895–1914*, Göttingen, 1976.

Heinz Josef Varain, *Freie Gewerkschaften, Sozialdemokratie und Staat. Die Politik der Generalkomission unter der Führung Carl Legiens (1890–1920)*, Düsseldorf, 1956.

Heinz Oskar Vetter (ed.), *Vom Sozialistengesetz zur Mitbestimmung. Zum 100. Geburtstag von Hans Böckler*, Cologne, 1975.

Thilo Vogelsang, *Reichswehr, Staat und NSDAP. Beiträge zur deutschen Geschichte 1930–1932*, Stuttgart, 1962.

Wilhelm Vogler, "Probleme des Klassenkampfes zwischen den Landarbeitern und Gutsbesitzern im Regierungsbezirk Merseburg (1918–1923)," Ph. D. diss., Halle, 1973.

Ludwig Volk, *Der bayerische Episkopat und der Nationalsozialismus, 1930–1934*, Mainz, 1966.

Heinrich Volkmann, "Modernisierung des Arbeitskampfs? Zum Formwandel von Streik und Aussperrung in Deutschland 1864–1975," in Hartmut Kaelble et al., *Probleme der Modernisierung in Deutschland*, Opladen, 1978.

Herwart Vorländer, *Evangelische Kirche und soziale Frage in der werdenden Industriegroßstadt Elberfeld*, Düsseldorf, 1963.

Karl Vorwerck, *Die wirtschaftsfriedliche Arbeitnehmerbewegung Deutschlands in ihrem Werden und in ihrem Kampf um Anerkennung*, Jena, 1926.

Eberhard Voß, "Revolutionäre Ereignisse und Probleme des Klassenkampfes zwischen Landarbeitern und Gutsbesitzern in den Jahren 1921 bis 1923 in Deutschland," Ph. D. diss., Rostock, 1964.

Oswald Wachtling, *Joseph Joos. Journalist, Arbeiterführer, Zentrumspolitiker. Politische Biographie 1878–1933*, Mainz, 1974.

Eberhard Wächtler, *Zur Geschichte des Kampfes des Bergarbeiterverbandes in Sachsen. Evangelische Arbeitervereine und gelbe Gewerkschaften als Instrumente der Zechenherren*, Berlin, 1959.

Hermann Weber, *Kommunismus in Deutschland 1918–1945* (Darmstadt, 1983).

Richard Webster, *The Cross and the Fasces: Christian Democracy and Fascism in Italy*, Stanford, 1960.

Bernd Weisbrod, *Schwerindustrie in der Weimarer Republik. Interessenpolitik zwischen Stabilisierung und Krise*, Wuppertal, 1978.

Udo Wengst, "Schlange-Schöningen, Ostsiedlung und die Demission der Regierung Brüning," *Geschichte in Wissenschaft und Unterricht*, September 1979.

—————, "Unternehmerverbände und Gewerkschaften in Deutschland im Jahre 1930," *Vierteljahrshefte für Zeitgeschichte*, 25 (January 1977).

Wilhelm Wiedfeld, *Der Deutsche Gewerkschaftsbund*, Leipzig, 1933.

Heinrich A. Winkler, *Mittelstand, Demokratie und Nationalsozialismus. Die politische Entwicklung von Handwerk und Kleinhandel in der Weimarer Republik*, Cologne, 1972.

Jonathan C. Wright, *"Above Parties": The Political Attitudes of the German Protestant Church Leadership 1918–1933*, London, 1974.

Peter Wulf, "Die Auseinandersetzungen um die Sozialisierung der Kohle in Deutschland 1920/21," *Vierteljahrshefte für Zeitgeschichte*, 25 (January 1977).

Friedrich Zunkel, *Industrie und Staatssozialismus. Der Kampf um die Wirtschaftsordnung in Deutschland 1914–1918*, Düsseldorf, 1974.

—————, *Der Rheinisch-Westfälische Unternehmer 1834–1879. Ein Beitrag zur Geschichte des deutschen Bürgertums im 19. Jahrhundert*, Cologne and Opladen, 1962.

Index

Arnold, Karl, 107n., 226, 233–34

Bachem, Carl, 26, 139n.
Baltrusch, Friedrich, 57, 97, 211, 222; and party reform, 38, 43–44; as advocate of planned economy, 55, 59–60, 180, 214; role in ZAG, 77–78, 91–92; cofounder of State Party, 147–48, 153, 165
Bang, Paul: as patron of Yellow unions, 118, 130–31, 191, 197; supports Hugenberg in DNVP, 127, 129
Bauer, Gustav, 28, 34, 57–59 passim
Bavarian People's Party (BVP), 40, 64, 133–34, 223
Bebel, August, 3–4, 8
Bechly, Hans: as DHV leader, 22, 46–47, 189; alliance with Christian unions, 38, 46–47, 72; friction with DVP, 123, 128–29, 171; friction with NSDAP, 205, 221
Becker-Arnsberg, Johannes, 39, 115
Behrens, Franz: as Stoeckerite Christian Social, 13n., 21, 41–42; heads Protestant wing of GcG, 22, 23, 91, 99, 111, 194; heads left wing of DNVP, 42–43, 64, 69, 73, 106, 152; heads Christian farmworkers' union, 50–53, 82–83, 131, 167; cofounder of CSVD, 152, 166, 211; submits to DAF, 222
Berlepsch, Hans von, 13, 18
Bernstein, Eduard, xiii, 17–18
Borsig, Ernst von, 92, 95, 163, 169
Brauer, Theodor, 57, 66, 86; opposes Christian socialism, 68, 180; analyzes decline of trade unions, 101; response to Third Reich, 218–20, 222
Braun, Otto, 62, 70, 108, 214
Brauns, Heinrich: early clerical backer of GcG, 15, 20, 65; influence in Center Party, 39–40, 73, 96; as Reich labor minister, 60, 62, 79, 83–90, 94, 100, 116, 125–26; supports coalition with DNVP, 100, 103–06 passim, 113–14
Brentano, Lujo, 7–8, 18, 20, 33
Brüning, Heinrich: influence in DGB, 46, 61–62, 71–72, 82; political views, 46, 86, 157–60; rise in Center Party, 114, 138,

141, 153–55; as Reich chancellor, 153–60, 167–72, 175–80 passim, 184–85; response to Nazism, 200–01, 212, 223n.
Brust, August, 14, 16–18, 19

Catholic Action, 136–41
Catholic workers' clubs: formation, 11, 16, 20; relations with Church hierarchy, 27, 30–32, 65, 107–08; relations with Christian unions, 64–66, 72, 138, 140–41, 180–81; response to Nazism, 194, 223, 225
Center Party: as patron of Christian unions, 9–11, 19, 23–24, 26–31; postwar reorganization, 39–40, 55–56, 66–70; coalition with DNVP, 84–86, 103–06, 114–15; and anti-union backlash, 119, 121–22, 134–41, 222–23; dissolution of, 222–23
Christian farmworkers' union, 50–53, 82–83, 101, 194, 211
Christian metalworkers' union, 15–16, 37, 62–63, 90, 141–43
Christian miners' union: formation, 14–15, 19; relations with Free unions, 23, 53–54, 93–97; relations with bourgeois parties, 44–45, 59–61, 134; campaign for nationalizing mines, 59–61, 178–80; urges militant policies on GcG, 85, 87–88, 93–97, 173–74
Christian railroad workers' union, 49–50, 58
Christian Social Commonwealth, 96, 106
Christian Social Party (Stoeckerite): early history, 21–22, 29, 33; as faction within DNVP, 41–42, 127, 132–33, 143–44, 150–51
Christian Social People's Service (CSVD), 152, 165–66, 180, 186, 210–11
Christian Unions, League of (GcG): formation, 16–19; social composition of, 16, 47–48, 134, 228–29; membership trends, 18–19, 90, 107, 176; programmatic debates, 34–35, 96–99, 180–81, 195
civil servants: relations with Christian unions, 49–50, 119–22, 138; resist *Notopfer*, 158, 162–63; response to Nazism, 211, 223
Communist Party (KPD): influence on union members, 73, 78, 80–81, 92–93, 107–09

255